TANGLED WEBS

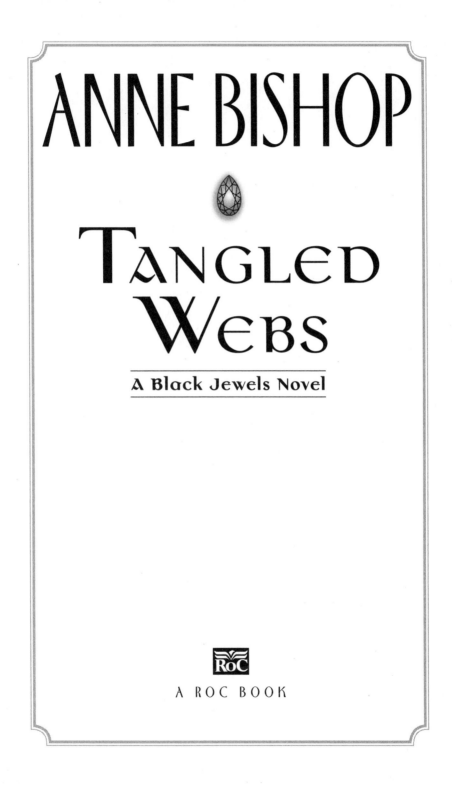

ANNE BISHOP

TANGLED WEBS

A Black Jewels Novel

A ROC BOOK

ROC
Published by New American Library, a division of
Penguin Group (USA) Inc., 375 Hudson Street,
New York, New York 10014, USA
Penguin Group (Canada), 90 Eglinton Avenue East, Suite 700, Toronto,
Ontario, Canada M4P 2Y3 (a division of Pearson Penguin Canada Inc.)
Penguin Books Ltd., 80 Strand, London WC2R 0RL, England
Penguin Ireland, 25 St. Stephen's Green, Dublin 2,
Ireland (a division of Penguin Books Ltd.)
Penguin Group (Australia), 250 Camberwell Road, Camberwell, Victoria 3124,
Australia (a division of Pearson Australia Group Pty. Ltd.)
Penguin Books India Pvt. Ltd., 11 Community Centre, Panchsheel Park,
New Delhi - 110 017, India
Penguin Group (NZ), 67 Apollo Drive, Rosedale, North Shore 0632,
New Zealand (a division of Pearson New Zealand Ltd.)
Penguin Books (South Africa) (Pty.) Ltd., 24 Sturdee Avenue,
Rosebank, Johannesburg 2196, South Africa

Penguin Books Ltd., Registered Offices:
80 Strand, London WC2R 0RL, England

First published by Roc, an imprint of New American Library,
a division of Penguin Group (USA) Inc.

First Printing, March 2008
10   9   8   7   6   5   4   3   2   1

Copyright © Anne Bishop, 2008
"By the Time the Witchblood Blooms" copyright © Anne Bishop, 2000. First published in *Treachery and Treason*, edited by Laura Anne Gilman and Jennifer Heddle (New York: Roc, 2000).
All rights reserved

ROC REGISTERED TRADEMARK—MARCA REGISTRADA

LIBRARY OF CONGRESS CATALOGING-IN-PUBLICATION DATA:
Bishop, Anne.
Tangled webs : a Black Jewels novel / Anne Bishop.
p. cm.
ISBN: 978-0-451-46160-5
1. Witches—Fiction. I. Title.
PS3552.I7594T36 2008
813'.6—dc22   2007034107

Set in Bembo
Designed by Ginger Legato

Printed in the United States of America

PUBLISHER'S NOTE
This is a work of fiction. Names, characters, places, and incidents either are the product of the author's imagination or are used fictitiously, and any resemblance to actual persons, living or dead, business establishments, events, or locales is entirely coincidental.
   The publisher does not have any control over and does not assume any responsibility for author or third-party Web sites or their content.

FOR

JULIE E. CZERNEDA

AND

JAMES ALAN GARDNER

HERE'S TO ANOTHER TEN YEARS OF

FRIENDSHIP AND GOOD STORIES.

ACKNOWLEDGMENTS

My thanks to Blair Boone for continuing to be my first reader, to Debra Dixon for being second reader, to Doranna Durgin for maintaining the Web site and for providing puppy information, to Candice Cavanaugh and Julie Green for helping me keep fit, to Pat Feidner just because, and to all the friends who make this journey with me.

JEWELS

WHITE
YELLOW
TIGER EYE
ROSE
SUMMER-SKY
PURPLE DUSK
OPAL★
GREEN
SAPPHIRE
RED
GRAY
EBON-GRAY
BLACK

★Opal is the dividing line between lighter and darker Jewels because it can be either.

When making the Offering to the Darkness, a person can descend a maximum of three ranks from his/her Birthright Jewel.

Example: Birthright White could descend to Rose.

AUTHOR'S NOTE
The "Sc" in the names Scelt and Sceval is pronounced "Sh."

BLOOD HIERARCHY/CASTES

MALES

Landen—non-Blood of any race

Blood male—a general term for all males of the Blood; also refers to any Blood male who doesn't wear Jewels

Warlord—a Jeweled male equal in status to a witch

Prince—a Jeweled male equal in status to a Priestess or a Healer

Warlord Prince—a dangerous, extremely aggressive Jeweled male; in status, slightly lower than a Queen

FEMALES

Landen—non-Blood of any race

Blood female—a general term for all females of the Blood; mostly refers to any Blood female who doesn't wear Jewels

Witch—a Blood female who wears Jewels but isn't one of the other hierarchical levels; also refers to any Jeweled female

Healer—a witch who heals physical wounds and illnesses; equal in status to a Priestess and a Prince

Priestess—a witch who cares for altars, Sanctuaries, and Dark Altars; witnesses handfasts and marriages; performs offerings; equal in status to a Healer and a Prince

Black Widow—a witch who heals the mind; weaves the tangled webs of dreams and visions; is trained in illusions and poisons

Queen—a witch who rules the Blood; is considered to be the land's heart and the Blood's moral center; as such, she is the focal point of their society

Dear Readers,

In the Realms of the Blood, the war has been fought, the battle has been won, and the epic tale has been told. But life goes on, so there are other challenges to face, smaller battles to be fought, and other stories to tell.

This is one of them.

PROLOGUE

He laid his hand on the cover of his latest book, closed his eyes to shut out the world around him, and savored this new reality that was still so painfully sweet.

They had embraced his previous story about Landry Langston. They had read his thinly veiled discovery about himself and had bought more copies of that book than any other.

He was one of them. Cheated out of his heritage for so many years and discovering his true nature only by accident, now he could stand among them as an equal. Some—themselves insignificant—had thought him worthy enough to be a casual acquaintance because his writing skills had earned him fame and wealth, had earned him invitations to parties and literary discussions that would otherwise be closed to a landen.

Now they would welcome him simply because of the power that flowed in his veins.

He'd been overwhelmed by his discovery and had kept it a secret for all these months. Well, an open secret, since he'd put it down on paper for all to read. But now he was ready to walk among them, to be acknowledged by them. Not just by the society sparklers, but by the true aristos. He'd even taken the first step to indicate he would welcome just such an invitation.

He could see himself sitting at the dining table at SaDiablo Hall, one of a small number of select guests. He would entertain the other guests with amusing stories, and he would flirt with the Lady—but not so much that he would offend his host. He'd heard rumors about a fool who had offended Daemon Sadi in *that* way.

Had Sadi really burned out the man's brain using witchfire? How intriguing. Perhaps . . .

There was so much to learn now that he was one of them. *So much.* And there was so much he could do now that he was no longer shackled by landen law. So much he couldn't have tried before. Except in stories.

For a long time he'd feared there was something wrong with him that made him crave the violence that had no outlet except by being poured into his stories. Now he knew that violence was simply part of his nature.

Oh, yes. He was one of them now. One of the ones who walked the Realms in all their dark glory.

He was no longer an insignificant landen, chained by someone else's rules.

He was Blood.

PART ONE

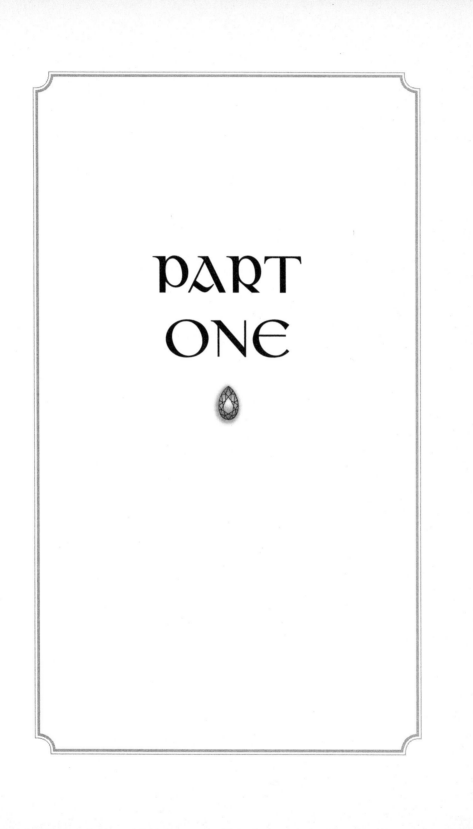

ONE

"Hell's fire." Surreal SaDiablo stared at the page she was currently reading, then let the book drop into her lap. "A body in a closet? What kind of idiot leaves a body in a closet?"

"Someone who doesn't have large furry friends who think 'human' and 'snack' mean the same thing?" Daemon replied in an offhand way that told her he was paying some attention but not really listening, his thoughts still on the papers spread out around him.

Another woman might have been insulted by that lack of immediate attention. Knowing the man, Surreal just waited.

Looking at Daemon Sadi wasn't a hardship at any time, but at the moment, he was comfortably rumpled, which made the picture even more delicious. His thick black hair was disheveled from his fingers running through it while he read reports and made notes of things he wanted to discuss with Dhemlan's Province Queens. His white silk shirt was partially unbuttoned, giving her a view of toned muscles and golden brown skin, as well as little flashes of the Red Birthright Jewel that hung from a gold chain around his neck. His bare feet rested on a pillow he'd tossed onto the low table in front of the sofa.

His deep, cultured voice always had a sexual edge that made a woman's pulse race—even when the look in those gold eyes promised pain instead of pleasure. He had a face too beautiful to be called handsome, and he had a temper typical of his caste.

Since he was one of the two males in the entire history of the Blood to wear a Black Jewel, he was as lethal as he was beautiful. And, may the Darkness help her, he was family.

It was that last part that assured her she'd have his full attention before much longer. It was the nature of Warlord Princes to be protective and territorial—as well as violent and deadly—so it was pretty much a given that a Warlord Prince was going to pay attention to the women in his family.

That thought had her narrowing her gold-green eyes as she considered why he was settled in the sitting room of the family's town house in Amdarh, Dhemlan's capital city, instead of doing paperwork in his own study at SaDiablo Hall. Where he belonged.

"Hell's fire, Sadi," she growled. "Now that you're the Warlord Prince of Dhemlan, don't you have enough details to keep you occupied without keeping track of my moontimes?" Which reminded her of the problem that was going to be filling up the sitting room if he was still there in an hour.

He set aside his papers and looked at her, his gold eyes full of warmth and amusement.

"You're married," she said, as if he needed the reminder of an event that had taken place a few weeks ago. "You should be keeping track of your wife, not me."

No answer. Just that annoying amusement.

"Why don't you keep track of Marian too while you're at it?" she muttered.

The warmth and amusement in his eyes deepened.

Shit shit shit. He *did* keep track of his brother's wife.

Her stomach gave a funny little twirl as she considered that. Daemon Sadi. Lucivar Yaslana. Half brothers linked through their Hayllian father, who was the Prince of the Darkness, the High Lord of Hell. Men who were ice and fire, working in tandem to look after the women in the family—especially during the few days of each moon cycle when those women couldn't use Craft and might be vulnerable.

Which made her wonder about the Warlord she had met at a party shortly after Daemon became the Warlord Prince who ruled the Territory of Dhemlan in the Realm of Kaeleer. The man had managed to maintain the mask of an interesting companion until she agreed to go to the theater with him. Then his true personality began to seep through. She would have gone with him anyway to find out what he really wanted, but he'd canceled, sending a note to offer his regrets and apologies for being called away unexpectedly. She hadn't thought anything of it; just figured he'd found out a little more about her and decided not to risk being gutted during the play's intermission. After all, men who were willing to escort a former whore who was connected to the most powerful family in Kaeleer tended to get nervous when they discovered the former whore was also a former assassin.

Now she wondered whether the little prick-ass had canceled to avoid having a few bones broken (Lucivar's method of dissuading fools) or whether he had run from a much scarier threat (if the prick-ass had ended up having a chat with Daemon).

"What body in which closet?" Daemon asked.

It took her a moment to remember.

"This one." She finger-snapped the offending page of the book. "What's wrong with these people? Why are they leaving bodies around for other people to find instead of disposing of them in some sensible way? And what's wrong with the person who found the body? With help, I should add, from a cat. What does he need help for? Even a human nose can smell that much rotting meat."

"What are you reading?"

There was a hint of wariness mixed in with Daemon's amusement. Which was fair, she supposed, since she'd made a good living as an assassin before she moved to Kaeleer and acquired too many powerful male relatives. Not that he'd be concerned about that. After all, he'd taught her most of the nastier tricks of that particular trade.

She held up the book so he could read the title.

"Ah. That book."

Definite wariness now, as if he had measured the distance between her chair and his place on the sofa and was determined to maintain it.

"Is there something I should know about this book? And what kind of name is Jarvis Jenkell? Do you think that's his real name?"

"I wouldn't know," Daemon replied dryly. "I do know that since he came out with this new series of books, Jaenelle isn't allowed to read his stories in bed anymore. She starts laughing so hard, she ends up flailing."

"What . . . ? Oh. Caught you, did she?"

Stony expression.

Oh, yeah. Back to the first subject. "So why don't these people have brains enough to bury a body where it won't be found? Nooo, they'll put a body in a closet . . . or in an old trunk in a spare bedroom—not even up in the attic, where it might be harder to find—or in the shed out back, where it attracts critters that want to take home some carrion for dinner." She clapped her hands to her cheeks, widened her eyes, and wagged her head. "Oh! Look! It's the gardener. Who is dead. And look! There's blood on the hedge clippers. Do you think it's a clue?"

Daemon snorted out a laugh, tried to regain control, then just slumped back and let the laughter roar.

She laughed with him, then shook her head. She was too much a professional to be able to dismiss sloppy work, even in a story. "Really, Sadi. Granted, a landen would have to work harder than we do to dispose of a body, but they do have shovels."

"It's a mystery, Surreal," he said when he could talk again. "That's the whole point of the story. A person discovers a body, gets caught up in the events surrounding the death, and has to figure out why the person died and who did the killing—usually while trying to avoid being killed himself. Until you've got a body, there's no reason to look for clues."

"And no point to the story." She nodded, since that part made sense. "That still doesn't explain this character who is supposed to be Blood—or the cat. A species of kindred who have chosen to remain hidden while pretending to be larger-than-usual domestic cats, except for this one rogue feline who has decided to help the poor, dumb, smell-impaired human figure out murders?"

Daemon got up and went over to the corner table that held an open bottle of wine and glasses. He lifted the bottle and gave her a questioning look. She shook her head.

After pouring a glass for himself, he returned to his place on the sofa. "It hasn't been that many years since the kindred dogs and horses made their presence known, so it is possible that a species chose to remain hidden when the rest of them decided to let the human Blood know the kindred existed. Not likely, but possible. As for the human side of the partnership, this is the second book with these characters. The man discovered his Blood heritage in the first story and is still learning how to use his power."

"Doesn't that sound a bit too much like the stories Lady Fiona writes about Tracker and Shadow?" Surreal asked.

"I believe it was Fiona's success that spurred him to write this new story line. Jenkell is a well-known writer in landen artistic circles, and he's become quite wealthy writing his mysteries. I've read a few of the books in the other series; they're entertaining stories."

She huffed out a breath and shook the book. "But this! The man has never been in the same room as one of the Blood. At least, not the kind of Blood he's trying to write about. You can tell he doesn't understand a damn thing about us."

Daemon smiled. "I know. For years he's been considered the top writer in his field, mostly because his characters were clever and found imaginative ways out of difficult situations."

"And entertained both landens and Blood."

Daemon nodded. "Then ego or temper overwhelmed sense when Fiona's Tracker and Shadow stories became popular with landens as well as the Blood, and he began writing this new series about a Blood male and his kindred partner."

"And he's still popular with the Blood?" She put as much disbelief in her voice as possible.

"He is, but not because he's telling a good story anymore." Daemon lifted his glass in a salute. "His portrayal of the Blood is so bad it's hysterically funny. At least, a good number of people have thought so."

Apparently Daemon wasn't one of them. "Does he know the Blood are buying the books to laugh at the characters? That must be biting his ass." She riffled a few pages until she got to the next chapter.

"I imagine it is. What are you doing?"

"I wanted to see what other Blood things he's doing wrong."

"The point of one of these stories is to read it in order to see the clues as they're revealed."

He was getting that bossy tone in his voice. She wasn't sure if it was family bossy or Warlord Prince bossy, but he'd stare her down if she tried to ignore him. Once he went home, she could . . .

Shit.

She glanced at the clock on the mantel, considered the man now studying her, and decided not to waste time being subtle.

"You have to go home now."

"No."

She hadn't thought giving him an order would work, but he didn't have to sound so politely unyielding about it. Now the only way to get rid of him was to tell him why he had to go.

"Rainier will be here soon," she said.

"So?"

Something under the pleasant tone made her think of a cat sharpening its claws before it went out to play with the mouse.

"You like Rainier," she said. "He *works* for you."

Daemon settled back on the sofa, making himself more comfortable. "I'm aware of that." He waited a beat. "Why is he coming here this evening?"

For the same reason you've got your ass snuggled into the sofa. Which was not something a witch said to any male relative who was bigger than she was and wore darker Jewels than she did.

"Doesn't he have family of his own to fuss over?"

Hell's fire. He was going to get pissy about this.

"Actually," she said, "he doesn't." A flicker in Daemon's eyes warned her he was aware of the lie within the words—he knew perfectly well Rainier had family living in Dharo—but he didn't know why the words were also true. And she wasn't looking forward to being the one to tell him. "His family prefers that he stay away."

"Because he prefers to warm a man's bed rather than a woman's?"

It was like seeing a storm coming and knowing you couldn't get out of the way in time.

"No," she said softly, "it's because he's a Warlord Prince."

A heartbeat. That's all it took. Daemon, the amused male relative, was gone. The Warlord Prince who looked at her . . . Not the Sadist, who could be so elegantly vicious. Thank the Darkness, it wasn't *that* facet of Daemon's personality that had surfaced. No, this was Prince Sadi, ruler of Dhemlan, who was considering the depth of the insult contained within her words.

"They aren't like our family," she said hurriedly.

A moment of silence. Then, too softly, he said, "Explain."

She didn't dare look at the clock to see how much time was left. It didn't matter. This discussion had to be over, done, *fast*.

"Most of the males in the SaDiablo-Yaslana family are, or were, Warlord Princes. So none of you are different from the rest. You know how to live with a Warlord Prince. The women in this family know how to live with a Warlord Prince. But Rainier . . . From what I gathered, there had been a couple of Warlord Princes in the family bloodlines over the generations, but they'd worn lighter Jewels, so the more aggressive, predatory nature"—*Shit! Don't remind him of that!*—"of a Warlord Prince was balanced by not having as much power. But Rainier wears an Opal Jewel that's considered a dark Jewel. His family didn't know what to do with him when he was young and wore Purple Dusk as his Birthright, and as sure as the sun doesn't shine in Hell, they don't know what to do with him now."

"So they turn away from him."

Oh, yeah. This was turning into a *fun* discussion.

"To his benefit, since they don't deserve to have him." She put some snap in her voice, hoping for a flash of amusement from him.

Nothing.

"A Warlord Prince needs a female to fuss over—if not family, then a friend," she finished quietly.

"Having his company for the evening is fine, Surreal, but—"

"He'll be staying for breakfast."

Long pause. "You trust him that much?"

Now they had gotten to the core of it. Did she trust a man who wasn't family during the hours when she was asleep and would be the most vulnerable? "Yes, I trust him that much. So go home to your wife, Sadi." *Then I can read this book however I want to.*

Another pause. Then the Warlord Prince of Dhemlan took a deep breath—and Daemon let it out in a sigh as he stood up.

"All right, then." Using Craft, he vanished all the papers and called in his black jacket. He slipped on the jacket, then ran his fingers—with their long, perfectly manicured, black-tinted nails—through his hair. Now the hair looked bedroom-disheveled. Now the partially unbuttoned shirt looked like a lure to attract and entice.

Which was insane, because the only woman who could safely have Daemon Sadi as a lover was Jaenelle Angelline, since she was the only woman he *wanted* for a lover.

Don't just sit here. Get up. Move. You've got no fighting room in this position.

Then a little flash, a blink of light near the floor. Nothing there, but . . .

He was still barefoot. There was something too sensual about him still being barefoot when he was wearing that silk shirt, the expensive jacket, and the too-well-tailored trousers that taunted women with a hint of what they couldn't have.

She pondered the feet and not the significance of their movement until he was leaning over her, one hand resting on the arm of her chair, the fingertips of the other hand drifting down the page of her book, then over her thumb and wrist.

She actually felt her heart skip a beat in anticipation of a kiss before it began pounding like a rabbit's.

Why was he doing this? What did he want from her? Those golden eyes held hers, demanding her attention. The way his mouth curved in a hint of a smile seemed to promise all kinds of delights. Which was probably the exact look the Terreillean Queens who had used him saw right before he killed them.

Then his lips brushed her cheek and lingered there as his chained sexual heat washed over her.

"Enjoy your evening, cousin," he said.

He eased back—and glided out of the room.

Had he used Craft to open and close the door, or had he used the power that lived within him to simply pass through the wood? She didn't know, didn't care. She felt a bit breathless—and more than a little scared. When Daemon was the Sadist, he used sex as a terrifying weapon. She felt as if she'd brushed against that side of his temper, but she didn't know why he'd be angry with her.

Maybe nothing. Probably hadn't even been aimed at her. Just feeling pissy about Rainier's family was all.

Which reminded her.

Shaking off the sexual haze—which she wasn't in any mood for anyway—she glanced at the clock. Rainier was late. Wasn't that lovely? Now that she knew the book was meant to be silly, she wanted to read a little more. And she wanted to flip through and discover some of the other stupid things this Jarvis Jenkell thought the Blood did.

She picked up the book and tried to flip through the pages.

Tried to flip through the pages.

Tried to flip through the pages.

"That whoring son of a whoring *bitch*!"

As he walked down the town house's steps, Daemon reached inside his black jacket. Then he stopped, baffled that he'd been reaching for a cigarette case he hadn't carried in several years.

He couldn't remember when he'd stopped smoking the black cigarettes. Sometime during the years when his mind had been shattered and he'd wandered the paths of madness the Blood called the Twisted Kingdom. During the years when he was slowly regaining his sanity and lived in hiding with Surreal and Manny, it hadn't been prudent to call attention to themselves by adding an expensive item to their supplies when the invalid—and fictitious—owner of the island had never ordered cigarettes before. Now the only way to get the things would be to buy them from a supplier in the Realm of Terreille, and there was nothing he wanted from Terreille. Nothing.

Which didn't explain his suddenly slipping into the movements of an old habit.

Then he looked up at the town house's sitting room windows—and smiled.

His reaching for a cigarette had been a response to memories of the hundreds of times he and Surreal had spent an evening together in exactly the same way—enjoying each other's company while pursuing individual interests. Which meant the two of them had finally circled back to being the friends they had been once upon a time.

She was twelve when he first met her and her mother, Titian. A pretty, leggy girl with the Hayllian coloring of black hair and light brown skin that had come from her sire, Kartane SaDiablo. But her eyes were gold-green instead of pure gold and larger than usual, and her ears were delicately pointed. The slightly oversized eyes and the ears, along with a slim body that was stronger than it looked, came from Titian, who had been a Black Widow Queen of the Dea al Mon, one of the Children of the Wood.

So Surreal had a dual bloodline, as it was politely called in Kaeleer. Hayllians were one of the long-lived races; the Dea al Mon were not. Her body had matured closer to the pace of the short-lived races, but her emotions . . .

Because he'd seen her only for an evening here and there, and because she'd had to grow up hard and fast after Titian was murdered, it hadn't occurred to him that Surreal's emotional maturity might develop at a slower pace, that even after a few centuries of being a whore and an assassin, she had still been more of an adolescent girl than a mature woman. So in a way, the night that had broken their friendship was as much his fault as hers.

She'd been young and foolish and drunk the night she had asked him to show her what Hayll's Whore could do in bed. She'd said it would be a feather in her cap because no whore who worked in a Red Moon house could claim actual experience in bed with him. And he, who had thought of her as a young cousin, had been bitterly hurt at what he'd seen as a betrayal of his trust. So he had responded with a cold fury, and he had shown her what it was like to dance with the Sadist.

That night changed things between them, and it was only because of Jaenelle that their friendship began to mend. Jaenelle, who was Witch, the living myth, dreams made flesh. She had been a child when they had both met her. She grew up to be an extraordinary Queen. Then she sacrificed herself to stop the war being orchestrated by Hekatah and Dorothea SaDiablo—the High Priestess of Hell and the High Priestess of Hayll, respectively.

Because of their mutual commitment to Jaenelle, he and Surreal had found their way back to being friends—and family. Maybe it was because they were finally comfortable with each other again that his leave-taking had been as much warning as distraction. Even Surreal couldn't afford to become complacent and forget what he was.

Now there was another connection he had to consider: Rainier.

Prince Rainier had met Jaenelle and the coven when he'd been hired to be their dance instructor. Unlike the instructors who had come before him, he had been no more than a few years older than them and had thrived on the contact with the young Queens who, not many years later, would rule Kaeleer. When Jaenelle formally became the Queen of Ebon Askavi, Rainier joined her court as a Second Circle escort, although he'd continued to make a living as a dance instructor.

Now there was no court at Ebon Askavi. Not officially. And that was the problem. The Warlords and Warlord Princes who had served in the First Circle already had a connection to other courts—usually the court of the Queen they had married or were related to in some way. But Rainier had served in the Dark Court, and when it ended, he could no longer legitimately claim to be serving a Queen. Oh, no one had pushed it during that first year, especially after they'd heard Jaenelle had survived. No one had disputed Rainier's claim that he still served Witch in an unofficial capacity. But the day had been coming when other Queens wouldn't have considered that a valid reason to refuse service in another court.

That was why he had hired Rainier and given the man a five-year contract, duties to be flexible and as needed. While no male born in the Shadow Realm was *required* to serve, it was assumed that most would spend some time serving in a court at one point in their lives or another. And Warlord Princes, who were considered a dangerous asset because of their tempers and nature, were sometimes treated as outcasts if a Queen wasn't holding the leash. Even in Kaeleer.

Despite his family's opinion of him, a man like Rainier would be a prize. He was a fine-looking man with a dancer's lean build, fair skin, green eyes, and a mane of brown hair. He had an easy manner and a mild temper for a Warlord Prince. But while he made a delightful—and protective—companion, he wasn't suited for bedroom duties. Even if Rainier had taken a contract with one of the coven—and because he was a friend, they had all offered him a contract—service in the bedroom for the other Ladies in the Queen's First Circle would have been unspoken but understood.

Serving the new Warlord Prince of Dhemlan was the best solution. There was no court, so there were no Ladies who could demand service. And yet no one was going to argue that service to *him* wasn't sufficient to control another Warlord Prince.

So the arrangement promised to work well for both of them.

And here comes the innocent now, Daemon thought, suppressing a grin as Rainier turned a corner and walked toward the town house, his stride easy and graceful.

"Prince Sadi," Rainier said when he reached the town house's steps.

"Prince Rainier," Daemon replied.

Rainier's eyes flicked to the town house's door before focusing on the Prince he served.

"I'm on my way out," Daemon said. "I understand that you're on your way in. For the night."

"Is that a problem?"

"Not for me." Daemon stepped aside and waited until Rainier had climbed the stairs and raised the knocker on the door. "How are your reflexes this evening?"

Rainier twisted at the waist and looked down at him, clearly puzzled. "They're fine. Why?"

"You may need to be fast on your feet."

With that, Daemon walked away. It was a pleasant summer evening. Since he wasn't expected home, he'd walk to his favorite bookshop and see if there was anything new that might whet Jaenelle's appetite for stories.

Then he'd go home and see what he could do about whetting her other appetites.

"I saw Prince Sadi on my way in," Rainier said as he walked into the sitting room. "He seemed amused about something."

"Let's see how amused he is when I put his balls through a meat grinder! *While they're still attached!*"

To give him credit, Rainier didn't turn and run out of the room. But he also didn't come any closer. Surreal wasn't sure if the wariness was sincere or a sop to her ego, since he was the dominant power right now, despite the fact that she wore Gray Jewels and he wore Opal. She didn't care if it was sincerity or sop. She just wanted someone to howl at.

"Look what he did to my book!" she wailed, shaking the book at him. "Look!"

Cautious, he came closer. Encouraged that she wouldn't lose her audience, she tried flipping through the pages to demonstrate.

"The pages are stuck together," Rainier said. "Is the book defective?"

"*He* did this." She turned the page, as if she'd finished reading it. *That* she could do. Then she tried flipping through pages and all the pages stuck together. "I can turn one page at a time, but if I want to skip around to—"

"Wouldn't that spoil the story?" Rainier asked, breaking into her rant.

"Stop thinking like a male," she snarled.

He grinned at her. The grin didn't last long when she just stared at him.

"Sorry," he said, doing his best to sound meek.

She looked down at the book, and her eyes filled with tears. Stupid to get weepy over something so foolish. Moontime moodies. Didn't hit her often, thank the Darkness, but she was entitled to a mood or two when she didn't feel well and couldn't use Craft on top of it.

A tear plopped onto the back of her hand. She sniffled—and heard a low sound rumble through the room. Growl? Snarl? She looked up to ask Rainier and . . .

"He made you cry," Rainier said, staring at her through the glazed eyes of a Warlord Prince who had risen to the killing edge. "The bastard played a cruel trick and made you cry." He took a step toward the sitting room door.

Hell's fire, Mother Night, and may the Darkness be merciful. He was going after Sadi. He saw tears and gut instinct kicked in, and he was going after Sadi, who was the most powerful male in the Realm. And Daemon, when challenged, would give Rainier a chance to back down—and then would lash out in response to his own predatory nature, destroying the other man completely.

"No." The book went flying as she propelled herself out of the chair and grabbed his arm. "You're not doing this."

"He made you cry."

"He pissed me off, and I got weepy. He wouldn't have done it if he'd known I'd get weepy." Which was true. On any other day, she would have raged for a few minutes and then tried to figure out how the spell worked. Or she would have stomped over to the nearest bookshop and bought another copy of the damn book.

"Rainier."

At the moment, she had some sympathy for his family's inability to deal with a Warlord Prince, but she wasn't going to let him leave. She could think of a lot cleaner ways to commit suicide than challenging Daemon. If that meant channeling her power when her body couldn't tolerate being the vessel for that power, so be it. She'd slap enough shields around Rainier to cage him for a while. It would hurt like a wicked bitch, but she'd do it. And then she'd grab the fastest messenger she could find to ride the Winds to Ebon Rih and deliver a message to Lucivar. He'd arrive with that Eyrien temper of his stoked to the point of explosion and yell at Rainier for considering something so stupid. He'd yell at her too, for hurting herself by using Craft when she shouldn't. And then he and Rainier would be merciless about fussing over her because, to their stone-headed way of thinking, she *needed* to be fussed over.

What did Jaenelle keep telling her? Work *with* a Warlord Prince's nature instead of trying to work against it.

She sagged against Rainier so suddenly, he grabbed her to keep her on her feet.

"Surreal?"

Razor-sharp tone, but not the killing edge. This was worry now, focused completely on her.

Good.

"You promised to stay with me tonight," she said. *Don't sound pathetic. He won't believe it for a moment if you sound pathetic.*

"I know but—"

"A mood, Rainier. Just a mood. You don't ask a man to step onto the killing field for a mood." At least, not in Kaeleer. The bitches in Terreille had done it all the time.

He studied her, and she could feel the tension in him slowly fading.

"That's all it is?" he finally asked. "Just a mood?"

She nodded, then rested her head on his shoulder. It was nice to have a male friend. Her one attempt at a romantic relationship with a man had left her with a heart bruised badly enough to wither any sexual interest she had in the gender. At least for the time being. So it was nice to spend time with a male who didn't want her to be more than a friend.

All she had to do was avoid getting him killed.

"Was there anything you wanted to do this evening?" Rainier asked.

The brilliance of an idea dazzled her for a moment.

"Well," she said, "I was curious about that book, especially now that I know the things in there about the Blood are very silly. But I don't want the frustration of those stuck-together pages." And she was going to send Daemon a blistering letter about tricks that almost backfire.

No. Not Daemon. She'd send a note to Uncle Saetan. He may have retired from being the Warlord Prince of Dhemlan, he may have taken up residence at the Keep as a retreat from the living

Realms, but he was still the patriarch of the SaDiablo family, and no one could flay an erring son with a look or a phrase as well as the High Lord of Hell.

Cheered by the thought, she almost didn't respond in time when Rainier said, "I could read the story to you, if that would be pleasing."

"I'd like that." She stepped back. "I'm going to freshen up first. Could you see about getting some food we could nibble on?"

A relaxed smile and a look of pleased anticipation in his eyes. "I could do that."

As she climbed the stairs to her room on the second floor, Surreal considered how annoying the evening might have been. She would have wanted to read the book; Rainier would have wanted some way to look after her, and his need to fuss would have scraped on her temper. Now, with him reading the story to her, they could talk about it and laugh over it, and they would both have an enjoyable, entertaining evening.

She paused outside the door of her room to consider everything that had happened.

One spell, designed to annoy her just enough. One man, who understood the nature of Warlord Princes all too well.

Since Daemon had found a clever way to take care of her *and* Rainier, maybe she wouldn't send that note to Uncle Saetan after all.

She shook her head and smiled as she walked into her bedroom. "Sneaky bastard."

TWO

Early morning. Cool air against his bare skin—air that held the promise of heat later in the day.

No longer sleeping and not quite awake, Daemon breathed in the scent of his wife, his love, his Queen, and breathed out a sigh of contentment. His hand caressed Jaenelle's thigh, traveled up her belly. Not to arouse, just to confirm that she was here, was real. It wasn't something he took for granted.

Then his hand moved higher, curved around a breast, and he smiled with pleasure at the feel of that warm, round flesh against his palm and the caress of soft, thick fur against the back of his hand.

Fur?

Fully awake now, he opened his golden eyes halfway. He tried straightening his legs, but the weight that was pressed against the back of his knees gave an annoyed grunt followed by a sleepy yawn.

Ladvarian. The Sceltie was a Red-Jeweled Warlord and the most trusted liaison between human Blood and kindred, who were the Blood of the nonhuman races that lived in Kaeleer. He'd been a puppy when he'd decided Jaenelle belonged to him as his

Queen and had come to live with her at the Hall. Years later, he'd been the stubborn heart that had rallied the kindred to do the impossible and save Jaenelle when she'd been torn apart by the power she had unleashed to stop a war.

The kindred had developed a fine sense of when *not* to come into the bedroom, but Daemon had gotten so used to some of their psychic scents that their presence no longer roused him from sleep when they slipped into the room.

Didn't mean it didn't annoy him to wake up and discover company in his wife's bed. Especially since the bed was big enough to be a small room and there was no reason to be crowding him. Unless . . .

He raised his head and looked at the bed's fourth occupant.

Kaelas lay on his back, sprawled over the large bed. Eight hundred pounds of limp Arcerian cat. An enormous blanket of white fur.

Kaelas stared at him through half-lidded eyes. Daemon couldn't decide if it was a deliberate imitation of his own look or lazy arrogance.

Daemon bared his teeth, a show of dominance.

Kaelas bared his teeth, leaving no doubt that *his* teeth were more impressive.

Contentment vanished. Temper scratched. It didn't matter that Kaelas wasn't a rival lover. It didn't matter that he usually tolerated the cat's presence, acknowledging that the Red-Jeweled Warlord Prince was one of Jaenelle's fiercest protectors. What mattered was that on this particular morning, he, who was Jaenelle's husband, didn't want to share her bed with *a damn cat!*

The feelings swelled, bubbled up, demanded an outlet.

Daemon snarled, using Craft to let that soft sound roll through the room like thunder.

Kaelas snarled, not needing Craft to fill the room.

Then Jaenelle snarled.

Suddenly he was the only male in the bed.

We'll tell Beale you need coffee, Ladvarian said, using a psychic spear thread to keep the comment just between the males.

You do that, Daemon replied, watching the way Kaelas shifted from one paw to the other, as if uncertain whether to stay or run.

Jaenelle stirred.

Kaelas sprang toward the glass doors connected to the balcony that looked out over Jaenelle's courtyard. He passed through the glass, leaped over the balcony railing, and landed in the courtyard two floors below.

Ladvarian ran straight for the inside wall and passed through it to the corridor, no doubt racing to find Beale and inform the Hall's butler that the Lady was awake.

Which left him to deal with his wife, who was not the friendliest person first thing in the morning.

He kissed her bare shoulder, an acknowledgment that he knew she was awake. "Good morning."

He'd been a pleasure slave for centuries when he'd lived in Terreille. He knew all the nuances for playing bedroom games. The rules were different for a husband, but a lot of what he'd learned about women still applied. So he kept his voice warm and loving, with just a husky hint of sex—enough to tell her she was desirable but not enough to imply he had any expectations.

She shifted. Turned toward him. There was nothing loving or loverlike in the sapphire eyes that stared at him.

"You woke me up."

A shiver of fear went down his spine. He had seen her in the Misty Place, that place deep in the abyss where she appeared as the Self that lived within the human skin—a Self that clearly revealed that not all the dreamers who had woven this dream into flesh had been human.

Despite the fact that the body still looked like Jaenelle, it was Witch who stared at him. And Witch was *not* pleased.

"Sorry," he said, brushing his fingers over her short golden hair. "Didn't mean to."

She braced one hand against his shoulder and pushed.

He could have resisted, physically, but he'd waited seventeen hundred years for her, and he could no more disobey her than he could stop loving her. So he rolled onto his back, passive, knowing he wouldn't defend himself from anything she did to him.

She settled over him, her nails lightly pricking his shoulders. She rubbed against him—and his cock responded with enthusiasm.

"You woke me up."

She nipped his lower lip, then settled in for a long, slow kiss that had his blood pumping. The scent of her arousal, both physical and psychic, filled him until there was nothing but need and desire.

Then she ended the kiss and her teeth closed over his throat. Not a love bite on his neck, but a predator's hold meant to strangle the prey. No pressure, no real menace from her, but the hold—and what it stood for—shredded the chains that usually held a Warlord Prince within the boundaries of civilized self-control.

His long nails whispered down her back, encouraging her to take him. His hands rested on her ass for a moment. Then he pricked her with his nails just hard enough to have her hips pushing down against him.

Snarling, she raised her head.

"You woke me up," she said for the third time.

This wasn't lovemaking, and it wasn't just sex. He wasn't sure there was a word for where they were at that moment.

And he didn't care.

Lifting his head, he licked her throat as he shifted her hips and sheathed himself inside her. Then he purred, "I guess I'll have to make it up to you."

Daemon watched his hand as he poured a cup of coffee, pleased to see that the uncontrollable shakes had settled down to little tremors.

Their mating had been a combination of unrestrained arousal mixed with dollops of fear, which, because of the woman, had intensified his excitement. Sex that was savage and yet still tender, that was all physical and yet was possible only because of the depth of their feelings for each other. When they were done, Jaenelle had staggered into the bathroom, and he, braced by self-discipline and sheer stubbornness, had stumbled his way to the bathroom in the adjoining Consort's suite. In safe privacy, he had braced his hands against the shower walls, and while the hot water poured over him, his body shook in response to what he'd been doing in bed with the woman who was his wife and Queen.

He sincerely hoped they would enjoy each other like that again in the future. And he hoped, just as sincerely, that it wouldn't be anytime soon.

"I thought men liked morning sex," Jaenelle said, looking baffled.

"We do," Daemon replied. Of course, "sex" was a pale word to describe what they had been doing, but he wasn't about to debate her choice of words. Especially since she was watching the hand holding the coffee cup. Had noted the tremors. "Of course we do."

The baffled look changed to something that was almost angry, almost hostile. "You said it didn't matter. You said you could accept that I no longer wore Ebony Jewels, was no longer dominant."

Her quiet intensity alarmed him. He set the cup down. "It *doesn't* matter. I *can* accept it. What is this about?"

"It's about that." She waved a hand to indicate his own. "It's about pretending that you were with a witch who was stronger than you, and now acting all shaky and nervous."

Sweetheart, you didn't see the look in your eyes when we were in bed. But he saw the problem now. Despite having gotten married twice—once in a private ceremony and again in a public ceremony a few weeks later—she still wasn't certain he had accepted the choice she had made.

After he'd dealt with the witches who had tried to stop the wedding by hurting her, Jaenelle had brought him to the Misty Place and shown him the truth. So he *knew* she could have been exactly the same as she had been before she'd sacrificed herself to save Kaeleer. She could have worn the Ebony Jewels again instead of Twilight's Dawn, which had only a hint of Black. But she hadn't wanted that much power, had never wanted to be so different and so distant from everyone else. And everyone around her, everyone who had loved her, was still adjusting to what they thought of as a loss.

"I'll agree with the part about my being shaky, but I'll dispute the accusation that I'm pretending to be nervous." He put enough punch in his voice to assure he'd have her attention.

"Men pretend sometimes. You can't tell me they don't."

He acknowledged that fact with a nod. "Sometimes a man does pretend he's a little intimidated by the woman he's bedding, even if he's the one wearing the darker Jewels." And sometimes it wasn't pretense; men just didn't argue with women's incorrect assessment—mostly because they figured women wouldn't understand that the power that was sometimes being wielded had nothing whatsoever to do with the Jewels.

To give himself a moment to collect his thoughts, he picked up the cup and took a sip of coffee.

Damn. If he'd known they were going to have *this* kind of discussion, he would have put a warming spell on the cup. He swallowed the cold coffee and set the cup down.

"Would you say our enjoyment of each other this morning was intense?" he asked. "Because I would."

A blush stained Jaenelle's cheeks. She nodded.

Daemon sighed, a sound of strained patience. Or patient exasperation. "Sweetheart, sometimes the body reacts. Should I apologize for feeling weak in the knees and quivering? I'm your husband, and I'm your lover. Being both—being *able* to be both—still takes my breath away."

She studied him a moment longer, then reached across the table. He clasped her hand, craving the touch.

And that touch was enough to rekindle his arousal. He let his chained sexual heat wash over both of them, leaving her with no doubt that if they ended up in bed before the breakfast dishes were cleared, *he* would be the dominant partner.

She offered him a small, embarrassed smile before she released his hand and picked up her fork, a clear signal that she wasn't ready for another romp in bed.

Then again, neither was he. Not really.

Relieved they could change the subject, he poured more coffee and gave his attention to his own breakfast. Since he'd already had his exercise for the day—and more—he was ravenous.

"What are you planning to do today?" he asked.

"I'm meeting Marian. We're going to walk through the building we're going to transform into a spooky house." Jaenelle gave him a bright smile that said, *Ask me. Come on, ask me.*

No sane man with any kind of functioning brain would go

near that statement. But he knew his duty as a husband, so he said, "Spooky house?"

Jaenelle swallowed a bite of omelet. "I was visiting one of the landen villages that's located near the family vineyards, and I got to talking to some of the boys. They had the strangest ideas of what the Blood are like—especially since common sense should tell them the things they think can't be true."

"They're boys," he said. "They don't have common sense."

"No doubt, but I thought it would be fun to create a house based on all the silly, spooky things they think we live with day to day. There are usually harvest festivals in the late autumn. We could have it ready by then as an entertainment."

"An entertainment." Hell's fire, Mother Night, and may the Darkness be merciful. "Where is this entertainment?"

"We got a big old house in a landen village located in the central part of Dhemlan. Well, I bought it. It's structurally sound, but it looks . . ." She shrugged.

There was something stuck in his throat. He was pretty sure it was his heart. "You bought a house?" *And didn't tell me?*

"Yes."

She gave him an unsure but game smile—and he had a sudden understanding of the terror his father, the powerful, Black-Jeweled High Lord of Hell, must have felt during Jaenelle's adolescence when greeted by that smile.

"What are you doing today?" Jaenelle asked.

Had Marian told Lucivar about this spooky house? Surely the lovely Eyrien hearth witch hadn't kept it a secret from her own husband! Which was a thought he wasn't going to follow to its logical conclusion because then he would start to wonder why his own lovely wife hadn't informed *him* until now.

But if Lucivar *had* known, why hadn't the prick sent a warning?

A man did *not* need to be blindsided by something like this at the breakfast table. Or any other time, for that matter.

"Daemon?"

"Uh?" *Pay attention, fool.* "Oh, I have some paperwork to finish up for my meetings with the Province Queens." He focused on his coffee cup and added, oh so casually, "And I thought I would drop in at the Keep and see how Father is doing."

"Uh-huh." Jaenelle sliced her omelet in half, put a half between two pieces of toast, and wrapped her breakfast in her napkin. "I have to run if I'm going to be on time to meet up with Marian. She's a little nervous about doing this."

I wonder why. "Are you taking one of the Coaches?"

"No, I'll just ride the Winds." She drained her coffee cup and stood up.

Something not quite right here. "It shouldn't take that long to reach the landen village, should it?"

She came around the table and gave him a sweet kiss. "No, it won't take that long." Then she gave him a wicked grin. "But first I have to yell at the cat for waking me up."

THREE

How did I get talked into this? Marian wondered as she followed Jaenelle into the next gloomy room of the old landen house that had sat empty and neglected for the past decade or more. Of course, based on what she'd seen so far, the house hadn't been cared for even when people had lived in it.

She waited until Jaenelle nudged open one of the slatted shutters to let in dingy light through the grimy window. Then she looked around and decided this was the worst room yet. Judging by the furniture, this must have been the dining room. Judging by the wallpaper, the people who had lived here must have wanted to discourage everyone from lingering over a meal.

"Cobwebs," Jaenelle said, looking at the corners of the room.

Marian winced as she forced herself to take a closer look around. She was here because her hearth witch practicality provided balance for Jaenelle's more whimsical ideas. Besides, they were family. Jaenelle had been adopted by Lucivar's father when she was twelve, so even though there was no bloodline connecting them, Jaenelle was Lucivar's sister—and Lucivar's Queen. Since Marian was Lucivar's wife, that meant Jaenelle was also *her* sister now.

And there was another connection between them. If Jaenelle hadn't saved her and brought her to Kaeleer, she wouldn't have survived the attack by five Eyrien Warlords, and if she hadn't survived, she wouldn't have fallen in love with a strong, wonderful man, and she wouldn't have a son.

So she owed Jaenelle. But debt or not, family or not, there was only so much *ick* a hearth witch could handle.

"Yes," she said. "Those cobwebs definitely will have to be cleaned out."

"No. Well, yes, *those* will have to be cleaned out, but we'll put new cobwebs in the corners. Black, sooty strands. Clots and layers. Maybe add an illusion spell in a couple of them so it looks like there's something moving."

Marian shuddered. Her membranous wings, shades darker than her brown skin, were pulled in tight to her body, an instinctive response to make herself look smaller. "They think our homes have cobwebs?" She wasn't sure if she was insulted or appalled.

"And rats," Jaenelle said cheerfully as she called in a list and handed it to Marian. "I took notes when I was talking to the boys."

Those weren't boys, Marian thought darkly as she studied the list. *Those were maggot-brained little beasts.* "We can't have rats."

"Not real rats," Jaenelle conceded. "But we can create a skittering noise so it sounds like there are rats in the walls." She looked around, considering, then frowned as they both heard a *skitter skitter.*

Marian closed her eyes for a moment. They'd bring some of the kindred wolves with them the next time to deal with the rats already in residence.

"So these"—*maggot-brained beasts*—"boys think the Blood live in moldy rooms with creaking doors and squeaking floors and furniture that hasn't been dusted in a decade, and we eat in rooms that have cobwebs in the corners and rats in the walls."

Jaenelle smiled brightly. "Yes. Exactly."

Marian walked around the table that clogged the center of the room. What would it take to clean that thing? Maybe a chisel. Or a sledgehammer. She stopped at the serving board and stared at the silver serving tray set just off center enough to make her grit her teeth.

At least, she thought it was silver under all that tarnish.

Seeing it made something in her brain fizzle. She turned and marched to the closest door, baring her teeth in a silent snarl as she turned the grimy doorknob. It took some muscle to open the stuck door, but when she finally succeeded, she discovered it wasn't a way out of the room. It was a storage cupboard with shelves that had more blackened silver and bug-infested linen. And she couldn't take any more.

"Why not a rotting corpse?" Marian said in a voice so snippy she didn't recognize it as her own. "Wouldn't we lock our enemies in a cupboard and let them starve to death while they watch us dine?"

"Well . . . ," Jaenelle began.

"You said you were thinking of ghostly narrators. So just tell the"—*maggot-brained beasts*—"boys not to open that door. If they're anything like Daemonar, they'll open the door as soon as they can just to find out why they're not supposed to."

"But these aren't little children Daemonar's age," Jaenelle protested. "These children will be old enough to have gone through the Birthright Ceremony—or would be if they were Blood. A child that age is *not* going to open a door after he's been told not to."

"Then have an illusion of a boy the right age. Have *him* be the one who opens the door. In fact, don't even have a knob on the door until the ghost boy appears. Then a ghostly knob will appear that only he can turn."

"He'd been told not to open the door, but he did—and the knob came off in his hand, breaking the locking spell on the door," Jaenelle said. "The ghost boy will back away, and visitors will hear a malevolent laugh as the door slowly opens."

"And that's when they'll see the skeleton of the boy who had been told not to open that door and had disobeyed."

And, apparently, would still be disobedient even as a ghost.

"The skeleton," Jaenelle said softly. "Yes. A boy's skeleton. With just enough scalp left to hold a little hair, but otherwise ragged clothing over clean bones."

"Isn't that what we all have in the closet that holds the tablecloths and napkins?"

Silence filled the room. Then . . .

"Marian," Jaenelle breathed, "that's brilliant. We'll have to figure out why he wasn't supposed to open the door, but . . . It's *brilliant.*"

That would teach her to try to be bitchy. Obviously she didn't have the temper for it.

"Come on," Jaenelle said, heading for the hallway. "Let's see what sort of nonsense we can come up with for the upstairs rooms."

Marian stared at the empty doorway and considered what would be upstairs. Bedrooms. Bathrooms. Closets. And above that, the attic.

As she reached the doorway, she heard the loud creak of the old stairs. Heard Jaenelle's delighted laugh. She looked at the list Jaenelle had made based on how landen boys thought the Blood lived.

May the Darkness have mercy.

Daemon carefully leaned back against the large blackwood table that provided a work space for the scholars who were permitted to use the material in this part of the Keep's library. A sore muscle in his back. Nothing more than that. All things considered, he'd gotten off lightly.

Damn cat.

"What brings you to the Keep today?"

Affection. Dry amusement. Love. He heard all those things in the deep voice. He turned his head to look at the man sorting the books stacked in the center of the table.

A handsome Hayllian whose thick black hair was heavily silvered at the temples. His face was beginning to show the weight of his long life, but it was the laugh lines fanning out from the golden eyes that cut the deepest in the brown skin. He was a Guardian, one of the living dead, and had walked the Realms for more than fifty thousand years.

He was Saetan Daemon SaDiablo, a Black-Jeweled Warlord Prince who was the Prince of the Darkness, the High Lord of Hell, the High Priest of the Hourglass. Formerly the Steward of the Dark Court at Ebon Askavi—and still the unofficial Steward of that same unofficial court—he was now the assistant librarian/historian at Ebon Askavi.

He had one other title, the one Daemon considered the most important: father.

They hadn't known each other for that many years. The Birthright Ceremony, where a child acquired the Jewel that indicated the power born within that young vessel, was also the time when paternity was formally acknowledged or denied. At Daemon's Birthright Ceremony, while he'd stood proudly holding his Red

Jewel, paternity had been denied. Saetan had been stripped of all rights to his son, and they had been lost to each other—until the need to protect a powerful but fragile girl brought them back together.

Now he had a father, someone he could talk to, someone who, being the only other male who wore Black Jewels and was also a Black Widow, understood his nature better than anyone else could. Even Lucivar.

"Do I need a reason to visit you?" he asked.

"Certainly not," Saetan replied, walking to the far end of the table and putting three books next to another stack.

Daemon shifted a little to get a better look at the stacks. Were those the books to be discarded or the ones Saetan and Geoffrey, the Keep's historian/librarian, were trying to preserve?

Old books, from the looks of the covers. Most were so old the titles had faded and the bindings had become fragile despite the preservation spells that must have kept them intact for so long. Culling the volumes in the Keep's vast library was an ongoing project, and every book had to be handled with care.

"I'm always delighted to see you, Daemon," Saetan said, returning to the stacks in the center of the table. "But I recognize the difference between a casual visit and when one of you drops by because you have something on your mind."

Caught. But he wasn't ready to ask the question. So he lobbed a different conversational ball onto the table. "Have you heard about the spooky house?"

"The what?"

With perverse glee, Daemon told his father all about Jaenelle's plans to create a house based on landen children's ideas of how the Blood lived—and watched the High Lord of Hell pale.

"You're joking," Saetan said hoarsely.

Daemon shook his head. "Jaenelle and Marian are there right now, inspecting the property."

"Can't you stop this?"

"Would you like to suggest how?"

Absolute silence.

For a minute, Daemon watched his father sort books, certain the man wasn't paying any attention to what was being placed where and would have to sort them all over again.

"Wasn't there anything else you wanted to discuss?" Saetan asked, picking up a stack of books.

It was that tiny hint of desperation, the little undercurrent of a plea, that made it possible to ask the question. But he turned his head and stared at the wall instead of the man.

"When I was a pleasure slave in Terreille, I woke up each morning and wondered who I needed to kill that day, or what kind of vicious game I would have to play, or if I'd be the one who was killed. I lived on the knife's edge every waking moment, and I honed my own temper on that edge. I earned being called the Sadist."

"And now what's the most frightening thing you face?"

"Morning sex."

Saetan dropped the books.

Daemon cringed, hoping none of the volumes had been damaged.

Saetan fussed over the books, then stopped. Just stopped.

"I'm your father," he said quietly. "And I am Jaenelle's adopted father. So there are aspects of your marriage I would prefer to remain ignorant about unless necessity requires me to know about them. But I'll ask you: Do you need a Healer?"

The question startled him. "No."

"You're favoring your back."

"That's not because of Jaenelle; that's because of the damn cat. She yelled at him, and he got upset."

Saetan sighed, a quiet sound full of relief. "Kaelas is a Red-Jeweled Warlord Prince who is eight hundred pounds of muscle and temper. It always amazes me that all it takes to turn him into an anxious puddle of fur is for Jaenelle to say 'bad kitty' and rap him on the head with her fingertips."

"She did a bit more than that, actually. She *yelled* at the cat."

"Why?"

"He woke her up."

Another silence. "You were in bed with Witch?"

Sharp concern, Steward of the Court to Queen's Consort. And the understanding that Jaenelle, allowed to wake up by herself, woke up grumpy. When startled awake, Witch was the side of her that woke first—and Witch woke up deadly.

"Then I'll ask again, Prince," the High Lord said. "Do you need a Healer?"

Daemon shook his head.

"Your back?"

He raised a hand, then let it fall to his side. "Just a bruise. I was sitting at the desk. He came in too fast. I didn't expect Kaelas to completely lose his brains and try to climb into my lap while I was sitting in the chair!"

"You shielded?"

"Kept me from getting impaled," Daemon replied dryly. Didn't do him much good otherwise. Lying there on the study floor, a little stunned, getting smashed between broken chair and anxious cat, whose huge paw—with claws thankfully sheathed—patted at his head while Kaelas's thoughts batted at him. The Lady was upset. Daemon was the Lady's mate. Daemon would make things better.

At the time, Daemon had been a bit busy trying to breathe.

Saetan rubbed his chin. "That was a nice chair. Wasn't meant to take that kind of weight, though."

Neither am I, Daemon thought.

"The name of the craftsman who made it is in the household files."

"I'll contact him to make a replacement."

Another silence. Then Saetan said, "What else?"

"I like my life now. I truly do. I like waking up in the morning knowing the day will be full of small challenges and pleasures, that I'll spend part of the day tending to the family properties and finances, as well as my own business ventures, and part of the day tending to Dhemlan. And through it all, there is being with Jaenelle. There is the wonder, and the joy, of being with Jaenelle."

"But?"

"But sometimes I wonder if I'll lose the edge that makes me who and what I am. Sometimes I wonder, when the day comes for me to stand as defender, if I'll have become too soft, too tame, to protect what matters most. Is that the price I'll have to pay to have a pleasant life?"

There. He'd said it. Asked the question.

And Saetan just stood there, staring at the books, his fingertips gently brushing the topmost cover.

"You'll never lose that edge," Saetan said suddenly, quietly. "Daemon, this life you have now is everything I could have wished for you, and I hope you have decades where the worst challenges you face are morning sex with your wife and dealing with an anxious cat. But I can tell you, here and now, you will never lose that edge. No matter how long who and what you are remains sheathed in that pleasant life, when the day comes for you to draw that cold blade of your temper, it will be as sharp and as honed and as deadly as it is now. Maybe even more so."

A tension he hadn't been aware of drained out of his muscles. This was the question he'd come to ask. This was the answer he'd hoped to hear.

"Now," Saetan said, giving him a dry smile, "why don't you go tend the family business and let me—"

The door opened. Lucivar walked in. Daemon felt his body freeze, felt Saetan stiffen beside him. Not because of Lucivar, because of—

"Unka Daemon! Granpapa!"

Daemonar held out his arms, little feet braced and pushing on his father's hip, little wings flapping. A happy bundle of Eyrien boy . . . in a room full of priceless books.

The thought terrified Daemon.

"Hey," Lucivar said, trying to control the squirming boy without setting off a full-scale tantrum. "Have you two heard about this spooky house Jaenelle and Marian are planning?"

Suddenly Saetan had Daemon by the arm and was hauling him toward the door with enough speed to have Lucivar backing up into the corridor.

"Yes, Daemon was just telling me about that. I think this is something the two of you should discuss, since this is something that should be dealt with by husbands rather than a father. But if I think of anything that might help, I'll be sure to let you know."

And somehow he was standing in the corridor, staring at a closed door, listening to the distinctive *snick* of a lock.

"Well," Lucivar said, "I guess that puts us in our place."

Lucivar's mouth was curved in that lazy, arrogant smile that usually meant trouble, but the tone of voice was wrong.

Daemon studied his brother. Half brother, but they had never made that distinction. What made the difference obvious was that Lucivar had the dark, membranous wings that distinguished Eyriens from Hayllians and Dhemlans, the other two long-lived races. And he had all the arrogance and attitude that came naturally to an Eyrien male—especially one who was a Warlord Prince and wore Ebon-gray Jewels.

"Do you want to—?" Daemon began.

"No." Too sharp, almost cutting, even though the smile didn't change. "Have things to do."

Daemon felt a sudden distance between them. Why it was there, he couldn't begin to guess. "Could we get together for a drink this evening? I could come—"

"I'll come to the Hall. See you then, Bastard."

"Take care, Prick."

"Bye-bye, Unka Daemon! Bye-bye."

He waved bye-bye until Lucivar and Daemonar disappeared around a curve in the corridor. Then he looked back at the locked door and sighed.

He might not need to dance on the knife's edge the way he did when he lived in Terreille, but it didn't look like his life was going to get complacent after all.

Saetan leaned against the locked door and stared at the ceiling.

Why did I want children?

He'd been rattled by the conversation with Daemon, had reacted instead of thinking. And the look in Lucivar's eyes just before he'd closed the door had shown him the depth of his error. He'd fix it. He would stop by the eyrie this evening, and he would fix it.

He wasn't sure how to fix the other problem. Spooky house. The words had become a sharp bone stuck in his throat, an insult to everything he believed in. An insult inflicted by his Queen.

He had two choices. He could swallow the bone or he could cough it out. Either way, it was going to hurt. He just had to decide which choice he could live with.

Pushing away from the door, he returned to the blackwood table just as Geoffrey stepped through one of the archways that led to the stored books. The other Guardian looked sympathetic and amused as he watched Saetan shuffle a few books.

Geoffrey approached the table, picked up a book, then opened it to read the title page. "How long do you think you'll be able to keep this up?" he asked. "Sooner or later one of them is going to figure out these are new books with an illusion spell on the covers to make them look old, and you're just using them for a prop."

"None of them have figured it out so far," Saetan replied, tugging the book out of Geoffrey's hand. "If I'm occupied, they can take their time working their way around to whatever they've come to talk about. None of them look closely enough to notice that the condition of the paper doesn't match the supposed age of the books."

"And you used some of the real books to create the templates for the spell. Quite ingenious, Saetan. But from what I overheard before I retreated, you do have a problem."

"I do." The bone in his throat scraped a little more. "Yes, I do."

Lucivar landed in the small courtyard outside his eyrie, shifted his grip on his bundle of boy, then turned to look at the mountain called Ebon Askavi.

He wasn't like them. Could never *be* like them. His father. His brother. Two of a kind. The difference wasn't so sharp when it was one of them or the other. But when they were together . . .

Educated men, with a passion for books and words and learning. He was the outsider, the one who didn't fit.

It hurt. No matter how often he tried to shrug it aside, it still hurt. And now the hurt went deeper. Because of the boy.

He rubbed his cheek against Daemonar's head, felt the sweet ache as little arms reached up to hug.

He knew why he'd been locked out of the library. Knew why he'd been excluded. But if he had to choose between them, he would choose the boy he held in his arms.

Giving his son a kiss, he said, "Come on, boyo. You get to play with your papa today."

FOUR

The clatters, bangs, and curses coming from the eyrie's kitchen were not sounds Lucivar usually associated with his darling wife. He hesitated a moment, then set Daemonar down near the side door that opened onto the part of the yard that could withstand the rough-and-tumble play of an Eyrien boy and a litter of wolf pups—and had a domed shield around the whole thing to keep boy and pups from tumbling down the mountain.

"Stay here," he said.

Another hesitation as he stepped over the threshold. The command would keep the boy out for a minute or two, but not much longer. But if he shut Daemonar outside, he wouldn't have even that much time to assess what was upsetting Marian before Daemonar voiced his unhappiness loud enough to be heard all the way to Riada. So he left the door open and strode across the large entry room to the archway that led to the kitchen.

"Marian?" he said softly.

His voice startled her enough that she kicked one of the metal buckets—and said words he'd *never* heard her say before.

"Your sister," she panted as she gathered up rags and mops and brooms. "Those maggot-brained little *beasts*."

He flinched a little over the word "maggot," then shifted into a fighting stance. Just as a precaution. He wasn't sure why looking at an old house would cause this reaction, but—Hell's fire!—*something* had her riled up.

"My home is going to be *clean*."

He wasn't sure if that was a wail of despair or a declaration of war.

"Our home is clean," he said calmly.

She turned on him so fast, he took two steps back before he was aware of moving.

"Don't you patronize me, Lucivar Yaslana. Don't you dare!"

He raised his hands chest high in a gesture of surrender and kept his mouth shut. There was no point trying to reason with her until she started sounding a little more like Marian and less like some hysterical, mop-wielding Harpy.

"My h-home does *not* have cobwebs in the corners or rats skittering in the walls or decaying bodies."

Just as well he hadn't told her about the partially eaten rabbit the wolf pups had left in one of the out-of-the-way rooms. He'd gotten rid of the carcass—and the maggots—hadn't he? And he'd scrubbed everything down to get rid of the smell.

Maybe he hadn't scrubbed everything down quite well enough?

"Mama!"

Lucivar shifted just enough to block entry into the kitchen. Daemonar, who was pelting toward the opening, smacked into his leg.

Before the boy could voice his displeasure, Marian wailed, "They think we live like that!" Then the wail changed to a snarl as she added, "I need to clean."

Since he'd spent the past few years teaching her how to defend herself with objects she would normally have at hand, he was looking at a pissed-off woman whose hands were full of potential weapons.

"All right." He nudged his son back with his foot. After Daemonar heard his mother snarl, instinct had kept the boy silent and cautious—and watching everything while hiding behind his father. "Why don't I stop by The Tavern later and pick up something for dinner?" When she bared her teeth, he added, "It's just a suggestion, Marian, not a criticism."

The wild look in her eyes finally faded enough for him to see the wife he loved in the riled woman standing before him.

"That would be good," she said.

Still watching Marian, Lucivar crouched and picked up Daemonar. "We'll get out of your way for a while."

He didn't wait for an answer, just turned and headed back out to the yard. Once the door was closed and he was moving toward the far end of the lawn, he began to relax.

That's when he fully realized what he'd done, and he jerked to a stop.

He was an Eyrien Warlord Prince. He wore Ebon-gray Jewels. He was the third most powerful male in the Realm of Kaeleer. And he'd just run from a hearth witch who wore Purple Dusk Jewels.

Of course, the usual rules of battle didn't apply to a wife, which put him at a distinct disadvantage when it came to dealing with her.

A little hand pressed against his face, so he turned his head and looked at his son.

"Mama was scary," Daemonar said.

"Ooooh yeah." He gave Daemonar a smacking kiss that made

the boy laugh. "Come on, boyo. We'll just play outside for a while longer."

And, he hoped, wife and son would both be tired out in a few hours, so he could tuck them in before heading to the Hall for his chat with Daemon.

"The house has a lot of potential," Jaenelle said as she faced the mirror over her dressing table and fastened a sapphire and ruby earring to her left ear. Her eyes met Daemon's as she smiled. "But I think the condition of the house had Marian a little upset."

Damn. He'd hoped the lovely hearth witch would be able to calm her husband a little before Lucivar got here. If Marian was upset, Lucivar would arrive at the Hall as a walking explosion.

"So you're going to do this." He'd thought about it all afternoon. There wasn't anything dangerous about this spooky house; it was just a silly amusement. The Darkness knew the Queens in Terreille had done some vicious things in the name of amusement, and this wouldn't hurt anyone. But something about it bothered him. He just couldn't figure out *why*.

"Yes, Daemon, we're going to do this."

She fastened the other earring to her right ear, and his attention was caught by something much more interesting than an old house.

He'd loved her long golden hair, had loved the feel of it in his hands or when it brushed over his skin. But the short hair, properly cut and styled thanks to Surreal's badgering, nicely framed her face and revealed her neck. And *that* was the fascination.

There was something about the spot where her neck and right shoulder met. Not the left side, just the right. An enticing scent.

A special taste. It wasn't something she put on her skin, and there wasn't a scent gland under the skin. But for Warlord Princes, that particular spot was like catnip. They wanted to breathe in the scent of it, lick it, close their mouths over it, and—

Down, boy. Don't start what you can't finish until much, much later.

He hadn't thought about how often he came up behind her and kissed that spot, lingering for a moment to get the taste of her, until he realized Lucivar did the same thing, except the kiss was quick and friendly. Until he noticed all the Warlord Princes in the First Circle did the same thing, even Kaelas and Jaal, so the fascination wasn't just to human males.

And it wasn't exclusive to Jaenelle. He hadn't noticed this behavior in Terreille, but every Queen in Kaeleer had that special little spot—a spot that appealed only to the Warlord Princes who served her.

Which had him circling back around to Jaenelle's hair. Long, it had hidden the enticement unless she put her hair up or braided it. Now the short golden hair led the eye down her neck right to that spot and—

"Are you all right?" Jaenelle asked. "Your eyes are glazing."

It took a little too much effort to leash his libido, but he managed to do it. Or to be more precise, Jaenelle's slightly puzzled, slightly amused look managed to do it. Besides, this wasn't an evening to let his mind wander.

"I'm fine." He hesitated, then decided he'd better warn her. "Lucivar will be coming over after dinner."

She picked up a bottle of perfume he'd given her recently and applied a drop to her pulse points. "Is he upset about something?"

"Yes." No point in denying it.

She set the bottle on the dressing table and turned to face him.

It had been easier talking to her reflection than being pinned by those sapphire eyes.

"Do you know what it is?" Witch asked.

He shook his head. "But it's . . . between brothers."

She turned back to the mirror and put on the multigemmed bracelet he'd given her before they were married, during the weeks when he'd been afraid she was going to turn away from him forever. "Then I'll stay in the suite this evening. It sounds like this discussion would be easier if there are no distractions."

"I think so." He wouldn't have asked her to stay away, but he was relieved that she understood her presence would hinder any attempt at getting to the root of the problem.

She walked over to him and gave him a soft kiss. "You'll work it out. The two of you always do."

Giving in to one need, he wrapped his arms around her and nuzzled that special spot on her neck.

The psychic scent rolled through the lower rooms of the Hall, announcing Lucivar's temper before he crossed the study's threshold. Arrogance. Anger. And hurt.

Daemon leaned back against the blackwood desk and waited for his brother to smash through the door.

On second thought, enough things had already gotten smashed that day. He used Craft to open the study door just ahead of the Eyrien's entrance.

Lucivar's temper was leading, and most people would have scrambled to get out of the way of the storm that was about to shatter everything in its path. That anger didn't bother him. They had clashed before and would, no doubt, clash again. And the arrogance was simply Lucivar being Lucivar. But the hurt . . . That was the wound they were going to have to lance.

"Bastard," Lucivar said as he began prowling the room.

"Prick." He watched Lucivar take in the room, assessing it as a battleground.

Unless he was completely relaxed and in a familiar place, Lucivar made that same assessment. He didn't see the furniture for its craftsmanship or the decorations for their aesthetic value. He didn't look at the space of a room in terms of its comfort or pleasing dimensions. He saw weapons, traps, and defense. The fact that he was making that assessment of the study did not bode well for this discussion.

"What's wrong with your back?" Lucivar asked as he prowled past the desk, his gold eyes taking in the details of a potential enemy with one slashing look.

Should have realized he'd notice, Daemon thought as he braced his hands on the desk. "Jaenelle yelled at the cat." Even though Jaal was around as much as Kaelas was, everyone understood "the cat" referred only to the big white feline and not the tiger.

"If you don't have brains enough to shield, you deserve to get hurt."

He felt his temper flex, lightly testing the leash of self-control.

"I know why we were closed out of the library today."

Daemon blinked. Worked to shift his mental balance.

"Daemonar's just a little boy," Lucivar growled. "He doesn't understand about the thrice-damned precious books."

There was the hurt, suddenly bubbling up to the surface. And there was something more under the hurt. Something that worried him.

"That's right," Daemon said carefully. "He's just a little boy. That library isn't an appropriate place for him."

"Isn't appropriate for an uneducated Eyrien, isn't that what you mean?"

Someone had managed to hit Lucivar in one of the few places where the man was emotionally fragile.

Daemon's temper unsheathed its claws. He pushed away from the desk. "Who took a jab at you?"

"What?" Lucivar stopped prowling. His wings opened slightly for balance. And wariness was now added to the messy stew of emotions that filled the room.

"*Who?*" Because whoever had hurt his brother would find herself in a deep grave—and the bitch wouldn't necessarily be dead when he put her there.

"I'm not like you! I can't *be* like you. Either of you."

A mental skid on emotional ice. Trying to restrain a temper that wanted to snap the leash. So this was about him after all.

The truth of it was like a knife slicing his heart.

"No, you're not like me, any more than I can be like you." He went back to the blackwood desk and leaned against it, clamping his hands on the edge of the wood. "What is this about, Lucivar? You were pissed at me when we were at the Keep; you're still pissed now. Why?"

Vulnerable. Fragile. He couldn't stand seeing Lucivar like this.

"I don't have the schooling you do," Lucivar said, looking at the wall, not meeting his eyes.

Do I hug him or kill him? "Eyriens don't value that kind of schooling. I absorb information from books for the pleasure of it, but it's also another kind of weapon." He paused to assess the battleground and the man, and then added, "Besides, you don't like to read."

"I can read." Quick, automatic defense.

"I know you can," Daemon said dryly. "From the first time I met you—or the first time I thought I'd met you—I pushed and bullied and bruised your ego until I goaded you into learning. In the same way that you pushed and bullied and bruised my ego until I learned a few basic moves with hand weapons."

During the centuries they had been enslaved and had clashed over and over again, they hadn't understood why they felt compelled to push at each other to share the knowledge and skills they had acquired. Even after they had learned they were brothers, they hadn't realized that this need to protect each other's weaker side had begun in a childhood they didn't remember.

Lucivar's shoulders relaxed a little, and the smile was fleeting but genuine.

"You can read," Daemon said, "but you don't enjoy reading. It was always difficult for you. Maybe that's not just you, Lucivar. The Eyrien race has a strong oral tradition to pass on stories, but they don't put much value on the written word."

"Marian reads a lot," Lucivar mumbled. "She likes books."

"Then maybe it's cultural. Reading is a female entertainment, something the males can sneer at indulgently."

"I don't sneer," Lucivar said. Then added under his breath, "Wouldn't dare."

They were circling around the heart of the wound now, so Daemon just leaned back and waited. And felt memories stir awake.

"Maybe it is a part of being an Eyrien male," Lucivar said. "Like being stronger and having more muscle than females."

"Maybe."

Lucivar took a deep breath and let it out slowly. Daemon almost sighed with relief. They'd gotten past the worst of this without too many bruises.

Then Lucivar looked him in the eyes and the words burst out. "I want that for Daemonar. The education. That kind of knowledge. I don't want him to feel hobbled. I don't want him to feel like he's . . . less."

Daemon snapped upright. Then sucked in a breath as his back protested. But his voice held a chill and an edge not quite honed enough to cut. "If that's your way of saying you feel inferior to me in any way other than that I wear darker Jewels, I will beat you to a bloody pulp."

Lucivar smiled that lazy, arrogant smile. "You could try."

They were on even ground again. Just that simple.

Since they were on even ground again, he allowed himself a huff of exasperation. "I'm not blind, Prick. So you don't read for pleasure. The mountains won't fall down because of it."

"Daemonar was shut out of the library."

Daemon threw up his hands. "He's a little boy. The only value those books have for him right now is they're things he can throw or tear or chew. Lucivar! His grandfather is the High Lord of Hell and the assistant historian/librarian at the Keep. When that boy reaches an age when he can understand what is held between the covers of those books, do you really think you can stop his grandfather from taking him into that library and showing him all it can offer? For that matter, do you think you can stop me from buying him books and reading him stories and showing him the other side of his education?"

Lucivar tipped his head in a considering manner. "Other side?"

"You stand on a mountain and taste the wind. That's what you've called it when you've tried to explain it. You taste the wind. And you understand more about what is around you in that moment than I can ever hope to know. I can teach Daemonar about books, but you're the only one who can teach him that."

Lucivar mulled that over and finally nodded. Then he took a

step back and turned toward the door. "Why don't we get that drink?"

"That bitch is centuries gone. If you let her keep jabbing at you, you deserve to be hurt."

Damn. He hadn't meant to say that. Hadn't intended to share that memory. But he watched Lucivar turn. Saw the look in his brother's eyes that demanded an explanation.

"You were never good at reading," Daemon said. No. That wasn't the place to start. "I don't have many memories of my childhood before living with Dorothea. Didn't have any for most of my life. But sometimes now . . . It's more the feel of something remembered that opens up the rest."

Lucivar said nothing. Just nodded.

"I remember the feel of Father's arms around me. I remember the sound of his voice, the rhythm of it when he read a story." Daemon paused to sort out a jumble of images. "You weren't good at reading, but you soaked up a story if someone read it to you or told it to you. You remembered all kinds of things, saw all kinds of things in the story."

"And probably related everything in terms of a fight."

"Of course. You're Eyrien." Daemon shrugged. "There was a teacher. I don't remember her name and can't recall a face. I think she was tutoring me, but you were there a lot of the time too. She used to jab at you. Not physically, but she made it clear that you were a waste of her time.

"One day she gave us a story to read. Challenging for me; impossible for you. She did it so you would feel bad. And you were so miserable because you couldn't read it.

"You must have gone home until the next lesson, because I don't remember you being there when Father came to the cottage that evening. Instead of reading the next chapter of the story-time book, I asked him to read the story to me. At first he refused because it was my lesson, and I should read it myself. I pleaded with him, so he gave in and read it to me. But the third time I asked him to read it, he wanted to know why."

"Why did you ask him to read it more than once?" Lucivar asked. "You would have gotten the story the first time."

Daemon looked at the floor. "I wanted his cadence, his rhythm, his phrasing of the words." He looked up. "I wanted to read the story to you before the lesson, and I wanted the way *he* read the story."

Now Lucivar looked away.

"Father would let us get away with little fibs, but he wouldn't let us lie to him," Daemon said. "And he always knew. So I had to tell him why I needed to know the story so well. And I told him about the teacher being mean to you because you were Eyrien and you didn't read as well as I did. He didn't say anything."

Lucivar swore softly. "He's at his scariest when he doesn't say anything."

Daemon nodded. "He read the story over and over, then had me read it, working with me until I was satisfied."

"I think I remember this part." Lucivar sounded a little uncomfortable. He stared at nothing. "You grabbed me before the lesson and read me the story. She was pissed because I could answer her questions about what the story was about."

"He let her come back that last time because we were prepared to meet her on that battleground. But the next lesson, we had a different teacher."

They stared at each other. Prince of the Darkness. High Lord of Hell. They knew enough about the man now that neither wanted to speculate, even between themselves, what had happened to the witch who had been foolish enough to hurt one of Saetan's children.

"How about that drink, Bastard? Then you can tell me all about this spooky house."

Daemon pushed away from the desk to join Lucivar at the door. "Didn't Marian say anything?"

"Marian was too riled about cobwebs to have any kind of discussion. Hell's fire. The next time she gets that worked up about something, I'm dragging you over to the eyrie to deal with her."

"Drag Falonar," Daemon replied. "He still deserves to sweat a bit for bruising Surreal's heart."

"Nah. Marian would probably rein it in and be polite, since he isn't family." Lucivar gave Daemon a wicked smile. "I'll just make the son of a whoring bitch look after Daemonar for an afternoon."

A brush of bodies, shoulder to shoulder.

"You have a mean streak, brother," Daemon said as he opened the door. "I like it."

Lucivar slipped into bed and cuddled up against Marian, more relaxed than he'd been all day. He wasn't drunk. Far from it. But he was hoping she wasn't in the mood for more than a cuddle.

Marian stirred. Let out a sleepy sigh. "You're home."

He brushed his lips over her cheek. "Yeah. It's late, sweetheart. Go to sleep."

She shifted a little, snuggling closer. "Your father came by not long after you left."

So much for contentment. "Why?"

"I think he wanted to talk to you, but he wasn't surprised that you'd gone to the Hall to see Daemon."

Should he have expected Saetan to show up? Maybe. But there

were things he could say to a brother he'd known for centuries that he couldn't say to a father he'd known only for the past nine years.

"He spent the evening reading stories to Daemonar. He's got a wonderful voice for it. I think they read almost every storybook we own. Daemonar fell asleep halfway through the last one."

Lucivar smiled. "Gave you a bit of a rest, then."

A change in her breathing, in her body going from sleep relaxed to aware.

"Before he left, he said something interesting."

"He says interesting things all the time."

No amusement. Her body was telling him he didn't have to be concerned about her temper, but he wished there were a little more light in the room so he could see her face.

"He said children aren't the only ones who like to hear a story."

He tensed. Couldn't stop his body's response to the words. His father might say interesting things, but sometimes the man talked too damn much.

"No one valued reading in my family," Marian said. "Even when I asked for a book as a gift, it was viewed as wasted coin. So I was relieved that you were indulgent about my buying books and spending time in the evenings reading."

"I'm not indulgent," he growled. Envious sometimes because she got so much pleasure from blots of ink on a page while he struggled to read what he had to, but not indulgent. "Your coins, your time. You can do what you please with both."

"I didn't realize you would enjoy sharing those stories."

Embarrassment. A coating of shame. And a healthy sense of survival because he knew if Daemon and Saetan were aware of those feelings—or more aware than they already were—they would both pound on him.

"He suggested having a family story night once a week. Just us—you, me, Jaenelle, Daemon, and him. Surreal, too, if she's interested."

He shifted. All right. He squirmed. "You don't have to do this. You would have read the book. All of you would have read it."

"Not if we picked a new story. And maybe in the winter, when it's too cold to do much, maybe I could share some stories with you that I enjoyed. But not the romances. I couldn't read the . . ."

"The . . . ?"

"I couldn't read *those* parts out loud."

"Maybe I could read those parts for myself." At least he'd have incentive.

"Don't get ideas. It's late."

"Yes, Lady," he replied, chuckling.

He tucked them in and curled himself protectively around her.

"Lucivar?"

"Hmm?"

"I'd like to do that story night. It would be fun."

"I'll talk to Daemon about it." Who would pounce on the idea, so the decision was already made.

As he drifted off to sleep, he thought about his father coming here to talk with him, to read to Daemonar.

No, he hadn't been reunited with Saetan for that many years, but the man did understand his children.

FIVE

Sometimes the only way to deal with a Warlord Prince was not to let him in the door.

Surreal was so pleased with that solution, she repeated it to herself two more times while waiting for Helton, the town house butler, to open the front door.

"Now," she said, in a tone that held both warning and forgiveness. The warning was for the attempt to delay her departure until Rainier arrived. The forgiveness was because Helton wasn't half as scary as Beale, the butler at SaDiablo Hall, and she didn't want the man to resign because he felt unable to deal with her. He'd been fine serving the rest of the SaDiablo family, including the ones who had been demon-dead, but he seemed to find her more of a challenge.

She wasn't sure if that was flattering or frightening.

Helton hesitated a moment longer, then opened the door. Slowly.

Running out of patience, she slipped through the meager opening and stepped outside just as Rainier bounded up the town house's steps. When he saw her blocking his entry, he teetered on the edge of a step—as much as Rainier ever teetered—then settled one step below and gave her a look that blended a hopeful-puppy expression with the Warlord Prince I-am-a-law-unto-myself at-titude. The attitude came naturally to that caste of male. She sus-pected Rainier, along with the rest of the boyos, had learned the hopeful-puppy expression by studying his kindred brothers. It was damn hard to slap at any male when he had that look on his face. Even if he wasn't furry.

"We're going out," Surreal said pleasantly.

"No, we are not," Rainier replied just as pleasantly.

She saw that little extra something in his eyes now, that subtle difference in the way he held himself.

Jaenelle had told her once, *When a male sets his heels down with the intention of standing between you and whatever he's decided isn't good for you, he will remain pleasant and he'll sound agreeable—but he won't budge.*

Letting out a huge sigh, Surreal stepped to the side, giving Rainier clear access to the door. He smiled at her as he came up the last steps and reached for the door. She smiled at him—and raced down the steps.

She got to the house next door before he caught up to her.

"Surreal."

She clenched her hands and clenched her teeth. He had a shield fanning out on either side of him, effectively blocking the whole sidewalk. As long as he stayed put, she could dodge around the shield by going into the street. Since he wasn't likely to stay put, the only way to get past him would be to knock him down—which had a lot of appeal at the moment. Unless Rainier reported the incident to any male in her family.

Forcing herself to relax, she said, "I'm going out." She didn't give him the chance to snarl about it. "It's the fourth day, Prince. I can wear my Birthright Green without discomfort. I could wear the Gray if I needed to."

"You still—" He bit off the words. Hopefully that was all he bit off.

When they were in public, Blood males rarely admitted to having the ability to pick up something in a witch's psychic scent or physical scent that indicated her moontime. They considered it discourteous to remind a woman that she was vulnerable because she couldn't use her own power to defend herself. The Blood didn't talk about it very much, but that ability *was* silently acknowledged by everyone because Warlord Princes stood a heartbeat away from the killing edge during the vulnerable days of any witch to whom they had given their loyalty, and they were more inclined to kill first and ask questions later.

Still, there were limits to indulging the male temper.

"I had considered making a sign that said 'I have a sharp knife and a large Warlord Prince' and floating it over my head, but I don't want to tell anyone about the knife until after I use it, and anyone dumb enough not to notice you deserves to get knocked into a wall."

A twitch of his lips. A shift toward humor instead of temper.

"Where are we going?" Rainier asked.

Ah. Got him. "Bookshop. It's fun reading that Jarvis Jenkell book together, but I wanted something to read at other times."

"Well, that's convenient. I was asked to pick up some books."

Surreal hooked her long black hair behind one ear and narrowed her gold-green eyes. "You were going to suggest walking to the bookshop, weren't you?"

"Was I?"

Bastard. Prick. Arrogant, insufferable *Warlord Prince.*

When she moved forward, he dropped the shield and pivoted

in a graceful dancer's move to fall into step beside her. She took a couple of steps, then grabbed his arm to stop him as she swung around to put herself on his left, which was the subordinate position.

"Surreal."

She was just a witch and he was a Warlord Prince, but her Jewels outranked his, so he wasn't comfortable standing in the dominant position.

Good. He deserved to squirm a little.

"It rained last night," she said. "Puddles. Carriages. Splashing. Whether you create a shield or decide to take your chances, you being on the street side means I won't get splashed."

A male caught between Protocol and the desire to protect. He didn't like it, but he didn't argue about it and he didn't try to switch positions.

They walked in silence for a couple of blocks. Then Rainier said, "Have you heard from your cousins lately?"

"No." Thank the Darkness.

"Then you haven't heard about the spooky house?"

"Spooky house? What's a spooky house?"

Rainier just smiled.

It took several blocks and a few rash promises she shouldn't have made before Rainier told her about Jaenelle's little project.

"You're not serious," Surreal said as Rainier opened the bookshop's door for her. "You made this up."

He shook his head.

She stepped into the shop, then waited for her eyes to adjust to the dimmer light. "Does Daemon know about this?"

"Uh-huh."

"Lucivar? Uncle Saetan?"

"I would think so."

"Hell's fire, Mother Night, and may the Darkness be merciful."

"That seems to be the general reaction."

Surreal sniffed. She hadn't wanted Daemon or Lucivar showing up to fuss over her, but *one* of them could have stopped by to tell her about the spooky house. After all, she *was* family.

And that little thought made her scowl at Rainier. "When did you hear about this?"

"I was at the Hall early this morning."

Why?

Her expression must have conveyed the question, because he gave her a puzzled look. "I stop in a couple of times a week. I *do* work for Prince Sadi, remember?"

She remembered. Even though she'd met Rainier before he'd signed a contract with Daemon, she had to consider what kind of task a male cousin might give an unattached Warlord Prince.

"Am I a friend or an assignment, Prince Rainier?"

She saw the insult in his eyes, saw the way his jaw tensed with the effort to keep his anger leashed.

"You're a friend," he snapped. "At least, *I* thought we were friends. Picking up the books is an assignment."

"I'm sorry." And she was. "I just . . ." Oh, that particular wound was still more raw than she wanted to admit.

Rainier's look was too sharp, too understanding. "You just wanted to spend time with someone who liked you for who you are and didn't see you as a way to advance his standing in a court?"

A light touch of his hand on her elbow, shifting them both away from the door as a dapper-looking man entered the shop.

"I've had sex with a lot of men, but Falonar was my first lover.

It felt different, being with a man when it wasn't business of one kind or another. Maybe if we'd had a romp during the days after we arrived at the Hall and then had gone our separate ways— Falonar to Ebon Rih and me somewhere else—it might have been an easy good-bye. You know. 'Thanks for the hot ride in bed' sort of thing. But I ended up going to Ebon Rih too, and somewhere along the way, enjoying a hot ride turned into something else. At least, I thought it had. But toward the end, instead of having a lover, I felt like I was being serviced by someone who wasn't enthusiastic about the work." That wasn't the only bone still stuck in her throat where Prince Falonar was concerned, but that was all she was willing to share at the moment.

Rainier smiled wryly. "Your introduction to the courts in Kaeleer was the Dark Court. The men who served in Jaenelle's First Circle were the exceptions, Surreal, not the rule. The Consort of a Territory Queen is one of the three most influential men in that Territory. A man usually isn't offered *that* ring until he has credentials."

"So he sleeps his way into a position of power?"

"He doesn't do much sleeping in his Lady's bed, but, essentially, yes. Usually there is attraction, basic lust on both sides. Most often there is affection. Sometimes even love. And sometimes there is lust on the Lady's side and ambition on his—and nothing more."

She moved toward the shelves of books, wanting to be farther away from the counter and the other customers. "It was like that in Terreille, but I hadn't thought it was that way in Kaeleer." And Falonar had come from Askavi in the Realm of Terreille. Maybe he'd seen servicing her as a way of solidifying his position as Lucivar's second-in-command.

What bothered her more? That Falonar's interest in her could have been a combination of lust and a desire to have a connection with the witches who ruled Kaeleer, or that his interest in his current lover had nothing to do with ambition and everything to do with heart?

Let it go. He wasn't the right man for you anyway.

"What I'm trying to say is, I will stand as an official escort for you whenever you need one—or whenever it is required that you have one," Rainier said. "But I'm not here for the sake of ambition. I'm here because I like you. All right?"

She nodded, then puffed out a breath. "I guess I'm just being moody. Or bitchy."

A warm smile now. "I hadn't noticed."

He was teasing her, poking fun of her usual sharp tongue. Something a friend would do. Something a man *wouldn't* do unless he was sure the teasing would be taken as intended.

Cheered by the thought, she moved toward the back shelves. The dapper-looking man who had come in while she and Rainier were talking saw her coming toward him, flushed as if he'd been caught doing something dirty, and ducked out of sight.

Her cheerful mood vanished as she stared at the spot where the man had been. Something about him. Something not quite right. Like he'd dressed very carefully for an afternoon out, but it was a laboriously constructed costume, and he had missed some small detail that skewed everything else just enough to scratch her temper. Added to that was the suspicion that he'd been trying to eavesdrop on a conversation and hadn't been happy when she'd caught him at it.

She considered sending Rainier down another aisle and boxing the man between the two of them, but she had seen no Jewel, didn't get any sense of threat or power. In fact, she got so little sense of him, she wasn't even sure he *was* Blood. Was she going to scare the shit out of a man and spoil his pleasant afternoon of browsing in the bookshop just because she didn't like something about the way he dressed?

Since she couldn't say with certainty that her reaction wasn't the result of an edginess caused by talking about Falonar, she turned to Rainier and said, "Help me find the first Jarvis Jenkell story about the Blood. And while we're doing that, you can tell me again about this spooky house."

Late that evening, Daemon sprawled across the big bed, naked, sated, and blissfully content, his head pillowed in Jaenelle's lap. They had bathed after a hungry session of lovemaking, but he still caught a light whiff of their mingled scents beneath the clean smell of soap.

So tempting to turn his head and press a kiss on that triangle between her thighs. But a kiss through her nightgown would make him want to push up the fabric in order to taste skin, and that kind of kiss would lead to other kinds of kisses.

He'd already indulged himself with those other kinds of kisses.

Besides, she was reading a book and petting him, her fingers drifting through his hair, over his shoulders and back. He could float on that sensation, and he did, beginning to settle into sleep when . . .

tap. tap tap. tap. tap tap. Her finger against his shoulder.

He knew that rhythm. It seldom boded well.

"Are you asleep?" Jaenelle asked.

"Mmmm." Noncommittal response. Could mean anything.

tap. tap tap.

"Daemon?"

He opened his eyes halfway.

"When we have sex, does your penis weep with gratitude?"

A handful of answers flashed through his mind. If he said any of them, he would end up sleeping in the Consort's room. Alone.

"In what context?" he asked.

She lowered the book. Since he'd acknowledged being awake, he raised his head and read the passage. Then he read it again.

"Sweetheart, if my penis ever does that, you will be the first to know. Not as my wife, but as a Healer."

"That's what I thought, but I wanted to be sure."

Hearing the frown in her voice, he shifted, reluctantly, and propped himself up on one elbow. "What are you reading?"

She flashed him a guilty look. "A book by Jarvis Jenkell."

At least you didn't kick me this time. "That book doesn't start with a body in a closet, does it?"

"Yes, it does."

Hell's fire. Well, Rainier would get to deal with Surreal when they reached that part of the story. And wouldn't that be fun?

"Do you think there's something wrong with his brain?"

He studied her expression. Not a flippant question.

"Do you think there's something wrong with his sanity?"

Definitely not a flippant question when asked by a witch who was a Black Widow as well as a Healer.

"Are we talking about the writer or the character?" Daemon asked.

"I'm not sure," she replied, looking troubled.

Uneasy now, he pulled the sheet up to his waist, a defensive gesture. "Why are you asking? Because Jenkell wrote a bad sex scene?" Appalling was a more accurate description.

"No, I'm asking because he seems to think this is normal behavior for the Blood."

He hesitated a moment, then said softly, "It's not that far off from what was done in some of the Terreillean courts." Other places. Other beds. None where he served willingly. Those weren't memories he wanted to stir up and bring to the surface. Not now. Not ever.

Jaenelle looked at him with those sapphire eyes. Looked through him. Saw him in ways no one else ever had—or could.

She vanished the book, then shifted so that she was propped up on an elbow, close enough to him that all she had to do was lean a little to kiss him.

Memories swam up to the surface. Ugly, hateful memories. As he looked at Jaenelle, his heart pounded, but it wasn't from excitement or lust.

Submit. Serve. Play the whore.

He couldn't do it. Not even as a game. Not with Jaenelle.

"Daemon?" Her lips touched his in a soft kiss.

He couldn't do this, had to stop this before she became aroused. If he tried to oblige her while the memories churned inside him, it would damage the feelings between them.

"Do you want to sneak down to the kitchen and snitch whatever Mrs. Beale is hiding in the cold box?"

He blinked once. Twice. Waited for his heart to settle back down to a normal beat.

Love and mischief. That's what he saw in her eyes. She, too, had emotional scars that had come from violence in the bed. She would recognize when something came too close to one of his scars.

As she looked at him, waiting for an answer, different memories washed through his mind. Memories of Jaenelle when she was twelve and he had been her grandmother's pleasure slave. She had talked him into silly, mischievous adventures during those months, dragging him into the game like a well-loved toy that had half the stuffing hugged out of it. She'd given him a taste of innocent childhood.

She was making the same offer now.

"We do have our own kitchen and some food in the cold box." Well, *he* had his own small kitchen where he could putter around when he felt like cooking. That recent renovation was a very large thorn in Mrs. Beale's side, and he had the feeling that the negotiations required before she accepted that addition had just begun.

The fact that a Yellow-Jeweled witch, whom he paid very well to be the cook at the Hall, could make him uneasy about renovating his own home sparked a little, boyish flame of defiance in him.

"Do you think there's anything worth snitching?" he asked.

"This afternoon, when I went to the kitchen doorway to ask for a plate of fruit and cheese, she seemed more territorial than usual."

That was a terrifying thought.

He brushed a finger over Jaenelle's shoulder. "We do own the Hall, and we do pay for all the food, so we are entitled to eat anything we want from either kitchen."

"Uh-huh. If we're caught, you should try that argument."

A picture in his head: him with his hands full of pilfered food; Mrs. Beale and her meat cleaver, both wearing old-fashioned, frilly nightcaps, blocking the doorway and waiting for an explanation.

Mother Night.

Since they were partners in this late-night venture, he reached for Jaenelle's mind and lightly brushed against her first inner barrier. When she opened the barrier, he showed her his imagined picture of Mrs. Beale.

"Oh. *Ick.*" Jaenelle scrunched up her face and made gagging noises. Then she stopped making noises and looked at him, her eyes owl wide. "Do you think she really wears one of those things? Does anyone wear those anymore?"

"I have no idea."

"Beale sleeps with her," Jaenelle whispered. "Do you think the meat cleaver has its own little bed?"

He shuddered. "If I were Beale, I wouldn't share a bed with that meat cleaver." Although Beale might think the same about him occasionally sharing a bed with an eight-hundred-pound cat.

"They have sex," Jaenelle whispered.

"No. No no no. *That* is too scary to consider." He swung out of bed. "Come on. Let's do this before one of us remembers we're supposed to be adults."

She laughed, and that silvery, velvet-coated sound washed away the rest of the bad memories, leaving nothing but the anticipation of a mischievous adventure.

They were laughing at him.

He'd gone to the bookshop in Amdarh that afternoon to spend some time among his own kind, to give them a chance to recognize who he was—and to listen to their praise of his latest book.

The Blood hadn't recognized him, hadn't recognized the significance of his being in that store. As for praising his latest book . . .

Oh, they had liked him well enough when they had thought he was a clever landen who could spin a good tale, but when he had tried to show them who he really was, the truth about *what* he was, *they had laughed at him.*

Landry Langston wasn't just a character in a story. Landry Langston was *him.* A half-Blood raised by a landen mother. A half-Blood who had matured into a man strong enough to *be* Blood.

He didn't know their customs, didn't know their Protocol, didn't know what it meant to be Blood. *How could he?* He hadn't grown up in one of their precious villages, hadn't grown up surrounded by this dance, as they called the constant ebb and flow of dominance that depended on who was in the room. Instead of being trained all through his childhood and youth, as he should have been, he had to *pay* for information about his heritage. His "consultants" had been quick enough to take the gold marks he offered in exchange for "research," but he now wondered about the accuracy of their information—and wondered if they'd given him just enough to make him look foolish.

As for his other "consultant" . . . Well, he couldn't trust much of *anything* that came from *that* mind.

At the bookshop, they had laughed at his portrayal of the Blood, had laughed at him. But they had done much worse here at the hotel. Here, they *pitied* him.

Thank the Dark he hadn't used his real name when he checked in. After that humiliation in the bookshop, he didn't want anyone to know he was in this thrice-cursed city. He almost changed his mind about revealing who he was when the clerks at the desk *did* acknowledge him as Blood. Then he looked into their eyes and listened to their carefully phrased words . . . and realized they thought he was a *broken* male, someone who had been stripped of so much of his power, he was barely one of them anymore.

Didn't stop them from taking the gold marks. No, his lack of power didn't stop *any* of them from taking a hefty fee for the pittance they were willing to share.

Like this room. If he'd gone to a landen establishment in a nearby city, he could have had a better room for half the price. But he'd wanted to stay at a hotel that catered to the Blood. For what? The room he'd been given wasn't any different from rooms he'd had in landen cities—was, in fact, stripped of almost everything that required Craft. On purpose. Because they didn't believe he was capable of being like them.

And he wasn't capable. Not yet anyway.

They thought they were so special, so powerful, so superior.

Daemon Sadi, for example. He'd personally sent *Prince* Sadi a copy of his new book. The bastard hadn't even had the courtesy to write a sentence acknowledging the gift. And *certainly* hadn't sent the desired dinner invitation.

And then there was *Lady* Surreal. He'd heard of her. Who *hadn't* heard of her? Nothing but a whore, but she could stand in a shop and publicly laugh at an *educated* man for no other reason than because she wore a *Jewel*.

There was more than one kind of power. The Blood made the rules and ruled the Realm, but they weren't all-powerful, weren't invincible. A clever man could defeat them and prove he was worthy of notice, of respect.

Pitting one kind of skill against another, a clever man could defeat them. Even the most powerful among them.

Of course, it might not be prudent to admit being the author of such a scheme, but he'd know, for himself, that he could stand among them.

And Lady Jaenelle Angelline herself had provided him with a way of covering his tracks. He'd been a little upset when he'd thought she had stolen his idea and spoiled the setting for his next novel, but now that only meant that people could confirm he'd begun the new Landry Langston story *before* the tragic events took place.

Yes, there was more than one kind of power, and he had the means of weaving a wonderful plot.

He would give the Blood a story the SaDiablo family would never forget.

At least, the ones who were still alive.

SIX

"No, witch-child. I will *not* say *bwaa ha ha.*"

"But it's for—"

"No!" Saetan slammed the books down on the blackwood table in the Keep's library. "If you choose to insult what we are, that is your decision. But I will *not* participate."

Jaenelle stared at him, stunned. "It's just a little fun."

"Fun!" He choked on his anger, since it had no outlet that wouldn't end in fierce destruction. "You're turning what we are into a mockery, and you think this is fun?" He turned away from her, his daughter and his Queen, and pressed the heels of his hands against his temples as he struggled for control.

"Saetan . . ."

Bewilderment. Hurt. She'd come to the Keep to share something amusing and hadn't been prepared for him to turn on her. How could she? He wasn't sure if he was lashing out at her as her father or as her former, and still unofficial, Steward.

He turned to look at her, and he also wasn't sure if it was Jaenelle or Witch who now watched him. No matter. He would have his say.

"We are the Blood, the caretakers of the Realms. We come from various races, but we are no longer a part of those races. We have our own culture that spans those racial cultures. We have our own laws, our own code of honor that landens don't understand and couldn't live by even if they tried. We rule the Territories, and we control the lives of all the landens in those Territories. But we are the minority, Jaenelle. Despite the sometimes brutal way we deal with each other, we seldom need to unleash that power and temper against landens *because we are feared.* Because we are a mystery mostly seen from a distance. And now you are turning us into a *cheap entertainment.*"

He choked. Such a long, long life. So many things that he'd done, both good and terrible.

"By letting some children dictate what we are like, you turn us into a safe, insignificant fear. Cobwebs and creaking doors and funny sounds. We become something to laugh at. So I ask you, Lady. What happens when those boys who find us amusing become men and feel they can ignore the laws established for the landens? What happens when they challenge the Warlords who come on behalf of the Queens who rule over their villages? What happens when they gather in force to attack the Blood and discover how vicious—and how complete—the slaughter can be when we fight?"

A long silence. Then Jaenelle said, "Why didn't you mention this when you first heard about it? You haven't said anything in the past few weeks while Marian and I have been putting this together."

"It wasn't my place to say anything. And, frankly, it hurt too much that it was you, of all people, who was doing this to us."

Another long silence. "My apologies, High Lord," Jaenelle said quietly. "I didn't see this as you did, didn't consider the consequences if people believed this was anything other than make-believe. We'll close the house. Put an end to it."

He shook his head. "You can't. The idea has already taken root, and the news that *Lady Angelline*"—he saw her wince—"is creating a spooky house as an autumnal entertainment has spread to Blood and landen villages alike. I'm sure Daemon and Lucivar will help you control the crowds—"

"Crowds?" She looked alarmed.

"And Daemon will handle any complaints from the Queens who are dealing with the visitors flooding into the surrounding villages."

"Complaints? Visitors?"

He crossed his arms over his chest. "What did you expect? Just a handful of children from the landen village where the house is located?"

"Well . . . yes."

His heart ached with love and exasperation. "Then you really have no idea what you've done." Sighing, he ran his fingers through his hair. "Very well, witch-child. I'll give you your funny sound. But I want a favor in exchange."

She tipped her head and waited.

"Somewhere in your spooky house, let there be one thing that will show those children who and what we really are, that will show them what they face when they stand before the Blood."

"Done."

"Then let's find a room that's a little more private."

There were only the two of them in the library, but Geoffrey could return at any moment.

His face burned with embarrassment as he walked to the door, and he knew that, even with his light brown skin, color visibly flamed his cheeks. He would do this, not just because Jaenelle asked it of him, but because someone else's sensibilities were at stake.

"I promise, Papa. No one will know it's you," Jaenelle said as she stopped at the door.

"Thank you," he replied faintly.

She looked at him. Then she looked at the table stacked with books. Her lips curved in a wicked smile. "If you want us to keep pretending that you're sorting old books whenever we come by to chat, you shouldn't slam them on the table. We all know you wouldn't do that to a book that was truly ancient and fragile."

He closed his eyes and promised himself that he would not whimper. "You all know?"

"Well, I don't think any of the boyos have figured it out, but all of the coven knows."

May the Darkness have mercy on me.

"Come on, Papa. Let's go *bwaa ha ha.*"

Daemon tucked the tip of his tongue between his teeth and bit down hard enough to keep himself from saying something stupid.

If he'd walked in on his father having sex—when Saetan was still physically capable of having sex—it would have been less embarrassing than hearing *that* voice say *"bwaa ha ha."*

"What do you think?" Jaenelle asked.

Eyeing the audio crystal sitting on the corner of his desk, Daemon bit his tongue a little harder and counted to ten—twice—before he said, "It sounds like the High Lord."

She studied the audio crystal, clearly disappointed. "I don't want to lose the quality of his voice, but I did try to adjust it so it wouldn't be recognizable."

There's nothing you can do to disguise that voice, Daemon thought.

Then she perked up, looked more hopeful. "Of course, you *would* recognize his voice, but it's not likely that anyone else will. Not now that it's altered a bit."

Which was when Lucivar walked into the study, carrying Daemonar in a grip that indicated they'd already had one discussion about whether the little beast could run free in the Hall.

"I'm not sure what Marian is working on today, but we were strongly encouraged to leave home," Lucivar said. "So here we are."

★We can take him up to the playroom,★ Daemon said on an Ebon-gray spear thread.

★You've got plenty of shields there and nothing breakable?★ Lucivar asked.

★Oh, yes.★

"Well, you're just in time," Jaenelle said, beaming at her brother and nephew. "Listen to this."

"Bwaa ha ha."

Daemonar squealed and struggled to get free. "Granpapa! Granpapa!"

Not daring to look at anyone, Daemon stared at his shoes and began to understand his father's fascination with footwear.

Jaenelle sighed. "All right. I'll work on it."

Lucivar studied both of them and began backing away. "We'll just wait in the hall."

"Ba ha! Ba ha!" Daemonar shouted. "Granpapa, ba ha!"

Once Lucivar and Daemonar were safely on the other side of the door, Jaenelle said, "Do you think Daemonar will forget?"

Not a chance. "Of course he will. He's little."

She gave him a kiss that tasted of a promise for a very interesting evening, then said ruefully, "Thank you for lying."

He rested his hands on her waist. "You're welcome." He hesitated, but a nagging curiosity made him ask. "What were you going to do if he'd refused?"

Jaenelle looked at him and smiled.

Butterflies filled his stomach and tickled unmercifully before turning into heavy, sinking stones.

"Well," his darling said, "you have a wonderful deep voice too. So if Papa refused, I was going to ask you."

Saetan walked into the sitting room where he'd asked Geoffrey and Draca, the Keep's Seneschal, to meet him.

"My friends, this bottle of wine arrived this evening, compliments of Prince Sadi. Since it came from the wine cellar at the Hall, I can assure you it is a very fine vintage, one best enjoyed when shared."

He called in three glasses and opened the wine.

Draca said nothing until he handed her a glass. "What iss the occassion?"

Saetan grinned. "My son has just realized how much his father loves him."

SEVEN

Daemon walked out of the bathroom in the Consort's suite, noticed the look of apprehension on his valet's face, and approached the clothes laid out on the bed with a heightened sense of wariness. He studied the gold-checked shirt and dark green trousers, which were *not* his usual white silk shirt and black jacket and trousers. Then he looked at his valet.

"What are those?" he asked.

"Casual attire," Jazen replied. "You said you were walking down to the village. For exercise."

"I said I was going to walk to the village instead of taking a carriage because I could use the exercise." Which, in his mind, wasn't saying the same thing. "But I'm going down to the village to talk to Sylvia. The Queen of Halaway. At her request."

"But you're walking. So you'll need these." Jazen held up a pair of shoes that were not Daemon's usual black, polished-to-a-gleam footwear. "They go with the casual attire."

Daemon lightly scratched his chin with one black-tinted nail. "I've been an adult for quite some time and have handled all kinds of personal details all by myself. I am now the ruler of a whole Territory, which means I make decisions that affect the lives of thousands of people. So why am I no longer capable of choosing my own clothes?"

"You got married."

He studied Jazen's face. "That wasn't a smart-ass remark, was it?"

"No, Prince. The Lady thinks you look stunning in your usual attire, but she felt a change of pace once in a while would be good for you."

"I see."

While Jazen went into the bathroom to "tidy up," Daemon shucked off the bathrobe and got dressed. There wasn't much to tidy, but he didn't need an audience when he dressed or undressed—unless it was Jaenelle—and Jazen, who had been viciously castrated when he'd lived in Hayll, didn't need to see a whole male and be reminded of what he had lost.

By the time Jazen came back into the Consort's bedroom, Daemon was dressed and inspecting a cloth bag full of broken biscuits that had been left beside the clothes.

"No!" Jazen said a moment before Daemon popped a piece into his mouth.

His gold eyes narrowed. "Since they were here with my walking attire, I assumed these were treats for the walk."

"They are," Jazen assured him. "But not for you," he finished, hunching his shoulders.

Ah, Hell's fire.

Daemon opened the bedroom door and stood in the doorway, not ready to commit himself by stepping out of the room.

Five furry little bodies waited in the corridor. Five little tails wagged happy greetings. Five little Sceltie minds yapped at him just outside his inner barriers.

★Walkies?★ ★Walkies!★ ★We go with you!★

He got bumped into the corridor when Jazen shut the door behind his back.

"Fine," he said, vanishing the sack of treats. "Let's go for walkies."

The first challenge came when he reached the bottom of the stairs and was stopped by the wails and *arooos* coming from the top of the stairs. Apparently the puppies could get up the stairs by themselves but couldn't get back down.

So it was up the stairs, gather a pup in each hand, down the stairs, set the pups on the floor. He could have used Craft to float all five Scelties and bring them down at one time, but . . .

Exercise, Sadi. You were taking this walk for the exercise.

Two more trips, and they were all heading for the great hall and the front door.

Where Beale was waiting for him, holding a water dish and a pitcher of water. A footman opened the door, and five bundles of fuzzy scampered outside, yipping for him to hurry up.

Daemon vanished the bowl and pitcher. "Thank you, Beale."

"Enjoy your walk, Prince. I have asked Tarl to bring around one of the small gardening wagons."

Daemon just raised an eyebrow and waited.

"It is a long walk for short legs," Beale said. His expression didn't change, but there was a definite twinkle in his eyes. "I think you will find the wagon more convenient for the walk home."

When he'd be pulling that wagon full of five snoozing puppies.

"I am a Black-Jeweled Warlord Prince and the Warlord Prince of Dhemlan. I haven't imagined being those things, have I?"

"No, Prince," Beale replied. "You have not imagined those things. You are the most powerful male in Dhemlan."

Nodding, Daemon walked to the door.

"However . . ."

He stopped. Twisted at the waist to look back at Beale.

"After the Lady came to live with him here at the Hall, the High Lord quite often asked the same question."

Sylvia looked at the puppies. She looked at her younger son, Mikal. Then she pointed at the door. "Outside in the yard. And *stay* in the yard. That is not only a request from your mother; it is an order from your Queen."

Boy and puppies scampered outside.

"Does that work?" Daemon asked. "Using both titles?"

"It usually gives me an extra fifteen minutes before I have to check on him and stop whatever mischief he was about to get into." She brushed at her hair and seemed surprised when it came to an abrupt end.

"New haircut?" he asked, keeping his voice neutral. It was short and sassy and made her look more . . . athletic . . . than the longer, more elegant style he was accustomed to seeing on Lady Sylvia.

"New clothes?" she countered.

"I got married," he replied dryly.

"We did notice."

Shadows in her eyes behind the amusement.

"Why?" he asked softly, looking at her hair. But he knew.

"I needed to look different." She touched her hair again. "I didn't want to look in the mirror anymore and see the woman who had been the High Lord's lover."

She walked into the family parlor. He followed.

"I loved him," she said. "I still do. I've sat in this room through a lot of long nights, thinking about what happened last year and why he chose to step away from day-to-day living—and from me."

"Sylvia . . ."

"No. Let me say this to someone. Please?"

He slipped his hands in his trouser pockets and nodded.

"Saetan showed me what I deserve from a lover. Not just skills in bed, but the genuine affection, the interest in my life and my concerns. That mix of tenderness and amusement he would have when I raved on about something. That look that said, whatever was going on, he understood it was female and he would just ride it out." She pressed her lips together and closed her eyes for a moment. "I finally realized he left. . . . It wasn't just because of what was done to him when he was tortured in Terreille. He really needed to go, to step away from the living Realms."

"Yes," Daemon said softly. "He really needed to go."

He watched her eyes fill. Watched one tear roll down her cheek.

"We were friends before we were lovers." She wiped the tear and sniffled. "I miss my friend. More than the lover, I miss my friend. I wrote him letters on some of those long nights. Just newsy things about Halaway or the boys."

"But you never sent them."

"No."

He held out a hand. "Give them to me."

"Oh, no, I—"

"Give them to me. I can't tell you that he'll welcome them or that he'll read them. But I'll offer them."

She opened a drawer in the rolltop desk and took out a packet tied with a rose-colored ribbon. "There are a couple of letters from the boys, too. Maybe . . ."

He took the packet and vanished it before she could change

her mind. "He did love you, Sylvia. He still does. But he's not coming back."

"I know." It was a trembling smile, but it was still a smile.

"Well, I'd best gather the furry children and—"

"No." Sylvia made a face. "I didn't ask you here to talk about your father. It's your mother we need to discuss."

Daemon studied the fronts of the two cottages, then slowly circled the buildings, checking to see that everything was well tended. Saetan had purchased one cottage fourteen years ago as a home for Tersa. Daemon had purchased the neighboring cottage for Manny, the servant who had been his caretaker when he had been an enslaved prize living in Dorothea SaDiablo's court. More than that, Manny had raised him, had loved him, had been the one good constant in his childhood.

When he immigrated to Kaeleer, he brought Jazen and Manny with him, not willing to leave them to the mercy of the Queens in Terreille. Jazen remained as his valet. Manny, after a few weeks at the Hall, wanted a place of her own—and work of her own. He bought her the cottage next to Tersa's, and Manny gradually took over as housekeeper and cook for Tersa and Allista, the journey-maid Black Widow who was Tersa's current companion.

He rounded the corner and stopped, counting silently to see how long it took the young couple locked in an ardent embrace to become aware of his psychic scent and, therefore, his presence.

He reached twenty before the boy's body jerked with awareness and the couple jumped away from each other.

He stared at the girl first, letting instinct rule temper. Her embarrassment came from *who* had caught them kissing, but he didn't pick up any of the bitch-pride feeling that came from witches who enjoyed putting males in a compromising position.

And the shy smile she gave the boy before bolting out of the yard made him feel easy enough about her to relax about the boy. This wasn't a conquest; this was young love. Most likely, Manny would have shooed the girl out of the yard—after giving the couple enough time for a few unchaperoned kisses.

As he walked toward the boy, he wondered if Manny had taken up her other occupation—village matchmaker.

"Prince Sadi," the boy stammered.

Sleeveless undershirt, dirt-smeared and sweaty. Wheelbarrow, hoe, rake, shovel. No doubt one of the youths who earned a few coins by helping out with the heavier chores.

"We were just . . . I was just . . ." Flustered, the boy looked at the tools and the ground as if an answer would suddenly appear.

"I noticed." He smiled, letting dry amusement clearly show. "The next time you want to kiss the girl in a public place, stay aware of what is around you. And try a little less tongue next time. Never hurts to have the girl wanting more than you're giving. Especially in these circumstances."

The boy looked at him, shocked delight lighting his face be-cause the Warlord Prince of Dhemlan—and more importantly Jaenelle Angelline's husband—had offered sexual advice.

Suppressing the urge to sigh, and feeling much older than he had felt when he woke up that morning, Daemon walked to the back door and knocked.

When Allista opened the door, she didn't seem overly anxious, but he did pick up an undercurrent of concern as he stepped into the kitchen.

"Tersa is up in the attic," Allista said. "She's put locks on the attic door, and she's secretive about what she's been doing for the past few weeks."

"Why wasn't I informed about this?"

"It's odd, but there doesn't seem to be any harm in it or any danger to Tersa. In fact, she's quite pleased about . . . whatever this is."

He felt the edge of his temper sharpen. Tersa was his mother, a broken Black Widow who, seven hundred years before, had surrendered her already-tenuous hold on sanity in order to reclaim her power as a Sister of the Hourglass and see the dreams and visions that foretold the coming of Witch. She had given him hope the night she had told him about the vision she'd seen in her tangled web. But the price of seeing that vision was that her life became as shattered as her mind—until Jaenelle brought her as far out of the Twisted Kingdom as Tersa was able to go, and brought her here to live under the care and protection of the High Lord.

"I am here at least once a week," Daemon said, his voice strained by the effort not to lash out at Allista. "I should have been informed if Tersa was acting unusual in any way."

Allista stared at him, clearly struggling with the need to balance loyalties. Being here was part of her own education—all Black Widows took the risk of becoming lost in the Twisted Kingdom—and in that, her loyalty was to the Hourglass Coven and to Tersa. But he ruled Dhemlan, and he was the one who provided her with a quarterly income to show his appreciation of her care—just as his father had done before him.

She came to a decision. She raised her chin, squared her shoulders, and said, "She didn't want you to know."

He was out of the kitchen and bounding up the stairs before Allista could sputter a protest.

The physical lock on the attic door was undone, but when he tried to open the door, he heard the rattle of another lock on the other side. And he felt the tangle of a Craft-shaped lock. If Tersa had made it, that lock was potentially dangerous, even to someone with his power.

"Tersa?" He pounded on the attic door. "Tersa! Open the door!"

Go away, she replied on a psychic thread.

No, I will not go away.

Annoyance came through the thread. And a trace of fear.

Wait.

He paced the upstairs hallway, and he waited. Five minutes. Ten minutes. Fifteen minutes.

Finally the attic door opened and Tersa slipped into the hallway. She was as thin as she'd always been, despite the regular meals, but her clothes were new and her hair, still as tangled as her mind, was clean.

"Tersa." He couldn't read her emotions, couldn't untangle them enough to get a feel for what was going on. That she was unhappy about his presence hurt, but he set the hurt aside.

"It's a surprise," she said, a pleading note in her voice that he'd rarely heard before. "For the boy. Just a little surprise for the boy."

The boy. Meaning him. He often wondered what she saw when she looked at him. Was it like looking into a shattered mirror with each piece holding an image from the past? Sometimes he *knew* she was seeing him as the child he had been before Dorothea took him away from her and drove her out of Hayll. Sometimes she saw him as the youth he had been when he'd met her again, thinking it was the first time because he didn't remember who she was. And sometimes she saw him as he was here and now. But within all the broken pieces of her mind, he was always the boy.

Knowing why she didn't want him there eased the hurt. She

was making something for him, and she was afraid he would insist on seeing it before she had finished it.

He ducked his head and looked at her through his lashes. "When do I get my surprise?"

A moment's startled hesitation. Then her gold eyes narrowed. "You are teasing me?"

"Just a little." He gave her his best boyish grin.

Her eyes narrowed a little more, but he noticed the change in her psychic scent as she absorbed the fact that he was being playful instead of demanding answers.

"When do I get my surprise?" he asked again.

"Soon. But not today."

He waited, watching her make the effort to hold on to the ordinary world.

"Today you can have nutcakes." Tersa took his arm and tugged him toward the stairs leading to the first floor—and away from the surprise in the attic. "And milk."

"I don't need milk," he said, hustling down the stairs to keep up with her.

"Boys get milk with nutcakes. It's a rule. Manny told me so."

He clamped his teeth together. He couldn't argue with a rule that gave Tersa a way to cope with something other people saw as simple and mundane, not when he knew Sylvia's son Mikal was a frequent visitor. Manny, no doubt, had established the rule for Mikal's benefit.

"Fine," he said, trying not to snarl. "I'll drink the"— *damn*—"milk."

Tersa stopped just inside the kitchen and shook her finger at him. "And no using Craft to vanish the milk. That's fibbing."

A mother's gesture. A mother's scold. Such an extraordinary thing to come from Tersa because it was so ordinary.

It almost broke his heart.

There were so many things he couldn't say to her, his mother, because they would confuse her, tangle her up, threaten her fragile connection to the mundane world. But there were other ways he could tell her he loved her.

So he raised her hand to his face and pressed a kiss in her palm. "All right, darling. I'll drink the milk. For you."

"So," Jaenelle said as they inspected the dining room in the spooky house. "We have the skeleton in the closet, the critters in the cobwebs, the snarl in the cellar, the glowing eyes and smoke, and the laughing staircase."

Marian shuddered. "Can't you fix that laugh to just one stair?"

Jaenelle turned to her and grinned. "It is much creepier now that I took the original laugh and played it in a cavern to get the final sound. But we don't want it fixed to one spot. The next set of visitors would anticipate hearing it when they reached the sixth stair."

"Exactly." She'd almost wet herself when she'd carefully avoided stepping on the sixth stair and then had that sound rising up under her feet when she stepped on the eighth stair. "At least, fix it to one stair while we're still working on the house."

Jaenelle gave her one of those long, assessing looks. "Admit it. This has made you shudder and shiver a lot of the time, but you've also had fun."

"I don't have to admit anything," Marian replied. But she smiled when she said it. Just outside the dining room, where people would be waiting for their turn to enter, was a dusty table with a vase of dead flowers. Swipe a finger in the dust—or even better, have one of the landen boys write his name in the dust—and the next thing that appeared was the words "hello, prey."

She'd thought of that one all by herself.

It was the mix of the absurd, the creepy, and the real that was making the spooky house more than the dumb ideas the landen boys had originally told Jaenelle. Now there were ghostly guides directing people through the house and telling them bits of stories so they would know what to look for in each room. There were phantom shapes that would appear in one of the mirrors, but the spell didn't engage until someone looked in the mirror. As you walked down one part of the upstairs hallway, you heard a heart-breakingly beautiful voice singing—Jaenelle's voice, in fact—but if you backtracked to hear it again, it was gone.

And then there were the other guides.

"Nobody is going to be scared of a Sceltie," Marian said as the two illusion-spell dogs—one black with tan markings on his face, the other brown and white—trotted into the dining room and stared at the humans, their expressions just a little too gleeful.

"That's because these people don't live with a Sceltie," Jaenelle replied.

Marian studied the illusions, whose tails began to wag now that she focused her attention on them. "How complex a spell is this?"

"They'll be able to interact with the visitors in the most usual ways."

A wicked cheerfulness shivered through Marian. "In other words, they're going to herd the landen children going through the house."

"They can touch you; you can't touch them," Jaenelle said, tipping her head toward the dogs. "Your hand will pass right through, but you'll certainly feel it if one of them nips you."

She was starting to like this house better and better. Those landen boys wanted to see how the Blood lived? They thought it was all cobwebs in the corners and rats in the walls? Ha! Let them try to deal with the kindred!

"How *did* we end up with Sceltie ghosts?" Marian asked.

A blush stained Jaenelle's cheeks. "When I went to Scelt to ask Fiona to polish up the little story bits we wrote, Ladvarian and Shadow heard us talking. And since Kaelas got to be the snarl in the cellar and the ghost cat that's seen from one of the upstairs windows . . ."

"They nipped at you until you gave in, didn't they?"

"Badgered. There were no teeth involved. Mine or theirs."

Oh, the sour note in Jaenelle's voice.

Marian turned away to hide a grin. The powerful men in Jaenelle's life didn't often win an argument with her. On the other hand, *she* seldom won an argument with Ladvarian. Did it annoy Lucivar, Daemon, and Saetan to see a dog that didn't come up to their knees cornering Jaenelle into agreeing to things when they couldn't get her to budge, or were they grateful that *someone* could successfully herd their darling Queen when herding was required?

"All right," Jaenelle said briskly. "We have one more room that needs significant work." She left the dining room and led the way to the room that must have been a parlor. "This will be the scariest room in the house."

Marian looked at the furniture and wallpaper and thought the room qualified without their doing anything to it. "What's going to be in here?"

Oh, the look in Jaenelle's eyes as she said softly, "A promise."

Entering one of the small parlors that were in Witch's private section of the Keep, Daemon used Craft to move another cushioned footstool next to the one that held Saetan's socked feet. Then he sat down and studied his father as Saetan closed the book he was reading and took off the half-moon glasses.

"Nice sweater," Daemon said dryly, eyeing the long black sweater Saetan was wearing over a white silk shirt.

"Nice shirt," Saetan replied just as dryly, confirming Daemon's suspicion that Saetan owned the sweater for the same reason he now owned this shirt. "The gold looks good on you."

"I have other clothes besides white shirts and black trousers," Daemon grumbled.

"If you don't, you will." Saetan smiled. "Have any of your silk shirts found their way into your Lady's closet?"

"No." Daemon felt amusement bubble up. "My shoulders are broader than yours, so my shirts don't fit as well as yours did. I gathered this was a disappointment. In terms of the shirts, not the shoulders."

"Lucky you."

He grinned at the sour note he heard in Saetan's voice. Then his amusement faded as he called in a packet of letters tied with a rose-colored ribbon. "Sylvia wrote these," he said softly. "There are a couple from the boys as well. I told her I would offer them, but you don't have to take them." Especially now when he could see the pain gathering in his father's gold eyes. "I can keep them, or destroy them, or read them if you feel someone needs to know the contents. I will do with them whatever you want me to do."

"I can't take them," Saetan said, his voice strained. "It's selfish, I know that, but . . ."

Daemon vanished the packet and rested a hand on Saetan's ankle. "You're entitled to make that choice."

"There are reasons why the demon-dead have their own Realm. There are reasons for the dead to step back from the living. And those same reasons apply to Guardians."

Step back from whomever you must, Daemon thought. *Except me. Except Lucivar.*

"You and Lucivar . . ." Saetan smiled that dry smile. "When I first told the two of you I was retiring from the living Realms, I heard the unspoken warning about what you'd do if I tried to shut myself too far away from all of you. And I wouldn't have tried to shut you out. Not my children. Not you or Lucivar or Jaenelle. Not from the coven or the boyos, since they, too, are my children in a way."

"They've taken the lessons and the love and gone on with their lives. They aren't placing any demands on you. Just small expectations, when there are any at all."

Saetan hesitated. "At this point, my darling, you and the others are fine entertainment most of the time. Not just for me. For Geoffrey and Draca as well. Even Lorn. Once a week, I go down to visit and read him the letters from the coven. The Darkness only knows what the legendary Prince of the Dragons thinks of the content." Another smile, there and gone. "But it's not the same with Sylvia."

"No, it's not the same." It could never be the same with a lover who truly touched a man's heart. He gave his father's ankle a friendly squeeze, then sat back on the footstool. "There are going to be some changes in her household. That may not be easier for her initially, but it will be different."

"Oh?"

"I walked down to the village with five Sceltie puppies. I came back to the Hall with four."

"And the fifth?"

"By now, I'm sure Sylvia has convinced the little bitch to let go of Mikal's trousers. And Mrs. Beale promised to send her recipe for puppy biscuits to Sylvia's cook."

"Mrs. Beale agreed to share a recipe," Saetan said slowly.

"Mrs. Beale agreed that I could pay for . . . I'm not sure what it is except that it's something she wanted for the kitchen but couldn't justify as a normal household expense."

"And you agreed to fund this in exchange for a recipe?"

Daemon stared at his father for a long moment before he muttered, "She sharpened the meat cleaver before coming to talk to me."

One beat of silence. Two. Then Saetan burst out laughing.

Almost time. Everything was almost ready. Big surprises soon. Just a few details left to handle.

Almost ready.

Soon.

And then they would see how many of his surprises the Sa-Diablo family could survive.

PART
TWO

EIGHT

Lucivar braced his elbows on the kitchen table, clamped his hands on either side of his head—and squeezed.

What was wrong with Rihlanders that they had to put *everything* down on paper? And why send this crap to *him*? If Jhinkas were attacking a village in Ebon Rih—or any part of Askavi for that matter—he wanted to know about it because he would be the one stepping onto the killing field to take care of it. But why in the name of Hell did he need five pages of scribbles from some Queen's Steward to tell him *nothing was wrong*? And if he *had* to get stuck in this bog of words, why couldn't the fool who wrote it have the courtesy of having penmanship that a person could read?

Thank the Darkness Daemon took care of all the family business. For reasons he had never understood, Daemon *liked* paperwork.

He didn't mind the twice-a-month meeting to review the properties and wealth held by the SaDiablo family. They were necessary, and the Dhemlan estate that was part of his inheritance and the people who worked on that land were his responsibility.

But Daemon didn't make him read all those damn bits of paper just to tell him nothing was wrong.

Normally he thought of the paperwork that came with being the Warlord Prince of Ebon Rih as the equivalent of having a smashed toe—you just gritted your teeth and limped your way through it. But today it was raining, Marian was gone, and Daemonar and a wolf pup were entertaining themselves by making a lot of noise in the next room. If this had been summer, he would have stripped off the boy's clothes and chucked those two outside, figuring a little water wouldn't hurt any of them—as long as he got boy and pup cleaned up and dried off before their mothers returned. But it was a chilly autumn day and a cold rain, so he was stuck with paperwork, noise, and—

bang bang bang

"I open it!" Daemonar shouted, scrambling to his feet and running for the door. "I open it!"

Sure you will, boyo, Lucivar thought as he pushed away from the kitchen table. *Just as soon as you're tall enough to reach the latch—and the extra locks.*

He simplified his life by containing boy and pup inside a protective shield that kept them from racing out the door as soon as he opened it.

The Dhemlan youth standing at the door was a Summer-sky-Jeweled Warlord wearing a messenger's uniform.

"I have a special delivery for Prince Lucivar Yaslana," the Warlord said, holding out a cream-colored envelope.

As he reached for the envelope, he used Craft to create a skin-tight, Red-strength shield around his hand and forearm. Creating a shield before taking something from a stranger was second nature to him. The fact that the Warlord's eyes widened told him it wasn't second nature to the boy.

"You don't shield before taking something from someone you don't know?"

"They're messages!"

"And packages?"

"Yes, sometimes."

Lucivar stared at him.

"It would drain my Jewels faster if I shielded every time I handled a message," the Warlord protested. "Besides, everything is checked at the message stations before we're given our bundles to deliver."

Lucivar just stared at him.

Beads of sweat popped out on the Warlord's forehead.

"First of all," Lucivar said, "it requires very little power to maintain a shield after you've created it, unless the power is being drained because something is striking it in an effort to get to you. Second, since the danger *is* minimal and you look old enough to have made the Offering to the Darkness, there is no reason why you can't use your Birthright Jewel to shield and tap into the reservoir of power in your Summer-sky Jewel to ride the Summer-sky Wind and deliver your messages at your best speed. Third, even if you believe the danger is minimal, walking into an unknown without shielding is a stupid kind of arrogance—and not an arrogance I'll tolerate where I rule." He continued to stare at the Warlord and waited.

"So all messengers coming into Ebon Rih should shield before handling the messages?" the Warlord finally asked.

"That's right. And if it's shrugged off, I'm going to kick someone's ass—and I'm not going to be particular about whose ass gets kicked. Make sure you deliver *that* message to whoever is in charge of the message station."

"Yes, Prince."

The Warlord managed a stiff-legged control all the way across the courtyard, then raced headlong down the stairs to the landing area, where he could catch the Summer-sky Wind and get out of Ebon Rih.

Lucivar closed and locked the door, released Daemonar and the wolf pup from the protective shield, and walked back into the kitchen muttering, "No shields? What are they teaching these boys?" Since the messenger had come from Dhemlan, he'd talk to Daemon about this. No, he'd *write* to Daemon, who would understand the effort required. And *that* would guarantee the message would get the sharp edge of his brother's attention.

Just look at that, Lucivar thought as he opened the envelope. *Now that I'm settled down and respectable, more or less, I can be twice the prick I used to be and not even have to leave my own home.*

A glance at Daemonar and the pup, who were sitting close to each other and were quiet. The quiet wouldn't last more than another few moments, so he pulled the heavy paper out of the envelope and tossed the envelope on top of the other papers spread out on the kitchen table. Then he gave his attention to the words.

" 'Your presence is requested at a private viewing of The Spooky House,' " he read aloud. An invitation from Jaenelle and Marian. More than an invitation. "Your presence is requested" was a phrase used in Protocol, and the gentleness of the wording didn't change the fact that it amounted to a command. Especially when it came from his Queen and his wife. But . . .

Lucivar twisted around to look at the clock on the other end of the kitchen counter.

"Hell's fire, Marian," he muttered. "You didn't leave me much time to find someone to watch the little beast and reach a village in the middle of Dhemlan."

He read the invitation again, and the insult under the words pricked his temper. He was a Warlord Prince, and he was the ruler of Ebon Rih. And this . . . invitation . . . despite the formal, and correct, wording, left a taste of *slave* in the air.

Sending this shit piece of paper to him was selfish, especially since Marian could have told him about this viewing yesterday so he wouldn't have to jump on command and scramble to find someone to watch the boy. If it had been anyone but Marian and Jaenelle, he would have told her to take a piss in the wind. And he still might, even though one woman was his wife and the other his sister.

And *that*, damn it, was the bone that stuck in his throat. Jaenelle and Marian were both originally from Terreille, but they had never acted like the bitches who lived in that Realm. Until now.

He closed his eyes and forced himself to breathe slow and easy. A man didn't make decisions because of an insult hidden within words. A man made decisions based on honor—and Protocol. So he would heed the command, even though it rankled. He wouldn't disappoint his wife, and he wouldn't disobey his Queen. But . . .

He hadn't seen the spooky house—the Ladies had insisted that he and Daemon not see the place until it was completed—so he didn't know the exact location of the damn village.

First things first. He needed to find someone to—

The wolf pup yipped. Daemonar yelped.

Opening his eyes, Lucivar flipped the invitation toward the counter as he moved to separate boy and pup, but before he'd completed that first step, he knew this wasn't one of the usual boy-and-pup tussles. Something more had happened during those moments of inattention, because Daemonar's fist was raised in real anger and the pup's teeth were bared with intent to harm.

And he, seeing a disaster in the making, made a sound that thundered through the eyrie—the primal, undiluted roar of a furious adult male.

The three of them froze.

As Lucivar stared at the boy and pup, who were staring back at him, he thought, *Mother Night. I sound like my father.*

The thought, like the stone that starts an avalanche, broke open something inside him. He felt the cascade, felt the pressure of the storm on his skin, in his bones. No telling what was coming or how long he could hold it back. But the children had to come first.

So he moved, scooping up Daemonar in one arm and the pup in the other. He vanished the papers on the kitchen table and plunked boy and pup down—and faced the next problem as he kept pushing back that storm, that *sound*.

There was one of him and two of them—and a truth that would sink into the marrow of their bones and remain long after the actual memory was gone. No matter which one he tended first, the other "child" would always know he wasn't as important, didn't matter as much. And things would never be the same between boy and wolves.

So one hand examined the pup and found a sore spot that could have been caused by a kick, while the other hand pushed down the boy's sock. The pup had caught Daemonar enough to scrape the skin on the inside of the boy's ankle. Lucivar rubbed his thumb over the scrape, wiping away the blood before Daemonar noticed it.

"You're all right," he said, trying for soothing but not able to keep the grim temper out of his voice. "Nothing punctured, nothing broken." And neither more damaged than the other, thank the Darkness.

Keeping a firm grip on both of them, he stopped trying for soothing. "I don't care what you did. I don't care who started it. If this happens again, you won't be allowed to play together."

Whimpers from the pup. A poked-out, quivering lower lip from Daemonar.

Hearing the click of nails on the stone floor, Lucivar turned his head and looked at Tassle, who was standing in the archway. Using a light psychic touch, he showed the wolf the memory of what had just happened.

Tassle bared his teeth and snarled at both children.

"Here," Lucivar said, setting the pup on the floor. "Why don't you take care of yours this afternoon, and I'll deal with mine."

At least, he hoped he'd be able to take care of his son. He hoped the emotional storm produced by that sound wouldn't cripple him.

Tassle grabbed his pup by the scruff of its neck and stalked off.

Lucivar looked at the dribble trail of puppy urine he would have to clean up, then looked at his son, whose eyes were now swimming in tears. Sighing, he picked up Daemonar and rubbed the boy's back to comfort him.

"Want Mama," Daemonar sniffled. "Want Mama *now*."

"Me too, boyo. Me too."

He took Daemonar into the parlor and settled into the rocking chair. Between the rocking and the soothing spell he wrapped around the boy, it didn't take long before Daemonar was sound asleep.

Once he was sure the boy wouldn't wake, Lucivar called in a bottle of ointment Jaenelle had made up for "everyday ouchies" and rubbed some on the scrape to clean the wound while he used basic healing Craft to make "everything all better."

Then he vanished the bottle, rocked his son . . . and faced the storm raging inside him.

Not a memory. Not exactly. More like reliving a *feeling*. He didn't know where or when, but he was young. Older than Daemonar, but not by much. He was in that small-boy body, sitting on a bench, hunched around himself as the echo of that *sound* pressed down on his skin, on his bones. Pressed into his heart.

His father's voice. But there had been something terrible in that sound.

There had been agony in that sound.

His fault. He couldn't remember why, but he was certain of that.

Prothvar would know.

The thought brought tears to his eyes. He blinked them back.

Prothvar was gone now. Truly gone. He had died on a killing field over fifty thousand years before, in the war between Terreille and Kaeleer, but he had remained, along with Andulvar and Mephis, as one of the demon-dead who continued to guard the Shadow Realm. In a way, the war that Jaenelle had stopped last year had been an extension of that first war, since Hekatah had been behind both conflicts.

In a way, when Prothvar gave himself to Jaenelle's webs to help protect the Blood when she unleashed her full power, he had stepped onto the last battlefield of that old war.

So Prothvar was gone now. Truly gone. So were Andulvar and Mephis.

Whatever had happened the day Lucivar had caused that *sound* to thunder out of his father had changed his life, had changed *him*. He was sure of that. Now he needed to know why.

There was only one person he could ask.

He closed his eyes—and felt a single tear roll down his face.

He wasn't sure if the tear was for the boy he had been or the family members who were gone.

As he rocked his son, the weight of that old memory that was only a feeling settled over him—and smothered everything else.

Surreal pulled Rainier into the town house's sitting room the moment he arrived.

"Did you get one of these?" she asked, holding out a cream-colored invitation.

"No," he replied after he read it.

She watched his expression change into a thoughtful frown. "What?"

"Well, Jaenelle and Marian both know anyone they invite to view the spooky house will show up—especially anyone from the family—so why set this up like a test of obedience?" He studied her deliberately blank expression. "Queens—especially young Queens—sometimes test their First Circle by making demands that aren't harmful but also aren't considerate. The phrasing on this invitation makes this a command to attend, and since the viewing is for this evening, you're expected to cancel whatever plans or commitments you had made and obey."

"Maybe they wanted to make sure the invitations wouldn't be ignored."

"Maybe." But Rainier didn't sound convinced.

It didn't sound like something Jaenelle or Marian would do, but they could have gotten the jitters about showing the spooky house and hadn't thought out the phrasing of the invitations.

Surreal hooked her hair behind her pointed ears. "Doesn't matter. There isn't much time to get there, so I've asked for a quick meal. We'll eat in a few minutes. I'm going to change clothes. You talk to Helton and find out where this village is."

"Surreal." Rainier looked a little embarrassed. "I wasn't invited."

"Did you or did you not tell me you would stand as an official escort whenever I needed one?"

"Yes, I did."

"Then it's settled. I'm going to change, and you're going to find out how to get to the spooky house."

He flashed a smile at her as he opened the sitting room door. She returned the smile as she walked past him. Then she bolted up the stairs. But she paused when she reached her bedroom, bothered by Rainier's comment that the phrasing of the invitation sounded like a test—especially since the invitation arrived just a few minutes before he did, and barely gave them time to grab a quick meal before they had to leave.

What bothered her even more was the feeling that she'd recently read or heard about someone who had been given a similar kind of test, but she couldn't remember where—or why.

The eyrie was quiet. Much too quiet. And there wasn't a single lamp or candle in use even though the rain and clouds here in Ebon Rih had brought on nightfall sooner than usual.

Leaving the front door open, Marian removed her cape and hung it on the coat-tree. Using Craft, she created a small ball of witchlight, which she tossed into the middle of the room. Then she called in the hunting knife Lucivar had given her. She handled knives all the time in the kitchen, which was why he'd decided this was a practical weapon for her to carry.

It felt different—because it was meant for something different. She could accept that. Even embrace it. She had changed enough from the timid hearth witch she had been when she'd first come to Kaeleer that she could—and would—use that knife to protect her family.

Using Craft to keep the witchlight moving in front of her, Marian crept toward the kitchen. Then she stopped. Sniffed. Brought the witchlight closer to the floor and studied the telltale spots of dried pee that hadn't been wiped up. She raised her hand and gave the candle-lights inside the lamp on the kitchen table a touch of power.

The lamp's soft light filled the kitchen.

Nothing out of order.

Moving farther into the eyrie, she passed the room where Lucivar conducted the formal business of being the Prince of Ebon Rih, and continued on into the family rooms.

And then she found her husband and son in the room they used as a family parlor—a room that was comfortable for adults but could withstand the rough-and-tumble play of an Eyrien boy. Lucivar was in the rocking chair. Daemonar was on his lap. Both were sound asleep.

Marian studied the doorway. Felt the light presence of power. The shield around this room would alert Lucivar to someone's presence the moment anyone or anything crossed the threshold. And the moment that happened, even before he was fully awake or had opened his eyes, he would be primed to attack.

Lucivar, she called softly on a psychic thread.

A change in his breathing, telling her he was awake and aware. He didn't open his eyes, but he dropped the shield, allowing her into the room.

She entered the room, brought the ball of witchlight back to her hand, then set it in a bowl made of stained glass that sat on a table near the doorway.

As she crossed the room, Lucivar opened his eyes. For a moment there was baffled annoyance, as if he'd been angry with her for some reason but now couldn't remember why. Then he looked at her right hand—and smiled.

Puzzled by his amusement, she looked down.

"It was dark and quiet," she said, huffing out a breath as she vanished the hunting knife.

Lucivar's smiled widened. "Worried about me, sweetheart?"

"Maybe." She leaned down, resting one hand on his shoulder while the other hand lightly touched her son's head, and gave Lucivar a soft kiss. "Should I ask why the two of you are tired enough to be asleep at this hour?"

"You don't want to know."

She'd take his word for it.

Lucivar turned his head and looked out the window. "Sun's down."

"It is, yes."

He looked down at Daemonar. "Should we wake him up so he'll sleep later or just put him to bed and accept that tomorrow will start in the wee hours of the morning?"

"Are you up to dealing with him?"

"No." That sounded like a groan. "Besides, I need to fly over to the Keep and see the High Lord."

"Then let's put him to bed. I stopped at The Tavern and picked up some food. We can eat when you get back."

Lucivar shifted Daemonar and stood up. "Fair enough." When they reached the doorway, he stopped.

"What?" Marian asked.

Lucivar stared at nothing. "Don't know. Just . . . It was an eventful afternoon, and I feel like I've forgotten something."

Lucivar walked into the small parlor at the Keep and did a quick assessment. Drapes drawn. Fire going, with plenty of wood in the copper basket. A cozy feel for a chilly, rainy night. His father wearing a wool dressing gown over shirt and trousers. Slippers instead of shoes. Hair that was clean but looked as if it had been finger-combed instead of brushed.

Not unkempt, he decided. Just comfortable.

"I wasn't expecting company," Saetan said dryly.

Lucivar shrugged, then eyed the book in Saetan's lap. "Is Marian going to want to read that book?"

"Probably."

"Is it going to make her cry?"

"Probably."

"*Tch.*"

The sound made Saetan smile as he closed the book and set it on a table beside a tray that held a decanter of yarbarah, a decanter of brandy, and two ravenglass goblets. "If you want to live with a woman, you have to ride the currents of her moods, boyo."

Lucivar picked up a wooden chair that was tucked against the wall, brought it over to where Saetan was sitting, and straddled it, resting his arms on the back. "We now have a code. If she suspects the story is going to make her cry, Marian puts a polished rock on the table next to her chair. When I see the rock, I'm supposed to let her cry and not make a fuss about it."

"Can't stand to stay in the room when that happens, can you?"

"No."

A long pause. Then Saetan said, "What's on your mind, Lucivar?"

He told Saetan about Daemonar and the wolf pup—and saw wariness flicker in his father's eyes.

"I don't remember you," Lucivar said, feeling cautious. "I don't remember the early years when you were there. Daemon remembers a little more, I think, and when he tells me about something, I can sometimes fill in the rest, like a story I've heard a long time ago." He paused. "I don't remember you, but I remember that sound. Even though it came from me this afternoon and it wasn't the same, not really, I could feel the memory of that sound. It's more than the usual roar that will stop a boy before he does something stupid."

No answer. Just a vicious—and visible—effort at self-control.

"Come on," Lucivar said. "You've told us plenty of stories about when Daemon and I were young."

Still no answer. Then, too softly, "And you need to know about this one?"

Oh, he didn't like the phrasing, and he heard the warning, but he nodded. "Yes. I need to hear this one."

Saetan turned his head and stared at the fire. Lucivar waited.

"Even as a little boy, you were a brilliant warrior," Saetan said, his eyes still focused on the fire. "Andulvar said you were the best he'd ever seen, and when you matured and were a physical match for your instincts, nothing would be able to stand against you."

A significant compliment, especially coming from the Demon Prince, but there was more than one kind of fighting, and Andulvar hadn't looked into Daemon's eyes when the Sadist had turned cold. If he had, he would have known there was one thing even an Ebon-gray Eyrien Warlord Prince couldn't stand against and survive.

"You and Daemon . . ." Saetan rubbed one finger against his forehead as his mouth curved in a grim smile. "Even so young, you recognized each other's weakness—or what you thought of as a weakness—and you worked with it. For you, it was words. For him . . . Mother Night, Lucivar. There were times when I couldn't decide if I should laugh myself silly or strangle both of you. You tried to teach him how to fight. And there was so much frustration on both sides because you couldn't understand why your brother couldn't do what you could do in terms of using physical weapons."

"He's less resistant to learning that side of a fight than he used to be," Lucivar said. Of course, Jaenelle needing a sparring partner every day in order to continue regaining her strength and muscle was the prime incentive for Daemon learning a few routines that used the Eyrien sticks. And the sparring sticks were only a short step away from learning to use the bladed sticks, which could be as elegantly vicious a weapon as any sword.

Not that he was going to mention that part to Daemon. Not yet.

Saetan's response was a soft snort of laughter. But he still kept his eyes fixed on the fire. "At that time, Daemon wasn't able to hold his own with you, so Prothvar worked with you, teaching you the moves and how to hold the weapons. He'd even gotten Eyrien weapons made for you, with unhoned blades, so they would be balanced for a child's hand."

Prothvar hadn't told him that. Oh, he'd been told his demon-dead "cousin," who was Andulvar's grandson, had been his sparring partner when he was a child, but he hadn't known Prothvar had been *that* involved in his early education. And he wondered what had happened to those small weapons. His mother had probably thrown them away when she'd given him to the High Priestess of Askavi in order to hide him from Saetan—and then had lost him herself.

"You were staying at the Hall with me for a few days, and Prothvar was staying as well to work with you."

A quiver in Saetan's voice, quickly banished by that vicious—and visible—self-control.

"He had always been so careful around you and Daemon to use illusion spells to hide the worst of it, even though he always wore a leather vest as well. I don't know how you did it, but you talked him into showing you his death wounds. I suppose that was inevitable. He was an older cousin, a seasoned warrior who had died on a killing field, and you were still young enough to see the romance of battle rather than the grim and bloody reality."

Lucivar didn't move. Hardly dared to breathe.

One hundred men walked off the field. Fifteen of them were dead.

The opening lines of the story of the Demon Prince's last battle, the decisive battle in the war that had almost destroyed Terreille and Kaeleer fifty thousand years ago. Eyriens had been telling that story for generations, but he had heard a little of it from the men who had been there. So he knew about Andulvar and Prothvar fighting in the battle—and being the leaders of the army that had stood on the pivotal killing field that had ended Hekatah SaDiablo's attempt to take control of the two living Realms. They were both so immersed in riding the killing edge and winning that battle, they never felt the blows that should have brought them down, just made the transition to demon-dead between one heartbeat and the next—and tore out their enemies' throats, gorging on the blood to sustain their own dead flesh as they kept killing and killing and killing.

Only one side walks away from a killing field. Even though they were no longer among the living, the fact that Andulvar and Prothvar Yaslana walked off that field changed the history of two Realms.

"Nothing would have come of it," Saetan said softly, "if you hadn't come running into my study right after that. You looked so excited, I thought you were coming in to tell me about a new move you had learned or to watch some flying trick you had mastered. Instead, you asked me when you could get your own death wounds. And in that moment, looking at my brilliant little boy, I saw Andulvar and Prothvar as they had looked when they walked off that killing field. I saw Mephis when he first arrived in the Dark Realm, having died that same day. And I remembered the pain of searching for Peyton and Ravenar—and never knowing what had happened to either of them. But it was Andulvar and Prothvar I saw most of all, and I could see you with them—as a boy, as a grown man—walking off a killing field but no longer among the living. And there were no words for that kind of pain. Just a sound."

Lucivar closed his eyes. The words squeezed his chest until he ached.

He had stood on killing fields—and sometimes he had been the only one to walk away. So he could see it clearly. No visible lines defined the space, but a warrior could feel it, knew exactly where the line began, knew the shape of the field. Once a man stepped onto one of those fields, he was committed to the battle. There was no turning back, no walking away. Because of that, a killing field embraced a savagery that transcended anything that could be found on a battlefield. For Warlord Princes, there was a clear distinction between those two things.

After he'd come to live at the Hall and serve Jaenelle, he'd walked in on Prothvar one evening before his cousin was dressed. Before the illusion spells were in place. He had looked at those wounds with the eyes of a warrior—and the fact that Prothvar had walked away from that killing field had told him more about the man as a warrior than all the stories he'd heard in the hunting camps. As a youth, he'd thought those stories about Prothvar's abilities had been exaggerated, as stories tend to be.

As a man, seeing his cousin's body, he'd understood those stories hadn't told the half of it.

He could picture Prothvar and Andulvar as if he were standing next to Saetan waiting for them to cross the line and step off the killing field.

Waiting for them.

In that moment, as a suspicion floated through his mind, he imagined he could feel the brush of Daemon's lips against his ear and hear his brother's voice.

Words can be a weapon, and our father is very skilled with that particular blade. Look—and see clearly. Within what he didn't say is the reason he didn't want to tell you the story.

So he considered the story he'd just heard. And he considered the few things Andulvar had said about that battle.

Then he looked at his father and thought, *Liar.*

While Saetan called in a handkerchief and delicately blew his nose, Lucivar went to the table and poured yarbarah into one of the ravenglass goblets. He warmed the blood wine over a tongue of witchfire, then held out the glass.

Saetan vanished the handkerchief and took hold of the goblet.

Lucivar didn't let go.

The resistance was enough to assure he'd have Saetan's attention when he released that goblet, picked up the other—and poured and warmed another glass of yarbarah.

Eyrien warriors drank small glasses of yarbarah as part of some of their ceremonies, but drinking a full goblet wasn't something a living man would normally do.

He returned to his chair and took a sip of the blood wine, his eyes never leaving his father's face.

"Uncle Andulvar told me you had refused to fight in that war. You had said that, as a Guardian, you had no right to interfere with the living Realms."

"Yes," Saetan replied, his voice barely a whisper. "That's what I said."

"Must have galled him when he walked off that field and saw you standing that one careful step away from the line—the step that kept you out of the fight."

A ghost of a grim smile, there and gone. "I don't think he ever forgave me. Not completely."

"Funny that he never considered why you were there."

"It was a killing field, Lucivar. A slaughter of thousands."

"So the High Lord of Hell was there to meet his closest friend and that friend's grandson to help them make the transition to demon-dead."

"Yes."

Lucivar smiled and said, "Liar."

No answer. Just that vicious—and visible—self-control.

"I *am* brilliant on a killing field, and I think I can see you more clearly than Andulvar ever did."

Still no answer. He didn't expect one.

"The pivotal battle," Lucivar said softly. "The place—and the men—who could break Hekatah's bid to control the Realms. The *man* who could break Hekatah's bid. As long as Andulvar Yaslana, the Demon Prince, could lead warriors into battle, Hekatah's chances of winning grew less with every fight. So she had to eliminate him, destroy him completely.

"You had declared yourself out of the fight. A Guardian has no right to interfere with the living Realms. That's what you'd said.

You hold to your code of honor, no matter the cost. Hekatah and Andulvar both knew that."

"What's your point, Lucivar?"

He heard the warning. Saw something lethal flicker in his father's gold eyes before Saetan regained all of that formidable self-control. But he was going to finish this, was going to acknowledge something that had remained hidden for fifty thousand years.

"The army that faced Andulvar and his men that day. All those men on that killing field. They were fodder. They were there to drain the power in Andulvar's Ebon-gray Jewels, to wound him, weaken him, eliminate the men around him. But Hekatah hadn't expected *them* to win. Another army was supposed to reach that field. Fresh warriors primed for a fight standing against survivors who had been fighting for hours. *They* were the warriors who were supposed to win the battle. *They* were the ones who were supposed to walk off the killing field.

"But they never got to that field, did they? Because they met another enemy. One whose presence hadn't been anticipated. One who didn't fight with a blade. One whose power and skill and temper . . . Well, as you said, it was a slaughter of thousands."

No response. He didn't expect one. And he wasn't sure he actually wanted Saetan to admit to breaking the code of honor that kept the man from being a monster.

"If Andulvar, Prothvar, and their surviving men hadn't been the ones to walk off the field that day, Hekatah would have won the war between Kaeleer and Terreille, and both Realms would have become the nightmare Terreille became all those long years later." He took a swallow of yarbarah as a private salute to the warriors who were gone. "So I won't ask why you were there that day. But I thank you for being there—and for standing that one careful step back from the killing field."

They looked at each other, and there, within the silence, ac-knowledged a man's betrayal of himself—and a secret that would remain a secret.

"Anything else?" Saetan finally asked.

Lucivar stared into the goblet. Easy enough to shrug it off, let it pass. After all, they were both feeling a little raw. But . . .

"I don't remember you, but you shaped the core of me during those early years, and your passion and honor were the forge that made that core unbreakable, despite everything that came after. I don't know what I would have become without that, but I'm certain I wouldn't have been worthy of serving Witch. So I thank you for that, too, and . . . I'm proud to have you as my father."

"As I am proud to have you as a son," Saetan replied softly.

Time to go, boyo, before you get weepy. He used Craft to float the goblet back to the tray, then stood up and stretched. "Well. I'd better get back. If the little beast wakes up and Marian has to deal with him on her own . . ." He frowned.

"What?" Saetan asked.

Lucivar rubbed the back of his neck. "I have the nagging feel-ing that I've forgotten something."

"Hmm. Well, you'll either remember it on your own, or you'll remember it when whatever you've forgotten comes back and bites you in the ass."

Lucivar laughed. "I guess that's something to look forward to."

NINE

Standing at the edge of the street, Surreal studied the three-story house that looked like it had seen better years. Better decades, actually. There was a shabbiness to it that felt like neglect rather than the decline that comes with age. But it must have been a prominent house in the village at one time, since it was standing on a plot of land that was significantly larger than its neighbors.

She didn't know much about landen architecture or landscaping, but the whole thing struck her as being off-balance, as if the right side of the land were about to tip up from the weight of the house on the left side. And why would anyone surround property with a waist-high wrought-iron fence that followed the property line at least on the two sides but split the front yard in half between house and street, making it useful for nothing?

"It might have been attractive at one time," she said, not bothering to keep the doubt out of her voice.

"You mean before it was built?" Rainier replied.

She huffed out a laugh.

"There are plenty of Blood mansions that have a tower,"

Rainier said. "But the tower attached to the right side of this building . . ."

"Looks like a fat penis with pretensions."

Rainier choked. And because he choked, she couldn't resist.

"Really," Surreal said. "It reminds me of the cock decorating that was done in a Terreillean Territory a few decades ago. Didn't stay in fashion for long, but it was amusing while it did."

"Cock decorating."

She couldn't tell if he was amused or appalled. But he didn't sound suspicious. "Feathers, ribbons, netting that acted as a sleeve so that seed pearls and sequins could be added."

"I can't imagine any of that would be comfortable, and I also don't see the point."

"Well, it's not like they kept it stuffed in their pants." She bit the inside of her cheek.

"But . . . In a social gathering, it's much better for a man to imply what he's got rather than actually *show* it."

Did men use undergarments that enhanced their cocks the way women sometimes used corsets or specially constructed brassieres to enhance their breasts? She'd have to ask him sometime.

"Besides, a man can't sustain an erection for an entire evening," Rainier said.

"That's true. And there was an ebb and flow to the festivities for a while." Oh, he was definitely appalled now. "That's why most men started wearing a stiff covering over their asset and decorating that."

"How could you tell it was a covering?"

"Has your cock ever turned purple?"

"No."

"Well, then." She grinned. Couldn't stop herself. Besides, he sounded like he was being lightly strangled, so it was time to stop teasing. "Now that you're warmed up for it, shall we go view the rest of the evening's horrors?"

"*Surreal.*"

Laughing, she ignored the muttering coming from her companion.

"It really was done in a Terreillean Territory, but not to that extent," Surreal said.

They both pondered that, and she suspected her perception of that particular fashion was very different from his.

Then Rainier said, "If it *had* been done like you described, do you think Sadi . . . ?"

He looked at her. She looked at him—and knew they were both picturing that elegant, beautiful man moving across a ballroom with lethal, feline grace. If Daemon had been forced to display himself during the years he'd been a pleasure slave, he would have done it right. Nothing garish for Sadi. Seed pearls and silk. Maybe a small ruby strategically placed to catch the light—and a woman's eye. A fatal lure that promised unimagined pleasures, despite his lack of arousal. But the look in Sadi's golden eyes and his cold, cruel smile would have made a very different kind of promise—and *that* was the promise the Sadist always kept.

And *that* thought got her moving up the broken, weedy flagstone walkway at the same moment a man came out of the house and lit the lanterns that hung on either side of the door.

"Think that's the equivalent of the houselights going down in a theater?" Rainier asked as they stopped at the gate in the fence.

"Could be." A movement near the edge of the property had her dropping back a step, giving Rainier fighting room as she turned.

"Just children," Rainier said, turning with her. "One of them must have been keeping watch. Or else they planned to meet here at dusk."

"Makes sense. After all, they're probably the ones who provided the inspiration for this place." And imagining them all getting close enough for her to give each one of them a hard whack upside the head as payment for that inspiration pleased her so much she smiled and waved at them.

"Don't encourage them," Rainier warned. "They'll think you're inviting them to come with us."

"Don't be daft. Landens stay away from . . . Hell's fire." They *had* taken her wave as an invitation.

"Told you," Rainier said, grabbing her arm as he pushed the gate open. It swung easily enough but creaked as if it hadn't been used in years.

"How was I supposed to know?" Surreal grumbled, caught between going through the gate, which she didn't want to do, and being trapped against the fence by a pack of children.

"You were that age once."

"I wasn't like them at that age."

Rainier made a scoffing sound. "Being Blood doesn't make us *that* different when we're young—at least in terms of behavior."

That wasn't what I meant. But she didn't contradict him because the children were approaching too fast—and because her relationship with her ex-lover Falonar had taught her that a man who could accept she'd been a whore might have a problem when he discovered *when* she'd become a whore.

There weren't many outside of the family who knew the details of her past, and she preferred it that way.

"Let's get inside," she said.

They went through the opening. Then Rainier swore fiercely.

So did she as she wiped her face. Nothing there, but the sense that she'd walked into a big cobweb lingered.

"I guess the fun begins even before we get into the house," Rainier said, sounding cross.

"It explains why the fence is here instead of bordering the edge of the property," Surreal said. "Jaenelle and Marian must have moved it so they could attach this illusion spell to the gate and still leave some open ground where visitors can gather."

"Maybe getting a face full of cobwebs is meant to discourage people from going farther?" He sounded like he'd be quite happy to be discouraged from going farther.

"Are you telling me an Opal-Jeweled Warlord Prince is going to be put off by a few cobwebs?"

He just looked at her.

"Right. We're here—and we're stuck." Surreal rubbed her hands over her face to get rid of the lingering feeling. Then she sighed. "And we should accept this as part of a performance." A glance at the children, who were hovering on the other side of the gate and seemed to be rethinking the wisdom of approaching two of the Blood. But once she and Rainier reached the house, it was a fair bet that the children would come through the gate to get a closer look. After all, this place was probably irresistible to their maggot-filled little minds.

As she and Rainier walked up to the covered entryway, she listened for the squeals. Landen or not, those children weren't going to shrug off getting a face full of cobwebs.

"Well, that's a bite in the ass," Rainier said, looking back when they reached the steps. "Damn illusion stopped us cold, and they didn't even notice."

"Maybe that says more about landen housekeeping than about the illusion," Surreal replied before giving her attention to the man who had lit the lanterns and now appeared to be waiting for them.

"A good evening to the Lady and gentleman," the man said. "Or a frightful, fearsome evening if you're not careful. Strange things go on in this house." A hard look at the children who were now standing close enough to hear him. "Yes, strange things."

Nervous giggles from the girls in the group.

If we really want to scare them, we shouldn't bother with this spooky-house stuff, Surreal said on a psychic thread, tipping her head to indicate the children. *We should just throw a couple of them into the kitchen at SaDiablo Hall.*

While Mrs. Beale is in there? Rainier asked. *That's vicious.*

I know.

"And who might you be?" Rainier asked, looking at the man.

"The resident caretaker," the man replied. "And a resident ghost."

"Ghost?" Surreal asked.

The man nodded. "One of them who was enslaved to serve the ruler of the house."

"The Blood—" She bit back the words. This was Jaenelle and Marian's performance. If they wanted landen children to think the Blood kept enslaved ghosts as servants . . .

Maybe this version of the Blood was going to be harder to swallow than she'd imagined.

A ghost is one of the demon-dead whose power has faded to the point where there is still a shape without substance, Rainier said. *What possible use would one be as a servant?*

Apparently they can light lamps, Surreal replied. *Although you would think they could just stand out of the way and glow.*

*I don't think they can do that. And even if they could, *he* isn't glowing.*

She wasn't even inside yet and the place was already scraping on her nerves and temper. The sooner they fulfilled their obligation and could leave, the better she'd like it. "Has anyone else arrived?" she asked the caretaker.

"No, Lady," he replied. "You and the gentleman are the first."

"What time is it?" she asked Rainier.

He called in a watch, opened the cover, and held it in the light for her to read.

Somewhere in the house, a gong sounded.

"What's that?" Surreal asked.

The caretaker shrugged. "Nothing that concerns the likes of me."

Rainier closed the watch and vanished it.

The gong sounded again.

Some kind of clock? Frowning, Surreal stared at the street. Where in the name of Hell were Lucivar and Daemon?

"Well, shall we go in?" Surreal asked Rainier.

"Oh, best to wait for the whole party," the caretaker replied. "Won't be as much fun if there's just the two of you."

Since she wasn't expecting to have fun, that wasn't an incentive to wait.

"How many were you expecting?" Rainier asked.

"Only twelve people per tour," the caretaker said.

"Twelve people were invited?" Surreal asked.

The caretaker shrugged. "Was told only twelve to a tour."

They stood outside, waiting. To give herself something to do, Surreal pictured a straw dummy of Falonar—and thought she deserved a lot of credit for picturing a straw dummy. Then she pictured herself throwing lovely, shiny knives at the target.

The third time she got to one hundred, she huffed out a sigh. Rainier must have taken that as his cue to do something.

"What about them?" Rainier asked, tipping his head to indicate the children.

No, Surreal said. *I don't want to be responsible for them. I'm not a Sceltie who enjoys herding idiot sheep.*

Tomorrow they could come here on their own, so by letting them come with us tonight, we're nothing more than token escorts, Rainier replied. When she hesitated, he added, *Do you want to be done with this family obligation or not?*

Put *that* way . . . *Yeah. All right. Fine.*

"How about if seven of them come on the tour with us?" Rainier asked the caretaker. "That would make nine in the house and enough places left open so the others can join us when they arrive."

The caretaker shrugged.

I guess ghosts are as good with providing information as you are with adding, Surreal told Rainier. *When Sadi and Yaslana arrive, that will make eleven, not twelve.*

I was assuming the High Lord was also invited.

Mother Night, I hope not.

A flash of amusement along the psychic thread, but Rainier kept a straight face as he turned toward the children. "All right, then. The seven oldest of you may come with us."

The next few minutes were filled with arguing, bartering, and negotiating.

Rainier said, *I thought this would be the simplest way, since the younger ones will be able to come on another night.*

Surreal studied the group of children as if she were at an aristo party. *Nothing is going to be simple. You've got a dominant cock and a bitch who's the dominant female among this group.

But not all the children here follow those two, so cock and bitch are trying to ignore your age requirement in favor of having their followers tour the house with them.*

Rainier didn't respond to her assessment directly, but his sharp whistle got the children's attention. Within moments, Rainier had eliminated the younger children, selected the six oldest—three boys and three girls—and was about to toss a coin to decide between the two remaining children when Surreal gave him a psychic tap on the shoulder.

One more, she said, looking at the boy lingering on the other side of the fence. Not like the others. This one was an outsider who might be included when another body was needed for a game, but he wasn't someone any of the others would include for any kind of treat.

"What about it, boy?" Rainier said, holding up a copper. "We could do a second coin toss for the last spot."

A hesitation. Then the boy looked at the other children and backed away, shaking his head.

The crest side of the copper won the toss, and the fourth boy joined the others.

"This way now," the caretaker said, opening the door but carefully staying outside.

An odd sensation as she passed through the doorway, as if the threshold required more than one step. Maybe it was all the illusion spells that had to be woven throughout this place. Would Blood who wore lighter Jewels be more or less affected? She'd have to ask Marian, since the hearth witch was the only one in the family who wore lighter Jewels.

"Sitting room is that doorway to the right," the caretaker said.

Since the children were crowding in behind her, she moved farther into the hall—and caught a whiff of something unpleasant.

"Just wait in the sitting room," the caretaker said, still standing outside.

The last one of their group to enter the house, Rainier was now the first to enter the sitting room.

As she waited for the children to follow Rainier, she caught another whiff of . . . something . . . and looked around. Seemed to be coming from the area around the stairs, but it was there and gone before she could pinpoint the source, and there was nothing else in that part of the hall except a mirror on the wall opposite the stairs. The only other thing in the hall was a coat-tree, and the smell wasn't coming from that.

Sighing, she went into the sitting room. An hour from now she would have completed her duty to family, Rainier would have completed his duty to Queen, and they could go back to a clean dining house in Amdarh and have a late meal while they figured out how to avoid saying anything about this damn place.

They weren't coming. *The bastards weren't coming!* How could either of them have ignored that summons? He'd been so careful with the wording to make sure they couldn't wiggle out of attending the evening's activities.

There had been some risk in sending the invitations so late, but he'd had to balance the delay against the risk of them talking to each other or, worse, talking to the *Ladies*. Still, he'd given them enough time—*if* they were as devoted to their wives as they professed.

Bastards. He recognized the male who had come with *Lady* Surreal as the man who had been with her in the bookshop that day in Amdarh, but he didn't know who he was. Probably no one important. Probably just the stud Surreal was currently riding. He'd been in the wrong position to see the Jewel in the male's ring, so there was no way for him to tell what kind of power had just walked into the house.

No matter. He'd prepared this entertainment for the SaDiablo family. No other male could compare with *those* two, so the bitch's escort posed no threat to his plans.

At least the male had been obliging enough to invite some of the children. It was necessary for a few of them to be involved in this entertainment, and as the kindly caretaker, he would have let some of them go in with the Blood. But now the Blood would feel responsible for the children's welfare, since *they* had extended the invitation.

Assuming, of course, that the Blood ever felt responsible for anything they did.

No matter. The children were in the house by the Blood's invitation, and that should work out better than he'd anticipated.

He looked at the street, his eyes passing over the boy still standing on the other side of the gate, and hoped to see one of *them* appear. Once he closed the door, all the spells would be in motion—and would stay in motion while any of the guests lived.

Sadi and Yaslana weren't coming. So be it.

Let the game begin.

The outside of the house had peeling paint and some shutters that looked like they were holding on by a single nail. The sitting room was a good match for the exterior—peeling wallpaper that was thankfully so faded it barely had color, lace curtains that looked like they would shred as soon as any attempt was made to clean them, and overstuffed furniture that, judging by the chew holes, housed several generations of mice.

"It's awful," the oldest boy said, sounding thrilled.

"The Blood don't live in places like this," Rainier said, sounding less than thrilled.

"I have," Surreal said as she wandered around the room. A wave of annoyance coming from Rainier washed over her, but she continued to study the room. Wasn't there supposed to be something spooky? Although she'd bet just looking at this place had given Marian shudders.

"Lady Surreal, neither of us live in a place like this."

More than annoyance. Rainier was pissed that anyone, even landen children, would think the Blood would consider this place homey.

"Not now," Surreal said, focusing on a portrait over the fireplace. Was there something queer about the man's eyes? "But when I was preparing for a kill and didn't want anyone to know I was in that part of a Territory, I would stay in an abandoned place like this for a few days."

Sometimes she preferred secrecy to staying at a Red Moon house and providing services as a whore, which had been her other profession—until her recently acquired male relatives calmly told her that any male who got into her bed from now on had better be there for her pleasure or he would live just long enough to regret using his cock. So that ended *that* career. All right, she'd already walked away from that part of her life even before she came to Kaeleer, but it was still annoying to be *told* she was retired.

Becoming aware of the silence, she turned away from the portrait and found seven children staring at her.

"You kill people?" the youngest girl asked.

"I was an assassin," Surreal replied cheerfully. "And a damn good one. I know all kinds of death spells."

★That might have been a little more than they needed to know,★ Rainier said.

Since they were looking at her the way a rabbit looks at a wolf, Rainier was probably right. On the other hand, they would probably want to stay away from her and would attach themselves to him during the tour, and that was all right too.

Then she looked at Rainier. His expression strongly suggested that she soften her statement.

"But I'm retired now," Surreal said. "I don't kill people anymore." *At least, not for money.* "I'm Lady Surreal, and this is Prince Rainier."

"Those are funny names," the oldest boy said.

"Really?" Rainier sounded like he was gritting his teeth hard enough to break a few.

★You were the one who invited them to join us,★ Surreal said, earning a searing look from Rainier before she focused on the children. "So who are you?"

The oldest boy, the one she'd labeled the dominant cock, was Kester. His friend was Trist. The other boys were Haywood, who was called Henn for reasons she didn't understand, and Trout, whose face reddened when the other boys sneered at him, but who gave her a polite bow nonetheless.

The bitch was named Ginger. Her pal, the aspiring bitch, was Dayle. The youngest girl was Sage.

★Is it common for landens to name their children after foods and spices?★ Surreal asked Rainier.

★I don't know. Maybe their mothers were hungry when they had to choose a name. Or they could be lying about their names because they think it's amusing.★

A door slammed. The house shuddered.

"I'll check," Surreal said, crossing the room, her hand curled in just the right way if she needed to call in her stiletto. But when she reached the sitting room doorway, there was only the care-taker in the hallway, turning away from the closed front door.

"So discourteous," he muttered as he walked past her. "So *dis-obedient*. Not what I expected."

"When does this tour begin?" Surreal asked him.

He didn't stop, didn't turn. "Find the first clue, and you'll know what to do," he snapped. He slammed through a door at the end of the hallway.

She was trying to be tolerant of this place because it was Jae-nelle and Marian's idea, but she was going to talk to them about that little bastard. Performance or not, if he tried that pissing con-test with the wrong Blood male, he would end up very very dead.

And speaking of Blood males . . .

She headed for the front door.

"Anything?" Rainier asked as he stepped into the sitting room doorway.

"I'm going to check for late arrivals," Surreal said. "You look for the first clue. It must be in the sitting room, since we were directed there by that little piece of walking carrion."

"Surreal." Rainier tipped his head to indicate the children.

She turned and gave him a look that had him backing up a step. Then she yanked the front door open—and stared at the brick wall in front of her. She reached out cautiously, sure her hand would pass through the illusion—or trigger something "spooky." But it was solid brick against her palm.

"Hell's fire," she muttered. "Guess we don't leave through the same door we entered." And now that the door was closed, that smell in the hallway was getting stronger—and more familiar.

Near the stairs. But where . . . ?

Using a few drops of her Birthright Green power, she created a ball of witchlight—and frowned as a gong sounded somewhere in the house. But the sound was forgotten when the light revealed a door under the stairs. No obvious knob, but there had to be a latch that was easy enough to find and open. Otherwise, the space would have no use.

As she moved closer, the smell got stronger.

Yes, there was the latch, made to look like a knot in the paneling. She shifted the witchlight so she could see inside as she opened the door and . . .

"Well, shit."

"Did you find the clue?" Rainier asked, crossing the hallway to join her.

She pulled the door open a little farther so they could both see inside. "I don't know if it's a clue, but I did find a body in a closet."

TEN

Daemon approached the Consort's suite with weary eagerness. He usually enjoyed the business side of ruling Dhemlan and taking care of the family property and wealth, but today each thing had felt like a handful of grit being sprinkled over him. Before he gave himself to the best part of the day—those hours he would have with Jaenelle—he wanted a long, hot shower. No. A bath. The luxury of soaking away all the nattering voices he'd dealt with throughout a long morning's worth of meetings and all the paperwork he'd waded through during the past few hours. The Dhemlan Queens were still nervous about dealing with him, and he understood that. When Jaenelle's life had been threatened by a witch obsessed with having *him*, he'd made it brutally clear what he would do to protect someone he loved. So he understood why the Province Queens were anxious to assure him that they *did* have control over the territories they ruled within his Territory.

But he really didn't need to know all the damn details.

And he really didn't need anyone else trying to wheedle an invitation out of *him* to the private viewing of the spooky house, which everyone seemed to know about. Except him because, after all, why should *Jaenelle's husband* know about a private viewing? Hell's fire! He'd come back to the Hall to find a note from Lord Khardeen, who wanted to talk to him about the damn place—and Khary lived on the other side of the Realm!

Rumors, he reminded himself. Just rumors, which were to be expected. Everyone was curious about this entertainment Jaenelle and Marian had created.

When he saw the envelope on the dressing table, he huffed out a sound that was part sigh, part annoyance. No doubt it was another invitation to some kind of autumnal festivity. He'd have to ask Jaenelle how many of these things she was willing to attend. Even better, he'd ask the High Lord how many the ruler of Dhemlan was *required* to attend.

He picked up the envelope, noting it was good-quality paper, then turned it over. Just a simple, decorative seal pressed into the wax. Nothing that belonged to an aristo family or a court. At least, not one he recognized. The writing had been done by an unfamiliar male hand.

He opened the envelope and withdrew the invitation. Moments later, his anger arrowed toward one mind. *Beale!*

While he waited for the Hall's butler to answer the summons, he paced around the room, too upset to stand still and yet feeling more and more caged by his own need to move. Damn and damn and damn!

The knock on the door was tentative, which told him how much his lash of temper had unnerved Beale.

Since it was too tempting to rip through the door—and then rip through the man—he forced himself to stand still and used Craft to open the door with obvious control.

"Prince?" Beale said when he entered the room. No sign of

nerves in voice or stance, but in the eyes . . . Yes, there were nerves. After all, a Black-Jeweled Warlord Prince could do a vicious amount of damage to a Red-Jeweled Warlord—especially if the intent was to maim rather than kill.

"Explain this." Daemon held out the invitation.

Beale came forward just far enough to take the invitation and read it. Then he glanced at the small clock on the dressing table. His skin turned gray as he looked at Daemon in horrified apology.

"I have been down in my study doing paperwork for the past several hours," Daemon said through gritted teeth. "I was home, Beale. I have no excuse for ignoring this invitation." Summons, actually. They both understood what the wording meant.

"The messenger was quite specific," Beale said, stammering. "The invitation was to be delivered to the Consort's *room*. He specified a place, not the person. So I thought, since it was for the *Consort*, the Lady was planning a private evening and had asked a friend to address the envelope so the contents would be a surprise for a little while longer."

Hell's fire. Beale was a romantic. Who would have guessed? He'd brought up the message thinking the Queen wanted a sensual evening with her *Consort*.

Daemon took a moment to consider the implications of that. "Dinner?"

"Since we weren't expecting you downstairs this evening—"

Or even out of bed, Daemon added silently.

"—Mrs. Beale planned some dishes that would not be spoiled if the meal was . . . interrupted."

He really didn't want to think about Beale and Mrs. Beale discussing his sex life.

"I *am* sorry, Prince," Beale said. He turned his head, and the

slight change in his expression indicated he was talking to someone on a psychic thread. Then he relaxed a little as he turned
back to Daemon. "Mrs. Beale is packing up the meal. I had already selected some bottles of wine, so she'll pack those as well.
You will arrive a little late, but perhaps a celebratory moonlight
picnic will be sufficient apology?"

They both heard it at the same time—the sounds of someone
moving around in the next room.

Jaenelle was home. The fact that she was here instead of overseeing the first viewing of her precious entertainment meant his
absence had been noticed and he was in for a rough night.

Don't do that, he warned himself. *Don't smear her with the memories of how other women would have reacted.*

It was a fair warning, but it didn't lessen his feelings of bitter
unhappiness.

"I will explain to the Lady," Beale said, squaring his
shoulders.

"No." Daemon took the invitation. "No matter the reason,
I'm still the one who is accountable."

"But—"

"No." He hesitated. "I do appreciate the offer, Beale."

He waited until Beale left before he approached the connecting door and knocked.

"Come in."

As he walked into the room he usually thought of as their
bedroom and now hesitated to think of at all, Jaenelle gave him
a puzzled look, then turned her attention back to the dress box
on the bed. "I stopped in Amdarh on the way home. I wanted to
see if the dress was finished, and it was." She seemed happy and
excited as she tossed the top of the box aside. "Why were you
knocking?"

"I wasn't sure if I would be welcome."

She stopped unwrapping the dress, straightened up, and faced him. Her sapphire eyes were filled with a chilling blankness.

They were still working through some difficult patches in their relationship, raw spots created during the months she had been healing—when neither of them had been sure of still being wanted by the other. So his words were a warning that he had done something that could end with her locking him out. Forever.

"Meaning what?" she asked too softly.

He felt a desperate need to hold her, to assure himself that it was, after all, a small mistake. But it wasn't. Not for a Blood male who wore a wedding ring. Not when the marriage was so new he still wasn't accustomed to the feel of that ring on his finger—or the joy of knowing that it was there at all.

So he couldn't touch her as he wanted to. Couldn't even beg to be forgiven until he received some sign from her that she would permit him to beg. Because it wasn't just his wife he had disappointed; it was his Queen.

He held out the invitation. "I'm sorry." Inadequate words, but all he could offer at the moment.

She stared at the invitation for a long time. Then she looked at him.

Her sapphire eyes blazed with anger, but it was the icy slash of temper swirling deep in the abyss, almost to the level of the Black, that told him he was in serious trouble.

Sweet Darkness, she was *pissed* at him.

"Do you know where this village is located?" she asked, handing the invitation back to him.

He nodded.

"Then get a Coach ready. Something big enough to

accommodate several people. I need to gather a few supplies." She headed for the door leading to the corridor.

"Jaenelle . . ."

"*Now,* Prince."

Her voice made his heart race as the sound sizzled down his spine like cold lightning. There were caverns and sepulchres—and a whisper of madness—in that voice.

Midnight whispered in that voice.

Witch, not Jaenelle, had just issued that command. And the Lady wasn't pleased.

Since there was nothing he could do about her anger, he went downstairs to prepare the Coach so they could ride the Winds to the landen village where that damn spooky house was located.

"That's not a fresh kill," Rainier said, holding a hand over his nose and mouth.

Surreal stared at the body in the closet. "Nope. Been here long enough to start to smell. But someone wearing the illusion of that face let us into this house and passed me just a minute before he went through the door at the end of the hallway." The shields had kept the smell to a minimum until she opened the door. Now there was no doubt they were looking at carrion.

"What door?" Rainier asked.

She looked at the end of the hallway. "The door that's no longer there."

"Hell's fire," Rainier muttered. "What's going on here? And where are Jaenelle and Marian?"

She shook her head, then took a step closer to the body. Was that . . . ? Yes. There was a folded piece of paper tucked between the dead caretaker's thigh and hand. Naturally it was between the body parts farthest from the door.

She reached in, pulled the paper free, shook off a couple of maggots, and then stepped back, closing the door to cut down on the smell.

"It's getting dark outside—and even darker in here," Rainier said. "Let's go into the sitting room and light a couple of lamps before we have to deal with frightened children."

"We're going to be dealing with frightened children whether we light lamps or not," Surreal replied.

"I just don't understand what Jaenelle and Marian were thinking."

Surreal waggled the paper. "Since I think I found the first clue, let's light the lamps and find out."

The moment they walked back into the sitting room, Dayle said, "Where is the spooky stuff? This place is boring." Then she poked her lower lip out in a pout.

Maybe landen adults thought pouting was cute. As far as Surreal was concerned, if you were old enough to stand up by yourself, you were too old to pout and have it look cute.

Don't even consider it, Rainier said.

I wasn't considering anything.

You were going to tell her to open the door under the stairs.

Of course she was. *If she doesn't stop pouting, I'm going to put maggots in her hair.*

A hesitation. Just long enough to tell her he was picturing the possibility—and enjoying it.

Since that cheered her up, she waited while Rainier used Craft to light two of the oil lamps in the room.

Somewhere in the house, a gong sounded twice.

Rainier held one lamp while she opened the paper.

THERE ARE THIRTY EXITS FROM THE SPOOKY HOUSE, BUT YOU
WILL NEED TO LOOK CAREFULLY TO FIND THEM, FOR THEY ARE
WRAPPED IN DANGER. EVERY TIME CRAFT IS USED, AN EXIT IS
SEALED, AND THAT WAY OUT IS LOST. WHEN THE LAST EXIT IS
SEALED, YOU WILL BECOME PART OF THE HOUSE—AND STAY
WITH US FOREVER.

"What in the name of Hell . . . ?" Rainier said, following Surreal as she moved away from the children.

"The gong," she whispered once they were standing near the
door. "It sounded twice when you created the tongues of witchfire and lit the lamps. I heard it when I made the witchlight."
Which was still floating in the hallway.

"When I checked the time, I called in and vanished the pocket
watch," Rainier whispered back.

"So that's five times we've used Craft since we went through
that gate in the fence."

"Five times that we remember."

He had a point. The Blood—especially darker-Jeweled Blood—
were so accustomed to using Craft as a way to siphon off the power
that flowed within them, they weren't even aware of using it half
the time.

"The gong must be a signal that Craft was used," Surreal said,
glancing at the children to make sure she and Rainier were still
out of hearing.

"Or a signal that one of those exits closed because Craft was
used." Then Rainier added on a psychic thread, *But communicating like this doesn't appear to trigger . . . whatever this
is.*

They waited, but no gong sounded.

She read the note again and considered the implications.

⋆Rainier . . . I couldn't have been the only one to receive an invitation.⋆

⋆An invitation to a trap, from the looks of it.⋆

⋆Yeah.⋆ She gave him a moment to consider that. ⋆The others haven't shown up yet, and we don't know how many invitations were sent.⋆

⋆Fair bet invitations were sent to Yaslana and Sadi. And the caretaker, or whoever he is, did say there were twelve visitors per tour.⋆

⋆Doesn't mean twelve of us were expected.⋆ She studied the note. ⋆Every time Craft is used, an exit is sealed, and there are thirty exits. That sounds like the total number of times Craft can be used between all of the Blood in the house. Which means the more Blood in this place, the less chance we have of finding a way out while there still *is* a way out.⋆

⋆Agreed,⋆ Rainier said. ⋆What are you suggesting?⋆

She handed the note to him. ⋆That we not play the game and try a direct approach for getting out of here.⋆

Returning to the hall, she opened the front door. Still had solid brick behind it. But brick was no match for a punch of Gray power.

Turning inward, she made a fast descent in the abyss until she reached her inner web and the full power of her Gray Jewels. Then she turned and rose like an arrow of psychic power released from a bow.

She raised her right hand, aiming it at the bricks framed by the doorway. The Gray Jewel in her ring flashed as she unleashed a punch of power that would blow out the whole damn wall.

Or should have.

She stared at the undamaged bricks. Then she heard an odd crackle. A sizzle.

"Surreal!"

No time to reply. Some kind of webbing suddenly wrapped around her head and torso. She couldn't see it. Her fingers couldn't feel it. But it felt like a web made out of lightning and wire that passed through her skin and tightened until it squeezed her lungs, closed her throat.

Her heart thundered in her ears as she fought to breathe, fought to stay alive.

"Surreal!"

Rainier's arms around her.

She heard him snarl in frustrated rage. Heard a door slam. Or maybe that was her heart.

Then she heard the gong.

Suddenly the webbing was gone and she could breathe again.

"Mother Night," she gasped.

"Are you all right?" he asked.

No. "Not sure." Shit shit shit. That *hurt.*

"What happened?"

She was on the floor. Didn't remember going down. Since Rainier was being so obliging about propping her up, she leaned against him.

"Backlash," she said, wincing when she swallowed. "There must be spells that have formed a cage around this place. I punched them when I tried to open the wall. They punched back."

She tried to get up—and wasn't happy that she needed Rainier's help.

If Sadi and Yaslana were invited, then this cage was designed to hold the Black and Ebon-gray, Rainier said.

Yeah. And that wasn't good news for her or Rainier.

"Come back into the sitting room," he said, leading her to the room. "You should sit down."

"I'm all right." Had to be. "I don't need to sit down." More to the point, she didn't want to find out she was too shaky to get up by herself if she did sit down.

★Looks like we're going to play the game,★ Rainier said. ★The only way out is to find one of those exits.★

Surreal nodded. ★But first, we have to find a way to warn the others before they walk into this place. Then we get us and the children out of here.★

★Without using Craft.★

★Without using Craft.★

Rainier hesitated. ★Do you think Jaenelle and Marian did this?★

★Doesn't matter at this point, does it?★

Everything has a price. That was a common saying among the Blood. Everything has a price.

And the price for trying to leave his game by cheating was pain.

The caging spell had worked exactly as he'd been told it would, using the witch's power against herself to inflict a great deal of pain.

But not enough physical damage to take Surreal out of the game.

Unfortunately, the caging spell wasn't as effective if it was challenged a second time, but that was why the pain was so vicious—to discourage anyone from trying to break through the spell a second time.

Why were Surreal and Rainier just standing there? Why weren't they doing anything? They had the first clue. Had the *only* clue.

He'd debated giving them even that much, but it seemed

necessary. If his character Landry Langston was going to get ensnared by a house that would tighten the trap every time he used his newly learned Craft skills, he had to have a chance to escape the danger—and readers had to be *aware* of the danger.

Besides, having the gong sound every time one of them used Craft meant none of them could deny using it—and, by using it, taking away another chance for all of them to escape.

But why . . . ?

Damn! They were using those psychic threads to talk to each other! He hadn't thought of that. Hadn't done anything to penalize them for doing that. How was he supposed to make notes for dialogue if he couldn't hear what they were saying?

No matter. He was betting the Surreal bitch and her stud would have plenty to say once they started seeing his little surprises.

Surreal turned to the children and held out one hand with her fingers slightly curved. "We need to find something about this size—a whatnot or rock or, Hell's fire, even a loose brick. Start looking."

Trout and Sage immediately headed for the crowded tables, but Kester asked with a sneer, "Why? Will we finally see something spooky if we look?"

"If you don't look, you'll see me kicking your ass hard enough to bounce you off the ceiling." Right now, she'd end up on the floor if she didn't keep both feet planted, but no one but Rainier realized that. "Do as you're told, boyo. We've got trouble here."

"I don't like this place," Dayle whined. "I want to go home."

Surreal looked at Rainier.

They didn't notice the cobweb feeling, he said.

This place was a trap for the Blood. Maybe the children would be allowed to leave.

She looked at Dayle. "Sure. Go ahead. Go home." She stepped away from the door, giving the girl a clear path to the hallway.

"This is a stupid house," Trist said as he and the two younger boys followed Dayle and Ginger into the hallway.

Sauntering out of the sitting room, Kester paused in the doorway and gave her a look that would have earned him bruises from the adult males in a Blood village. Lucky for Kester, Rainier hadn't caught that look. Under the circumstances, she didn't think her Warlord Prince escort would have much tolerance for any kind of cock wagging from a boy old enough to use his brains instead of showing off his balls.

She gave a moment's thought to shoving the little prick-ass in the closet under the stairs to see how he liked spending time with a corpse, but she was still too wobbly to take him on without using Craft, so she dismissed the idea. Besides, once all the children were out of the house, it would make things easier for her and Rainier.

Finally the only child lingering in the room was Sage.

The girl looked up at her, genuine concern in those young eyes. "You fell down before. I saw it. Are you hurt?"

She almost dismissed the concern, almost offered a lie in order to reassure. Then she thought of what she would have said to a Blood female that same age.

Glancing at Rainier to make sure he was out of hearing, she leaned toward Sage and said quietly, "Yes, I'm hurt. But right now, that can't matter." She tipped her head to indicate the door. "Go on. Join the others. You need to get out of here if you can."

Moments after Sage left the room, Dayle said in a loud, whiny voice, "Where's the door?"

Shit shit shit.

"You go," Surreal said to Rainier. "I'll look for what we need."

On a table in the farthest corner of the room, she found a hefty glass paperweight. In the center of the glass was a slightly squashed baby mouse.

She decided not to wonder why anyone would find that appealing.

Rainier's expression was grim when he came back into the room followed by all seven children.

"Couldn't get past the bricks blocking the doorway?" she asked, holding the paperweight just behind her hip to avoid upsetting the children.

"No doorway," he replied. "No door. And nothing to indicate there ever was one."

Great. Wonderful. "All right. Let's wrap up our package and figure out a way to deliver it. Do you have a handkerchief?"

"A hankie?" Henn said. "Does it have boogers on it?"

Trist stared at Rainier as if he were part of the entertainment. "Do the Blood make boogers?"

"Some things that are tolerated when said among males are *never* tolerated when said in the presence of a Lady," Rainier said too softly.

★They're landens, not Blood,★ Surreal reminded him.

★They're males,★ he snapped.

Shit. If Rainier was going to divide acceptable behavior by the criterion of penis or breasts, they were all in trouble.

Hoping to shift his mood, she said with blatantly false cheerfulness, ★We could just kill them now. It would make everything so much easier.★

★Don't tempt me,★ Rainier replied as he took a clean handkerchief out of his pocket.

Hell's fire. He might be serious. About the boys anyway. A

Warlord Prince didn't put up with much of anything from a male who didn't outrank him.

But that caste of male was also primed to defend and protect. If she could get Rainier focused on duty, that would turn his temper toward the problem of getting out of the damn house.

We invited them to join us, Rainier.

I invited them, you mean. He took a deep breath—and puffed it out in a sigh as he nodded acceptance of the reminder.

Nothing more needed to be said, so Surreal looked at the double strand of blue ribbon Ginger was using as a hair band. "I need those ribbons."

"I don't have to give them to you. I don't have to do anything you say." Ginger fisted her hands on her hips. "You make the door open so we can go home."

Surreal caught the quick look Ginger gave Kester. Oh, yeah. Impress the dominant cock by playing the bitch. Or keep the cock impressed by squaring off against a witch. Since she'd seen plenty of variations of that theme when she lived in Terreille, she knew one thing for certain: Ginger was going to be a pain in the ass she didn't need.

"Give me the ribbons," Surreal said calmly. "If you don't, I will rip them off your head—and rip most of your hair off with them."

Ginger's face paled, then flushed with embarrassment.

Lesson one, bitch. Don't start a pissing contest with someone who has the strength and temper to hurt you.

Ginger pulled off the ribbons and threw them on the floor. "You're bad! You're just like my mother says you are!"

"Well, sugar, that's something you should have remembered before trying to act like the dominant bitch around someone like me," Surreal said softly. She took a step toward the girl—and felt a tapping against her fingers. No, that wasn't quite right, but . . .

She brought her hand around to look at the paperweight and felt a jolt of revulsion followed by a sick tickle in the belly.

No longer solid glass. Now it was a glass dome over a solid base. Now the baby mouse, still looking slightly squashed, was on its hind legs, its front paws pounding on the glass as it squeaked for help.

Her hand shook, but she didn't drop it. It was the only thing she'd found that would serve her purpose, so she didn't drop it, didn't throw it against the fireplace.

"Ew," Dayle said, her eyes wide and excited. "That's *creepy.*"

My apologies, Lady Surreal, Rainier said. *I shouldn't have discouraged you from showing them the closet. They'd probably find a dead body and maggots entertaining.*

"What was it before the illusion spell started?" Rainier asked out loud.

"A dead mouse in a glass paperweight." She hesitated but had to ask because there was something about the skewed nature of the illusion that made her uneasy. *When you were a boy, would you have found this entertaining?*

The mouse? Hell's fire, no.

Would boys in general find this entertaining?

Rainier studied her but must have sensed she didn't want to share the reason for her questions. *Maybe. Our companions seem to, at any rate.*

Mother Night.

She started to bend down to pick up the ribbons, but Sage scooped them up and handed them to her. Thanking the girl, she perched on the arm of the overstuffed sofa, unwilling to sit on the cushions in case the mouse's relatives were still in residence.

The paper with the warning about the nature of the spooky

house was wrapped around the paperweight. The handkerchief was wrapped over the paper. Everything was tied securely with the ribbons.

"Now what?" Rainier asked.

"See if that window is still a window."

She watched him pull aside the lace curtains—and then jump back, swearing viciously, when black, beetlelike things fell from the curtains as they shredded.

Her heart jumped in her throat as the damn things scurried into cracks in the baseboard. She couldn't tell if the beetles were real or illusion—and since seeing them made her skin crawl, she really didn't want to know.

"Still a window," Rainier said, peering through the glass. "At least, I seem to be looking out over the front lawn."

She moved until she was just a little more than an arm's length from the window.

Rainier studied the glass panes. "We could open the window and climb out."

"Which might trigger a spell that will put more than glass in our way."

"It might."

The look in his eyes. Assessing. Considering. Weighing his desire as an escort to get her out of danger regardless of the cost against his responsibility for getting the children out safely, since they were here because of his invitation.

Just as he was here because of *her* invitation.

We walked in together, Prince Rainier. We will leave together.

Another assessment. Then he nodded.

"Stand to the side as much as you can, but hold what's left of that curtain out of the way," she said.

"Surreal, maybe I should . . ." He looked at the paperweight and didn't say anything more.

"You wear Opal; I wear Gray." And there was the simple fact that the Dea al Mon side of her heritage made her a lot stronger than she looked.

"You've already taken a hit," Rainier said.

"Yeah." And that was pissing her off because breathing still hurt like a wicked bitch.

Not that far from the house to the wrought-iron fence. Fifteen paces at the most. She could throw a stone that far.

She waited while Rainier fetched the poker from the brass stand on the hearth. Hooking some of the material, he pulled back the remains of the shredded curtain.

She stared at the window. Dark outside now. She couldn't see the fence or the street. Just her reflection in the glass. If she broke the glass . . .

A sensation at the back of her neck, like delicate legs brushing, crawling.

Letting instinct decide, she channeled her Gray power into her hand and then wrapped it around the bundle before she cocked her arm back and threw, using Craft to pass the bundle through the glass.

Somewhere in the house, the gong sounded.

"Did it get out?" Surreal asked, stepping closer to the glass. "Can you see if the bundle got past the fence?"

Her reflection in the night-darkened glass. And then it wasn't her reflection. Another woman's face stared back at her and . . .

The woman's arm shot out of the glass. Her nails, shaped like dagger points, slashed at Surreal's face.

Surreal turned her face away and flung up an arm as an instinctive defense. And felt those nails tear through her jacket sleeve before Rainier yanked her out of reach.

"Should have gone through the window," the woman said, her voice a malevolent singsong. "Should-a, could-a, too late now. Find an exit and don't use it, it's gone forever. Gone gone gone. Like you'll be. You'll join me soon enough. And your face won't look so pretty when you do."

"Who are you?" Surreal asked.

"He paid me. And then he killed me. And then he chained me to this house. But he's letting me play with all the tricks and traps. Don't die too soon, Lady Bitch. Not until you've seen my *best* surprises."

"Who is he?"

"You'll find out." The woman's face began to fade. "When you're chained to the house too."

Surreal stared at the window. Nothing in the glass now but her own reflection.

"We could have gotten out," she said. "Could have opened the window and climbed out."

"While trying to avoid the slashing nails?" Rainier countered. "I doubt she would have watched us leave."

"Assuming she wasn't lying about that being an exit." Surreal fingered the tear in her jacket. "What was she? Demon-dead? Illusion?"

"Both?" Rainier released a breath in a grim sigh. "Did she cut you?"

She shook her head. "Came close, though. And *that* wasn't meant as a bit of fun."

"Agreed." He hesitated. "Does this seem familiar?"

"How so?" she asked warily.

"Body in a closet. Clues."

They looked at each other.

"Ah, shit," Surreal said. "Someone set us up in a mystery? We're the dumb characters who walk into the Bad Place?"

"Looks like it." Then Rainier added on a psychic thread, ★And we helped by bringing victims with us. Fodder for the game.★

★Then it's time to stop thinking in terms of what we expected and really look at what we walked into.★

Dropping down from the Black Wind, Daemon guided the Coach as it coasted the rest of the way to the landen village. It wasn't hard to figure out where the spooky house was located. It was the only source of power pulsing through the village.

He and Jaenelle hadn't spoken since leaving their—her—bedroom. But as he settled the Coach gently on the opposite side of the street from the house, he'd had enough of her silence and her anger.

She surged out of her seat and headed for the Coach door—and then stared at it when it didn't open.

Moving with lazy, predatory grace, he rose from the driver's chair—and smiled at her. "Can't get through a Black lock?" he asked, his voice laced with nasty pleasantness.

"Open the door."

"Not until a few things get said." He moved toward her but stopped out of arm's reach. She was still a powerful Black Widow, and he had no desire to get pumped full of her venom by accident or otherwise. "I'm sorry I missed the viewing. I am, but—"

"You think that's why I'm angry with you? Because you didn't answer the invitation?"

His temper grew fangs. "If that isn't the reason, then why don't you tell me why you're so pissed off at me?"

Her sapphire eyes blazed. "I'm pissed off, as you so elegantly put it, because you think I am so shallow and so selfish that I would issue that kind of finger-snap summons and expect you to drop everything and obey."

"What?" Female was an alien language, but he usually could translate it well enough to understand what was being said. But this . . .

"You must think I'm completely unaware of what is required to rule a Territory or oversee the SaDiablo family. You must think I'm ignorant of how much work you do or the demands that are now made on your time since you became the Warlord Prince of Dhemlan. Or do you have another explanation for being so damn stupid?"

His temper strained against a fraying leash.

"When did that invitation arrive?" Jaenelle demanded.

"This afternoon. It was brought up to the room instead of being delivered to me."

"And if it *had* been delivered to you, you would have dropped everything and run to obey."

"I love you," Daemon shouted. "What in the name of Hell is wrong with wanting to please you?"

"What's wrong with it is that you never considered it odd that I would send such an invitation," Jaenelle shouted back. "Instead of using your brain, you would have obeyed and walked into that house! Now open the damn door!"

Because he couldn't think of anything else to do, he released the Black lock and opened the door. He was wrong. He still didn't know why, but somehow he was wrong.

She barely waited for the door to open before she was out of the Coach—and he was barely a step behind her. He grabbed her arm, knowing full well another kind of woman would rip his face for touching her during a quarrel.

"Jaenelle . . ." He loosened his hold, making it easy for her to pull away from him if she chose. Angry and confused, he wasn't sure if he should fight or surrender. And he wasn't sure what either choice might cost him. "You're angry because I would have answered the invitation?"

"Yes."

The ice in her voice chilled his heart. "Why? Please tell me why."

She pointed at the house across the street from where they stood. "Because that's not my spooky house."

ELEVEN

Cloaked in a sight shield, he watched them from the peep-holes in the portrait, secure in the knowledge that he would remain undetected. These hidden corridors and his little hidey-holes weren't bound by the spells constricting the use of Craft in the rest of his "entertainment." He'd made sure of that before he settled his account with the Black Widow who had added the final, deadly layer to his version of the spooky house. Of course, she hadn't intended to become part of that final, deadly layer.

Now that he'd taken care of all his "partners," there was no one to connect him to this place. Well, he'd taken care of almost all of them. *That* one hadn't shown up for her payment. Just as well. He'd sweated through the whole business of dealing with the Hourglass Coven, but *that* one had been creepier than the others. Still, even if she did talk about making illusion spells for a spooky house, who would *listen* to her, let alone believe her?

"All right," Surreal said, hooking her hair behind her ears. "Some-one has cast us as the lead characters in a mystery about a house that's trying to kill us. Does that about sum it up?"

"The house itself is wood, glass, and stone," Rainier said. "It's not trying to do anything. But based on the clue and the witch in the glass, it does seem like someone is trying to kill us. Hurt us at the very least. That same someone hired a Black Widow to create illusion spells—and probably other things—that we'll assume will try to harm us while we look for a way out."

More than one Black Widow, Surreal thought. That was something she was going to keep to herself a little while longer. After all, she could be wrong.

Sweet Darkness, please let her be wrong.

"We've got two lamps and the witchlight," Rainier said.

"And one weapon," Surreal said as Rainier handed her the poker. "I didn't put much power into the witchlight when I made it, so it won't last long."

Rainier picked up a small box that had been next to one of the lamps. When he opened it, he frowned thoughtfully at the contents.

"Those are matches," Kester said, rolling his eyes. "You scratch one on the rough side of the box to get a little fire to light the lamp or kindling."

"I know what matches are," Rainier said, slipping the box into his coat pocket. Then he looked at Surreal. ★Do we shield?★

If they didn't, they were vulnerable. If they did . . .

★Just us or the children?★ she asked. The landens wouldn't have any control over the shield or be able to replenish the power in it, but she and Rainier could place one around each child to protect them from the first few attacks. Except . . .

★If we shield everyone, that's nine more uses of Craft. Counting the times we've already used Craft, that would eliminate more than half the possible exits from this place,★ Rainier said, saying exactly what she had been thinking.

⋆And most likely, the easier exits to find are the ones that will close first.⋆ Like the front door. And the window there in the sitting room. "How many rooms?" she asked. "I wasn't paying a lot of attention, but the house looked like it was a good size without being *that* big. A dozen rooms in all?"

Rainier nodded. "Plus attic and cellar."

Was there another exit in that room?

⋆If the intention is for us to face the traps, there won't be more than one or two exits in the front rooms,⋆ Rainier said. ⋆And if this *is* based on a mystery story, we've already seen the clue and been shown a sample of the danger that will be triggered if we find an exit and try to use it.⋆

Unfortunately, she agreed with him. No one would have gone to this much trouble to create this place and then risk the possibility of their finding an exit quickly.

Surreal studied the room, looking for a potential exit or anything else that might be useful—and seeing nothing that would work to their advantage.

She had dressed casually in trousers, shirt, and jacket, and was wearing the boots Lucivar had given her at Winsol. Too bad she hadn't called in her stiletto and the palm knife before going through the gate. The boots were designed with sheaths for both knives. She would have felt more comfortable if she had a couple of honed blades within reach. Well, they were still within reach, since she could call them in, but she wouldn't be the only one penalized if she used Craft, so she would have to wait until she needed a blade.

⋆You know, we'd better get out of this place in one piece,⋆ Rainier said.

⋆For other than the obvious reason that I don't want to get stuck living here if I end up demon-dead?⋆ Surreal asked, still turning slowly as she studied the room.

*Do *you* want to explain to Lucivar that you didn't shield before walking into a strange house?*

Ah, shit. Maybe getting stuck in the house wouldn't be so bad after all.

Do we gamble and not create shields? Rainier asked.

For now. Let's gather up our flock of idiot sheep and herd them over to the room across the hall.

They're not idiot sheep; they're children.

That's what I said. Her study of the room finally brought her back to the portrait over the fireplace.

Something wrong with the eyes. Then there was something wrong with the whole face as the illusion spell started. The portrait's head shifted to look down at her. The mouth curved in a leer as the man said in a harsh whisper, "I know what you are."

Something inside her stilled. Something that had gotten bruised when Falonar's interest had waned in response to her wanting to hone her fighting skills. No. Not her fighting skills. Her killing skills. There was a difference, even to an Eyrien warrior. She had never been a warrior, but she had been a damn good assassin.

Now she felt as if she were drawing a blade from its sheath. Shining. Deadly. Her.

"I know what you are," the portrait said again.

"No," she told it. "You don't."

Just his luck to get the least interesting member of the SaDiablo family. An uneducated whore. That's all she was. No flair, no drama.

Or were they using those psychic threads to say all the interesting things?

No matter. He hadn't arranged this to collect dialogue. This was to observe the Blood and how they would deal with the little surprises.

And when his next book came out, *no one* would be able to say his character Landry Langston lacked authenticity.

That's not my spooky house.

Daemon let the words seep into his mind like rain softening earth.

Not hers.

An invitation sent to bring him to this place, worded in such a way that he would respond without questioning. A gut-level reaction that didn't take into account the personality of the woman. Jaenelle was right about that—if he had stopped to think for even a minute, he would have wondered why she had sent it.

Finger-snap summons, she'd called it. That was exactly what this had been. She was capable of issuing that kind of command and expecting it to be obeyed without question, but he had a feeling that if he asked any of the boyos in her First Circle how they had responded to that kind of summons, every one of them would have said they would have shown up fully shielded and ready for a fight.

Jaenelle Angelline had never been an inconsiderate or insensitive Queen. And she wasn't an inconsiderate or insensitive wife.

He took a deep breath and blew it out in a sigh as he stared at the house across the street. "If I admit to being an ass, could we finish this disagreement after we figure out what's going on here?"

"If there's any disagreement left to finish."

When she slipped her arms around his waist, he wrapped his arms around her—and felt the tight muscles in his chest and back begin to relax.

Until she smiled at him and added, "Just how guilty do you feel about being an ass?"

His spine quivered. His knees turned to jelly. "Why?"

"I need your help to finish the last part of my spooky house."

Hell's fire, Mother Night, and may the Darkness be merciful.

"Aren't you going to ask what I want you to do?"

Everything has a price, old son. Just consider this the equivalent to a kick in the balls. "No."

"I see." She gave him a light kiss, then stepped back. "You *really* feel guilty."

Don't think about it, don't think about it. "Shall we?" He tipped his head to indicate the house.

By the time they reached the other side of the street, he could feel the spells, like pins lightly scratching his skin. Tangled webs of dreams and visions. Illusion spells. Layers of them.

He'd been born a Black Widow—the only natural male Black Widow in the history of the Blood. The only other male to be made a Black Widow was his father. Whatever was around this house was the work of Sisters of the Hourglass—and that wasn't good. The other thing that wasn't good . . .

His heart jumped when he realized he recognized the feel of some of the spells.

"Three of them," Jaenelle said, taking a step toward the wrought-iron fence.

"Shield," Daemon snapped, creating a Black shield around himself. It was tempting to put a shield around her, but that would be like stuffing her into a sweater instead of letting her put it on by herself.

She blinked at him, then muttered something under her breath in a language he didn't know as a defensive shield formed around her. Not a bubble; this was a full cloak of power that followed her shape a hand span above her skin.

He was still learning to read Twilight's Dawn, the Jewel she now wore, but the shield seemed to have the equivalent strength of an Ebon-gray Jewel. That would do for now.

"How do you know there were three?" he asked, returning his attention to her earlier comment.

The look she gave him was Mentor to Student, since she was the one who was overseeing most of his formal training in the Hourglass's Craft.

The High Lord of Hell was overseeing the rest of it—which was something neither he nor Saetan mentioned to anyone.

"There are three distinct feels to these spells, three distinct temperaments that went into their making. We haven't reached the spot where the spells actually engage, but we're close." Jaenelle hesitated. "Daemon . . ."

"I know." And it made him heartsick because the closer he got to the gate in the fence, the more this place felt *wrong*. "I know, Lady. I didn't pick up that there were *two* more, but I recognized *her*." Then he added, *We've got company.*

They continued to study the house, giving no sign they were aware of the person moving toward them.

A landen, which wasn't surprising since they were in a landen village, but that's all Daemon could sense because his Black-Jeweled power was too dark and potent for him to touch a landen mind without destroying it.

So they waited until a young voice hesitantly asked, "Are you going into the spooky house?"

Now they turned, but Daemon shifted just the little bit needed to place Jaenelle partially behind his left shoulder, still giving her a view of the boy while acting as another shield.

He felt resigned amusement coming from Jaenelle, but no protest, no attempt to brush off that instinctive defense.

The boy was at that awkward age of being no longer a child but not quite a youth. Between his age and the fact that he was landen, he was an unlikely threat to either of them. That didn't make any difference.

"The other Lady and gentleman took some of the children with them," the boy said, sounding hopeful.

Daemon crooked a finger and made a "come here" gesture. Better to let the boy come to them. Something shy about this one, something . . .

He's been hurt, Jaenelle said.

Daemon clamped down on his temper. Coming from someone with Jaenelle's past, "hurt" and "wounded" didn't mean the same thing. Hell's fire, someone coming from *his* past recognized the difference. *Abused physically?*

Not sure. But there's a feel to such children. Like recognizes like.

He heard the pain under the words.

"What's your name?" he asked the boy.

"Yuli."

"You said a Lady and gentleman went into the house? How long ago?"

"Not long."

"What did they look like?" Jaenelle asked.

"The Lady was pretty," Yuli said. Then he lifted a hand and added hesitantly, "But I think her ears looked a little funny."

"Pointed?"

"Uh-huh."

"The gentleman," Daemon said. "Did he have wings?"

Yuli shook his head. "He wasn't from Dhemlan either, 'cause he had light skin."

It sounded like Rainier had come with Surreal. Which meant Lucivar hadn't arrived yet. Unless he'd come before the children had gathered to watch the house.

"If they took some other children, why didn't you go with them?" Daemon asked.

He saw the flinch, felt the tremor of hurt.

"I live at the orphans' home," Yuli said. "The others don't want . . ." The words faded into a pained silence.

"Well, then," Jaenelle said, "that's fortunate for us."

Her voice was like a summer breeze washing over the boy, but Daemon heard the ice underneath the warmth.

"Someone threw a stone out the window," Yuli said. "Just before your . . ." He frowned and looked across the street.

"Coach," Daemon said.

"Your Coach appeared." Yuli swung around and pointed to the lawn on the other side of the fence. "It's over there."

"Once we cross that line, the spells will engage," Jaenelle said.

Daemon didn't bother to argue about the "we" part of that sentence. He'd fight her into the ground before he let her cross that line and get tangled up in those spells.

"I'll get it!" Yuli said. The boy slammed through the gate, sending it crashing back against the fence as he sprinted to a spot in the lawn.

Jaenelle hissed. "Power."

"How . . . ?" Daemon glanced at her. Her Jewel, which usually looked like Purple Dusk with streaks of the other colors of Jewels, now glowed Rose. She was at the lightest end of her range of power.

"There's a hint of Blood in him," she said. "He's not pure landen."

Damn it! "Does he have enough power to trap him in those spells?"

"Don't know." She paused, her attention focused on the boy. "No. He's not strong enough to do Craft, so he's not strong enough to trigger the spells."

Daemon held his breath anyway until the boy raced back through the gate, holding out a bundle tied with ribbons. Murmuring thanks, he took the bundle, then used Craft to put a knife-edge on his right index fingernail. As he cut the ribbons, Jaenelle created a globe of witchlight.

That's not the most practical light, Daemon said, glancing at the globe that was a swirling rainbow of colors.

It serves the purpose, Jaenelle replied with a touch of tart sweetness.

A glance at the boy, whose eyes were wide with delight. Daemon offered no other comments as he unwrapped the handkerchief and vanished it. When he held a piece of paper in one hand and a paperweight in the other, the globe changed to a soft white light.

The three of them stared at the paperweight—and then watched the illusion spell change a dead, slightly squashed baby mouse trapped in solid glass into a creature pounding on a glass globe while squeaking for help.

Daemon stared at the globe. There was something grotesquely fascinating about the spell, something that appealed to a part of him he was sure was not appropriately adult.

Daemonar probably would love watching the mousie. So would the wolf pups who lived at the eyrie. Marian, on the other hand, would most likely grab a mop and try to beat him to a pulp with it if he gave this little grotesquerie to her boy.

"The illusion must be triggered by the warmth of a person's hand," Jaenelle said. "It stays dormant until someone picks it up."

"The confused Lady must have made that," Yuli said. "The others weren't nice, but she was."

The boy's words were a verbal knife in the gut.

"She talked to you?" Jaenelle asked.

Yuli nodded. "She said the spooky house was an entertainment, like Jaenelle was making. Something fun for children. A surprise for the boy."

"A surprise for the boy," Daemon murmured. He handed the paperweight to Yuli, then held the paper up so he and Jaenelle could read it.

Then he swore softly, savagely.

"Mother Night," Jaenelle said, looking at the house. "It sounds like this entertainment has a few teeth and claws."

"My apologies, Yuli," Daemon said. "I neglected to finish the introductions. I'm Daemon Sadi, Warlord Prince of Dhemlan. This is my Lady, Jaenelle Angelline."

Yuli's jaw dropped. "The *Lady*?"

Well, that told him where he stood in the pecking order. "Yes, *the* Lady." He paused. "I have a favor to ask of you. I have some urgent business and must leave immediately. Will you keep the Lady company until I return?"

"Yes, sir!"

★You're leaving a boy here to protect me?★ Jaenelle asked.

★I'm giving him an excuse to stay with you—and the hamper of food Beale placed in the Coach. I figure by the time I get back, you'll know everything this village knows about that house.★ *And everything the villagers might not want you to know about that orphans' home and this boy in particular.* ★Besides, if I can't warn him off in time, someone has to be here to stop Lucivar from going into that house.★ *And if you use that Witch tone of voice on him like you did on me, you'll stop him in his tracks.*

"All right, I'll stay," Jaenelle said. "And I welcome Yuli's company." ★You're going to talk to her?★

He gave her a light but lingering kiss, needing the feel of her. ★Yes, I'm going to talk to her.★

TWELVE

The only thing they found of interest in the parlor across the hall was another poker that Rainier now carried as a weapon. No tricks or traps. At least, none that they triggered. No exits either.

Using the poker to hook back the lace curtain hanging over the window, Rainier studied the bricks that replaced the window's view. As he let the curtain fall back into place, he said, "Seems odd to waste a room."

"Too close to the starting point of the game?" Surreal replied. She'd been standing behind him, ready to help if the woman with the dagger-point nails appeared in the window like she'd done in the sitting room.

"We're bored," Trist said.

"We want to go home," Dayle said.

"We don't like this place," Henn said.

She turned and walked over to the flock of idiot sheep, ignoring Rainier's quiet warning. She stared at each of them. They stared back. Even Sage and Trout just stared.

Did they think they were immune to harm because they were children? They weren't immune to anything. Especially harm.

"We're trapped in here," she said. "Someone played a nasty trick on all of us, and we're trapped in here until we find one of the secret ways out. Until we get out, you do as you're told. If we tell you to stay away from something, you stay away from it."

"Why can't you do your witch stuff to get us out?" Kester asked belligerently.

"We can't. That's part of the trap."

"I guess the Blood aren't so special after all," Ginger said, glancing at Kester.

"If that's what you think, why were you so eager to see this place?"

No answer. She didn't expect one.

She looked at Rainier. "Let's try the back rooms before going upstairs." Which would also give her a little more time to recover from the backlash. If Rainier heard her puffing after she'd climbed one set of stairs, he'd know she still wasn't breathing properly.

He joined her. "It would be easier to get everyone out if we're still on the first floor—providing the exits are actually doors and windows that are meant to let us out of the house."

"What else would they be?" Surreal asked.

"Exits from the game. What if 'exit' simply means the game ends and the spells go dormant so that doors and windows do work?"

"Then any kind of opening that a person could walk through—"

"Or crawl through," Rainier said.

Oh, she didn't want to think about that, not when the odds were good that any space that required crawling would also have something nasty waiting for them. "—or crawl through might be an exit."

"Yeah."

She considered the possibilities in the parlor again and shook her head. Nothing there. At least, nothing she could sense. Too bad she wasn't interested in training to be a Black Widow, despite her interest in poisons. Maybe she could have . . .

"Hey," she said. "Do you think a Black Widow would be able to feel more than we can? Would someone else from the Hourglass be able to see these spells or sense them? Or eliminate them?"

The arrested look on Rainier's face told her he hadn't considered that. "Maybe," he said slowly. "A Black Widow might have been able to recognize where the spells were to avoid triggering them."

"Then why—" She stopped and switched to a psychic thread. *If that's the case, why would anyone invite Sadi?*

We don't know he was invited. He shrugged when she just looked at him. *I don't think there is anyone beyond Jaenelle's friends and the Dhemlan Queens who know he's a Black Widow. But I don't see your point.*

I'm wondering if whoever created this game counted on one of us being a Black Widow—or if he'd counted on none of his guests being part of the Hourglass. Are we missing things we should be seeing?

"Mystery books." Rainier raked his fingers through his hair. "Sometimes there are clues that aren't recognized when they're first seen."

"And maybe we're basing our assumptions on our own intelligence instead of considering the intelligence of whoever put this together." Surreal grabbed one of the lamps and headed for the door. "Let's take a look at the next room. Gather up the sheep."

"Our enemy seems to be fairly intelligent," Rainier said, raising his voice over the children's *baa*ing and snickers.

She stopped in the doorway and looked at him. "Do you think so? Would *you* want to give Yaslana and Sadi a reason to be coming after you?"

Bitch. She'd actually given him a shiver down his spine. But he'd covered his tracks. They wouldn't find him. Even when his next book came out, they wouldn't connect Jarvis Jenkell, renowned author from Little Terreille, with the tragedy that took place in a landen village in the middle of Dhemlan.

But because she'd given him that momentary shiver, he really hoped *Lady* Surreal was the person who found the first big surprise.

Power and temper blew the message-station door open, almost ripping it from its hinges, but the Station Master held his ground behind the counter as the Warlord Prince of Dhemlan strode across the room. The gold eyes were glazed—a warning to everyone that a Warlord Prince was riding the killing edge—and that beautiful face was a cold, cold mask.

The Prince placed a piece of paper on the counter, folded and sealed with the SaDiablo crest pressed into the bloodred wax. "Assign your fastest messenger to deliver this. Send him now." He turned and walked away. As he reached the door, he added, "And may the Darkness have mercy on you if that message doesn't reach my brother in time."

The Station Master's hand shook as he picked up the paper and read the name and location of delivery just to be sure. Not that he had any doubt about *who* was supposed to receive the message. Then he looked at the young men watching from the doorway of the room where they sorted through their messages or waited for an assignment.

The Station Master pointed to a messenger. The young Warlord came forward, shaking his head.

"Not me," the messenger said. "I've already been there once today. I've completed my assigned runs. I've—"

"Do you want to tell the man who walked out of here that the message wasn't delivered in time?" In time for what, none of them would ever ask—and most of them hoped they would never find out.

He watched, puzzled, as the messenger shielded himself before taking the message, then put a shield around the message before putting it into his carry bag as if it were a sack full of poisonous snakes instead of a piece of paper, and *then* put *another* shield around the carry bag.

The messenger looked at him and grimaced. "*You* didn't deliver the last message." Then he added under his breath, "And I don't want *him* kicking my ass."

The Station Master decided not to ask. He just patted the Warlord's shoulder. "Good lad. Get moving."

And may the Darkness have mercy on all of us.

A dining room. Table, chairs, and a rug that had swirls of colors that had been muddied by age and dirt—or had been like that in the first place. No tools by the fireplace. She was hoping for another poker to start arming the children. They might not have any skill, but she figured anyone could whack at something that was trying to hurt them.

Guess we only get two weapons, she thought as she set her lamp at one end of the table and began a slow counterclockwise circuit around the outside of the room while Rainier made the same circuit in the opposite direction.

Three windows. The two along the side of the house had been bricked over. The one in the back, if she could trust what she was seeing, looked out on some kind of veranda. A doorway that opened into a small storeroom and an entryway with a door that *might* work. And a closed door.

Surreal studied the door, then looked at the room again. A triangular hutch in one corner, but it held nothing but teapots and matching cups and saucers. So behind the door was probably the storage cupboard for dishes and linens.

She reached for the knob. Any door might be an exit, right?

Her hand froze above the knob. Instinct? Or something less easy to define? Didn't matter. If she'd been fully shielded, she might have opened the door just to find out what was making her skin crawl—and then kill it. As it was, she backed away from the door, raising the poker like a sword.

"Surreal?" Rainier asked, stopping his circuit to watch her.

"Something here," she said.

"Is it something spooky?" Trist asked.

The children had been nicely huddled together when they got into the room. Now they were starting to spread out and explore.

She gave them all a hard look. "Stay away from this door." She put enough bite in her voice so there wouldn't be any question that this was a command and not a suggestion. Put enough snap in the words so that none of the children would think she was playing "spooky house" with them.

As she looked at them, she remembered another boy, a little

Yellow-Jeweled Warlord who had been a killer's intended prey. That boy had survived because he had obeyed her orders.

She felt some of the tension in her shoulders ease.

These children were old enough to understand they were in a dangerous situation. Despite the verbal pissing contests they seemed to want to engage in, and despite her calling them idiot sheep, they were smart enough to realize she and Rainier were trying to keep them safe.

And they *would* keep the children safe—at least as long as she and Rainier were both standing.

But there was something about the buzzy-buzz whispering between Dayle and Ginger that annoyed her. And the mumbles and snickers coming from Kester and Trist made her edgy.

Were the buzzy-buzz and the snickers something all children did, or just landens? She didn't know, wasn't sure how to ask. When she'd worked in the Red Moon houses as a whore, she'd refused to work in any house that used younger girls, and as an assassin, she had never accepted a contract to kill a child. So she'd had no reason to be around children and plenty of reasons to avoid them. If she'd had friends her own age when she was very young, she didn't remember them—and by the time she was Ginger's age, she'd been whoring on the streets in order to survive and had already killed her first man.

She turned away from the children and tipped her head toward the back window, a signal for Rainier to meet her there.

"I didn't feel anything when I passed that door," Rainier said quietly.

"I know that," Surreal replied. "You would have said something if you had." She caught a movement out of the corner of her eye and turned her head.

Trist was drifting toward the closed door. He stopped when he realized she was watching him. She waited until he retreated a couple of steps and began another whispered conversation with Kester before she turned her attention back to Rainier.

"Maybe the distaff gender is more sensitive to this spell than the spear gender. Or maybe I do have a bit more feel for what's here because my mother was a Black Widow. Either way . . ."

She glanced at the children in time to see Trist grab the knob of the closed door. He gave her a defiant smirk, then turned the knob and pulled the door open.

Disbelief froze her for a moment. Then she and Rainier leaped forward.

The girls screamed. Trist stared at whatever had been waiting in the cupboard. Then hands covered with burned, blackened skin grabbed the boy and yanked him inside.

The door slammed shut.

Trist screamed. And screamed. And screamed.

Rainier reached the door a step ahead of her. He grabbed the knob and tried to open the door, but it was locked, sealed from inside.

"Do it!" she yelled.

Using Craft, Rainier ripped the door off the hinges and threw it aside at the same moment Surreal dropped the poker and leaped into the cupboard, calling in her stiletto since that was a better weapon for close fighting.

No one else inside the small space. Just shelves of old dishes.

But she could still hear the boy screaming and then she heard . . .

She knew those sounds. She'd made enough kills to know what those sounds—and the sudden lack of screams—meant.

Rainier lobbed the ball of witchlight through the doorway.

She saw the wet spot growing on the wall between a tureen and another serving dish. Pushing them aside, she touched two fingers against the spot, then withdrew her hand and held it so Rainier could see the fresh blood.

A plopping sound. Movement on the shelf had her jolting back a step.

Then something small rolled off the shelf and landed on the floor between her and the door.

She stared at it—and felt that stillness inside her grow sharper and more deadly.

As she stepped over the freshly plucked eye, something inside her snapped. Rainier saw it, recognized it—and moved aside.

Kester, on the other hand, moved toward her when she walked out of the storage cupboard. His fists were clenched, and his expression was a blend of fear and fury.

"You bitch!" he yelled. "You're supposed to protect us!"

There was something about that blend of fear and fury. . . .

Knowing she was too close to using it on the boy, she dropped the stiletto. Then she grabbed Kester by the shirt, swung him around, and slammed his back against the narrow piece of wall between the cupboard and the passageway.

"Listen to me, you little piece of shit," she snarled. "You were told there is danger, you were told someone is trying to hurt all of us, and you were told to stay away from that door. But you had to play 'Who's got the biggest balls?' and you dared your friend to open the door. And now he's dead. So listen up, sugar. That little fool shouldn't have disobeyed me. Have you got that? If he had done what I'd told him to do, he would not have died. Not here. Not like that."

She let go of Kester and stepped back. "I hope he's dead. I really do. But if the rules of this house hold true, you'll see him again because now he'll be one of the things that will be trying to kill *you*."

She spun around, grabbed the lamp off the table, then strode down the passageway.

His hand shook so much with excitement, he had to force himself to slow down. No point taking notes if he couldn't decipher them, and this particular dialogue was too good to waste.

Oh, yes. This exchange was *excellent*.

But one thing did worry him.

Seeing how easily she handled a knife, he began to wonder if maybe, just maybe, the Surreal bitch hadn't been lying when she'd told the children she used to be an assassin.

Surreal passed the back stairs and ended up in the kitchen. She set the lamp down on the worktable and looked around—and wondered if whoever had prepared this house had been foolish enough to leave any knives she could use.

On the other hand, she'd walked into a strange room, alone, with only a lamp. She'd dropped the poker when she'd leaped into the cupboard. And she'd dropped the stiletto too. So who was the real fool?

Stupid boy. Stupid, *stupid* boy to die that way.

Her eyes filled. Her throat closed.

No. *No.* No tears. No grief. Not here. Not yet. But . . .

The boy had disobeyed. He'd defied a straight order. What in the name of Hell had he been thinking? That this was a game? Well, it was that. A bloody, vicious game. The rest of them knew that now, didn't they?

That won't save them from getting killed, she thought. *Won't save Rainier and me either.*

She looked around the kitchen and said too softly, "I'll find you, you son of a whoring bitch. I may not still be among the living when it happens, but I will find you. And when I do, I will rip you into small pieces and feed you to whatever you've put into this house."

She laughed, barely making a sound. "You don't think I can do it? Sugar, I skinned my own father and fed him to the Hell Hounds. If I can do it to him, I can do it to you."

THIRTEEN

Lucivar stared at the messenger and didn't laugh. Didn't even grin. The effort hurt his muscles, but he kept a straight face as he accepted the shielded message from the heavily shielded young Warlord.

"Thank you, Warlord," he said.

"It was my pleasure, Prince."

I doubt it, Lucivar thought as he watched the messenger walk across the courtyard—and then scamper down the stairs to the landing web. Maybe he'd sounded a *little* too threatening the last time the pup was at the door.

He frowned as he closed the door and locked it for the evening. There had been a message.

The one he held now was in Daemon's handwriting, but not the careful script he was used to seeing.

He looked at the back side of the message. Official SaDiablo crest pressed into the red wax.

He broke the seal and opened the paper.

Lucivar,
If you're home, stay there until you hear from me.
Daemon

"Stay there" had been underlined three times.

"Wasn't planning to go anywhere," Lucivar muttered, walking toward the kitchen, where Marian was putting away the remains of their meal.

Something niggled his memory. Something about Marian and a message.

Then his darling hearth witch turned away from the sink and looked at him.

"Who was that?" she asked.

"A message from Daemon. He told me to stay home this evening."

"Why?"

"No idea." Although . . . He *almost* knew. The message *almost* made sense.

Then Marian took a step toward him. Something about the look in her eyes. Something about the way her wings flexed open slightly and then closed. Something about her psychic scent—and her physical scent. Something that had changed in the time since she'd come home.

He vanished the paper as his hands caressed the sides of her hips and urged her closer until their bodies were just brushing. He gave her a lazy smile. "Want to snuggle?"

She rolled her hips, pushing into him as her arms wrapped around his neck.

His blood went from warm to sizzle in a heartbeat.

"I was hoping you'd want to do more than that." She slid one leg along the outside of his, then hooked that leg behind his thigh, pushing herself up against him even more. Opening herself for him.

As her tongue caressed his mouth, demanding entry, he counted days and put the pieces together. She became a bold, aggressive lover during her fertile days. He was pretty sure she didn't realize there was a pattern to the times when she sought him out for sex instead of him issuing the invitation, but it was a pattern he recognized—and thoroughly enjoyed. Since they weren't ready to have another baby, he needed to steep his contraceptive brew a little longer for the next few days. Just to be safe.

Then he opened his mouth for her—and lost his ability to think.

"Marian?" he gasped when she broke the kiss and clamped her mouth on his neck. "Come with me, sweetheart. I'll give you whatever kind of ride you want."

She nipped him. "I thought we could start here and work our way to the bed."

Hell's fire, Mother Night, and may the Darkness be merciful.

"We could do that," he said as she lowered her leg and backed him toward a chair. "Oh, yeah. We could do that."

The ball of witchlight floated into the kitchen, followed by Rainier. He laid the two pokers and her stiletto on the kitchen table.

"The witchlight is dimming," he said. "Did you check in here to see if there was anything useful?"

Surreal stared at the passageway, then looked at Rainier.

"I left them the other lamp," he said.

"Left them the . . . You left them *alone* in there?"

His face hardened with the kind of anger that made her want to take a step back, but she held her ground. She had to. She out-ranked him, at least in terms of the Jewels each of them wore, and she had to show her faith in his self-control—even when it didn't look like he had any.

"I'm your escort, not theirs. They disobeyed you. If they want to stay with us, we'll give them what protection we can. If not . . ." He shrugged. "Their choice."

She hadn't expected Rainier to draw such an unyielding line. Of course, he wouldn't have been that unyielding if the chil-dren had disobeyed *him* rather than *her*. But the Blood males in Kaeleer—especially the Warlord Princes—drew a hard line when it came to disobeying a witch unless she was asking for something they considered unreasonable.

"They're children," she argued, knowing it was pointless to argue. "We invited them to join us."

"We made it easy for someone, but I think those children would have been part of this sick game regardless. How did they know this would be the night the Blood would be coming here?"

"No sign of workmen?" Surreal paused. Would there have been workmen? Or just the Black Widows? Would children just wait around an old house after dark unless someone had given them a hint that they would see something of interest? She wouldn't have—unless she was meeting someone in order to kill him.

"All right," she said. "Let's see if we can find anything useful in here. A market basket, carry sack. Anything we can use to haul around what we find."

She walked over to the sink. Water would be good. She had a jug of fresh water stored in her "personal cupboard," a place cre-ated by Craft and power that allowed the Blood to carry things without being physically burdened with them. At least Lucivar couldn't chew on her about not having supplies, and Rainier probably had a jug of water as well. Maybe even some food. But they'd have to use Craft to call in things from those personal cupboards, and she'd rather wait until there wasn't a choice before doing something that would close another exit.

She turned both taps and waited. The water pipes clanked and gurgled—and finally produced a gush-and-trickle rhythm of rusty water that stank. Letting it run in the hope that she'd eventually get clear water, she started to turn away to help Rainier check drawers and cupboards. Then . . .

Plink-plink. Plink-plink-plink.

Tiny white nuggets fell from the tap along with the water, *plink*ing into the sink. Minerals in the pipes, knocked loose when she turned on the water?

Instead of being washed down the drain, the nuggets shifted and began to form a pattern. Began to form a tiny hand.

"Well, there *was* a carry basket here," Rainier said as he closed a lower cupboard door and stood up. "But it looks like mice have been nesting in here for some time."

Not mineral nuggets coming out of the faucet. She was looking at tiny bones. But how could mice get into water pipes?

Same way anything else could. They had help.

Maybe the main water supply wasn't contaminated. Maybe it was just the kitchen pipes. Rainier had said mice had been nesting in one of the cupboards. If there was a bathroom in another part of the house, they might be able to get fresh water from there.

"No water we can use here," Surreal said, moving away from the sink.

"All right," Rainier replied as he opened a drawer. "We can—"

She yelped and leaped back, banging into the sink as large,

hairy-legged spiders poured out of the drawer Rainier had just opened. He danced back, swearing, as spiders fell to the floor and ran in all directions. And as the spiders ran, they . . . giggled.

Surreal stomped on the one closest to her—and felt nothing under her boot. Saw nothing on the floor when she raised her foot.

Illusions that disappeared within moments of leaving the drawer. Just enough time to scare the shit out of anyone in the room.

She felt as if she'd been slammed against a wall. In a way, she had been. Under other circumstances, she would have created a protective shield around herself and known she was safe from the spiders. The tight muscles came from denying instincts and training by *not* creating a shield.

"You all right?" Rainier asked, his voice sounding sharp.

"Yeah." *No.* The damn things *giggled.* "Is that all of them?"

Rainier approached the drawer and bent just enough to look inside. Then he took one of the pokers from the kitchen table and used it to push the drawer closed. "There's one left in the back. Since it's dining on a mouse, I think it's the real one." He looked around the kitchen and blew out a breath that might have been a softly muttered curse. "What in the name of Hell . . . ?"

★It's Tersa,★ Surreal said. They were alone, so she wasn't sure why she didn't want to say the words out loud. Except that she really *didn't* want to say the words out loud.

★What?★ Rainier asked, following her lead.

★The spiders. The mouse in the glass. I'm pretty sure those spells were made by Tersa.★

★Are you saying Daemon Sadi's *mother* is part of this twisted place? That *she's* one of the people trying to kill us?★

★No! Tersa wouldn't . . .★ How much did Rainier know

about Tersa? He must have met her, but how much did he know? *Someone must have tricked her into creating illusions for this place. She wouldn't harm children, Rainier. And as sure as the sun doesn't shine in Hell, she wouldn't hurt Daemon.*

So we're going to run across things that are weird and creepy but mostly benevolent, while other things are really trying to hurt us?

She hesitated.

No, Rainier said softly. *It won't be that simple. By serving in the Dark Court, I've had the privilege of spending time with three of the most brilliant and creative Black Widows in the Realm. So I know, from listening to Jaenelle, Karla, and Gabrielle, that illusion spells and tangled webs can be layered and blended. It doesn't matter what Tersa intended. A death spell hidden in one of her harmless illusions is still going to kill us.*

I know. Glad that Rainier had retrieved all the weapons, she slipped her stiletto into the sheath in her boot, then picked up the other poker and used it to pry open a cupboard. "Let's see what else is in here."

Spider, spider. Who found the spider?

Not so brave when someone crippled their power, were they? Not so brave, not so fierce, not so damnably arrogant.

Maybe he should base a character on the Surreal bitch. After all, even with danger all around them, the Blood would still be hot for *some* sex.

Landry Langston could have her for a lover while they were trapped in the haunted house. Hot, fast sex. She'd have to have a climax. Female readers expected *that*. Landry would get out alive, of course, but not be able to save her from the last trap. Would he regret her loss?

Or maybe he should show how cruel witches were when they used males. The witch in the story could *use* Landry, adding another level to his own torment as he tried to find a way out of the house and keep the people trapped inside with him safe. Then, when he had to choose between sacrificing himself in order to save her and getting out of the house alive, he'd be justified in leaving her to the fate she deserved.

Yes. Leave her behind, as if she were worthless, less than nothing.

After all, wasn't that what the Blood had done to him?

"Six candles," Rainier said, laying them on the kitchen table. "Too bad I didn't find any candleholders."

"I did." Surreal set two chipped cups on the table.

He looked at them, then at her.

She bit her tongue to keep from calling him an innocent. "I told you—I've stayed in places like this at times. You've got the matches?"

He took the matchbox out of his pocket. She held up a candle and waited for him to light the wick. Then she tilted the candle just enough for the wax to drip into one cup. As she started the same process with the other cup, she took another candle, set it in the cooling wax, and lit it.

When she set the first candle into its "holder," Rainier lowered the flame in the oil lamp.

"Hopefully we'll find more supplies in other rooms, but this will do for now," Surreal said.

A sound in the passageway.

Rainier grabbed one of the pokers and moved toward the sound. She slipped her stiletto out of the boot sheath and waited.

The children scuffled into the kitchen, looking scared and

defiant. She understood both feelings, but right now defiant wasn't going to make Rainier warm up to them.

When no one said anything, she walked over to the farthest door and opened it cautiously.

Nothing fell out or sprang at her. In fact, she had no idea what the little room was used for. She closed that door and tried the next one. Pantry. That was promising—especially when she saw a few canning jars on the shelves. She closed that door too, then tried the last one, on the other side of the kitchen.

The moment she touched the doorknob, she felt uneasy. "Rainier."

He came over and settled into a fighting stance. She opened the door slowly, prepared to resist anything that tried to push it open fast.

Nothing.

As she pulled the door all the way open, Rainier took a cautious step forward. Then another.

"Looks like we found the way down to the cellar," he said.

A vibration in the doorknob, in the door's wood, as he took another step closer to the top of the stairs.

"If we were in a book," he began.

"One of us would be dumb enough to take a candle and go down into the dark, scary cellar, where something would be waiting to gut the dumb one." The doorknob rattled, pulling against her hand. "Rainier, get away from there!"

He spun and leaped clear just as the doorknob yanked out of her grasp and the door slammed shut.

"And the dumb person, having reached the bottom of the stairs when the door mysteriously slams shut . . . ," Rainier said.

"Is not only locked in with one of the Bad Things, he's also in the dark because the *whoosh* of air blows out the candle."

Rainier raised his eyebrows. "He?"

She smiled at him. "Of course the dumb one is a male."

"Of course," he replied sourly. But he smiled.

She took one of the chairs that were around the kitchen table and wedged it under the doorknob. When she looked at Rainier, he was no longer smiling. "There's a spell on that door," she said.

She saw his hesitation, his frustration. He wanted to Craft-lock that door and keep the nastiness that was hiding in the cellar locked in the cellar.

She glanced at the children. They'd come closer to the table—and the available light—but still hadn't said anything.

Back to the pantry. Neither of them sensed any power or Craft around that door, but Rainier still braced himself against the door to hold it open, and she didn't argue with him.

She slipped the stiletto under her belt, took two jars off the shelves, and returned to the table. Using her jacket sleeve, she wiped off the jars, then held one closer to the candles to get a good look at what was inside. "Peaches."

How long had the jars been there? How long did canned fruit last? Not much dust on them. The witches who had created this place would have wanted food handy in case they got hungry. Most likely, these were leftover supplies.

Using the tip of her stiletto, she pried the lid open on one jar. The *pop* of the seal breaking was a good sign, so she picked up the jar and sniffed. Smelled like peaches, but . . . Was she getting a whiff of something else?

After wiping her stiletto on her trousers, she poked at the peach slices on top.

"Why are you poking those with that dirty old knife?" Ginger said.

"Mind your tone, girl," Rainier growled. Then he added on a

psychic thread, ★Why *are* you poking around? The seal was good, wasn't it?★

★It was good,★ Surreal replied. ★But do you really want to trust a good seal when there were three Black Widows in this house?★

"I'll find a bowl," Rainier said.

He did, and used his shirttail to wipe the dust out of it.

Wasn't much food to share between them, Surreal thought as she dumped the contents of the jar into the bowl. But a little food and liquid would help postpone the time when they'd have to use Craft to get to the supplies they were carrying and—

"What's that?" Sage asked, leaning closer to the bowl. "Are those grapes in there?"

"Mother Night," Rainier said, turning away.

She felt her gorge rise, but she stared at the mouse heads mixed in with the peach slices.

"So," she said too softly, "no water, no food. And nothing we can trust." She set the jar down, then slipped her stiletto into the boot sheath and picked up one of the candles. "Time to see what's upstairs."

"What's down there?" Ginger said, pointing to the cellar door. "You didn't go down there."

"And we're not going to," Rainier said. He picked up the oil lamp, then used the poker to point at the table. "One of you take the other candle."

"There might be food down there," Ginger said. She walked over to the door and pointed dramatically. "*I'll* go down there if *you're* too afraid."

"You do that, sugar," Surreal said. "But I'll only tell you this once. From here on, we'll do our best to protect you from whatever is in this house, but we won't protect you from your own stupidity. You want to open that door after we've told you not to, you go right ahead. If something comes after you, you deal with it or die."

"You have to—"

Something on the cellar stairs suddenly hit the door hard enough to rattle the hinges.

Ginger ran back to the other girls.

"Guess that answers the question, doesn't it?" Surreal said.

"Guess it does," Rainier replied. "I'll take point. You watch our backs."

"Done."

They didn't get to see the first big surprise. No matter. There would be plenty of opportunities for them to meet *that* one. And now that they were climbing the stairs to the second floor, they were finally starting the interesting part of the adventure.

FOURTEEN

Using Craft, Daemon flung open the Hall's front door, almost hitting the footman, who scrambled out of his way. Beale, wary but determined, stood in the center of the great hall. A prudent position, Daemon thought as he strode toward the man. He couldn't avoid noticing the butler's presence and yet the man wasn't in his direct path.

"Lord Khardeen has been waiting to see you," Beale said.

"Not now," Daemon growled as he headed toward his study. He needed a few minutes to settle himself before he went to Halaway—and also take care of the other worry that had occurred to him on his way back to the Hall.

Hell's fire! He hoped that message reached Lucivar in time. He could have contacted Yaslana on a psychic thread before leaving the landen village—he was strong enough to reach the Ebon-gray from any part of Dhemlan when his brother was at home—but they didn't use that kind of communication for casual matters at that distance. Sensing that something was wrong, Lucivar would have ignored the words and responded in typical Eyrien fashion: he would have headed for the location from which the message had been sent—and he would have ended up at that damn house. Sending a written message had been a gamble, one Daemon hoped he wouldn't regret.

Before he reached the study, Khardeen stepped out of the informal reception room.

"We need to talk," Khary said.

"I don't have time, Warlord," Daemon said as he opened the study door. "Beale, I need to get a message to the Keep. Find the fastest messenger within easy reach."

"Make time," Khary said.

He choked on the instinctive desire to lash out at any Warlord insolent enough to use *that* tone of voice when addressing a Warlord Prince. But because this was Khardeen, Warlord of Maghre and husband to the Queen of Scelt, he held on to his temper with all the slippery self-control he could command at that moment.

Last year when Jaenelle was secretly building the webs of power that would cleanse Hekatah's and Dorothea's taint from the Blood, he had stood as a wall between her and her First Circle—and had broken the trust of every other male who served her. It had been Khary's willingness to accept him again that had persuaded the other men in Jaenelle's First Circle to give him another chance. The friendships were still tentative, but they wouldn't exist at all if Khary hadn't made that first gesture. So he looked back at the man who still had a powerful influence with the rest of the dominant Warlords and Warlord Princes in Kaeleer.

"Give me five minutes, and I'll deliver your message myself," Khary said.

Khary wore the Sapphire Jewel. Except for Beale, who wore Red, there was no one at the Hall who could get a message to the Keep faster. And there was one advantage to sending this particular Sapphire-Jeweled Warlord instead of a Red-Jeweled butler—

Beale would have to talk to the High Lord, but Khary could talk to "Uncle Saetan."

"Five minutes," Daemon said as he walked into the study.

He hurried to his desk and pulled out a sheet of paper. By the time Khary walked into the study, he'd scribbled his message and was sealing the folded paper with wax.

"If this is about the spooky house . . . ," Daemon began as he pressed the SaDiablo seal into the wax.

"In a way, but mostly it's about Jarvis Jenkell and the *other* spooky house. The one I don't think is meant as an entertainment for children."

Daemon froze for a moment. Then he wrote a name on the front side of the message before saying, "What do you know about the other spooky house? And why would a landen mystery writer be involved?"

"Maybe because the writer was raised as a landen but is actually Blood."

Daemon straightened up and watched Khary pour two glasses of brandy from the decanter on the corner of the desk.

Khary handed a glass to him, then took a sip from the other and shrugged. "It happens. Not all the Blood live the way you do. Or the way I do, for that matter."

"And how do I live, Lord Khardeen?" Daemon asked a little too quietly.

"This is a dark house. The people who live here use Craft for all kinds of mundane things without thinking about it—lighting fires; using candle-lights, which require power, instead of candles or oil lamps; warming spells to supplement heat from fireplaces in the winter; cooling spells to make things comfortable in the summer. Anything a landen needs fire or ice to accomplish we can do with a spell and power. This place was designed as a home for dark-Jeweled Blood, and the reason so many things here require Craft is because you all need safe ways to siphon off some of the power. The Jewels provide a reservoir, but even they only hold so much."

Khary paused and took a long swallow of brandy. "But as deep as your power is, there are others on the opposite end of that scale. They're Blood, but their well of power is very shallow and is used up quickly. They would be almost as helpless as a landen in a house like this that requires using Craft for even simple things. Those Blood often form their own community within a Blood village in order to harness their limited power to better advantage."

Khary sat down, stretched out his legs, and crossed them at the ankles.

Since it looked like Khary was settling in until they discussed all he came to discuss, Daemon gave in and sat in the chair behind the desk.

"Fine," Daemon said. "Not all the Blood have a seemingly inexhaustible well of power. Not all the Blood live in mansions the size of a small village. Not all the Blood are wealthy or come from aristo families. I am aware of all that, Khardeen. What does any of this have to do with Jenkell?"

"There's a wide, deep chasm between a dark-Jeweled Blood and a landen," Khary said.

"That psychic chasm is just as deep and wide between a half-Blood and Blood," Daemon said.

Khary shook his head. "That's what the Blood in Terreille may have been taught, but it's not the reality. At least, not here in the Shadow Realm. In truth, when you're looking at the difference between someone who is full Blood with very little power and a half-Blood, that psychic chasm is more like a rift that can be spanned, and it's more like a crack between a half-Blood and a landen. There's a difference between Blood and landen, to be sure, but that difference isn't always as noticeable as you might think. So sometimes, for whatever reason, Blood will live in a landen village. They can pass for landen in ways that you or I never could. And since they *do* have just that little bit of something extra, they usually live quite comfortably."

"They take control of a landen village?"

Khary made a dismissive sound. "They're no doubt successful enough in their chosen work, but most prefer to live quietly and not call too much attention to themselves. since calling attention to themselves by trying to dominate a landen village would also bring them to the attention of the more powerful Blood living in the same part of the Territory. You'd have to check with the Dhemlan Queens, but in Scelt the Queens are aware of any Blood who have chosen to live in landen villages."

"So they live in a landen village; they marry—and have children," Daemon said, beginning to see where Khary was heading.

"They do. And if the full Blood was a generation or two back and the secret was kept a secret . . ."

Daemon considered that. Two half-Bloods marry—and neither has power, so neither is aware of the potential for power. No reason for them to think their children would be Blood. No reason to recognize a spark of power and train that child as even the weakest Blood child would be trained.

"How would Jenkell have found out he was Blood?" Daemon asked.

"Maybe it started as professional jealousy when Lady Fiona's stories about Tracker and Shadow became popular. It was after her books began receiving as much notice as his that he began writing his books with a Blood character." Khary's eyes took on that distinctive twinkle that was usually a prelude for his causing a little mischief—or just enjoying someone else's efforts. "Fiona tends to avoid Jenkell at literary gatherings. It seems he resents the fact that she was able to 'acquire' one of the kindred and he could not, despite his considerable success as a novelist."

Daemon felt a flicker of dry amusement in response to that twinkle. "Hasn't anyone told Jenkell that the acquisition isn't done by the human?"

"Even if he knows, I'm not sure he cares," Khary replied. "This is guesswork and most of it comes from Fiona, based on things she's observed or overheard at gatherings where Jenkell has also been present. Fiona says he changed while he was writing his first Landry Langston story. That he seemed more demanding and yet less confident."

"The first story was the one where the Langston character discovers he's Blood."

Khary nodded. "Wouldn't be that hard to find someone who would tell Jenkell how to make the Offering to the Darkness—at least in general terms. Some might have been willing to tell him because they like his work and enjoyed the thought of providing research for a story. And there are always some who will do a great many things in exchange for a generous stack of gold marks."

"So Jenkell made the Offering, thinking he was just going through the motions—and discovered he was Blood." Daemon shook his head. "Damn fool was lucky to come out of it in one piece."

"If he did come out of it in one piece." Khary drank some brandy, his blue eyes fixed on Daemon. "He didn't expect anything to happen. He wasn't *prepared* for anything to happen. And he did grow up in Little Terreille, so he may not realize—or believe it even if he was told—that after he discovered what he was, the Blood would help him understand the power that flowed in his veins, even teach him some basic Craft so he could use that power safely."

Daemon drained his glass, then set it aside. "This is all very interesting, but what does it have to do with the other spooky house?"

There was no twinkle in Khary's eyes now. "We think Jarvis Jenkell is creating a place as vengeance against the Blood."

A short flight of stairs to a landing. Turn and go up the other flight of stairs and reach the second floor. How in the name of Hell could it take so long, and why did the stairs seem to be going off at an angle? And where did the damn draft come from that blew out the candle, leaving her in the pitch-dark since she was *not* going to use Craft to relight it? And why couldn't she see the lamps or the other candle?

And if he was at the top of the stairs waiting for her, why didn't Rainier answer her?

Daemon poured another brandy for himself, refilled Khary's glass, then settled back in his chair. "Explain."

Khary scrubbed his curly brown hair with the fingers of one hand, then cupped his glass with both hands. "This is guesses based on rumors and hints. Fiona kept insisting that she didn't *know* anything."

"But . . . ?"

"Since Jenkell's other books were read and well received by

both Blood and landens, he was stunned by the Blood's reaction to the Landry Langston stories."

"Because we found his portrayal of the Blood so excruciatingly bad it was amusing?" Daemon paused and considered. "If he'd just found out he was Blood while he was writing the first story . . ."

"Then the story was a barely disguised announcement to the entire Realm that he was Blood—and no one realized it. Especially the Blood." Khary drank some brandy. "So a few months ago, Jenkell began hinting about the story for his next Landry Langston book."

"His character gets trapped in a spooky house?" Daemon guessed.

"I believe he called it a haunted house, but the same idea. Except that his character would be fighting for his life against traps and dangers instead of being entertained by a few illusion spells. Anyway, a few days after *that*, the story started spreading that Jaenelle was creating a spooky house—and before someone warned Jenkell to hold his tongue, he was spewing that Jaenelle had *stolen* his idea. Fiona was at that writers' gathering, so she approached Jenkell to assure him that his idea of a haunted house would be vastly different from anything Jaenelle would consider, since he was writing a mystery story and Jaenelle was creating an entertainment for children. But he seemed offended that a 'White-Jeweled bitch' would dare talk to him. Then he said something about how unjust it was that a mediocre writer like her could be acquainted with the Queen of Ebon Askavi and *he* wasn't even given the courtesy of an audience with the Lady. He left the party right after that and hasn't been seen since."

Daemon opened the bottom drawer of his desk and removed

the book he'd stashed there. A copy of the second Landry Langston novel, sent to him by Jenkell. The inscription read, "From one Brother of the Blood to another."

When he'd received the book, he'd thought Jenkell was being pretentious—or a complete fool—to send a message like that to a Black-Jeweled Warlord Prince. Had the man really believed they were equals just because Jenkell was Blood? Since he hadn't found the first book about the Langston character as amusing as other people did, he'd dropped the copy into the bottom desk drawer. Even after Jaenelle had wondered about the sanity of the character—or writer—he hadn't done more than skim a few chapters because the story was even less to his taste than the first Landry Langston novel.

Now he opened the book and stared at the inscription as Khary huffed out a breath and said, "Putting the pieces together, Fiona thinks—and I agree—that Jenkell is building a real haunted house somewhere and intends to pit some of the Blood against his creation."

"Is that what this is?" Daemon said as he put the book back in the drawer. "A pissing contest?"

Khary frowned. "What do you mean?"

He called in the invitation he'd been sent and the paper that had been wrapped around the mouse grotesquerie. Then he used Craft to float them over to Khary. While he waited for Khary to read them, he considered all the information he had—and didn't like the way any of it was adding up.

"Mother Night," Khary said. He leaned forward and tossed the paper and invitation back on the desk. "You're lucky you figured out it was a trap—although considering who the invitation was supposed to be coming from, the wording was sufficient warning that *something* wasn't right."

"I didn't figure it out," Daemon admitted. "I just didn't find the invitation in time."

"You can destroy that place."

It wasn't a question.

Daemon nodded. "If I unleash the Black, I'll burn out all the spells and destroy everything within the boundary of those spells. However, unless Jaenelle has discovered something she didn't notice about those spells initially—"

Khary made a soft snort of disbelief.

"—it's a good bet there isn't a way of breaking those spells from the outside without destroying everything in the building."

"Why would you even consider trying to break them when you can take the whole thing down?"

Daemon took a gulp of brandy. "Because Surreal and Rainier are trapped in that house."

FIFTEEN

Daemon knocked on the cottage door, thoughts and information swirling through his mind.

Jarvis Jenkell was Blood. That explained how he'd gotten two of the Black Widows to create the dangerous spells and the trap spell that would ensnare a person more and more with each use of Craft. A landen asking Sisters of the Hourglass to create those kinds of spells? The fool would be lucky if he left that meeting with his mind and body intact. But another member of the Blood, no matter how weak his own power, offering a substantial payment as the lure . . . Oh, yes, he'd find someone to help him play his game.

Jaenelle had cleansed the Realms of the Blood who had been tainted by Dorothea and Hekatah, but there would always be that kind of witch. Apparently Jenkell had found two of them.

By itself, the idea of a mystery story in a "haunted house" fueled by the illusion spells of a Black Widow was intriguing. If the witch had the skill, there would be no sure way outside of touch to know if something was illusion or real. And, of course, touching anything could be costly if not deadly.

Clues. Wasn't that what the mystery stories were about? Finding clues? If Jarvis Jenkell was behind this game and was playing it out like a story, there were some elements that should be part of the game. The stories began with a death—and usually ended with a death. The main character survived, but there were always more deaths before the enemy was defeated.

But it didn't sound like Jenkell had intended for anyone to survive his little game. Which meant Jenkell had intended to kill Surreal, Lucivar, and him. It didn't matter if this was meant as revenge against the Blood for not recognizing Jenkell as one of them, or a slap at Jaenelle for coming up with a similar idea at the same time and creating a spooky house as a harvest entertainment, or that Jenkell had wanted to indulge in a pissing contest with the SaDiablo family.

At the moment, only one thing mattered: Jenkell had used Tersa in order to harm her own family.

He was about to knock again when Allista opened the door. "Prince Sadi."

"Good evening, Lady Allista. I need to speak with Tersa."

Allista hesitated. "We were just about to have dinner. It's easier for her if I serve it at the same time each evening. Can this wait?"

Daemon stepped inside the cottage, forcing Allista to yield. "No, it can't. Ask her—"

"It's the boy." Tersa hurried toward him, her voice and face full of her pleasure at seeing him.

He was about to kill that pleasure. But he kissed her cheek and said, "Darling, we have to talk."

"It's time for dinner. No nutcakes until after dinner. Although . . . I think there is something chocolate for the sweet tonight." A distant look came into her eyes, as if she were about to follow a path only she could find.

"Tersa." He put enough bite in his voice to pull her attention back to him. "We need to talk. It's important." He took her arm and tried to lead her into the parlor.

"But . . ." Tersa pulled back, resisting. "Dinner is ready. We should eat dinner now."

"Prince," Allista protested. "Can't this—"

"Tersa!" Daemon snapped. "Surreal is in trouble. I need your help."

She cringed in response to his anger. Then she changed, and he saw a chilling lucidity in her eyes. He'd seen that look before. It never lasted more than a few minutes, and the effort to touch that place inside herself usually left her even more confused afterward, but in those minutes she was formidable. Whenever he'd seen that look, he'd wondered who she had been before she was broken—and before her mind had shattered into such confusion.

He released her arm and followed her into the parlor.

Allista hesitated, then shut the door, giving them privacy.

Tersa sat on the sofa. Daemon knelt in front of her.

Her mouth thinned in disapproval. "You're a Black-Jeweled Warlord Prince. You kneel to no one but your Queen."

He took her hands in his, a physical connection that would keep her grounded as long as she was able to hold on. "I kneel before my mother as a son pleading for her help."

She frowned, and a little of that lucidity faded. Too little time to find out what he needed to know.

"You helped a man build a spooky house," he said.

She nodded. "The Langston man. He was building a house like Jaenelle's and said I could help. It's going to be a surprise for the boy. And other children, too, but a surprise for the boy."

He was losing her too fast. "Who else was helping the Langston man? Do you remember?"

Confusion. "I made surprises. One of them . . ." That lucidity was gone. She looked at him through the clarity of madness. "No. If I tell you, it won't be a surprise."

"Can you remember what the surprises are? Can't you give me a hint?"

"*No.* You'll spoil the surprise for the boy." Now there was hurt in her voice.

He pressed his forehead against her knees, fighting to chain the frustration. "Tersa." She'd *worked* to create those illusion spells and that bastard Jenkell had used her.

He raised his head and looked at her. "Tersa, the Langston man is a *bad* man. He lied to you. He used your spells for his spooky house, but he also had two other Black Widows making spells for him, and *their* spells are meant to hurt whoever goes into his house. He wasn't making an entertainment for us like Jaenelle is making. He wants to *kill* us." He rubbed his thumbs over her knuckles, trying to hold her to this room and his words. "Tersa, Surreal is caught in that house. I need your help to get her out before she gets hurt."

He lost her. He'd told her too much—or not enough. No way to know with Tersa.

"Darling, is there anything you can tell me? *Please.*"

"They giggle," she said, her voice barely audible. "They're big and hairy and they giggle."

What giggles? Daemon wondered, but he didn't dare ask. She was pulling out whatever information she could. It would be up to him to figure out what it meant.

"Tippy-tap," Tersa said. She pressed her lips together and made a popping sound. Then she said, "The Mikal boy knows. He'll tell the boy about the surprises."

She looked crushed, defeated. Even if Jenkell did no other

harm, he was going after that son of a whoring bitch for the pain he'd just caused Tersa.

"Thank you, darling." Daemon kissed her hands and rose. "Thank you."

As he left the cottage and headed for the Queen of Halaway's home, he wondered just how much damage he'd caused.

"Here, Tersa," Allista said as she guided her Sister into a chair at the kitchen table. "Sit down and we'll have our dinner. Manny made a lovely soup for us this evening and a chicken casserole. Sit down, and I'll fetch the soup."

No response. Just silent tears. Tersa hadn't said *anything* since Prince Sadi left.

He was usually so careful with Tersa, so understanding about the fragile nature of sanity once a mind was shattered. So it was doubly cruel of him to rip Tersa up like this.

She would mention this in her weekly report to the Hourglass Coven, since caring for Tersa was part of her training, but what could they do? Daemon Sadi was the Warlord Prince of Dhemlan *and* a Black Widow. Who could reprimand someone like Sadi? Well, his father could. But she wasn't feeling quite brave enough to send a complaint to the High Priest of the Hourglass about his own son. Maybe . . .

"He spoiled the surprise," Tersa whispered sadly. "There won't be any surprises for the boy."

The surprises. Tersa had been working on these "surprises" for weeks.

"It doesn't matter now," Allista said. She put a bowl in front of Tersa. "Here, darling. Eat your soup."

Tersa didn't reply—and Allista watched a chilling lucidity fill the other woman's eyes.

"He wanted to hurt the boy," Tersa said softly. "The Langston man. He tried to use me to hurt the boy."

The moment came and went. But as they ate the evening meal, Allista was sure there was a storm brewing behind Tersa's quiet stillness.

Puffing from the effort to go up a few stairs, Surreal stood in the dark upstairs hallway and swore. This back hallway didn't feel big enough to hold six other people, let alone keep her from running into them. And a single lamp or candle should blaze in this dark.

"Rainier?"

No answer. No sound of body or breath. No sense of his presence.

Rainier? she called again, switching to a psychic thread.

Surreal! Where in the name of Hell are you?

I'm standing in the upstairs hallway.

No, you are not.

Shit. He really sounded pissy about it.

On the other hand, he might be right. She couldn't actually *see* where she was, and the stairs *had* seemed to go on too long and in a peculiar direction. *The candle went out, and I don't have any matches. I'm going to have to use Craft to light it.* And close another exit when she did. She wanted his agreement, since she wouldn't be closing another exit just for herself.

Put a tongue of witchfire on the candle, Rainier said. *Give it enough power when you make it to burn for several hours. You can light other candles with it when you find them, but at least you'll know nothing can snuff it out.*

*Nothing but getting doused with more power than I give

it,* Surreal replied. But he had a valid point. Witchfire was created with power and didn't need fuel or air. A draft wouldn't put it out. Neither would water. In fact, Marian sometimes shaped witchfire into a flower and floated it inside a glass vase filled with water. It was beautiful—and a little eerie—to see fire floating in the middle of water.

All right, she said. *I'll—*

Something there. A soft scuffle and a new, faint scent competing with the hallway's musty air.

She sidestepped to her right, away from the sound—and away from the possibility of someone shoving her down the stairs.

Something's here, she said.

What is it?

Don't know. Haven't made the witchfire yet.

She raised the poker like a shield in front of her, took another step to the side, and banged her hip on a table. She pivoted to bring herself around the table, extending her left arm to set the candle down. In that moment she felt the rush of air as something lunged at her, felt the swipe of knife or claws aiming for her exposed left side.

And she hesitated a moment too long before she created a protective shield tight enough to be a second skin.

A double slice through shirt and skin in that moment before the shield formed around her. A shiver along nerves that were uncertain if they should send a message of pleasure or pain. Then . . . pain.

She swung the poker, a backhanded blow that connected with someone hard enough to send the person slamming into the opposite wall.

A ball of witchlight floated above the table before she consciously decided to make one. But she saw her adversary—and silently swore when the light glinted off the hourglass that hung from a tarnished silver chain around the witch's neck.

A Black Widow who was very much one of the demon-dead, judging by how badly misshapen the head and face were from the blows that must have killed her. And not the same Black Widow who had attacked her downstairs.

"You want to tangle with me, you come ahead," Surreal said. "I'm in the mood to kill something."

The Black Widow laughed. "You think you can *kill* me? Look again."

"All right, maybe I'm too late to kill you, and maybe I won't even be able to finish the kill. But if you don't back off, I *can* arrange for you to become a permanent resident of a part of Hell that will make this place look like a high-class indulgence."

"Even when you become demon-dead you won't have that much power."

"Actually, sugar, since my uncle is the High Lord, I'll be able to send you anywhere I damn well please. He'll make sure of it."

The Black Widow hesitated, then smiled as much as her misshapen face allowed. "You won't be going anywhere, not even to Hell. I can wait to finish you, bitch." She passed through the wall and vanished.

"Shit," Surreal muttered. "Guess there's no penalty for using Craft once you're dead." Or part of the spells woven into the house.

She huffed out a breath and winced. First she needed to take care of the wound, figure out how bad it was—and whether she'd just been poisoned. Then she would deal with whatever came next. Right now she was certain of two things: she was in the upstairs back hallway and Rainier wasn't.

Rainier?

No answer. Nothing but a strange, gray blankness.

Rainier!

An aural shield must have been triggered, one that not only blocked out ordinary sounds but also prevented communication along psychic threads.

Had the gong sounded? She'd been too preoccupied to notice. Had Rainier heard it, or was that sound also blocked by the aural shield?

Leaving the unlit candle on the table, she took the poker and the ball of witchlight. The first door on her right was a bathroom. A narrow space with no room to maneuver if she had to fight. But it might have clean water, and that was something she needed right now.

"Wounded because I didn't shield and got separated from my escort," she said as she warily entered the bathroom. "Lucivar is going to be *so* pissed."

Interesting. Why was the witch so concerned about the opinion of a male who wasn't there? It wasn't like she was ever going to *hear* what he thought of her mistakes.

Yes. That was a thought. Those pointed ears would make a fine trophy. Something to remember her by when she was absorbed into the spells of this house.

And then she wouldn't have to worry about hearing *anything*.

Somewhere in the house, a gong sounded twice.

Surreal?

No answer. Nothing but a strange, gray blankness.

Surreal!

Rainier held his position. Waiting. Listening. Then he wove between the children and stopped at one of the hallway's openings and held out the lamp, trying to get a better look at the room.

Not a room. It was the front hallway.

He looked at Kester, then tipped his head to indicate the other children. "Stay here. Keep them together."

No sass from the boy. No arguments. No comments. Maybe it was finally sinking in that the children needed to do what they were told in order to survive.

He moved toward the front staircase. Could Surreal still be downstairs?

"Surreal?"

He peered over the banister. No sign of light down below.

The gong had sounded twice. One time would have been for the witchfire she needed to create in order to light the candle. The other?

She'd sensed something. Or someone. The second time the gong had sounded. Was that for a weapon or a shield?

Should have shielded when they first realized something was wrong. They had gambled on the degree of danger they were facing—and had underestimated their enemy.

She'd been coming up last, watching their backs. Should have been the safer position, since they'd already checked the kitchen.

Should have been.

What had changed in that moment between the last girl's starting up the stairs and Surreal's following her?

The last girl.

Rainier turned toward the opening leading to the back hall. Seven children had come up the stairs with him. But there shouldn't be seven anymore. The fourth girl. The last one to come up the stairs. She wasn't one of the children who had come into the house with them.

"Mother Night," he whispered.

He rushed to the back hallway and stopped at the opening

when he saw four children clustered around a closed door that Kester was trying to force open by slamming against it with his shoulder.

No sound. No warning of trouble. The girls had their mouths open and were probably yelling or screaming. The front hallway wasn't that big. He should have heard Kester trying to break down the door.

As soon as he crossed the threshold, he heard the screams.

Hell's fire.

"Get back!" Rainier shouted. He kept moving, building momentum with every stride. Kester saw him at the last moment and dove out of the way as Rainier turned the last stride into a leap and kick.

The door crashed open, revealing a room emptied of furnishings . . . but not empty.

For a moment, he froze at the sight of the burns and scars on the stranger's young body. An illusion spell must have hidden those injuries, just as it had hidden her ripped, dirty clothes. He felt sickened by what he saw—and even more sickened by what the girl had done.

The stranger wore openwork metal gauntlets, a kind of lethal jewelry witches sometimes wore. The fingers ended in razor-sharp talons. The ones on the girl's hands dripped with blood.

Her mouth was smeared with blood. It ran down her chin like juice at some kind of primal feast.

She was *cildru dyathe* now. A demon-dead child—and a deadly predator.

Ginger lay on her back on the dirty wood floor, her neck, chest, and arms ripped to shreds by the talons.

No sound from her.

No hope for her.

The *cildru dyathe* sprang to her feet and ran toward the back of the room.

Rainier sprang after her.

She fumbled at the wall, the talons on the metal gauntlets tearing the old wallpaper as she searched for something.

In the moment before he reached her, he was nothing but a Warlord Prince on a battlefield and she was nothing but an enemy. When he swung the poker at her back, it carried all his strength and fury in the blow.

He heard bone break.

She fell, no longer able to use her legs. Sufficiently Blood to become *cildru dyathe*, she didn't have the skill in Craft to use what power she had in order to get up.

He stood over her, looking at wounds that indicated torture. Looking at the madness and hatred in the girl's eyes.

"I'm sorry," he said.

"You're just like him," she said, her voice harshened by her hatred. "You're just like him."

"Who?"

She laughed. "I'll tell you once you're dead. I'll hook my pretty claws into your chest, and you'll have to carry me. Be my legs since you took mine. Hook my pretty claws into your eyes too. Just for fun."

Was that madness talking, or was that a reflection of who the girl had been?

He took a step back. Took another. Then he turned and walked back to Ginger.

So much blood, he thought as he knelt beside the dying girl. Too much damage. There were not enough moments left in her to even try a healing. There was not enough he could do for her with the basic skills he had to make a difference.

Her eyes stared at him but didn't see him.

Did landens have some place like Hell? They didn't become demon-dead. When their bodies died, they were gone. But did their spirits have a place where they spent some time before they were truly gone?

He didn't know, had never asked. And right now, he really didn't want to know.

"Her name was Anax," Kester said. "She lived at the orphans' home. She ran away a couple weeks ago."

Had she run away or had the people in charge of the orphans' home assumed that because Anax had disappeared? Someone had tortured the girl and killed her, leaving her in here to become one of the predators who hunted the "guests" trapped in this house.

"Did anyone else run away from the orphans' home recently?" Rainier asked, looking up at the other children.

"Three or four others," Kester replied, shrugging as if the loss made no difference.

Rainier choked back the urge to roar at the boy for being so cold and unfeeling. In order for Anax to become *cildru dyathe*, she had to be Blood. Which meant one of the Blood had been cold and unfeeling toward the girl long before Kester and his friends were.

No life in Ginger's eyes. No breath when he held a hand above her mouth and nose.

"She's dead," he said, getting to his feet.

"What . . ." Kester swallowed hard. "What do we do with her?"

Rainier waited a beat. "We have to leave her."

They looked at him.

"We *can't* just leave her," Sage said.

"You're welcome to carry her," he replied, retrieving the oil lamp. "I won't."

"So what are you going to do?" Kester asked.

Rainier tipped his head toward the wall. "Anax was searching for something. I'm going to find it."

There was water. Not as rusty as she'd expected, which maybe wasn't a good sign, since it meant someone had been using this bathroom on a regular basis recently. Of course, the Black Widows would have needed it before someone helped them into the first stage of being dead.

Surreal frowned at the toilet. Did the demon-dead need to pee? When they drank yarbarah, was there anything wasted, or did they absorb it all to sustain the dead flesh and their power?

Too bad she'd never thought to ask when she'd known some of them.

And what about Guardians like Uncle Saetan? He used to eat meals with the family, at least some of the time. So did he . . . ?

"No," she told herself firmly. If the High Lord of Hell did something so mundane as park his ass on a toilet, she did not want to know about it.

Besides, she had more immediate things to think about.

She turned sideways, her back to the bathtub, and studied the bathroom door. Should she close it and turn the lock to avoid a surprise attack from the hallway, or leave it open to give herself a fast way to escape?

"Don't close yourself in a box," she muttered, sucking in a breath as she removed her jacket. The shirt came next. She dropped both on the closed toilet seat. Then she braced the front of her thighs against the sink and stood on tiptoes to see her torso in the mirror.

Hell's fire. The blood was running between her skin and the shield, so she couldn't actually see the extent of the damage— and couldn't tell if the bleeding would stop on its own or if the wounds were something she needed to tend.

Rainier? she called as she lowered her feet.

No answer.

Dropping the shield would be one use of Craft. Restoring it, another. Calling in her kit of healing supplies, a third. Then another choice: vanish the kit and, therefore, close another exit, or leave it behind and hope she wouldn't need it again.

She couldn't reach Rainier. Would he hear the gong that signaled she'd used Craft? How many exits had they closed? How many were left?

If there had been any to start with.

It was ingenious, really. If this had been a story, she would have been intrigued, would have appreciated the struggle to avoid using Craft. Would have argued with Rainier about how and when Craft should have been used.

Since it wasn't a story, she was going to find the bastard who created this place and skin him, using nothing but a dull paring knife. Then she would crush all his bones into pebbles, leaving the spine and skull for last to be sure he got the benefit of all the pain. And *that* would be *before* Uncle Saetan got hold of him.

"Nice thought, sugar," she told her reflection, "but you have a few things to do first."

She called in the kit of healing supplies, swearing silently when she heard the gong. Taking the small pair of scissors from the kit, she cut off both sleeves of her shirt, then cut one sleeve in half. The jacket and shirt were hung on the bathroom doorknob. The healing kit was placed on the toilet lid.

She turned on the water in the sink and soaked one piece of

cloth. No hot water, and she wasn't going to use Craft for an indulgence, so she gritted her teeth against the shock of cold water on her skin as she dropped the protective shield and washed off the blood.

Up on tiptoes again to see the wounds as she cleaned that area.

Not too bad, she decided after a moment. A double swipe along her ribs from the bitch's nails. Deep enough that the wounds did need to be cleaned and sealed, but . . .

Dropping down again, Surreal frowned at her reflection. Why a double swipe? Why didn't the Black Widow hit her with all four nails, *especially* the ring finger that had the snake tooth and the venom sac under the normal nail?

"Not there," Surreal whispered, pressing the wet cloth against the wounds.

Last year, when Hekatah had captured Saetan and held him hostage, she had cut off the little finger of his left hand and sent it to Jaenelle.

Funny how the eyes stopped seeing the loss. Saetan no longer wore the Steward's ring on his left hand, so there was nothing to call attention to the missing finger. If someone asked anyone in the family about it, she'd bet they'd have to think for a minute to remember it was gone.

The Black Widow had been missing the little finger and ring finger on her right hand. That was why there was only the double stripe and no venom.

A lucky break for her, but she wondered if the loss had come before or after the Widow had worked on this house.

Surreal opened the jar of cleansing cream and dabbed the cream on the wounds. That would take care of ordinary infections until a Healer could take a look at the wounds. Then she took out a thin package the size of her palm and carefully peeled back one layer of paper. The spider-silk gauze was used by Healers in Kaeleer when they needed to close a small wound and didn't have time for a full healing or there was a reason to let the wound heal at its own pace. The silk was woven into a small web, and the strands helped keep the wound closed.

She pressed the spider silk against her side and didn't peel off the other piece of paper, using it as a bandage to absorb some of the blood.

Having done what she could, she closed up the healing kit, then reconsidered. She took out the scissors and slipped them into her trouser pocket. Even a small weapon was better than no weapon.

She was just about to create the protective shield when she looked at the toilet—and swore.

"Do whatever you can *before* you shield," she muttered. Sure, Lucivar had shown her a "shield with access," but it worked a lot better for someone who peed out of a pipe.

Not that she'd mentioned *that* to Lucivar.

She used the poker to lift the lid and seat. No nasty surprises, thank the Darkness, other than the kind that would give a hearth witch bad dreams.

But as she squatted over the toilet bowl, she thought she heard a sound coming from the bathtub drain. A funny sound. Like fingernail clippings being shaken inside a metal pipe.

It didn't take long to find the secret door. In fact, finding it seemed a little too easy.

Rainier lengthened the wick on the oil lamp to give himself better light.

Maybe it wasn't meant to be a secret door, just one that was supposed to blend in with the room. All he could see was a short hallway that ended in another door, and shelving on the right-hand side.

Folded blankets. Decorated paperboard boxes that women used to store hats and gloves or other small items that were used occasionally. Linens. Probably a mutual storage area for the bed-rooms on either side.

He didn't see anything sinister, didn't hear anything suspect. Of course, if the whole house was riddled with aural shields that kept people from hearing one another, not hearing anything wasn't actually comforting.

Linens.

He set the poker aside. Planting his right foot in the room they were in, he set his left foot in the storage room.

Something creaked. Might have been the floorboard under his foot. Might have been the door. But something creaked.

Rainier stepped back and studied the door.

Traps and games and illusions. The last time a storage room door was opened, a boy died.

"Kester," Rainier said. "You and the other two boys brace yourself against this door and hold it open."

While he waited for them to follow orders, he created a tight shield around himself, barely a finger width above his skin. Three openings in the shield—one for taking in sustenance, the other two for eliminating waste. Lucivar had taught him and the other boyos that particular trick, and they'd all gotten bruised enough times from Lucivar's surprise attacks to have learned that lesson very well.

Normally a tight shield was a subtle protection, since no one could know for certain it was there unless a person touched you. But . . .

Somewhere in the house, a gong sounded.

In this damn house, there was nothing subtle about using Craft.

He glanced at the boys and nodded, satisfied that he'd have plenty of warning if the door tried to shut. Then he stepped into the storage room, raising the lamp high.

Pillowcases.

"Girls," he called. "Come to the doorway."

He handed Sage the pillowcases, then gave Dayle a box of tapered candles and a globed candleholder. The candleholder would be easier to carry and shield the flame.

Stepping back into the room where the children waited, he set the lamp down near the poker. Taking the pillowcases from Sage, he shook them out to be sure there weren't any surprises hidden in them. Then he stripped the metal gauntlets off Anax's hands and took a good look at them before he dropped them into one of the pillowcases. Too small for his hand, but they weren't made for a child, so they would probably fit Surreal or Kester.

At this point, any weapon they could carry was a good weapon.

He fitted one candle into the holder and created a steady flame of witchfire to burn on the wick—and tried not to wince when the gong sounded.

"Bring that other candle over here," he said.

"It's almost gone," Henn said, handing him the candle in the cup.

Rainier stared at the candle. Almost gone. The bottom of the cup was filled with softened wax.

How long since they'd left the kitchen? Not long enough for a candle to burn down that much.

"Mother Night," he muttered. "Line up." He moved his hand to indicate a line in front of him.

When the children were lined up, he created a tight shield around each of them, leaving the openings for sustenance and waste.

"What did you do?" Kester asked.

"Created a shield around each of you," Rainier replied, trying to ignore the sound of the gong echoing in his mind. He lit a candle from the old one, then replaced the old one with the new. "It won't stop something from taking you, but it will keep you from being wounded or killed."

"Why didn't you do that before?" Kester demanded.

He put the box of candles and the second pillowcase in the one he was using for a sack. After closing his left fist around the top of the case, he hooked his finger into the loop on the candle-holder. "Sage, you carry that other candle. Kester and Henn, you take the lamps."

He walked back to the storage room door and picked up the poker in his right hand.

"Hey!" Kester shouted. "I'm asking you!"

"It takes Craft to create those shields. One use of Craft for each shield. And every time Craft is used, a way out of this place is closed off."

The boy didn't understand—or didn't want to understand.

"Why didn't you make these shields before Trist and Ginger got killed?" Kester said.

Because I thought we had a chance of getting out.

Rainier didn't answer. He just walked into the storage room.

Daemon sat at a round table in Sylvia's family parlor and stared at the piece of paper in front of him. He made hatch marks on the paper just to give himself time to . . . Not think, exactly. Just time to assure himself that he was maintaining the correct understanding-but-disapproving expression. Then he looked at Mikal, who sat opposite him. He didn't dare look at Sylvia, who was standing a full step back and to the right of her son's chair. He. Did not. Dare.

"Are these all the suggestions you can remember giving Tersa?" Daemon asked. These were bad enough. Skeleton mice that would scurry across a room, their little bones tippy-tapping on the floor. Big spiders that might drop from the ceiling or be hiding in a drawer. And the mousie in the glass.

"There was the eyeballs in the grapes," Mikal said hesitantly.

"The—" A quick glance at Sylvia. Oh, he should have insisted on talking to the boy alone. This was probably a lot more than a mother wanted to know about the workings of her male offspring's mind.

"The spell isn't triggered until someone starts eating the grapes." Mikal's voice held an excited enthusiasm. Apparently, since he couldn't see her, he'd forgotten about his mother being in the room. "Then some of the grape skins split and the illusion spell makes it look like there are eyes, all bloodshot and oozy."

Boyo, you may have just ruined your chances of ever seeing another grape in this house, Daemon thought.

"Did you *see* the mouse in the glass?" Mikal asked. "That one was—"

A growl, the voice barely recognizable as female.

Mikal hunched his shoulders and wisely offered no opinion about the mousie in the glass.

"I think I have everything I need," Daemon said. "Thank you, Mikal."

Mikal slid off his chair. Then he hesitated, leaned across the table, and said in a loud whisper, "Did Tersa tell you about the beetles?"

***

Surreal held her hands under the water running from the faucet, cleaning them as well as she could. Then she cupped her hands to fill them with water and took a cautious sip. No obvious foulness. Of course, if the water supply had poison or drugs dumped into it, she may have already done enough damage to kill herself.

That being the case, she drank another mouthful of water before turning off the taps.

She rubbed her wet hands over her face, trying to shake off the fatigue.

Shouldn't be this tired, she thought as she dried her face and hands on her shirt. *Shouldn't be this tired.*

She created a tight shield–with–access around her body and tried not to think about another exit closing because she had used Craft.

Then she heard it again. That funny little rattle coming from the bathtub drain.

With one hand resting on the sink, she turned toward the tub, wincing when the move tugged at her wound.

A little black beetle crawled out of the drain. It hustled toward the other end of the tub, making its little beetle noises.

It's just one, she thought as she tried to get her breathing under control. *It's just one, and it can't get out of the tub.*

A movement caught her eye.

Another little black beetle climbed out of the drain.

And another. And another.

Hell's fire, Mother Night, and may the Darkness be merciful.

She could put her hands on a body covered in maggots. She could cut up a man using nothing but a dull ax. She could skin a man and not shiver. She could scoop up a head that had been ripped off by a pissed-off cat and dump the damn thing in a bucket while the warriors around her wouldn't even touch it.

But she didn't like beetles. Didn't like the look of them, didn't like the clacking sound of their bodies. And especially didn't like the crunch they made when you stepped on them. *That* sound always made her stomach drop and filled her knees with jelly.

Her little secret. Everyone was entitled to one or two irrational fears.

Rattle. Rattle rattle rattle.

She watched them swell as they filled the tub, more and more of them coming out of the drain. Watched them swell, bigger and bigger, until they were the length of her palm and almost as wide. Bigger and bigger until . . .

POP! POP POP POP!

They burst. Their shells split down the middle and . . .

A sensation. On her hand. A light sensation, since it was against the shield and not her skin.

She looked at the hand resting on the sink. It was covered by a beetle.

Just one beetle.

She flung her hand up, sending the beetle flying through the air. And she *screamed.*

That piercing scream.

What in the name of Hell could make *Surreal* scream like that?

Rainier flung open the door at the other end of the storage room and rushed into an empty room similar to the one he'd just left.

"Surreal!"

He ran across the room, yanked open the door, and charged into the hallway just as Surreal rushed out of another room. He dropped the poker and grabbed for her, only realizing when he felt a shield hitting a shield that she wasn't wearing anything above her waist except a brassiere and her Gray Jewel.

"Surreal!"

"Be—be—be—"

He shoved the candle and pillowcase into her shaking hands, grabbed the poker, and strode into the room, ready to do battle with whatever had scared the shit out of her.

And found himself staring at a bathtub full of huge, split beetles.

"Be-be-beetles."

Relief made him giddy for a moment. Or maybe the giddiness was caused by his yanking himself back from the killing edge.

He glanced over his shoulder and fought not to grin. Damn things really must have startled her.

"Do you think they're edible?" he asked. The beetles were the size of a small lobster tail, and the meat looked like cooked lobster that had been pulled out of a split shell.

"Wh-what? That's not meat; that's exploded bug guts."

Rainier watched the beetles change back into little beetles that went scurrying down the drain. Nothing but an illusion spell. And most likely, even the little beetles were an illusion because they'd have to come out of the drain at the proper time. Since there wasn't much about dealing with blood and guts that usually threw Surreal off stride, it was his duty as a friend to tease her about getting excited over a bug.

"If you ignore the fact that they're insects instead of—"

"Say it, and I will rip your face off and shove it up your ass."

The threat sounded sincere.

Her tone pricked his temper, especially when he was still just one short step away from the killing edge, but he tried to cajole instead of squaring off with her, since that would lead to at least one of them getting hurt.

He turned toward her. "Come on, Sur—"

He reached up and shifted the ball of witchlight in order to get a better look at her.

Her gold-green eyes were glassy. Not glazed with cold rage, but glassy with shock. And she was breathing in these funny little hitches.

This had struck more than a nerve with her.

"Hey," he said softly, moving with a deliberateness that wouldn't startle her. "Illusion spell. That's all they were."

She was shaking. He could see the effort she was making to regain control, but she was shaking.

"Go back in the hallway," he said gently. "I'll get your clothes."

"Check them," she whispered as she stepped back.

He retrieved her shirt and jacket, pushed the witchlight out ahead of him, and left the bathroom.

He set everything on the hallway table next to the unlit candle, including the globe candle and pillowcase he'd handed her. Then he looked at her left side.

"How bad is it?" he asked, his fingers hovering over the blood-spotted paper covering the wound.

"Not as bad as it could have been. The Black Widow who attacked me had lost the finger with the snake tooth, so I don't have to worry about venom."

The bitch could have coated her other nails with poison. He was about to remind her of that—and then realized there was no point in telling her. She had been an assassin. She knew more about using poisons than he did.

"If there's any in me, I'll feel it soon," she said quietly, looking past him as the hallway got lighter.

"Whoever made this house trapped at least one *cildru dyathe* in here. Maybe more."

"Along with two demon-dead Black Widows. Not good odds if they all decide they want someone for dinner."

Rainier looked back at the children, then shifted closer to Surreal. *Any suggestions?*

She sighed. *I'm tired, Rainier. We've only been in this house a couple of hours, but it feels much longer.*

I think it has been longer, but we'll talk about that later.

My suggestion is to go back downstairs. We'll check that sitting room again for surprises. Then we'll put a shield around the room and a Gray lock on the door. That will keep out unwanted visitors.

That will close two more exits.

I know.

He nodded. *Main staircase should be that way.*

You'll take point? Surreal asked.

We'll take point. He shook out her shirt and jacket, then helped her into both. *Don't argue about it.*

She hesitated. *Wasn't going to.*

That told him more than anything else that she needed time to regain her balance.

They gathered up their various kinds of illumination and their weapons.

Rainier looked at Kester, put a finger up to his lips, then pointed at the doorway that would lead them back to the main staircase.

He and Surreal led. The children followed.

The front upstairs hallway looked just as he remembered it. That wasn't right, but he couldn't figure out why—and didn't care once they reached the bottom of the stairs.

Then Surreal said, "It's different."

Daemon capped his pen and vanished it. He folded the paper and tucked it in the inside pocket of his black jacket. Then he was up and moving toward the parlor door, slipping past the irate Queen of Halaway as he said, "Thank you for your assistance, Lady Sylvia. And Mikal's as well. I appreciate it."

As he opened the door, she balled up her fist and slugged him in the shoulder.

He turned on her, snarling.

"Don't you dare criticize Tersa," Sylvia said. "Don't you dare make her feel bad about what she's done."

His temper chilled, and he replied too softly, "You're out of line, *Lady.*"

"I saw your face, *Prince.* When Mikal walked out of the room and you didn't have to pretend to take a disapproving stand, I saw your face. Tersa may not understand the mundane world she tries to live in, but she understood her boy. If you were still Mikal's age, you would have been as fascinated by her spooky surprises as he is. Especially those damn beetles."

In that moment, he understood why his father had fallen in love with the Queen of Halaway. He could picture Sylvia squaring off with Saetan over whatever had lit her temper or nipped her sense of justice.

But he doubted Sylvia had ever slugged his father.

"No response?" Sylvia asked tartly.

"My father told me I should never lie to a Lady," Daemon replied.

"So?"

"So I have no response." Because he was *not* going to admit she was right. "Good evening, Sylvia. I'll see myself out."

She changed from irate woman to concerned Queen in a finger snap.

She touched his arm. Just a gesture of concern. "Good luck."

"Thank you."

As he left Sylvia's house and caught the Black Wind to return to the landen village, he knew it was going to take more than luck to get Surreal and Rainier out of that damned spooky house alive.

SIXTEEN

"There was a mirror on that wall, and a coat-tree near the door," Surreal said as she looked around the front-entrance hallway.

"That 'caretaker'—whoever he really is—might have moved things to cause confusion," Rainier said.

She frowned, then shook her head. "Wasn't really paying attention to the wallpaper, but I think that's different too."

"An illusion spell could change the wallpaper. A person could move a mirror and coat-tree."

Was it as simple as that?

"Does the front door work?" Kester asked.

The boy sounded upset, angry. She understood that. She'd had more than enough of dealing with this damn house and was feeling the same way.

"We'll check out the hallway and that sitting room to make sure we have some safe ground," Rainier said. "Then we'll check the door."

"Why wait?" Kester demanded.

"Because the odds are good that a door or doorway also has a trap," Rainier said with strained patience.

"You waited to make these shields to protect us, and Ginger and Trist died," Kester said. "Why wait for something else bad to happen?"

"Don't start a pissing contest, boy," Rainier warned. "Not here, not now. First we find some safe ground, and then we can— *Kester!*"

Kester bolted for the front door.

Rainier raised his hand, and Surreal felt the mental stumble as he stopped himself from using Craft to . . . Do what? Put up a barrier in front of the boy? Slam an Opal lock on the door, preventing it from being opened? Either action would have required a second use of Craft to undo what had been done.

But the moment passed when a choice might have mattered. Kester reached the door and pulled it open.

The thing on the other side . . .

Surreal's first impression was of an engorged, somewhat malformed Eyrien male combined with something made of smoke. Wisps of black smoke rose from its body, obscuring the separation between the male and the night. The eyes glowed red like stoked coals.

She saw those things in the moment before it grabbed Kester, before the Opal shield around the boy was shattered by a bolt of darker power. Before Kester's blood sprayed over the hallway.

Neither she nor Rainier had time to react, to strike back before the creature and boy disappeared—and she stared at a door that opened onto nothing but a brick wall.

"Mother Night," Rainier said.

"Well," Surreal said, wondering if anyone else could hear her heart pounding, "now we know someone who wore a Jewel darker than Opal was killed and trapped in this house."

Rainier looked at the remaining four children, who were just staring at the front door. Then he looked at Surreal, and she saw bleak resignation instead of hope. "Yeah. Now we know."

Nothing Rainier could have done. If the Eyrien could break an Opal shield, a blast of Opal power wouldn't have stopped him from killing the boy. A blast of her Gray might have stopped him, but like Rainier, she had hesitated, had choked back her natural reaction—and the moment when it might have made a difference was gone. Lost. Just like the boy.

Did you recognize the Eyrien? Rainier asked.

Surreal shook her head. *He wasn't from Ebon Rih, but there were plenty of Eyriens who came in during the service fairs and accepted service in other parts of Askavi—or other Territories altogether.*

Whoever devised this place killed two Black Widows and an Eyrien warrior.

An Eyrien isn't any harder to kill than any other man if you can slip a knife between the ribs when he's not expecting it.

I doubt we'll get that close, Rainier said. *If he comes at us, it will be a straight fight.*

And without Craft, neither of them had the training or skill needed to face an Eyrien who'd had centuries to hone his fighting skills.

Right now, there was nothing they could do about the Eyrien—or the other dead.

"Let's check out the sitting room," she said.

Rainier rounded up the children, and they all entered the sitting room in a tight little pack. Then Rainier swore softly.

"This *is* different," he said.

It should have been the same room, and it wasn't. Obvious differences, with no attempt to hide them.

"We should be in the sitting room where we started," Rainier said. "Since we're not, where in the name of Hell are we?"

She shook her head. "Don't know. But let's see what we've got in here."

They poked at sofa and chair cushions, swept the pokers under furniture to roust anything that might be hidden. There was a bowl of grapes on the table behind the sofa. Nothing noticeably wrong with them, but she said, "Hands off" when the children looked at them—and wondered if they'd actually obey her this time or if someone else would get killed.

The painting over the fireplace wasn't a portrait as such. It was a man and a woman. He stood behind his lover, his arms around her, his mouth pressed to her bare neck. But as Surreal watched, his arms tightened to restrain. The woman's eyes opened, and they were filled with fear and resignation. The man's kiss changed into a bite. No pretense of lover now, just a predator. Blood dribbled down the woman's pale skin and stained her white dress.

Surreal moved closer, raised her candle, and read the brass plaque attached to the painting's wood frame. Then she snorted.

"What?" Rainier asked, hurrying to join her.

"The painting is called *Rut*."

Rainier studied the painting for a moment, then turned away. "On behalf of my caste, I'm not sure if I should be insulted or relieved."

"Why?"

He gave her a look. Then he said, "Whoever painted that has never seen a Warlord Prince in rut."

★   ★   ★

Why? *Why?* He'd had that painting created based on solid information, and had paid extra for that particular illusion spell. Why was this male so dismissive of what he was seeing?

Warlord Princes were known to be extremely violent when they were caught in the sexual madness known as the rut. The women they used were brutalized for *days*. While the Blood didn't talk about it much, it wasn't one of their damn *secrets.*

Why had the whore dismissed the violent message of the woman's fate? She *had* to know the fate of such women. They were pampered and imprisoned—and used for the rut until their minds and bodies were too broken for even a sex-maddened beast to ride. That's what he'd been told.

On the other hand, he hadn't realized her companion was a Warlord Prince. Too bad there were still some children with them. Otherwise, he might have gotten some sizzling, firsthand information about Blood lust.

Then again, seeing as they were a Warlord Prince and a whore, maybe they wouldn't be inhibited by an audience—even the audience they could see.

They checked the room, then checked it again. Either there was nothing dangerous in the sitting room or they hadn't done the combination of things that would trigger it. There was wood for a fire, but they both felt uneasy about opening the flue. She didn't know if she and Rainier were sensing a real potential danger or if they'd just reached the point where they were spooked by *everything* in the house. But the uneasy feeling was strong enough that they decided to make do with the dusty, musty throws they'd found in a chest in one corner of the room.

Do we shield the room? Rainier asked.

She nodded. *A Gray shield around the room.*

They'd already seen that Rainier's power wouldn't be strong enough to protect them, so that would be her task. She would be the one closing off another potential way out of this damn place. But it needed to be done, and it was the smart thing to do.

She still flinched when the gong sounded after she shielded the room.

Rainier rested a hand on her shoulder, unspoken agreement and comfort.

They'd left the sitting room door open while they'd checked the room. Now they moved together to close the door and lock it.

As she started to push the door closed, Rainier sucked in a breath and swore softly.

Trist stood in the hallway. She could see the torn chest and belly through his ripped clothes. She looked straight at the face that was coated in blood on the side that had the empty eye socket.

But this wasn't Trist. Wasn't even *cildru dyathe.* This was an illusion spell called a shadow, an image created from a little blood and a lot of Craft.

Jaenelle could create a shadow that looked and acted and felt so real, even touching it didn't reveal the truth of its nature. But this . . . The boy stood with the woodenness of a puppet. Effective enough during that first jolt of seeing him, but clearly a trick just the same.

The shadow Trist smiled at them and said, "The worst is still to come."

Then it vanished.

Surreal closed the door—and swore when the door vanished too.

Rainier studied the wall, then shook his head and took a step back. "If that's an illusion, I can't tell without touching the wall."

"Which would put your hand on the wrong side of the shield."
Surreal looked around, swore, and pointed to the back wall. "That
wasn't there before."

A door. She had created her shield a hand span away from
the walls to avoid triggering any spells that might be *in* the walls.
Looked like she'd made the right choice. Still, in the morning,
the only way out of the room was through a door that held who
knew what on the other side.

She took a deep breath and let it out in a sigh. "Next?"

"Food and water," Rainier said. "We'll use my stash."

He didn't expect to get out of the house, Surreal realized. If he
died and made the transition to demon-dead, he might get pulled
into the spells and become an enemy instead of still fighting with
her. If that happened, she wouldn't have access to the supplies he
carried. That's why he wanted to use his supplies first. But neither
of them actually put that into words.

The other thing neither of them said was that she would be
able to destroy him, to finish the kill, but if *she* was the one who
died and turned on him, he wouldn't be able to survive her attack.
So keeping her alive was the only chance that one of them would
get out of this house.

He called in a jug of water and a chill box that was inside a
large wicker picnic hamper—the kind that had a separate compartment to carry dishes, glasses, and silverware.

Surreal blinked. She'd brought water, yes. Always carried some
with her. But her stash of food was four apples she grabbed from a
bowl in the town house's kitchen as she and Rainier were leaving.

"You carry a chill box?"

He looked puzzled. "Why not?"

She didn't answer that, too busy wondering if a chill box was
something all escorts kept with them or if this was just Rainier.

He opened the chill box's lid and pulled out a whole roasted chicken, a small wheel of cheese, and three apples.

"What, no sweet?" she teased.

"The chicken had already been cooked when we changed our plans for the evening. We didn't get much dinner, since we rushed to get here—"

She snorted.

"—so I figured a harvest picnic after viewing the house would be appropriate." *And I did bring a sweet,* he added, *but it's not in the chill box, so you'll have to do without.*

She grinned at him and opened the compartment that held the silverware and dishes.

They were joking, smiling, eating! How could they find anything amusing? Why weren't they *afraid*?

The worst was still to come, but they had managed to shut out all his pets. Nothing in that room but a couple of the little, creepy spells, and the bitch had already spoiled one of them by not letting the children eat the grapes. Unless the Warlord Prince insisted on sex, nothing interesting would happen while they stayed in that room.

But no. The Surreal bitch outranked the Warlord Prince, so he couldn't insist on being pleasured, even though she *had* been a whore.

No matter. When he wrote the Landry Langston version of this little adventure, he'd make things interesting. Besides, stories always needed an interlude before the final storm.

"So." Surreal bit off a piece of apple and chewed slowly. The wheel of cheese was gone, and the chicken was nothing more than a jumble of bones. With their tummies sufficiently full, the children had fallen asleep before they'd gotten to the apples. Just as well. She and Rainier needed the extra food, since their bodies, as the vessels of the power they wielded, burned up food faster. "If this was one of those mystery stories we've read, where do you think we'd be now?"

Rainier looked around the sitting room. "Well, we've had death and danger, we've been warned that there is worse coming, and we're barricaded in a room in order to get some rest. In terms of story, this is the place where the two main characters have fast, hot sex."

They looked at each other.

"So what do you want to do in the five minutes *that* would have taken?" Surreal asked.

Rainier huffed out a laugh. "*Surreal.*"

"What? Remember that one we read where the man's penis wept in gratitude? Personally, I thought he was just leaking, and that the woman, who swore it was the best sex she'd ever had, was being very polite. I know this because when I was a whore and had to be very polite in that way, I always charged a lot more."

"Hush." Rainier's face was turning red with the effort not to laugh loud enough to wake the children.

She looked at the painting above the fireplace mantel. Blood still oozed down the woman's chest from the wounds inflicted by her lover. Then Surreal looked at the children. They were all so exhausted, she doubted they were capable of overhearing anything, but she switched to a psychic thread anyway.

Has this all seemed odd to you? she asked.

In any particular way? Rainier replied dryly.

She hooked her hair behind one ear. *I don't know. It just seems . . . Not tame, exactly.*

Rainier looked away. ★Three children have died. That isn't tame.★

★And more died before we walked into this place. I know. But it's . . . clumsy. Deadly, yes, but . . .★ She wasn't sure what she was trying to tell him, wasn't even sure what she was sensing.

Rainier hesitated. ★Your family has a vicious elegance that is unmatched anywhere in the Realm. The only males and witches who come close are the ones who served in the First Circle at Ebon Askavi, and they rule the Shadow Realm now. These are your friends, your family. And frankly, Lady, that is the level of Craft that you yourself wield. This place may not be elegant, but it's a well-constructed trap.★

★Yes,★ she agreed. ★Well constructed but not elegant.★

★If any Black Widow in your family had built this place with the intention of destroying whoever walked in here . . .★

Surreal shivered. Seductive. Alluring. Lethal. Breaking a person down layer by layer. Weaving pain and pleasure together until both were a torment you would beg to feel.

Clickety-clack. Tippity-tap.

The sound—and Rainier's gentle nudge—brought her wandering thoughts back to the room and the potential danger.

Clickety-clack. Tippity-tap.

Something white, scurrying along the baseboard just inside her shield, tapping on the wood floor.

They watched the skeleton mouse scurry-scurry until it reached the corner of the hearth. Then it sat back on its haunches and turned its skull until it seemed to be looking right at them.

She wished she still had a crumb of cheese left to toss to it— just to see what would happen.

The mouse held its position for a moment longer, then scurried away.

Clickety-clack. Tippity-tap.

★Was that one of Tersa's spells?★ Rainier asked.

★Had to be.★ A good example of the elegance Rainier had pointed out. Bizarre? Sure. Even for Tersa. But the skill it took to create that bit of Craft was several levels above the nasty surprises.

And thinking about the difference in that level of skill made her very glad Tersa wasn't one of the Black Widows trying to kill them.

Daemon's frown deepened as he walked up to the Coach. Where in the name of Hell were the shields? Jaenelle *wouldn't* have been that careless. There was no reason to think the landens would challenge her presence in their village or even venture close enough to be a threat to the Coach and its inhabitants, but there was no reason to believe the person who had created that "entertainment" had kept the danger inside the fence.

Then he reached for the Coach's door—and felt power spiral up around his ankles, his calves, his knees.

No warning. He stood perfectly still while Jaenelle's death spells rubbed against him like a contented cat, sang over his skin like silk.

Recognition of his psychic scent, the Jewels he wore, him as a man.

The death spells released him, fading away with one final, playful, fingertip caress down his cock.

She was smiling when he stepped into the Coach, but he asked anyway. "Was that last bit especially for me?"

"Of course."

She was sitting at the small table in the Coach's sitting area. She'd opened a bottle of wine, and there was a glass, almost empty, near her hand. The table was covered with papers. He couldn't tell if they were notes to friends that she was writing to occupy the time or something else that fit the chill he detected in her psychic scent.

He braced one hand on the table, leaned over, and gave her a long, soft kiss. Then he looked over at the boy, Yuli, who was sound asleep on the short bench opposite the table.

"He has scars on his back—and a different kind of scar on his heart," Jaenelle said too softly.

"What do you want me to do about it?" he asked just as softly. A sincere question. If she wanted to unleash him as a weapon against whoever had harmed the boy, he would be her weapon.

"I think the District Queens should be encouraged to look more closely at the orphans' homes in landen villages. Especially the places that raise half-Blood children as an accommodation."

"Was anyone aware of this accommodation?" Meaning, had Saetan been aware of it when he ruled Dhemlan?

"Yes. The Blood parent is held responsible for the child, and there is a minimum allowance that must be paid for the child's support. If the parent can't pay the full amount, the Queen must make up the difference from the tithes that support her and her court. The penalty for not meeting that minimum allowance for each child is . . . severe."

He'd been ruling this Territory only a few months, and it looked like he was going to shake up—and scare the shit out of—the Dhemlan Queens once again.

Jaenelle rested a hand over his. "I don't think this is common. I know for a fact that Sylvia regularly inspects the orphans' home in the landen village under her rule, and she doesn't announce her presence until she's walking in the door."

"I see." He understood the message. He ruled the Territory,

but the District Queens—and the Province Queens above them—had to be allowed to rule their pieces of Dhemlan according to their own nature. He drew the lines of what he would and wouldn't tolerate in his Territory—and he would deal with anyone foolish enough to cross one of those lines, especially if it was someone who held power over others. But every Queen's court had a different tone, a different flavor. The Blood needed the flexibility of those differences just as they needed the implacable line.

And he'd needed the reminder that, while this particular District Queen might not be as diligent as she would need to be hereafter, most of the other Queens had not been so careless.

"Sylvia brought Saetan with her once," Jaenelle said, a mischievous sparkle in her sapphire eyes.

Picturing that amused him, as she'd known it would. "That must have been an exciting day for the administrators of the orphans' home."

"So I gathered."

He moved the other chair so he could sit close to her. "Did our young friend say anything else of interest?"

She filled the wineglass and offered it to him. He took a sip, then handed it back.

"Jarvis Jenkell, who is a famous landen writer—so famous even the Blood might have heard of him—used to be a frequent visitor at the school. Reading between the lines of what Yuli said, Jenkell was supporting one or more of the children who lived at the house, although it wasn't clear *who* he was supporting. I gathered he never claimed to be the father of any particular child, just claimed a fellowship with children who grew up in such places."

"I found out this evening that Jarvis Jenkell is Blood."

Ice and shadows came and went in the depths of her eyes. Despite no change in her appearance, he knew the difference—and knew who now spoke to him.

"I see," Witch said.

As a landen, Jenkell, if he was in fact the person behind this spooky house, would have been judged in keeping with the laws that governed landens, and the man would have been punished accordingly. As Blood . . . Well, the rules were different for the Blood.

"A girl named Anax claimed Jenkell was her father," Witch said. "But she has claimed a variety of men as her father, so it was difficult to judge her sincerity. However, based on the description I was given, she is like Yuli in that most of her heritage does not have its roots in the Dhemlan race."

"Jenkell was originally from Little Terreille."

"Anax and several other children from the house have 'run away' over the past few weeks."

He turned his head in the direction of the house, even though he couldn't see it through the walls of the Coach. "Maybe they didn't run far." He turned over the pieces of information and found more and more reasons to hone his temper. "Did you find out anything about the spells wrapped around the house?"

"The Black Widows were strong and quite talented. And they anticipated someone trying to pick their webs apart."

"So we can't work from the outside."

"Not if we want Surreal and Rainier to remain among the living. I'm still looking for a way to get around the trap spell without triggering the death spells."

He took Jaenelle's hand and kissed her palm.

Among the Blood, there was no law against murder. But that didn't mean payment wasn't extracted when required. While riding the Black Wind back to this village, he'd tallied up all the things he'd learned about this haunted house and what must have been done to create such a place. So he knew what would be required to pay the blood debt owed to him as the Warlord Prince of Dhemlan and to the people whose lives had been taken without good reason.

Since Jaenelle had told him they needed a Coach that would accommodate several people, they had used the one that was big enough to be a flying two-story flat.

"I have some work to do." He gave her hand one last kiss and stood up. "I'll work in one of the upstairs bedrooms so I don't disturb you or the boy." That wasn't the reason, but it was one of those lies that was understood for what it was—a public excuse for a private matter.

He didn't want to tell her what he intended to do. Didn't want to argue with her about it. The first stage of the punishment he was about to design would be brutal, but it was also just. And it was a side of him he was never comfortable letting her see.

His foot touched the first stair to the upper story when her voice stopped him.

"You should use the thicker-weight spider silk," Witch said. "It will hold up better for those kinds of spells."

SEVENTEEN

Marian drifted around the kitchen, feeling soft and delicious and powerful and female. She'd been so hungry for the man, and Lucivar had been so wonderfully *male* last night. And this morning.

It had been so satisfying to slide on top of him, and so flattering that his only response at first had been to wrap his arms around her. For a man with Lucivar's past, trusting a woman so much that he wasn't pulled from sleep when her body covered his told her how deeply he loved her. When she sheathed his morning-hard cock, she kept her movements quiet and controlled, enjoying the easy ride. And then she felt the excitement building as she watched his slow rise from sleep until he was fully awake and aware just moments before she was milking him with her climax.

She looked at the chair pushed back from the table and felt her body ready itself for a man.

Then she heard Daemonar's laughing squeals, followed by playful "papa growls" from Lucivar.

Time to be a mother instead of a lover.

Trying to focus on something besides the chair and what she

had done with Lucivar in the kitchen last night, she fixed her eyes on the corner cabinet. Years before, when she'd still been Lucivar's housekeeper, Jaenelle had decided Marian needed that corner cabinet—mostly because Jaenelle, who was incapable of doing something as simple as boiling an egg, had no idea what was needed in a kitchen. She hadn't been sure she'd ever use the thing, but now the shelves held little trinkets that warmed her heart—a pretty stone Daemonar had found for her; a seashell Lucivar had kept for her during a rare overnight stay he'd arranged with the dragons who lived on the Fyreborn Islands; and other things that reminded her each day that she was more than she'd thought she could be.

Because she was focused on the cabinet, she noticed the triangle of white sticking out from underneath it. When she pulled it out, she flushed with embarrassment that an invitation had gotten shoved under the cabinet. Lucivar never paid attention to such things, leaving it to her to decide what she'd like to attend or what he *had* to attend.

She read the invitation. Then she read it again.

She looked up when she felt his presence in the archway.

"Lucivar, what . . . ?"

He flinched. Her strong, powerful, arrogant, Eyrien Warlord Prince husband *flinched*.

"Marian . . . I can explain."

His distress was unnerving, especially when she didn't know *why* he was reacting so strongly to something that was, in the end, a simple miscalculation.

"It was sweet of you to prepare the invitations," she said, and then added silently, *Even if the wording needs to be softened.* "But, Lucivar, the spooky house isn't ready yet. We're still working on the last room and—"

"That son of a whoring bitch."

It was like watching a storm heading toward you. She could almost taste the violence that scented the air as he took the invitation from her.

"It's a trap," Lucivar said softly. "And he *knows* it's a trap. That's why he sent the message last night, telling me to stay home."

Marian said nothing. Just watched his eyes glaze as he rose to the killing edge and made the transition from fumbling husband to lethal predator.

"Pack a bag," Lucivar said. "Enough clothes for you and Daemonar for a couple of days. Do it now. I'll escort you to the Keep."

"And then?" she asked when it seemed like he wouldn't say anything more.

"And then I'm going to Dhemlan to have a chat with my brother."

"If you need to go, I can take Daemonar to the Keep as soon as we're—"

"No."

She looked into his eyes and saw the agony that still haunted him from the memories of what happened in Terreille last year. She was supposed to go to the Keep then too. Instead she and Daemonar had been abducted and taken to Terreille as hostages. Daemon had managed to keep them safe by playing out some savage games, but the emotional price for both Daemon and Lucivar had been brutally high.

She wouldn't risk her son again by thinking she was far enough removed from danger. And she couldn't risk the heart of either man.

"Give me ten minutes," she said.

He turned aside to let her pass. He didn't touch her. She didn't dare touch him. He understood something about that invitation that she didn't. Whatever he was facing, whatever he had to do, she wasn't going to be used as a knife held to Lucivar's throat.

Not again.

Surreal stirred, winced, swore softly. She didn't snarl at him when Rainier braced a hand on her shoulder and pushed until she sat up straight.

"How does your side feel?" he asked.

"Like I got ripped by some bitch with razor-sharp nails," she replied.

He slipped a hand under her shirt. She *did* snarl at him for that.

He ignored her, which was ballsy of him, since even without using Craft, she could do a considerable amount of damage to him before he could get out of reach.

Then she sucked in a breath as his fingers delicately brushed over the shield above the wound.

"Feels hot," he said, his green eyes filling with worry. "Might be infected."

"I cleaned it out," she replied, feeling defensive.

"You'll need to see a Healer when you get out of here."

A statement. One of those simple sentences that summed up the Blood in Kaeleer. Witches ruled. Males served. And somehow those two facts could add up to an escort hauling a witch to a Healer just because *he* decided she needed one.

And you couldn't even argue with him about it without having all the other males gang up on you.

She couldn't even argue with the other half of that statement—

the assumption that he was going to die getting her out of the house.

"Fine," she grumbled. "I'll see a Healer."

Rainier looked around. They had snuffed out all the candles except the one with the witchfire and had turned down the lamps to conserve the oil. The light didn't seem to illuminate as much now that it was competing with a room made up of shades of gray instead of true darkness.

"If we can trust the light coming from the windows, it's almost dawn," Rainier said.

"I wonder if we were supposed to survive this long."

"Probably not, but we had incentive."

"Yeah." When your uncle was the High Lord of Hell, becoming demon-dead for a stupid reason was not something you wanted to do. The lectures about it would go on for *decades*.

"There's water left in the jug," he said. "We should hold on to what's left of the food."

"And we need to make a decision." Surreal got to her feet and swore silently. She felt stiffer than she should, and her side hurt more than it should. At least her lungs seemed to be all right now. "We either need to go upstairs to use the bathroom or we need to pick a corner and pee on a carpet."

The children were waking up, so they would have to make that decision soon. Hell's fire, *she* needed to make that decision soon.

"Could the window be an exit?" Rainier asked. Taking one of the pokers, he approached the window. Then he gave her a considering look. "Your Gray shield will let things out but not in?"

She nodded. "Whatever goes out stays out."

He retreated, set the poker down, then selected a fork from the hamper.

"Doesn't give you much distance," Surreal said.

"No, but I'll still be behind the shield," Rainier replied. "Besides, we can't take the hamper or chill box with us, so losing the fork doesn't matter."

No, they wouldn't use Craft to vanish the hamper or chill box, and they couldn't carry it with them. While Rainier approached the window again, she selected the sharp knife and two forks. Any weapon was better than none.

Rainier hooked a bit of material in the fork's tines and pulled aside the curtain. "Surreal, look at this."

The window should have been facing the front of the house. She should have seen the wrought-iron fence and the street beyond. Instead, there were stone markers and, in three spots, freshly mounded earth.

"Graveyard," she said.

"Do those markers indicate how many people have died in this house and become fodder of one kind or another? Or are six of those markers reserved for us?"

She didn't know and didn't care. "If it's an illusion spell, we could try getting out through the window. If it's not . . ."

"We may not be in the same house anymore. Or even the same village."

She blinked. "You think someone shifted this whole house without us noticing? Without so much as one of those awful little statues falling off a table and breaking?"

He shrugged. "Jaenelle could have done it. She could pick up a house this size and turn it around without causing so much as a rattle. She could vanish something this size and set it down in a different village. Or in a finger-snap moment of the lights going out, she could swap a room right out from under your feet."

"You've never seen her do that."

Rainier released the fork, letting the curtain fall back into place. "Actually, I have. There's an odd sensation of the floor dropping out from under your feet in that moment when the lights go out. Then the lights come back on and you're standing in a different room—or sitting on a different sofa, which is actually more unnerving. We never could figure out if she shifted the people or shifted the room."

Surreal felt her jaw drop. Then she shook her head. Why was she surprised? Before she had shattered herself and her Jewels to save Kaeleer, there had been almost nothing Jaenelle couldn't do.

Except basic Craft.

"Which do we try?" Rainier asked. "Door or window?"

Sage's voice piped up behind them. "Lady Surreal? I need to pee."

"Well," Surreal said to Rainier, "unless you want to try holding her out the window, I guess we find out what's behind the door."

⁂

"He flinched." Marian glanced at Daemonar to reassure herself that he was still more interested in the plate of food Draca had brought in for him than the adults in the room. Then she focused on the High Lord. "Lucivar *flinched*."

Saetan looked solemn and serious—if she could ignore the laughter lighting his gold eyes. "Darling, I heard you the first time. It's the significance of the words that puzzles me."

"He *flinched*." Why couldn't she get through to him?

"And this upsets you. Why?"

"Because . . ." Flustered, she pushed her hair back. How could she explain if he didn't—or wouldn't—understand?

A twitch of his lips. A hint of a smile.

"It's a bit unnerving to realize you have power over such a powerful man, isn't it?" Saetan asked.

Thank the Darkness, he *did* understand. "Yes. I wear the Purple Dusk. I shouldn't have that kind of power over him."

"Marian, you're the woman he loves. There are very few things that can match that kind of power. Not even these." He tapped the Black Jewel he wore over the tunic jacket.

"Would you have reacted like that?" Marian asked. "If you had missed an engagement your wife had wanted you to attend, would you have flinched?"

She bit her lip when she saw the look in his eyes and wished she could take back the words. Considering who his wife had been, it was a bad question.

"No," he said. "I wouldn't have. Not for her." He took her face in his hands and kissed her forehead, a fatherly kiss washed in the sensuality that was inherent to the man. Then he added, "But if I had disappointed Sylvia by not remembering an engagement that I believed was important to her, then, yes, Marian, I would have flinched."

Draca,
The High Lord must not leave the Keep. Do whatever is necessary
to keep him there.
Sadi

Saetan handed the message back to Draca, then looked out the window and watched Marian playing with Daemonar in one of the Keep's courtyards.

After a while he raised his left hand. Most days he didn't think about that lost finger, but there were other days when he could still feel the moment when Hekatah put the blade against his skin.

"It's one thing for a man to say he's gotten old and has reached an age when it's time to step aside for those who are younger and better able to stand on a battlefield. But it humbles a man to realize his *sons* think he's too old."

"You were harmed the lasst time, Ssaetan," Draca said.

"Yes." And it wasn't just a finger that had been lost to Hekatah's torture. Oh, he hadn't lost anything else physically, but the damage to his body had been irreparable—and had weighed in his decision to step back from the living Realms.

Just because he couldn't use his balls didn't mean he didn't still have them when it came to temper and Craft.

"I am not without skills," he growled.

"They know that."

He snorted. "Do they? One son sends a message to *you*, asking you to lock me in the Keep—and sends the message with Khardeen, who latched on to me last night like a Sceltie who had found a meaty, unguarded soup bone. The other son shows up this morning and tells me to my face that he'll break my legs if I don't promise to stay here."

Draca made a soft sound that might have been laughter. "Lucivar hass alwayss been more direct."

You're amused. How delightful.

Draca reached out and touched his arm, a rare gesture for her. "Lucivar brought hiss wife and sson here becausse you are here. He dependss on you to protect what he holdss dear."

"And Daemon?" Saetan asked. "What is he protecting?"

"More than Lucivar, Daemon needss a father who undersstandss him. By keeping you here, he iss protecting hiss own heart."

Daemon put away the spider silk and the rest of his supplies, then vanished the debris, leaving no trace of his night's work.

Three tangled webs sat on a table, carefully protected by shields. These webs offered no visions. Nor were they simple dreams.

They were nightmare illusions combined with shadows. They were alluring and lethal—and exquisitely brutal. They would extract the debt owed to the SaDiablo family down to the last drop of blood and the last heartbeat of fear.

Now all he needed to do was find Jarvis Jenkell.

He vanished the tangled webs and went downstairs. They could all use some breakfast, and it would be better for the boy if Jaenelle was working on her second cup of coffee before Yuli woke up.

Then he felt the thunder rolling through the abyss.

He looked at Jaenelle.

She said, "Lucivar is here."

EIGHTEEN

The only thing behind the door was a dining room that wasn't the same as the one they'd seen last night. Nothing in the back passage, nothing on the stairs. No shadow illusions of dead boys. No Black Widows trying to take another slice out of her.

No damn beetles in the bathroom.

Surreal would have felt better if a hairy, giggling spider had been climbing up a wall or a skeleton mouse had been scurrying in the hallway.

The lack of small surprises could mean they were getting close to something big—and a lot more dangerous.

Daemon rushed out of the Coach and saw Lucivar walking along the outside of the wrought-iron fence, looking at the house and the land around it.

Looking relaxed, unconcerned, even friendly.

And underneath a surface that gave no warning, the man was so furious, he was capable of ripping a person's arm off before anyone realized his smile was feral and not friendly.

The fact that that particular flavor of Lucivar's temper seemed to be aimed right at him wasn't a good way to start the morning.

"Hell's fire," Jaenelle muttered as she joined Daemon outside. "He's really feeling pissy this morning."

Lucivar stopped at the gate and waited for them.

The lazy, arrogant smile. The glazed eyes. The explosive temper dancing one step away from the killing edge.

"Lucivar," Daemon said.

"Because you're my brother and I love you, I'm going to let you tell me why I shouldn't break your face."

"Lucivar," Jaenelle said.

He snapped his fingers, pointed at her, and snarled, "Stay out of this, Cat."

She blinked and actually took a step back in surprise. Then her eyes changed, the blue becoming a deeper sapphire. And suddenly Daemon could see his breath as the air around them turned cold.

"And put a warmer coat on," Lucivar snapped, still glaring at her. "It's cold out here."

The cold has nothing to do with the weather, Prick, Daemon said on a spear thread.

I don't give a damn. Cold is cold, and she's not dressed warmly enough to be standing out here.

"Prince Yaslana," Jaenelle growled.

"Don't get bitchy with me, or I'll knock you on your ass."

Have you forgotten that I'm standing here? Daemon asked.

No, it just means I'll have to knock you down first.

Yes, he knew that flavor of Lucivar's temper, and he knew the man. Lucivar was primed for a fight—and right now, the opponent didn't much matter.

"Lady," Daemon said, never taking his eyes off Lucivar. "Prince Yaslana and I need a few minutes alone."

She studied both of them for a long moment, then walked away, muttering something about snarly males that he couldn't quite hear. She stopped halfway between them and the Coach—out of earshot but close enough to quickly rejoin the discussion.

"Who's in that house?" Lucivar asked.

"What makes you think anyone is in there?"

"You're here, and it's still standing."

Daemon tipped his head to acknowledge the accuracy of that assessment. "Surreal and Rainier—and seven landen children."

Lucivar stared at him. "You knew it was a trap. Last night when you sent the message, you *knew.*"

"Yes, I knew," Daemon replied, letting his own temper sharpen. "Jaenelle figured it out before I did, but I knew it was a trap when I told you to stay home. I was afraid you'd just march in there if you found out Surreal and Rainier were caught in the spells that had been spun around this place."

"I am going in," Lucivar said.

"You *can't.*" He called in the paper that had the spooky house rules and waved it at his brother. "Damn you, Lucivar, according to the rules of this place—"

"Since when do we play by anyone else's rules?"

The words felt like a bucket of ice water thrown in his face.

Lucivar moved closer, until there was no distance between them. "Tell me, Bastard. Since when do *we* play by anyone else's rules?"

He floundered. Felt like he'd lost his footing, but he couldn't quite figure out why.

"This place was built as a trap to kill the three of us," he said, sure of at least that much. "You, me, and Surreal."

"Understood. What else?"

"We've figured out—or are almost certain, anyway—that Jarvis Jenkell is behind the creation of this place. He's recently discovered that he's Blood, and it seems he wants to test his newfound skills against the SaDiablo family."

"Which only proves he's a clever idiot. What else?"

Daemon held out the paper. "Read this."

Lucivar glanced at the paper, then looked at the house. "You read it."

"Lucivar . . ."

"Read it."

Daemon took a breath, ready to argue that Lucivar was perfectly capable of reading the rules by himself. Then he paused. Considered. This wasn't about Lucivar's resistance to anything "bookish." This was about what he absorbed from words when he heard them.

THERE ARE THIRTY EXITS FROM THE SPOOKY HOUSE, BUT YOU WILL NEED TO LOOK CAREFULLY TO FIND THEM, FOR THEY ARE WRAPPED IN DANGER. EVERY TIME CRAFT IS USED, AN EXIT IS SEALED, AND THAT WAY OUT IS LOST. WHEN THE LAST EXIT IS SEALED, YOU WILL BECOME PART OF THE HOUSE—AND STAY WITH US FOREVER.

Lucivar looked at the house, at the land, at the sky.

"Again," Lucivar said.

Daemon read it again—and watched his brother. That look. That stance. What was Lucivar looking at when he considered that house as a battleground? More to the point, what was Lucivar *seeing*?

Lucivar took a couple of steps away from him. "Read it again."

He read it a third time, then waited.

Lucivar took a deep breath and let it out in a gusty, annoyed sigh. Frustration filled his eyes, and Daemon recognized the feeling washing the air between them—their mutual desire to grab each other and shake some understanding into the other one's head.

"He hamstrung you, Bastard," Lucivar said. "He used words instead of a blade, but he hamstrung you. He counted on you doing exactly what you did—play by his rules. Surreal and Rainier, too, since they're still in there."

Jaenelle joined them. "There are three Black Widows who spun the illusions around this place. Every time Craft is used, the people in the house become more ensnared in the webs. And there are death spells tangled in with the rest. If you take a step over the boundary, you'll be caught in the spells."

"If you play by the rules," Lucivar said. "The sun's going to shine in Hell before I play by someone else's rules—especially some landen prick who wants one of us to help him commit suicide."

"He's Blood, not landen," Daemon said. "I don't think he expected anyone to know he was behind this game, so I doubt he anticipated experiencing a slow execution firsthand as fodder for one of his stories."

Lucivar stared at him as if half his brains had just fallen out of his ears.

"Even someone as strong as you can get caught by webs like this," Jaenelle said. "Have you forgotten when we got caught in the Jhinka attack a few years ago? Those weren't the same kind of webs, but close enough."

"No, I haven't forgotten," Lucivar replied. "I've learned a few things since then." He looked at Daemon. "That's why I know you can't go into that house—and I can."

"What makes you think—?" Daemon began.

Lucivar swung his arm out, shoulder high, his hand in a tight
fist.

Daemon felt the punch of Ebon-gray power as it hit the tangled webs that surrounded the house.

The house shook. It felt like a violent gust of wind—or a fist—had
slammed into the house, trying to knock it off its foundation.

"Hell's fire," Rainier said. "What was that?"

Daemon had been able to feel the webs around the spooky
house. Now he saw them. Lucivar's power lit them up—and revealed some of the things they hid. Just for a moment. Just long
enough.

"No wonder the house didn't look balanced on the land," Jaenelle said. "There's actually three attached houses here, and two of
them were sight shielded."

Lucivar nodded. "Spells wrapped around places of transition—
like a staircase or door—can be used to move people without
their being aware of it. The illusion spell preys on their sense
of where they are and how long they've been doing something
simple. They think they're going up a regular flight of stairs or
going through a door, but they're really being herded down a corridor that leads somewhere else. Surreal and Rainier are probably
in the second or third house by now."

"I've never heard of illusion spells that could do this," Daemon
said, glancing at Jaenelle. "Have you?"

"No," she replied, sounding as puzzled and intrigued as he
felt.

Lucivar looked at both of them and shrugged. "I guess it's not
part of the Hourglass's standard training."

"So where did you learn about this?" Daemon asked.

"From Tersa."

"I beg your pardon?"

"I learned about trap spells and transition illusions from Tersa."

"Tersa walks in the Twisted Kingdom," Jaenelle said. "You know that."

Lucivar shrugged again. "Most people think in straight lines; Tersa thinks in squiggles. Just means it takes a little longer to get an answer when you ask her a question."

Daemon rubbed his forehead, trying to dispel the headache that was brewing. "You talk to Tersa?"

"I visit her a couple times a month. I've done that for a few years now. We sit in the kitchen and drink ale and eat nutcakes."

He saw Jaenelle shudder at that combination of tastes. The combination didn't appeal to him either, but it brought up other questions. "Why don't you have to drink milk in order to get nutcakes?"

Lucivar grinned. "I told her ale *was* Eyrien milk."

You prick, Daemon thought, feeling resentful because he'd never thought of something like that. "You visit my mother."

"Yes," Lucivar replied.

"You never mentioned that."

"It's none of your business."

He rocked back on his heels, not sure how to respond. It *wasn't* any of his business as long as Tersa wasn't harmed by it.

"I don't know what you're fussing about," Lucivar said. "I drop in, ask a question, and just listen while I have a glass of ale. A lot of what Tersa says has nothing to do with the question, and some of it makes no sense to me at all, but she picks up all the scattered pieces of information as she wanders the paths within her mind. It's up to the listener to recognize what he needs and put the pieces together."

He could picture them in the kitchen of Tersa's cottage, with Allista hovering nearby. And it occurred to him that it might be a relief to Tersa to have the company of someone who could recognize her gifts of knowledge and experience without asking her to think in straight lines.

That was something he needed to consider more carefully at another time.

"You've been learning the Hourglass's Craft from Tersa?" Jaenelle asked.

"No, I've been learning *about* the Hourglass's Craft and how to defend against some kinds of spells," Lucivar replied. "You can punch your way out of a trap spell, but you have to do it fast and you have to do it before you use Craft enough times for the spell to hook into you and start feeding off your own strength. Of course, part of the point of a trap spell is to drain the prey's power, so there's a backlash spell attached to the trap. The first time you try to punch out, you'll get hit with a blast of power. It will hurt like a wicked bitch, even if you're shielded. And you might have to take a second hit. After that, it's strength against strength. The trap spell will keep trying to close up, so you just keep breaking through and moving forward until you're out."

"Mother Night," Daemon muttered as he stared at the house.

"One of them would have tried to break through the spells," Jaenelle said.

Lucivar nodded. "And took a hard enough hit to discourage them from trying again. So they're playing the game—and moving deeper into the trap. And that means whoever goes in to find them has to deal with whatever is in that house without using Craft. Which is why I can go in and neither of you can."

Lucivar unbuckled his everyday belt and vanished it. Then he called in the double-buckle fighting belt that Eyriens wore in battle. The hunting knife Eyrien males wore as standard dress was replaced by a hunting knife that was a little bigger, a little heavier, and a lot meaner. A palm-sized knife was slipped into a sheath between the belt buckles. Two more knives went into the sheaths in Lucivar's boots. Then . . .

"Wait wait wait," Jaenelle said. "What is *that*?"

Daemon felt the shield that formed around Lucivar like a second skin. He knew what it was. He'd just never expected to feel it again.

Lucivar frowned at her as he closed the leather gauntlets over his wrists and forearms. "It's an Ebony shield." Using Craft, he put chain mail over the light leather vest he was wearing in place of a shirt. "You may not wear Ebony Jewels anymore, Cat, but the power you put into the Rings of Honor is still there and the shields you built into those Rings still work."

Jaenelle stared at him. So did Daemon.

In Kaeleer, a Ring of Honor was given to every male who served in a court's First Circle. Worn around the cock, it was a symbol of the Queen's control over every aspect of a male's life. It also allowed her to monitor the emotions of her males, and the Rings were usually set to raise an alarm if anger, pain, or fear indicated the male was in trouble and needed help.

Lucivar attached a small bag of healing supplies to the belt. "The Ebony shield is the best protective shield a man can have going into a fight. *Nothing* can get through it."

"I didn't realize . . ." Jaenelle shifted from one foot to the other. "You still wear that Ring?"

Lucivar snorted. "We all do."

You do? Daemon asked.

Lucivar just looked at him.

"The Rings still work?" Jaenelle asked.

"In that the shields you put in them work and the males in the First Circle can sense if one of us needs help, yes."

But you can't read Jaenelle? Daemon asked, guessing at the reason for his Lady's dismay at learning the Rings hadn't been tossed into the backs of dresser drawers. Through a quirk in the way she had made the Rings for her court, the males in her First Circle had been able to read her emotions as easily as she could read theirs.

Not like we used to, Lucivar replied, sounding a little too evasive for a man who was usually blunt when answering a question.

Daemon decided not to ask anything else about the Rings until he retrieved his own from the velvet-lined box he'd had made for it and discovered for himself just how much connection the Rings of Honor still had to the former Queen of Ebon Askavi.

In quick succession, Lucivar layered an Ebon-gray shield, a Red shield, and another Ebon-gray shield over the Ebony. All of them followed his body rather than being a bubble around him.

He's preparing for a killing field, Daemon realized. "Lucivar."

Then he blinked as power coated Lucivar's hands. His brother could do enough damage just with muscle and temper. Boosted by the Ebon-gray, Lucivar could probably drive his fist through stone.

"You see, that's the thing," Lucivar said as he called in his Eyrien war blade and began coating the lethally honed steel with layers of Ebon-gray power. "This game depends on the Blood using Craft once they're inside the house, which works to the advantage of the spells woven in and around the place. Those spells can't do a damn thing to any Craft that's done *before* entering the house. So Surreal and Rainier should be safe from physical attack." He paused. His eyes narrowed. "If they didn't shield before they walked through that gate, I am going to beat the shit out of both of them."

"They thought they were going into the spooky house Marian and I made," Jaenelle protested.

"I don't care what they thought," Lucivar said. "They were entering an unknown building. If they didn't shield, they will regret it."

"What about you?" Daemon asked. "What are you going to do?"

"Based on those rules, this place was made to hobble the Blood from using Craft in order to fight whatever is in the house, so everything will be designed to push the Blood into using Craft. But it doesn't take into account what happens to the game when you throw a trained warrior into the mix. This place was designed to hamstring your way of fighting, not mine."

"Wait here," Jaenelle said. She ran back to the Coach.

"She's getting stronger," Lucivar said quietly as they both watched her enter the Coach. "Moving better. You must be letting her ride you half the time. Gives her leg muscles a good workout."

Daemon choked back a laugh. Then the humor faded. "What are you going to do?"

Lucivar tipped his head, as if he was conversing with someone. Then he looked at the house. "You said this place was built to kill us—you and me—so no matter what Surreal and Rainier have done to protect themselves and the people with them, not everyone has survived through the night. Anyone who was Blood probably made the transition to demon-dead and is now an enemy, and there must have been predators in the house in the first place. Surreal and Rainier are going to be moving, trying to find the way out. Whoever is alive is with them. So I'm going through the door, and I'm going to find Surreal—and I'm going to kill everything in between."

Daemon looked at his brother, armed for the killing field. "Are you sure you can avoid those ensnaring spells?"

"Don't worry, Bastard. I won't leave you to raise the little beast," Lucivar replied with a grin.

"I don't care about that," Daemon snapped. "I care about losing my brother."

The grin changed to a warm smile. "You won't lose me."

Jaenelle hurried back to them. She handed Lucivar a pack. "There's water, a couple of sandwiches, some fruit and cheese. Just in case it takes you a while to find them."

Daemon felt his gut clench when he saw the ball of clay she held out next. The last time he'd seen one of those, Jaenelle had prepared the balls of clay for the game he had played in Hayll to buy her the three days she needed to make a full descent into the abyss while keeping Marian, Daemonar, Lucivar, and Saetan from being killed by Dorothea and Hekatah. "What is that?"

"I asked Jaenelle to make a rough version of an air slide," Lucivar said.

Daemon looked at Jaenelle and raised an eyebrow in question.

"The coven and I used to use Craft to shape air into a slide," she said. "We'd add color so the formation would be easy to see, and we had spirals and loops and all kinds of things. This one is a straight slide that's already primed. Once it's triggered, people sit at the top, push off, and slide to the end."

"And the end will be on the other side of the fence," Lucivar said as he used Craft to set the pack on air before he slipped the ball of clay into the pouch attached to his belt. "I'm not going to look for one of the exits; I'm going to make one. Side wall of the third house is closest to the fence. I'll blow out the wall on the second floor and open the spell for the slide. You two will take care of whoever has survived once they're over the fence. Is that clear?"

Jaenelle stepped back. No embrace. No distraction. Not when a Warlord Prince was about to walk into a fight. "We'll be waiting for you, Prince."

Lucivar waited until she walked back to the Coach. *If I'm not out by sundown, you destroy this place completely. Take it down, Daemon. Don't leave one stone standing on another. Is *that* clear?*

*If I have to make that choice, I will find whatever is left of you and haul your sorry ass up to the Keep because *you're* going to have to explain this to our father.*

A quick grin was Lucivar's only answer.

Daemon pushed the gate open. Lucivar grabbed the pack in his left hand. With his right hand, he raised the war blade in a salute.

"Take care, Prick," Daemon said softly.

"My kind of fight, Bastard. I'll get Surreal and Rainier out of that house. You find Jenkell and take care of the debt on behalf of the family. You make sure the little son of a whoring bitch pays every drop of blood that is owed."

As he watched Lucivar walk up the path and open the front door, he felt Jaenelle come up beside him and slip her arm through his.

"Do you know the most annoying thing about him at times like this?" Daemon asked.

"That he doesn't gloat when he's right?"

He sighed. "Yeah. That's it exactly."

NINETEEN

Thunder rolled through the house, a messenger of fury. It shook pictures and mirrors off the walls, rattled windows, even knocked over curio tables filled with insipid porcelain figurines.

Surreal looked at Rainier and knew that he, too, recognized the dark-Jeweled power that had come to play.

"Oh, shit," she said. "It's Lucivar."

Lucivar? Had the uneducated Eyrien finally found someone to read the invitation to him? Or—and this was an even better thought—had he come to try to rescue the Surreal bitch and her companion?

Oh, this was excellent. Excellent! They were so unnerved by Lucivar being in the house! Maybe he would *finally* get some decent material to use for his book. Surreal and the limp Warlord Prince had made hardly any effort to find the exits. But the Eyrien was a warrior—and a *real* member of the SaDiablo family.

He had to hurry. Yes, he did. He didn't want to miss a moment of Lucivar trying to pit himself against the surprises in the house.

Lucivar set the pack down next to the wall. He'd issued the challenge. Now he'd wait a few minutes to see if anyone accepted the invitation.

Odd that he hadn't risen to the killing edge when he entered the house. He danced a heartbeat away from it, but he didn't have the cold purity he usually had when he stepped onto a killing field.

Which meant this place didn't offer a true killing field. It was a battleground, certainly, but it wasn't the kind of field Warlord Princes were born to stand on.

He wasn't sensing enough danger here. There wasn't enough threat to sustain that state of mind. At least, not for someone like him.

Which meant just being pissed off about someone setting a trap for his family would keep his temper sharp enough. At least for now.

He took another step into the front hallway.

Doorway on his left, with the door halfway open. Closed door on his right. A coat-tree next to the stairs leading to the second floor. A mirror on the wall opposite the stairs.

He took another step.

Why have a mirror there? To fix a collar or smooth a lock of hair after removing a coat? Or was there another reason for a mirror to reflect the side of the staircase?

The stealthy sound came from behind him, on his left. Then there was the rush of a body coming toward him, along with the putrid psychic scent of a malevolent mind.

He spun around, his right arm straightening as he became

a pivot for the death he held in his hand. He looked the Black Widow in the eyes as his Eyrien war blade sang through muscle and humbled bone.

The top half of her body fell in one direction, the lower half in another. Guts spilled out on the hallway floor, but not much blood. That meant the demon-dead witch hadn't been drinking blood or yarbarah and had become too starved to be cautious.

She screamed at him as she pushed herself across the floor, too furious to remember she could use Craft to float her body on air. Intent on reaching her prey, she followed him as he circled toward the room where she had hidden.

His inner barriers were locked tight, and he should be safe enough from any games a lighter-Jeweled Black Widow might try to play. But a man who got careless and underestimated an enemy was a man who usually died.

Switching his war blade to his left hand, he grabbed the Black Widow by the hair, flung her into the room, and closed the door. Then he walked across the hallway and kicked open the other door.

Nothing sprang out at him, so he grabbed one ankle and threw the lower half of the Black Widow into the sitting room.

It went against his training and his temper to leave an enemy at his back. Since she was already demon-dead, the Black Widow was still a potential enemy. But he would need power to burn out what was left of her power in order to finish the kill. That would feed into the spells woven around the house. So he would leave her, and deal with her again if he had to.

Then he stopped and stared at the hallway as a thought curled around his heart.

Three Black Widows had made the spells for this spooky house. It stood to reason that the little prick who had devised this game wouldn't want to leave any loose ends that could connect him to this place. Lucivar had no doubt at all that he'd just met one of the Black Widows—and he had no doubt he would cross paths with the second. But the third . . .

Daemon wasn't a fool. The feel of Tersa's spells was easily recognized by anyone who had spent enough time with her to know the woman. If she wasn't safely tucked in her cottage in Halaway, if she was trapped in the house, Daemon would have told him. And if . . .

Fury washed through him at the thought of anyone daring to harm Tersa.

He grabbed the coat-tree and swung.

The mirror exploded, showering that part of the hallway with glass. One foot of the coat-tree punched through the wall.

Lucivar pulled the coat-tree out of the wall, set it down, and said, "Why use Craft when a little temper will do?"

Wasn't likely he'd find Surreal or Rainier this close to the starting point of the game, but he'd check the back room and the kitchen before moving on.

One step. Two.

He caught a faint psychic scent, enhanced by a whiff of fear. It was gone before he could track the direction it came from, but it had been enough to warn him that Blood was nearby.

Not the Black Widow. This was someone else, someone who barely registered as Blood to his senses because that person stood so far above him in the abyss. Someone he hadn't detected at all until he punched a hole in the wall.

He stared at the wall and considered the game. Then he bared his teeth in a feral smile and walked back to the front door.

"Guess I'll play by your rules after all," he said softly as he pressed his right hand against the door. The Ebon-gray Jewel in his ring blazed for a moment as he put an Ebon-gray shield around the whole structure.

Somewhere in the house, a gong sounded.

He felt the bite of a spell as it hooked into the Ebon-gray power, but he fed the shield for a few heartbeats longer—giving it enough power to assure that it wouldn't be drained by the house before sundown. Of course, when he was ready to leave, he'd have to punch through spells that were bloated with his own Ebon-gray strength, and the backlash from that *would* hurt like a wicked bitch. So be it. He'd still be the one walking out. As for the little writer-mouse he suspected was hiding in the walls . . .

Lucivar picked up his pack and headed for the back room. As he passed the hole in the wall, he said in Eyrien, "You don't leave until I let you leave. So you keep watching—and prepare to die."

An illusion suddenly appeared in front of him. The boy had died a hard death, judging by the ripped torso and the missing eye, but he was just an illusion and not *cildru dyathe*, so he posed no threat.

"The worst is still to come," the boy said.

"No," Lucivar replied, walking right through the illusion. "I'm here now."

He secured the door, then pressed his back against the wall—and trembled.

Why use Craft when a little temper will do?

Lucivar had cut the Black Widow in half. The fight was over before it began because *he cut the witch in half.*

Without Craft.

Lucivar had swung a heavy coat-tree like it was nothing more than a stick and punched a hole in a Craft-protected wall.

Without Craft.

The hole had compromised that part of the secret passageway, making it vulnerable to the spells that chained the rest of the house. This just proved how right he'd been to install doors to divide these passageways into separate sections that had their own set of protection spells. The witch who had done those particular spells had been a sweet woman until he had tortured her and killed her in a way that made her a suitably vicious predator.

Of course, there was no law against murder, so he'd done nothing wrong. And the information he'd collected in the process would make his next novels wildly successful, surpassing any of his rivals'. Maybe even successful enough that he would be able to acquire one of the kindred as a companion.

There was just one little hitch in his plans.

He was beginning to understand why Surreal and her companion were afraid of Lucivar.

"He put an Ebon-gray shield around the house," Surreal said. "Hell's fire, Mother Night, and may the Darkness be merciful." How were they supposed to get past an Ebon-gray shield?

"Maybe Lucivar was trying to keep anyone else from coming in," Rainier said.

"Or he's trying to keep someone from getting out," Surreal replied. *Like us?* she wondered as she glanced at the children. They had come close to pissing out their brains when that thunderous challenge had rolled through the house. Now the four of them were staring at her and Rainier, looking pathetically hopeful that they could be protected.

As if any of them had a chance of surviving now.

"Last night, that boy said the worst was still to come," she said quietly. "What if Lucivar has been here all along?"

Rainier considered the question, then shook his head. "If he'd come in ahead of us, we would have seen some sign of his presence before now. A fist-sized hole in a wall, if nothing else."

That was true enough. Once he realized he was trapped, Lucivar would go through the house like a wild storm. They would have been climbing over wreckage instead of moving through untouched rooms. But . . .

"Someone managed to kill a dark-Jeweled Eyrien Warlord and trap him in the house's spells," Surreal said. "Could those spells be strong enough to trap an Ebon-gray Warlord Prince?"

"Based on the rules we read, I think trapping Lucivar and Daemon was at least part of the intention," Rainier replied. "But even if Lucivar is still just Lucivar . . ."

They looked at each other.

"Let's get moving," Surreal said. "We have *got* to find a way out of here."

Moments after Lucivar's Ebon-gray shield closed around the house, Daemon's Black shield surrounded the property, forming a dome over the house and sinking deep into the land.

Cold rage whispered in his blood, singing its seductive song of violence and death.

Then he felt Witch's hand on his arm, felt a cold in her equal to his own but still tempered by the fire of surface anger.

"Lucivar found something he wants to contain," Daemon said too softly. "Something not otherwise bound by the spells put on that house. He locked the house; I've locked the land."

She nodded. "Nothing will leave here without his consent—and yours."

And yours, Daemon thought. No matter what he and Lucivar thought, Witch would make the final decision.

Her hand tightened on his arm, a silent command to step back from the killing edge and the sweet, cold rage.

"Daemon, let's take care around the boy," Jaenelle said quietly.

That reminder helped him leash the rage and obey. He took a deep breath, let it out slowly . . . and regained control.

"Why don't we take a walk around the perimeter and look for something that doesn't feel natural?" Jaenelle suggested.

"Such as . . . ?"

"A tunnel. A passageway."

"An underground escape." Daemon nodded. His Black shield went deep enough to block such an escape, but the search would give them both something to do while they waited.

He looked at the Coach. "Should we bring the boy with us and let him stretch his legs? He hasn't left the Coach since you invited him in."

"He's afraid, Prince."

"Of us?"

Jaenelle shook her head. "Of being sent back to the orphans' home."

He hesitated, then said softly, "We can't keep him. The Hall is too dark. Our power is too dark. He would never belong. Might not even be able to survive."

"I know," she said. "But we can have him as a guest for a day or two while we decide what would be the best place for him."

Something in her tone of voice. Something that softened his temper and tickled his sense of humor.

"How do kindred puppies feel about young boys who may be half-Blood?" he asked.

Jaenelle just grinned.

Tersa stepped back from her worktable. She had worked through the night, building her tangled web strand by careful strand.

The Langston man had used her to hurt the boys. Her boy. And the winged boy.

She remembered the winged boy from the days when she had been less of a shattered chalice and had lived in a cottage with her boy.

Before Dorothea had taken her boy. Had used her boy. Had hurt her boy.

And the winged boy too.

But the winged one was strong now, powerful now—and still a boy when he came to visit. He thought she believed that foolishness about ale being Eyrien milk? Even someone who walked in the Twisted Kingdom could tell the difference between milk and ale.

He wasn't being mean, though. He wasn't making fun of her, thinking she wouldn't know the difference. He was teasing because he wanted ale, and his smile invited her to pretend she believed the fib.

He understood her. Daemon listened, and he loved her. Jaenelle listened too. And Saetan. But Lucivar rode her currents of words like he rode currents of air, following a path that wasn't meant for straight lines. So she told him things, taught him things that she couldn't explain any other way, and trusted him to eventually show the others.

His mother didn't want him. Couldn't love him because she hated him. All because he had those glorious wings that looked like dark silk when he spread them wide. What a foolish reason to hate a child.

So, in a way, he had become her boy too.

And Surreal. The girl child who had been forged into a warrior by pain and blood and fear. Never like a daughter, but always a friend. Someone who could accept what couldn't be made whole.

The Langston man wanted to hurt Surreal too.

Tersa gently touched the frame that held her tangled web.

She owed the Langston man for whatever harm she had done—and she would pay her debt.

TWENTY

Lucivar looked around the dining room. In the early light of a
gray autumn morning, an eyrie could look gloomy too, but
that was balanced by the fact that an eyrie was built of stone and
had the strength and character of being part of the land around it.

There was no excuse for *making* a room look like this.

No reason to linger, since Surreal and Rainier weren't there,
but he set his pack down on the dining room table and circled the
room anyway, just to see if he could sense anything of interest.

Like the reason someone had ripped the door of the storage
cupboard off its hinges and then replaced the door with enough
care that a casual glance around the room might not detect the
damage.

As he came abreast of the door, the knob rattled, as if someone
inside was trying to get out. Or trying to entice whoever was in
the room into *letting* him or her out.

Switching the war blade to his left hand, he stood on the hinge
side and closed his right hand over the doorknob, using the length
of his arm as a brace to keep the cupboard's occupant from simply
knocking the door down.

As soon as he started to open the door, something inside the cupboard slammed into it, trying to knock it down on top of him. He moved with the swing of the door, using it as a shield as the enemy rushed into the dining room, intent on finding its prey.

He tossed the door and flipped the war blade back to his right hand. The door's crash had the witch turning to face him, to find him—and his gorge rose.

Enough of her face was left for him to see that she had been pretty. Enough of her psychic scent was left, despite the layers of rage, for him to tell that she hadn't been a bitch when she walked among the living. In fact . . .

Hearth witch. She had been a hearth witch, and someone had burned her. Not a fast fire meant to kill, but a slow burning to torture the body and break the mind.

Her face blurred. Became Marian's.

She was on him before he could regain his emotional balance and evade her.

His heart went numb. Instinct and training took over. He caught her by the back of the neck and threw her against the wall. Before she could recover, he followed, pressing her head between his hand and the wall. Then he let temper and memories be the whip driving him as his hand smashed through bone and brains.

He kept his hand pressed against the wall, capturing bits of skull and brain while her body slumped to the floor.

Still there. Her Self was still there, chained to a demon-dead body that no longer functioned.

He shook the gore off his hand, then wiped off the rest on her dress.

As he crouched there, too close to the sight of her, the smell of her, memory took him back to the camp in Terreille and the nightmare that still haunted his sleep some nights.

*   *   *

Two naked . . . things . . . floated out of the hut into the light. An hour ago, they had been a woman and a small boy. Now . . .

Marian's fingers and feet were gone. So was the long, lovely hair. Daemonar's eyes were gone, as well as his hands and feet. Their wings were so crisped, the slight movement of floating made pieces break off. And their skin . . .

Smiling that cold, cruel smile, the Sadist released his hold on Marian and Daemonar. The little boy hit the ground with a thump and began screaming. Marian landed on the stumps of her legs and fell. When she landed, her skin split, and . . .

The Sadist hadn't just burned them; he had cooked them—and they were still alive. Not even demon-dead. Alive.

"Lucivar," Marian whispered hoarsely as she tried to crawl toward her husband. "Lucivar."

Lucivar stood up, backed away from the witch's body.

Daemon had tortured him with nothing but elaborate shadows, knowing that his response would convince Dorothea and Hekatah that the Sadist had actually cooked his brother's wife and son. That game had provided Daemon with the breathing space needed to get Marian and Daemonar away from the camp and keep them safe.

He and Daemon had both paid a high price for Marian and Daemonar's safety. He reminded himself of that often on the nights when he woke up in a cold sweat, certain there was a lingering odor of burned hair and cooked flesh in the bedroom.

But he also never forgot that, with the right provocation, the Sadist was capable of playing out that kind of game for real.

He studied the hearth witch. Was that why she had been killed this way? Had Jenkell been trying to kindle that memory, maybe turn him and Daemon against each other so they would focus thoughts and tempers on each other instead of this house? Who could have told Jenkell what happened in that camp?

Or had the little bastard killed the witch that way just for the fun of it?

"I don't know the answer, and I don't care," Lucivar said quietly. "Even if you pay for nothing else, you will pay for this witch's death. I'll make sure of it."

Picking up his pack, he headed down the passageway to the kitchen.

"The last time we used the back stairs, you got lost," Rainier said.

"I didn't get lost," Surreal replied, feeling testy. "I just didn't end up in the same place as you did." *And discovered those damn beetles because of it.*

"However it happened, we came up the front stairs and everyone is here. I say we go back down the same way."

But Lucivar is on the first floor. That couldn't matter. They hadn't found anything in their hurried exploration of the second floor. No clue that might indicate an exit. No trap that might indicate an exit.

They could pick a room and wait for something to come after them, or they could try to find a way out before someone else got killed.

Which meant going down.

"All right," she said. "We'll use the main staircase."

They went down in a tight little pack. Rainier led, taking it slow, testing each step just as he'd done on the way up. Henn held on to Rainier's jacket and Dayle's hand. Trout held on to Henn's jacket and Sage's hand. And Surreal held on to Trout.

Constant contact and a continuous roll call so they would know immediately if anyone suddenly disappeared.

How many times can you repeat six names? Surreal wondered. *It's not a big staircase.* But it felt like they had been going down those stairs *forever.*

She finally took the last step—and daylight vanished. The only light came from the witchfire on the candle Rainier held.

"Mother Night!" Surreal said. "Where are we now?"

Rainier looked over his shoulder at her. "I think we're in the cellar."

Lucivar took a mouthful of water, then corked the jug and dug an apple out of the pack.

The mice's heads floating in the jar of peaches was a bitch-mean trick. But the spiders . . .

Damn things gave him a jolt when they came pouring out of the drawer like that, big and hairy and *fast.* Of course, their scariness was greatly diminished by the fact that they giggled like a herd of little children who were playing "chase me."

"Not bad, Tersa," he said as he munched on the apple.

It had the feel of her, and it was what he'd expect from her efforts to build scary surprises for children. Strange? Yes. Creepy? Definitely. But benign.

He tossed the apple core in the sink and picked up the pack and war blade he'd set on the table. The doors that seemed to lead outside didn't interest him, so he considered the other door.

Cellar door? Probably. Even without the warning of a chair braced under the knob, he didn't need to get any closer to know something malevolent was on the other side of that door. Since they were trying to get out, Surreal and Rainier wouldn't head belowground. They'd stick to the parts of the house where they could make use of a door or window. So that left him heading upstairs.

Whatever was in the cellar held no interest for him.

Lucivar was destroying the predators! He was going to ruin *everything!*

At least the special one in the cellar hadn't been discovered yet. He wanted *that* one to survive for the story's climax.

"There's a tunnel here," Jaenelle said, pointing at the ground. "It's deep, so it must start in the cellar—maybe even in a chamber below the main cellar—and runs to there." Her finger traced a line that led to the stables behind the house.

Daemon pursed his lips, then let out a frustrated sigh. Give him a house party with rooms packed with people and he could pick out his prey and make the kill while gliding through the crowd—and more often than not, no one realized what he'd done. But this kind of tracking was as frustrating to him as reading was to Lucivar. And admitting he needed help was just as humiliating. "Does the Black shield go down deep enough to block the tunnel?"

Jaenelle's eyes had the unfocused look of someone deep in thought. "Not quite," she finally said. "There's enough space between the tunnel floor and the shield for someone to crawl out."

"Then I should extend the shield."

She gave him a sharp, feral smile. "I have a better idea. Yuli, take a look at this."

"How did you know there's a tunnel?" Yuli asked.

Good question, Daemon thought.

"The Arcerian cats build dens deep beneath the snow," Jaenelle replied. "Since some of the cats are my friends, I learned to recognize the feel of a tunnel or chamber that is deep underground. That was the only way I could find their homes."

So you've been finding tunnels like this since you were a child? Daemon asked.

Yes. "Speaking of Arcerians . . ."

Jaenelle held out her hand, palm up. A moment later, a small tangled web appeared, protected by a bubble shield that rested in her hand. A moment after that . . .

Yuli stared at the white cat that now stood on Jaenelle's hand.

"This is an Arcerian cat," Jaenelle said.

"It's so tiny."

I wish, Daemon thought.

Jaenelle gave him a sharp look, as if she'd heard the thought—or at least suspected what he was thinking.

"This is the first stage of the illusion," Jaenelle said. "This little cat will get as big as the real ones." With a fingertip, she stroked the tiny white head.

The purr that came out of that little shadow was that of full-sized Kaelas when he was being petted and was a happy, happy cat—the purr that was strong enough to make Jaenelle's spell-strengthened bed vibrate.

"You know Surreal," Jaenelle said to the shadow cat. "You know Rainier. You know Lucivar. You will not hurt them. If someone is with them and they tell you the person is a friend, you will not harm that person." She paused, then added too softly, "Kill everything else that tries to leave."

The tiny cat vanished. Because he was trying to sense it, Daemon felt the moment when the shadow cat reappeared deep in the ground beneath them.

"The shadow has slipped under your shield," Jaenelle said. "Now the next part of the spell will engage."

Yes, Daemon decided as the three of them walked back to the Coach. Jaenelle's shadow Kaelas *was* better than simply extending the shields. Anyone entering that tunnel would find an eight-hundred-pound cat waiting to kill him.

Try to touch it and it would be as solid as smoke. But when the cat struck . . .

Nothing was going to get out of that tunnel except the people the shadow had been told to recognize.

TWENTY-ONE

"It's solid," Rainier said, giving the ceiling above the stairs one last whack with the poker before joining Surreal and the children. "The spell must have been designed to let us pass through the floor."

"Damn dangerous thing to do," Surreal said. Using Craft, the Blood could pass through solid objects—like walls and floors—but it wasn't something that should be done carelessly. And passing flesh through a solid object without the person's being aware of the pass could be fatal.

Of course, that wasn't likely to be a consideration here.

Raising her arm to rub her forehead, she almost vanished the poker before remembering not to use Craft. She wasn't used to having her hands full all the time. She tucked the poker under her other arm, since that hand was holding the candle with the witchfire flame.

How many more times can we use Craft before we get locked into the spells in this house? she asked Rainier as she rubbed her forehead. *Have you counted them up? Could we make the pass and go back up the stairs to reach the first floor?*

⋆I'm not sure I've remembered all of them,⋆ he replied. ⋆I think we're getting close to "last one, the game is over." You and I could make the pass. If we each carried one, we could take two of the children with us. But that's all we could do.⋆

Which meant leaving two of the children behind, prey to whatever might be down here. Not a choice she wanted to make.

⋆And there's no certainty that if we did this, we would end up where we intended,⋆ Rainier added.

"Let's see what we can find down here," she said.

A few steps away from the stairs, the candles guttered and went out, except for the one holding the witchfire.

"Air currents," Rainier said, a hint of relief in his voice. "Maybe there's an exit down here after all."

A roar filled the cellar, both threat and warning.

"Do you think that's really one of the cats?" Surreal asked when she could hear again.

"Whoever built this place managed to kill two Black Widows and an Eyrien warrior, as well as who knows how many others in order to have predators for this game. Why not one of the cats? You wouldn't need one that wore Jewels, just one who was kindred and could make the transformation to demon-dead. Without Craft, it's our physical strength against the cat's."

"We'd have no chance," Surreal said grimly.

"None at all."

"I guess that's the direction we *don't* go in."

"Agreed. Now let's find a way to get back upstairs."

Lucivar grinned as he watched the little black beetles cover the bottom of the bathtub, then swell into big black beetles—and pop.

He hoped Rainier had been the first one to walk into this bathroom, because Surreal . . . She still believed that particular fear was her little secret, and neither he nor Daemon had any intention of telling her otherwise. But it wouldn't be a secret for long if she'd been the one to find *these*.

Tersa's work. Had to be.

Daemonar would love having a popping beetle. Of course, it couldn't be a free-roaming beetle. More like a bug-in-a-box. A well-shielded box, because if the boy managed to remove the beetle and leave it someplace as a surprise for his mama . . . Marian would *never* forgive him for bringing the thing home.

He'd talk to Tersa about making the beetle and talk to a carpenter in Riada about making the box. There would be plenty of time to get the thing made as a Winsol gift.

"Surreal, darling, you've got more spine than most of the Eyrien warriors I knew back in Terreille, but I bet you squealed when you saw these."

His amusement vanished when he walked out of the bathroom and saw the boy standing in the back hallway.

Not an illusion this time. The boy was *cildru dyathe*.

"I am going to bite you and drink your blood," the boy said.

Poor scared puppy. He must have been a sweet child. Even now he sounded like he was reciting a line for a performance at school—and stumbling over the words.

"The person who killed you . . . ," Lucivar began.

"He was a powerful Warlord."

The boy sounded more hopeful than sure that he'd been killed by someone powerful.

"Puppy, in terms of power, whoever killed you was a glass of water. I'm a stormy lake. You come at me, I will rip you apart."

"But . . . I'm just a boy."

"I know," Lucivar said gently. "I can't let that matter. Not right now."

The boy wilted.

A sweet child, killed for a game.

Lucivar set the pack down, then reached into the pouch of healing supplies he had hooked to his belt. He withdrew a small, stoppered bottle and held it out. "Here. It's lamb, not human, but it's undiluted blood. It will keep your power from fading, at least for a little while."

"Will you hurt me if I take it?"

His temper flashed to the killing edge for a moment before he chained it back. "No, I won't hurt you."

Wonderful dialogue. Just wonderful! Who would have thought such a gem would come from the *Eyrien*? He would have to put a scene in the book where Landry Langston meets the boy. It would be so sad, so moving, so . . . wonderful.

The boy took the bottle and gulped down the blood. Wasn't more than a couple of swallows, but he looked like he'd been given a feast. He almost started licking the inside of the bottle, then stopped as if suddenly remembering his manners. He replaced the stopper and handed the bottle back.

"Puppy, do you know who the *cildru dyathe* are?" Lucivar asked.

"Dead children," the boy replied. "If you're a good boy, you get to go to a nice place for a while before you become a whisper in the Darkness. But if you're bad . . ." He looked around the hallway.

You bastard. You not only killed this boy, but you told him he deserved to be here? Compared with here, he supposed, the *cildru dyathe's* island in Hell *was* a nice place.

"Who killed you?" The question was blunt, and his voice had

hardened with the strain of keeping his temper leashed. This boy didn't deserve seeing his temper.

Instant terror. The boy knew who had killed him, and even now was too afraid to say.

Not likely the boy had any training in the psychic communication the Blood used, but anyone who was Blood *could* do it to some degree. "Look at me and think the answer as loud as you can in your head."

Jarvis Jenkell.

Barely a whisper. If he hadn't been focused on the boy, he wouldn't have heard it. Now he had confirmation for Daemon about who had set up this trap for them.

"I don't remember his name," the boy lied, "but he's very famous."

"As of this moment, he's walking carrion. That's a promise." Lucivar took a deep breath and let it out slowly. "This is another promise. I have to help the living first, but if there's a way to break you free of these spells and get you out of this house before we tear it apart, my brother and I will do it."

"Okay."

Lucivar picked up the pack and moved into the front hallway, aware of the boy following him.

"Those are bad stairs. They have a trick."

He looked at the stairs, then back at the boy. "What's the trick?"

"You can see the hallway down there, but you can't reach it. You end up someplace else."

"Have you seen a witch and a Warlord Prince?"

The boy nodded. "They went down the stairs. They disappeared."

"They have any children with them?"

"Four."

Which meant three of the children who had come in with Surreal and Rainier were now among the dead.

"You didn't warn them about the stairs?"

"The lady witch was screaming and I got scared. So I didn't talk to them."

"I guess she saw the beetles."

A quick, boyish grin. "They pop real good."

Lucivar hesitated. "If there's a way, we'll get you out of this house." Then he went down the stairs.

Oh, this wasn't good. This wasn't good at all. If Lucivar caught up to the Surreal bitch and her companion, it would spoil the big battle at the end of the story. Just *spoil* it. And that boy! What was he doing? He should be *attacking* people, not *talking* to them.

Of course, he hadn't anticipated any of his "guests" coming in with bottles of blood to use as bribes.

Good idea, though. Probably have to give that idea to the witch in the story. Landry couldn't have *all* the good ideas. And she would be carrying blood because she always did—ever since her encounter with . . .

Well, he'd figure that out later.

Right now he had to provide his "guests" with the way out of the cellar and up to the final act.

And he wasn't going to think about that phrase Lucivar used: "walking carrion."

TWENTY-TWO

One minute there was nothing but a pile of storage boxes and broken furniture; the next, there was a set of stairs leading up to a door.

Surreal didn't much care where the stairs led as long as it got them out of the cellar, which was a warren of little rooms piled with debris—or barren in a way that made her think the space had been used to cage something. It went on too long, was too *big* for the house above them—and it also felt like it was shrinking around them.

Rainier looked at her. *The Black Widows who made the illusion spells were good at their Craft. The illusion that hid these stairs didn't stop working by chance.*

I know, she replied.

It feels like a grave down here. It feels like we're buried alive.

She wished he hadn't said that, since it matched her sense of the place closing in on them.

Do we go up? Rainier asked.

She nodded. Whatever was on the other side of the door would be easier to face than staying here.

They went up the stairs, Rainier leading while she guarded his and the children's backs. The door opened with a dramatic creak—and they were back in the kitchen.

And somewhere in the house, a gong sounded.

Good. Good. One problem solved. As soon as Surreal closed the cellar door, he reengaged the illusion spell that hid the stairs.

Now they would see how well Lucivar fared in the cellar.

The ball of witchlight floated on the end of his war blade, challenging the smothering darkness.

Lucivar hated the cellar. Too dark, too damp, too closed in for a man who belonged to a winged race.

Too much of a reminder of the salt mines of Pruul.

This Jenkell bastard. This writer. How much did he know about the SaDiablo family? Was he choosing some of the things in this house because he *knew* they would provoke memories, or was it all just chance? Did he know enough about Eyriens to understand the difference between living within a mountain and being trapped under the ground?

Didn't matter. There was a punch of fear that came from memories, so he let fear fuel temper. He'd gotten out of the salt mines of Pruul. He would get out of this house too.

The kitchen looked exactly the same—except for one thing.

"The bowl of peaches is gone," Surreal said, turning slowly as she looked more carefully at the room. "Did the 'caretaker' remove the bowl or are we in a different room despite how this looks?"

Suddenly all four children screamed. A moment later, the smell of urine stung the air.

Rainier gave her a sheepish look as he closed a drawer. "The spiders are still here."

Currents of air. Not fresh air, exactly, but different from the cellar. The witchlight revealed no opening, no difference in the walls. But there were those currents of air. And then . . .

The roar took him by surprise, had him shifting into a fighting stance.

No movement. No rushing attack. Just that warning.

"Jaal?" he called softly. "Kaelas? It's Lucivar."

It was possible that Jenkell had hired other Blood to hunt down a tiger or an Arcerian cat. As one of the demon-dead, either feline would be a lethal predator. Of course, either one would be just as lethal if it was dumped into the house alive. Wouldn't even need one of the kindred if it was a live predator.

But if the cat wasn't part of the spells in the house . . .

Using the air currents as a guide, he moved closer to the wall—and was rewarded by a snarl.

He'd heard it often enough to recognize that snarl and knew which cat he was dealing with. He just wasn't sure if the snarl was meant as a greeting or a threat.

"Kaelas? It's Lucivar."

What was there? A passageway that had been built when the house was inhabited so that servants could move back and forth from the house to another building? Or was it just a dirt tunnel that had been dug as an escape route when the house was being made into this nightmare?

Either way, he couldn't see Jaenelle asking one of the cats to guard a tunnel, and neither cat had been with her this morning, so neither was close enough to have reached the house this soon.

That left a shadow guarding the tunnel. Almost as deadly as the real thing. Maybe a little more so if Jaenelle made it. There was a faint hope of reasoning with the real Kaelas, since the cat knew he'd get yelled at if he attacked another male who belonged to Jaenelle. But a shadow followed a set of commands. Lucivar figured "kill" was the dominant command for anything Jaenelle had placed in the tunnel.

He was about to call again when the male rumble that was Kaelas's psychic voice thumped against his inner barriers. Kaelas's voice, but not Kaelas. So it *was* a shadow guarding the tunnel.

Do not eat Lucivar. Do not eat Surreal. Do not eat Rainier. The shadow Kaelas sounded grumpy about having his list of edibles restricted.

Damn shadow couldn't eat anyone anyway. Maul and kill, yes. Eat, no.

At least, he was fairly sure a shadow couldn't really eat someone. Then again, it wasn't smart to make assumptions about any shadows Jaenelle made.

"The Lady told you not to eat me?"

A pause. Then, reluctantly, *Lady said do not kill you.*

Hell's fire. He would have to tell Jaenelle she was giving these shadows a little too much of the original's personality. Unless it had been told to, a shadow shouldn't be making that distinction.

"Have you seen Surreal?"

Smelled her. Gone now.

"Out the tunnel?"

No.

Not surprising. Surreal and Rainier didn't know Jaenelle and Daemon were waiting outside, had no reason to think Jaenelle was responsible for the cat guarding the tunnel. Instead of heading out of the house, they must have headed back in.

Lucivar started to turn away, then stopped and considered that faint presence he'd sensed in the house—the little writer-mouse scurrying behind the walls, watching and listening. Then he considered that, shadow or not, it never hurt to make a large predator happy—especially if he might need to use the tunnel to get everyone out of the house.

He told the shadow cat, "If any other human tries to get out through the tunnel, you go ahead and eat him."

As he walked away to explore another part of the cellar, the shadow Kaelas's pleasure purred at him through the psychic thread.

Daemon circled the fence around the house, a slow prowl. Watchful. Aware.

There was no sign of anyone in the house. No movement of a curtain, no face at a window. Of course, he hadn't seen any lights last night, and there had to have been lamps or candles burning.

So he couldn't trust what he was—or wasn't—seeing.

But he had to trust that when Lucivar punched through the spells and opened up a way out of the house, he would see it.

He stopped over the spot where the tunnel was located and considered the shadow cat standing guard. Seemed a shame to waste such a magnificent predator. Maybe . . .

Instead of continuing his prowl, he retraced his steps and returned to the Coach.

"Mrs. Beale was very efficient," Jaenelle said when he stepped inside. "Yuli and I have discovered more food in the chill box and pantry. We're going to heat up some soup. Do you want some?"

He shucked off his coat and vanished it. "Yes, I want some, and I'll heat up the soup."

"I can heat up soup."

"I'm sure you can." Having made the attempt to teach her a couple of cooking basics, he wasn't sure of that at all.

She narrowed her eyes at him. *It's been years since I blew up a kitchen.*

Despite the boy watching wide-eyed, he gave her a simmering kiss—then nipped the jar of soup out of her hand. *All the more reason why we shouldn't take a chance now. You can slice up bread and cheese.*

Hurray for me.

He noticed Yuli's puzzled look and grinned. The boy was bright enough and observant enough to know something was going on but not what—or why.

After we eat, I'd like to talk about making a slight change in the tangled web that holds the shadow cat. I may have a use for a predator.

Can I at least stir the soup?

No.

A huff. *I'll talk to you anyway.*

As he heated the soup for the three of them, he put aside the worry and the anger. There would be time enough for both later.

It was time.

Tersa vanished the tangled web and turned away from the worktable.

She would go to the spooky house and talk to the Langston man. One . . . last . . . time.

TWENTY-THREE

"Surreal? *Surreal!*"

"Wha?" Why was Rainier sounding so cranky?

"Drink this."

A glass against her lips. A hand behind her head to keep her from pulling away.

The glass tasted dusty, and she had this odd memory of seeing Rainier flicking his wrist to toss out dried mouse turds before wiping the glass with his shirttail. Then the water, tasting like dust and bitter leaves, was filling her mouth. She swallowed the first mouthful because she needed the water.

"Drink it all."

He wasn't giving her much choice. Since he was being such a prick about it, it was either drink or drown.

"Hell's fire," she muttered when Rainier released her and set the glass on the kitchen table. She stared at it for a moment, then looked at him. "Did you toss mouse turds out of that glass and then give it to me without washing it?"

"No." His voice sounded odd, strangely hollow, and . . . yes, there *was* a slight echo. And something was going *gong* inside her head.

"Surreal!"

"Wha?"

"I gave you a general healing tonic. I'm hoping it will help enough so you can think clearly for a while longer."

The floor swished. Swishy, swishy, swish. She watched it until Rainier bent over so they were face-to-face. She didn't like the worry and fear in his eyes. She would rather watch the floor swish.

He grabbed her shoulders. She tried to pull back. It made her side hurt—and she felt like she was suddenly standing on a patch of clear ground surrounded by fog.

"We have to get out of here," he said.

"Sugar, we figured that out yesterday when we realized this place was a trap."

"We have to try harder," he said. "Surreal . . . I think you were poisoned after all."

Lucivar had shown such promise—and was such a disappointment. He was just wandering around the cellar, all woeful and lost. He wasn't even *trying* to get out.

At least the Surreal bitch was finally doing something interesting.

Death scenes were always gripping moments in a story.

Somewhere in the house, a gong sounded.

And overhead, a floorboard creaked.

The gong indicated Craft had been used. He remembered that from the rules of the game—and he'd heard it when he made the witchlight. The floorboard creaking . . . Might be real, might be illusion. No way to tell in this house.

Lucivar stared at the ceiling, waiting for another sound.

No staircases except the one he came down. There had to be others.

He took a sandwich out of the pack and ate while he prowled through the cellar again, looking for some indication of where Surreal and Rainier had gone.

The cellar under the two sight-shielded houses was connected, but it was split into a warren of small rooms that made it feel bigger and smaller at the same time, confusing a person's sense of where he was in relation to the ground floor. The cellar of the first house—the house that had been the lure—was closed off from the rest. And held something dangerous enough that Jenkell didn't want the thing roaming freely.

But there was nothing *truly* dangerous here. Not by his standards. On the other hand, there were plenty of things here that could do some damage if a person walked in unaware—or unprepared.

He washed the sandwich down with a long drink of water, then returned the water jug to the pack.

"Enough," he said as he walked back to the staircase. Most likely, the predators that were loose in this house were hunting Surreal and Rainier. It was time to give the predators a reason to come hunting him instead.

And it was time to remind them that they were also prey.

Enough? Yes, he'd spent more than enough time on the SaDiablo family, who were nowhere near as interesting as he'd been led to believe. They hadn't provided him with nearly enough material to justify the risks he had taken. Still, he *had* acquired a few good scenes, and he would flesh out the rest of the story.

Now it was time to unleash all the surprises and record the last moments of desperation before he got rid of the props.

A door creaked.

Lucivar turned away from the stairs and set the pack down.

Something had entered this part of the cellar.

Moving away from the stairs to the area that had the most open ground, he took the ball of witchlight off the end of his war blade, raised his arm, and left the witchlight floating above him.

A rank smell. Shuffling feet.

The man who came out of the dark topped him in height, weight, and muscle. But Lucivar saw no real intelligence in the eyes—and didn't get the sense there had been much, if any, even before the man was caged in this house.

Doesn't mean the bastard can't use the club he's carrying or the . . .

Leg bone in the man's other hand. Not an old bone. And not completely clean.

"Food." The man smiled, tossed the bone aside, and took a step toward Lucivar.

A glint in the eye. Not intelligence, just anticipated pleasure. This man liked to fight.

A club against an Eyrien war blade. A simple mind against centuries of training. An unshielded landen against a shielded Warlord Prince.

The fight would be over as fast as Lucivar wanted it to be.

He made the choice out of pity rather than practicality, out of Eyrien tradition rather than landen understanding. He would give the man the compliment of pretending that he, Lucivar Yaslana, was facing another warrior.

The man took another step toward him. And Lucivar rose to the killing edge.

The stuff oozing out from beneath the door looked like chicken fat and was so acrid it stung her eyes and made her nose run.

"Hell's fire," Surreal said, taking a step back. "What is that?" *And does anyone else see it but me?*

"Do you think it's one of Tersa's spells?" Rainier asked.

It did look as if what had oozed onto the kitchen floor was reshaping itself into arms and a bulby head.

"No," Surreal said. "It feels malignant. It feels like if it touches you . . ." Taking another step back, she put a hand over her mouth and nose.

"Shielded or not, I don't want to get near it," Rainier said. "Since it seems to be guarding the back door, I guess we try to go out the front."

She pressed her arm against her side. The flesh around the wound felt pulpy, pus-filled, not good. Didn't matter at this point if it was infection or poison or something else the Black Widow had dipped her nails in.

"Don't count on me to watch your back," Surreal said as Rainier guided her and the children to the front hallway. "I can't trust what I see, and you shouldn't trust me to stand with you."

If you need to, leave me behind. That's what she was telling him. Not that he would listen. He was a Warlord Prince who was her escort. He would fight to protect her with his last breath and beyond.

"I'll try the front door," Rainier said. He pointed at the children. "You four. Stand on the stairs. If something happens, you'll have more chance of getting away by going up. You too, Surreal."

She didn't argue with him. Couldn't. Not when the floor turned swishy again and beetles started oozing out of the walls.

She shook her head, hoping to clear it. Instead, the room seemed to melt around the edges—until the front door slammed open and her heart jumped.

No smoke and red-eyed illusions this time, but it was the same Eyrien Warlord who had killed Kester. He stepped into the hallway, looked at Rainier, and said, "Time for you to join the rest of us."

Lucivar wiped off the Eyrien war blade on his enemy's ragged trousers.

The man hadn't seen the killing blow, had died so fast there had been no moment of realization, no moment of fear. He'd never understood Lucivar was doing little more than sparring with him. He'd fought with more grace than expected, and it was clear that he was used to fighting in a confined space and used his size and reach to advantage.

He didn't have any chance against an Ebon-gray Warlord Prince, but he'd fought with a little boy's glee.

And now he was dead.

Lucivar returned to the stairs and looked up. He was riding the killing edge now, and he wasn't stepping away from it until he walked out of this house.

Lucivar raised his right hand and released a blast of Ebon-gray power from his ring. The hallway floor rained down around him, wood and tile reduced to the size of small hailstones.

He shook his arms and opened his wings to clear most of the

debris off his shields. Then he looked at the hole no illusion spell could hide—and he bared his teeth in a savage smile.

It was a fool's battle. Surreal knew it. So did Rainier. A man with a poker and a few years of training was no match for an Eyrien warrior and a war blade. Especially when the warrior was already demon-dead. It didn't matter that the Eyrien wasn't shielded, because a killing blow wouldn't kill him.

Might not even slow the bastard down.

She held her position at the foot of the stairs, mostly because she was afraid she'd get in Rainier's way. So far his Opal shield was holding—probably because the Eyrien wanted to stretch out the fight—but every blow the Warlord landed drained Rainier's shield a little more. Soon there would be one blow too many.

Rainier wouldn't use Craft to save himself. Not anymore. Whatever Craft could be used would be reserved for her.

Then something flew toward Rainier's head from the sitting room doorway. A momentary distraction. He barely flinched, despite the instinct to duck.

But barely was still too much. The Eyrien swung the war blade—and Rainier's shield finally broke. It held long enough to prevent the blade from going all the way through Rainier's left leg, but the wound still cut deep.

Rainier slapped his left leg, and the gong sounded as a tight shield encased his thigh. He retreated, struggling to stay on his feet as the Eyrien raised the war blade again.

"No!" Surreal drew the stiletto out of the boot sheath and threw it, a motion she had practiced for weeks until it was a single smooth move.

The stiletto pierced the Eyrien's neck. Should have been a

killing blow. All it did was piss him off—and buy Rainier the few
seconds he needed to reach the stairs.

"Up," she said. "All of you, go up."

"Surreal," Rainier began.

"Hop, crawl, I don't care. Get up those stairs. I'm still shielded.
You're not."

Using the poker as a cane, he hobbled up the stairs as fast as
he could.

The Eyrien Warlord pulled out her stiletto and dropped it on
the floor. The three-fingered witch came out of the sitting room.
And half a witch floated out of the door on her right.

"Surreal," Rainier said. "Come on."

The three of them moved toward her, sure they'd have her,
one way or another.

She was sure too—until a blast of power shook the house.

It was so damn frustrating, Daemon thought as he watched the
spooky house. When it came to communicating with someone
using a psychic thread, the Black gave him a long reach, and he
and Lucivar were usually able to contact each other over fairly
long distances. Now the tangled webs around that house separated them.

*Be patient, old son. He'll get out. Lucivar has stood on worse killing
fields and walked away. He'll walk away from this one too.*

Then he felt the blast of Ebon-gray power. Even the spells
around the house weren't strong enough to completely muffle
the temper behind that punch.

"Lucivar," Daemon whispered.

"Daemon," Jaenelle said, rushing from the Coach to join
him.

He touched her shoulder. "You check the point where he intended to come out. I'll circle around the house in case he needed to choose another exit."

She trotted toward the far side of the house. He went in the other direction.

And he tried not to think of what he'd tell Saetan if Lucivar *didn't* come out of that house.

Lucivar stood in what was left of the front hallway and listened. Waited. Then he frowned.

No gong. If the last exit had closed, wouldn't he sense something? Or . . .

"Every time Craft is used," he said softly. "Every time *Craft* is used." Craft, not power. Had the little writer-mouse made that distinction deliberately? Had the man even realized there was a difference? Probably not.

Of course, it was a subtle distinction, one that hadn't occurred to him when he'd heard the rules—and still wouldn't have occurred to him if he hadn't heard the gong confirm the use of Craft when he'd made the witchlight.

"My apologies, Bastard. I guess you could have played this game after all."

Lucivar waited. Listened.

The house felt oddly empty, the way a house feels when you've had a big gathering and the last guest is gone.

Had Surreal and Rainier gotten out? Was the game ended?

No. The game hadn't ended because *he* was still here. Which meant the little writer-mouse had been scurrying to herd all his predators to one particular spot.

But not in this house. And not in the first house. Pointless to drive Surreal and Rainier back to the starting point when there was one last possibility—the third house.

Lucivar opened his mouth and breathed in.

A taste in the air, coming from . . . that direction. Up there. In the third house.

He smiled and rolled his shoulders to loosen the muscles.

There was a killing field in this place after all.

They had followed the children into one of the rooms. The *cildru dyathe* had gathered in the adjoining bedroom, cutting off that possible escape. The Eyrien Warlord and the two Black Widows were standing in the doorway, savoring the moment when the fight began.

"So," Surreal said as she shifted to stand on Rainier's left and support his weak side as long as she could. "This is where we die."

Rainier shifted slightly to defend against the *cildru dyathe*. "Yeah. This is where we die."

TWENTY-FOUR

You have to shield again, Surreal told Rainier, shifting her weight as the predators moved forward, savoring the moment of attack. She cut him off when he started to protest. *We'll survive longer if you're shielded. Maybe long enough for Lucivar to join the fight.*

That may not work to our advantage, Rainier said. But he created an Opal shield around himself.

She didn't hear the gong. What did that mean? That it no longer made a difference if they used Craft? That the last exit had closed? That they were trapped in this house forever?

Forever meaning until Daemon unleashed the Black against this place and tore it all apart—and everyone still in it.

A sideways glance at Rainier. He was sweating heavily, his face tight with pain.

He was a dancer. And that leg . . .

The tight shield around his thigh was acting like a brace, which was the only reason he was still on his feet. She couldn't think about what it was going to cost him to fight.

★Have you ever seen Lucivar on a killing field?★ Rainier asked.

★I've seen him when he's riding the killing edge. Hell's fire, your caste of male rises to that edge as easy as you breathe. Maybe more so.★

★Not the same thing. I saw him, once, when he walked off a killing field.★ Rainier swallowed hard. ★May the Darkness have mercy on us if he sees us as an enemy.★

Not something she wanted to hear—especially when it was being said by one Warlord Prince about another.

A door suddenly appeared in the wall and swung open—and the demon-dead walked out. A dozen of them. None of them wore Jewels, but that didn't matter. Not in this fight.

★Now I know why we couldn't find any weapons,★ Surreal said. ★The demon-dead were hoarding them.★

Knives. Pokers. Clubs.

She spared one thought for the four children pressed into a corner behind her and Rainier. She hadn't liked most of them, wouldn't have spent an hour with any of them by choice except for . . .

She glanced at the children. Sage gave her a wobbly smile that seemed all the more brave because of the wobble.

Her chest ached.

She looked away.

Odds were good that the children would have been lured into the spooky house as fodder for the game, but she and Rainier had invited them in last night, and she felt the weight of their presence on her shoulders—and she would carry the weight of their deaths.

And his. Rainier, too, was here because of her.

I'm sorry.

Even more sorry because she knew the weapon that would kill her in the end. The *cildru dyathe.* She would do everything she could to destroy the adults, but not the demon-dead children. Memories of ghosts swam through her mind—and the night when she'd seen the truth about a place called Briarwood.

She couldn't raise a weapon against a child.

Then all the demon-dead attacked, and there was no more time to think—or regret.

Damn hard to win a fight when you could die and the enemy couldn't. No room to maneuver, no place to retreat.

The room swam and time became fluid as the poison inside her worked its deadly magic. Either blows came too fast or she made a defensive move for a blow that took too long to fall, giving another enemy an opening.

Her shields would fail soon, and the blows would start breaking bone, start breaking her down, start killing her for real.

A female grabbed her left wrist and jerked her arm up, throwing her off-balance and pulling the wound in her side.

A club came toward her head that she barely deflected with the poker.

Then something dark and fast and so damn *big* came toward her, shining in places where the sunlight caught metal and—

A hand shoved the female's head against the wall.

Surreal ducked as brains *splush*ed out of the shattered skull.

A movement in front of her. A scream of fear.

She looked up just as he spun to meet another of the demon-dead, and she saw him—the glazed gold eyes, the face carved from implacable stone. Here in this place, his life was about slaughter; his world was made of death. He was power and grace, savagery and skill—and no mercy.

Now she understood what Rainier meant about seeing Lucivar on a killing field.

He was so damn fast. He didn't bother to duck the blows from the demon-dead. He didn't even try to parry them. Their blows hit his shields and never touched the man. And any of the demon-dead who were close enough to strike at him . . .

It wasn't that large a room, and he seemed to fill it.

He severed heads, sliced through limbs. Or simply ripped off an arm and drove it into the next body.

And he was just as ruthlessly efficient when it came to eliminating the *cildru dyathe* from the fight.

Then there was only the sound of harsh breathing—hers and Rainier's—and the children whimpering in the corner.

Lucivar stood in front of them, those cold glazed eyes just staring at them. He pointed the war blade at her, then shifted the tip to a spot on her right.

"Move," he said.

She sidestepped to the right.

Lucivar pointed at the wall. The Ebon-gray ring flashed as a burst of power was unleashed.

The wall exploded, leaving a gaping hole.

An odd feeling, like netting tightening over bare skin.

Before she could cry out a warning, the spells around the house hit Lucivar with a vicious amount of power. Enough power that she felt his Ebon-gray shield break.

But he withstood the strike, never moving, and when that lash of power was done . . .

She could feel all the spells trying to close the gap in the wall, chewing on the Ebon-gray power shielding the hole, in an effort to cut off the possibility of escape.

Lucivar reached into the pouch hanging from his belt, pulled out a ball of clay, and tossed it to Rainier.

"Jaenelle made a slide. You need to rub blood on the clay to trigger the spell." Lucivar's eyes raked over Rainier. "That won't be a problem."

"No need to get pissy about it," Surreal muttered.

His eyes sliced over to her. "I'll deal with you later."

★Surreal, don't push him,★ Rainier whispered. He hobbled over to the hole in the wall and blooded the clay. When he set it on the bottom of the hole, the slide appeared, looking like a clay-colored cloud.

"Rainier, you take one of the girls and go," Lucivar said. "You two boys go next. Surreal, you'll help them get on the slide. Then you'll go with the other girl."

"I should—" Rainier began.

"Most wounded, first out," Lucivar said.

No arguing with *that* voice.

Rainier, the fool, argued anyway. "Surreal has been poisoned."

Oh, shit. If Lucivar was pissed off before, now he was *really* pissed off.

Lucivar stared at Rainier. "Go," he said too softly.

Surreal dropped the poker, dragged Dayle out of the corner, and brought her over to the hole.

Rainier was cursing softly and viciously as he got into position on the slide. She settled Dayle on his right side. As he put his arm around the girl, Surreal looked at the end of the slide and saw Jaenelle and Daemon waiting.

The poison blurred her vision, and she was glad. She really didn't want a clear look at Sadi's face right now.

She gave Rainier and Dayle a push, then watched them slide

on air until they passed over the wrought-iron fence and all the tangled spells that had held them captive in this house.

By the time she got the boys on the slide and started them down, the hole Lucivar had made in the wall was half the size. The spells around the house were closing the hole, and there was no doubt in her mind that anyone left in the house when that hole closed completely wouldn't be coming out. Ever.

"Lucivar . . ."

His head was turned, as if he was listening to something behind him. But there was nothing but blank wall behind him.

"Take the girl," he said. "Go."

"The hole is closing up. The three of us need to go *now*."

He looked at her and snarled.

She couldn't reach him. He would never listen. Not to her.

He'll listen to Jaenelle.

She grabbed Sage and hustled to the hole, ignoring the way her feet couldn't seem to find the floor. Since Lucivar wasn't going to leave until she was gone, she needed to get herself and the girl out *fast*.

The poison made the ride down a little too exciting, and she felt giddy when Daemon helped her off the slide and set her on firm, unspelled ground.

"What—?" Jaenelle said, her voice sharp.

Then Daemon roared, *"No!"*

She saw Lucivar framed by the rapidly shrinking hole as he turned back toward something in the house.

A moment later, the hole closed and the exit was sealed shut.

CWENCY-FIVE

He had time, Surreal thought as she stared at the solid wall. He could have gotten out. Why in the name of Hell had Lucivar turned back?

Thunder rolled over the house and shook the ground. She wasn't sure if that was Daemon's temper being given voice or Jaenelle's.

But it was Daemon who bared his teeth in a snarl and wrapped one hand around a wrought-iron spike. She thought he was going to rip away a piece of fence. He was furious enough that he might not even need Craft to do it.

Instead, a section of fence suddenly fell to the ground, nothing more than a pile of metal shavings. That was a quieter—and more frightening—indication of the power and fury that had just blasted out of the man.

Then Daemon was running toward the house's front door.

Jaenelle leaped to follow him, hit a Black shield, and bounced back. "Daemon! *Daemon!*"

He didn't stop, didn't even check his stride—but the shield came down, and Jaenelle ran to catch up to him.

"Go," Rainier said. "Help her stop him. I'll shield the children."

She ran. The poison seemed to slow her down a little more with every step, but she ran.

He'd reached the covered entranceway. Once he opened that door . . .

"Daemon!" Jaenelle shouted.

He spun to face her, his face filled with barely controlled fury. "I am *not* leaving my brother in that house!"

"Of course we're not leaving him in that house," Jaenelle snapped. "But—"

BOOM!

Surreal staggered. Stopped. Spun around as the side of the house exploded. *Rainier?*

I've got a shield around us. Shit! I'll layer the shields.

Debris rained down as a dark shape shot skyward with the speed of an arrow released from the bow. Past the fence and high above the trees beyond the property line.

Then those dark wings spread, pumped, caught the air, and began a wide circle back to the front door, where Daemon and Jaenelle waited.

"Who did Lucivar bring out with him?" Jaenelle asked, shading her eyes with one hand.

He's an idiot, whoever he is, Surreal thought, hurrying to join Jaenelle and Daemon. The man, who was held by one wrist, was flailing around trying to get free. Lucivar was still high enough to skim over rooftops. If he let go, the fool would end up with broken bones or get impaled on the fence.

A gliding descent. The man's feet barely cleared the fence. Then Lucivar backwinged, dropped his prey, and landed lightly on the walkway.

"Look what I found," Lucivar said. His mouth curved in a savage smile as he looked at Daemon. "I think it's a little writer-mouse who's been scurrying in the walls."

Daemon's golden eyes became glazed and sleepy. He purred, "Jarvis Jenkell."

"I built this house as research for a novel," Jenkell said, sounding belligerent. "No one was forced to go inside."

"You sent us invitations," Daemon said.

"But no one was required to attend," Jenkell replied.

Surreal thought about the wording of that invitation and snorted. Then she looked at Lucivar. He looked primed to crush another skull.

"That's true," Daemon said mildly. "We had a choice, even if the phrasing of the invitation implied otherwise. However . . ." He raised one eyebrow as he looked at Lucivar. "How many dead?"

"At least twenty," Lucivar replied.

"Twenty people were killed to provide the entertainment." Daemon pursed his lips, looked at Jenkell, and shook his head. "Somehow, I don't think they were given a choice."

Jenkell's forehead beaded with sweat, but he looked defiant. "Among the Blood, there is no law against murder. And I'm Blood, same as you."

Surreal stared at Jenkell. *Boyo, if you think being Blood makes you the same as Sadi, then you weren't paying attention to that little detail we call caste.*

"There is no law against murder," Daemon agreed. "But there is a price. So I think—"

"Langston man." The words came out in a vicious snarl.

Surreal took a step to the side to get a better look at the woman moving toward them in a predatory stalk.

Hell's fire. It *was* Tersa.

"You tried to hurt the boy," Tersa said. "And the other children, too. You lied to me. You said it was a surprise for the children."

It was that, Surreal thought.

"Tersa." Daemon turned toward Tersa, blocking her direct path to Jenkell.

She had known Tersa for centuries, had seen her when she was semilucid, lost in her visions, or just raving mad. But she'd never seen her when she was filled with a cold, wild fury.

Still focused on Jenkell, Tersa shifted to move around Daemon. "You tried to hurt the children. You tried to hurt my boys!"

She lunged at Jenkell, who squealed—*squealed!*—and turned to run.

Daemon caught Tersa. Lucivar caught Jenkell.

"Tersa, let me handle this." Daemon tightened his grip on Tersa's arms. *"Mother."*

Jenkell froze. Surreal wanted to slap him for being an idiot twice over. Hadn't he bothered to find out who she was *before* he lured Tersa into helping him?

"Mother, let me handle this."

They stared at each other, mother and son, and Surreal saw a truth about Daemon she'd never seen before. *Mother Night. What he is . . . Not all of it came from his father.*

Then Tersa held up something between them. Surreal couldn't see what it was, but when Daemon looked down, he smiled. A cold, cruel smile.

He stepped back and turned to face Jenkell. "There is no law against murder. But there is a price. I rule this Territory. The people you killed to fuel this entertainment? They belonged to me. The Warlord Prince who was wounded works for me. The witch who was injured is family. Not to mention the harm you've done to my mother by using her in a scheme to kill her own son. Everything has a price, Jenkell. It's time for you to pay the debt."

Daemon walked up to the front door, then looked at Jaenelle. "Lady, would you mind holding the door?"

Jaenelle followed him up the steps. *She* was the one who opened the door and kept her hand on the latch while he walked past her into the house. He stopped in the middle of the hallway, nothing more than a shadowy figure.

Somewhere in the house, a gong sounded. One, two, three, four.

I guess the count starts over when a new game begins, Surreal thought.

She lost count. She wasn't sure if there were echoes in her head or if the gong was really sounding that quickly.

Daemon walked back to the door, holding a pen in his hand. "Twenty-eight?" he asked Jaenelle.

"Twenty-eight," she agreed as he slipped the pen into a jacket pocket.

He nodded at Lucivar, who dragged Jenkell up to the door.

"According to your rules, there are thirty exits in this house. Twenty-eight have now been closed. You have seventy-two hours to find either of the remaining two. I guarantee that no matter what you meet in this house, you will live through those seventy-two hours."

Surreal shivered, hearing the threat beneath the words.

Jenkell, the idiot, looked relieved.

Then Daemon stepped out of the house, grabbed Jenkell by the shirt, and flung him into the front hallway.

Jaenelle released the latch and skipped back.

The door slammed shut.

Jaenelle and Daemon came down the steps to join her and Lucivar, and all four of them looked at Tersa.

"Why?" Jaenelle asked, her voice gentle. "If you wanted to help with the spooky house, why didn't you say something to Marian or me? We would have been glad to have your help. We would still like your help."

Tersa wrung her hands, looking lost. "I saw . . . in a tangled web. Surprises for my boys. Not to harm, just little surprises. But there were other boys. That's why I came to this place, this house. When the Langston man said he was building a surprise for the boys . . . I saw it in the web. One boy lost because I didn't make my surprises."

Lucivar looked back at the house, then looked at Daemon. "I think I met that boy. And he would have been lost in every way if it wasn't for one of Tersa's surprises."

Daemon studied Lucivar for a moment, then nodded before he looked at the Coach across the street. "And I think Jaenelle and I found the other boy who needed help."

"Yes," Jaenelle said. "I think you're right." She smiled at Tersa. "But you didn't answer the question. Would you like to help Marian and me finish up our spooky house? Maybe you could put in the same surprises."

No, no, no, Surreal thought. *Not the damn beetles.* "The skeleton mouse was kind of cute. Very clever."

"The spiders were good too," Lucivar said.

"But you can't have them pouring out of a drawer," Surreal said. "If you do, you'll need to assign someone to keep mopping the floor."

A beat of silence. Then Lucivar burst out laughing. "That explains why I smelled piss in the kitchen."

The ground melted. Suddenly Jaenelle was holding her up.

"We need to finish this discussion later," Jaenelle said. "I've done as much preparation as I can on Surreal and Rainier. Now we need to get them into the Coach so I can do the actual healing."

Preparation? Come to think of it, she *had* been feeling a phantom hand over the wound, easing the heat and pain.

"Yes," Lucivar growled. "Our little cousin got herself poisoned."

"You can't yell at me if I'm sick," Surreal said. "It's a family rule." And if it wasn't a family rule, it was damn well going to be—starting now.

"Since when?"

That was Lucivar. In a pissing contest, he not only stepped up to the line; he pissed on the other person's foot.

Since she was the other person, she balled up her fist, threw a punch—and didn't come anywhere close to hitting him.

"Lucivar and I will bring Rainier and the children to the Coach. Can you handle Surreal?" Daemon asked.

"Don't need to be handled," Surreal muttered.

"Do you really want Lucivar to help you into the Coach?" Jaenelle whispered.

"No."

"Tersa?" Jaenelle said. "Give me a hand?"

With Tersa on one side and Jaenelle on the other, she didn't trip or stumble on the way to the Coach. Of course, Jaenelle was floating her on air and they were just tugging her along, but that was a small and insignificant detail.

"How bad is it?" Surreal asked when the Coach's door opened and a young boy stared at her. "Really."

"You're going to be sick for a few days, but your body's been burning out a lot of the poison in the same way you burn up food. An advantage you had because you wear the Gray." Jaenelle hesitated, then added, "It was fortunate you were the one who was wounded that way. Rainier wouldn't have survived it."

Shit shit shit.

They floated her up the stairs to one of the Coach's little bedrooms. As they settled her into the bed, she said, "Since this is the first time I was really stupid, do you think Lucivar will overlook the fact that I didn't shield before walking into a strange place?"

Jaenelle looked at her and laughed. "Not a chance."

TWENTY-SIX

Jarvis Jenkell picked himself up and brushed off his jacket with shaking hands.

This wasn't good. This wasn't good at all. He hadn't anticipated the SaDiablo family linking him to the spooky house. He'd deliberately told a few people "in confidence" about the setting for his next Landry Langston story so that there would be independent confirmation that he'd begun writing his book *before* the tragic events that should have taken place here.

How had Lucivar known he was there? The passageways and observation posts had been carefully shielded. Had to be. Otherwise the demon-dead, chained to this house and craving fresh blood, would have been hunting *him*. But the protection spells hadn't been good enough to fool the Eyrien. Not at the end.

No matter. He had seventy-two hours to get out of the house. He wouldn't need an hour. The last two exits were actually in this first house. Not easy to find if you didn't know what to look for, but easy enough to reach.

He turned toward the door at the back of the hall—the door

he'd gone through in the guise of the caretaker in order to observe this game.

"Regrets?" a deep voice purred.

Jarvis spun around, his heart pounding.

Daemon Sadi leaned against the doorframe of the sitting room.

"I thought you had gone," Jarvis said.

"We still have a few things to discuss."

"What kind of things?" Jarvis asked as Daemon walked toward him. Such a beautiful man. It wasn't just his face or the way his body was put together. It was the way he moved.

A temptation—even if a man wasn't usually tempted by his own gender. A promise—but the sleepy gold eyes didn't reveal all that was being offered.

"A seduction?" Daemon's voice still purred, but it also held cold amusement.

When had Sadi circled around him, come up behind him?

He could feel the heat of the man pressed against his back, could feel the light prick of those black-tinted nails as a hand closed around his throat. Lips brushed his cheek as Sadi's other hand slipped beneath his shirt and began a slow caress down his chest, down his belly, stopping when the fingers slipped just below his belt.

Delight? Shame? He wasn't sure what to feel when his body responded, helpless to resist.

"Same game, Jarvis," Daemon whispered. "But the rules have changed a little."

No other warning before Sadi's nails ripped his belly open, tearing through muscle, slicing his gut.

He screamed in pain and terror. Struggled to get away from the hand digging deeper into his gut.

He twisted, determined to land one blow before he died. His hands shoved at Daemon's chest—and hit the wall.

He stared at his arms, which disappeared into Sadi's chest. He felt the wall under his hands. He looked at those sleepy eyes.

Daemon smiled a cold, cruel smile.

"A sophisticated shadow," Daemon said. "All part of the new game. You can't touch me, but I"—a nail flicked, slicing Jarvis's cheek—"can touch you."

Jarvis backed away. One arm cradled his ruined belly, while the other hand touched his cheek. He looked at his fingers.

No blood.

He dared to look down.

No wound.

"Feels real enough, doesn't it?" Daemon said pleasantly. "But it's all illusion. Well, the pain is real. The wounds are not."

"What's the point of that?" Jarvis asked.

Daemon looked surprised. "I did guarantee that nothing in this house would kill you. The predators you brought into this place might hurt you if they catch you, but I'll prevent them from killing you."

"Lucivar killed them all."

"Oh, no. Most likely, he ripped them up enough to take them out of that fight. Since his main interest was getting Surreal and Rainier out of the house, he wouldn't have bothered to finish the kill."

"But they're all still . . ." *In pieces,* Jarvis finished silently.

Daemon sighed and gave him an amused smile. "Jarvis, darling, a demon-dead witch who was beheaded will have to use Craft to float on air, but as long as there is some power still burning within her, she can hunt. And she does have teeth."

Jarvis shuddered. How was he supposed to survive something

like *that*? He'd hole up in the protected passageways. He had food and water, a mattress and blankets, even a few chamber pots. He could hold out for the seventy-two hours required, and then he would be free. Debt paid.

"About those things we need to discuss," Daemon said. "Since most of the original webs were destroyed when Lucivar punched free of the house, I've replaced them with my own illusion spells. You won't find my tangled webs, so don't waste your time searching. But I will tell you that one of them feeds into the hidden passageways. Yes, Lucivar did tell me about the writer-mouse's hidey-holes. So in our new game, those passageways will still keep you safe from your own predators, but not from mine. Not from me."

"Yours won't kill me?"

"I demonstrated what mine are going to do."

Another shudder went through him. Would the pain be any less because he knew the wounds weren't real? Or would it be worse when he knew that no attack would kill him, no matter how vicious?

"My darling, I think you're beginning to understand." Daemon drifted toward the sitting room door. "The next thing you should know is that using my tangled webs to fuel the game shuffled the exits. There are still thirty of them, although only two remain open, and they're still where they were. But the order in which they open was shuffled."

"But that means . . ."

"You're going to have to check every one of them in order to find the two that are still open."

He'd have to travel through the whole house—all three buildings—with the demon-dead hunting him, and Sadi . . .

"You wanted to dance with the Sadist," Daemon said too softly. "Now you will."

He'd wanted to *observe* the Sadist, which was altogether different.

"What else?" Daemon tapped a finger against his lips. "Ah, yes. My mother wanted me to tell you that she made some changes to her illusions. They're connected to my webs, and her little surprises are now more in keeping with your intentions for this house."

"And that means . . . ?"

"They all have teeth." Daemon smiled. "You wanted to play games with my family. Now we'll play, you and me." As the shadow Daemon faded, he added, "Watch out for the cat. He doesn't like humans—except when he's using them for a toy or having them for dinner."

Jarvis stood in the hallway, uncertain what to do or where to go. If he went into the sitting room, would the shadow Daemon still be there, waiting to play another round of the game? There was an exit in the sitting room. Maybe he should check the exits at the back of the house first. Or . . .

A rumble on the stairs, a sound that vibrated in his bones.

The white cat filled the stairs, and Jarvis wondered which was going to be worse—the illusions that couldn't physically hurt him or the predators that could.

Daemon stepped out of the Coach and felt some of the tension ease out of his muscles as he looked at SaDiablo Hall.

Jaenelle joined him, slipping her arm through his.

How bad is it really? He'd been busy with other things while they'd remained in the village, and then had to focus on driving the Coach home, so he hadn't asked before. Hadn't been ready to be told.

They'll both heal.

Rainier was a dancer. He remembered Lucivar's words before they parted. *With help from a good Healer, severed muscle will heal; a completely severed limb won't, no matter how good the Healer is.*

He's still a dancer, Jaenelle said. *He'll hobble for a while, but he'll dance again. I'll make sure of it.*

And Surreal?

After deciding that the four surviving children would be better off staying with their parents rather than being taken to another strange house, Jaenelle had quickly made up four packets of a mild sedative that would let the children sleep through the night. While Tersa looked after Surreal and Rainier, and Jaenelle dealt with the healings, Daemon and Lucivar had returned the children to their parents, and then went to the orphans' home to pick up Yuli's belongings.

A pathetically small bundle. A diminished life for a bright boy. Who was Yuli's mother, his father? Had they hidden him away because he had the potential to be Blood or because he didn't? Would he become a bitter man someday because his heritage hadn't been acknowledged?

Daemon could have sympathized with Jarvis Jenkell. He might have enjoyed discussing stories with him if they had met at a party. Or he might have hated the man for being a pompous ass. Either way, he would have acknowledged Jenkell as Blood.

If the man hadn't played out this game.

Even then, he might have been willing to overlook—to some degree—the man's suicidal attempt to play games with some of the darkest Blood in the Realm.

If the man hadn't killed children to do it.

If the man hadn't hurt Surreal and Rainier.

She'll heal, Jaenelle said.

She sounds like a cranky child. And that scared him because it made her sound weak and diminished. Once he was sure she would recover, she could bitch and whine as much as she wanted. Until then, the sound was going to scrape nerves already raw from worry.

She has a fever, the poison is draining out of those wounds and hurts, and she's feeling pretty miserable. On top of that, she thinks we're treating her like a child by making her stay here instead of letting her go back to the town house in Amdarh. Of course she's cranky. And she's figuring that as soon as she's feeling better, you and Lucivar are going to chew on her for getting hurt.

For a woman with a fever, Surreal did have a good grasp of where things stood. Which made him feel better. If she understood that much, her brain was still working.

Beale opened the door. Footmen hurried out to bring Surreal and Rainier into the house.

Daemon stepped aside, bringing Jaenelle with him.

"They're going to need me for the rest of the day," she said.

He nodded. "I have tasks of my own to deal with." Including figuring out what to do with a young boy.

Yuli followed Tersa out of the Coach. He looked so young, so scared, despite a fragile show of bravery.

"Boy," Tersa said. She walked up to Daemon, pressed a hand against his cheek, and smiled. "You did well, boy."

"Will you make some of your surprises for my spooky house?" Jaenelle asked.

Tersa looked at Jaenelle, then looked at him—and walked away without answering.

Jaenelle patted his arm and whispered, "If she answered, it wouldn't be a surprise." Then she held out her other hand to Yuli. "Let's find you a room for a day or two."

They'd barely gotten into the great hall when four Sceltie puppies came running up to greet them. Three bounced and yapped
and wagged tails at everyone before running back to whatever
puppy game they'd been playing.

The fourth one planted his little white feet on Yuli's foot and
said, *My boy!*

I guess that settles that, Jaenelle told Daemon.

I guess it does, he replied, watching the boy's face bloom
from shy smile to complete delight.

"Can I play with him while I'm here?" Yuli asked.

Oh, boyo, just try not playing with him. "Yes, you can. He still has
some trouble on the stairs, so why don't you pick him up while I
show you to your room."

Up! the puppy said. *Up!* When Yuli didn't immediately
respond, the puppy whined and looked at Jaenelle. *Boy has dead
ears?*

"He hasn't learned to hear kindred yet," Jaenelle said, slanting
a glance at Yuli. "But he'll learn."

"Huh?" Yuli said.

"Pick him up," Daemon said. *This is going to be a learning
experience.*

She pressed her lips together, fighting to keep a straight face.
For both of them.

As Yuli followed them, silent and wide-eyed, and the puppy
never shut up about what he would need to train his boy, Daemon thought, *At least something good has come from all that pain.*

TWENTY-SEVEN

Daemon filled time with paperwork while he waited for Jaenelle to return home.

He'd wondered if his father had been aware of the half-Bloods who were raised in orphans' homes in Dhemlan. He should have known better. His only excuse for not picking up the clues was his own emotional turmoil the previous year.

One of the vast estates owned by the SaDiablo family contained a self-sufficient community, including a school. When he'd taken over handling the family's property and wealth, Saetan had told him that community was required to support itself, but no income should be expected from it. Daemon hadn't questioned it or looked at the place beyond reviewing the quarterly reports to make sure the community *was* still supporting itself.

So when he and Jaenelle sat down to review possible new homes for Yuli, it was embarrassing to discover that the community's school was for half-Blood children who had the potential to become Blood when they reached maturity. Some of the children were there because their parents wanted them to have the dual landen-Blood education that matched their potential. Others were considered orphans—children who had lost their parents or children whose parents were nothing more than names that acknowledged family bloodlines. The children were educated and cared for, taught Protocol, and instructed in basic Craft if they developed the power to do simple spells. They were also given the opportunity to earn spending money by working within the community or on another part of the estate.

Two hundred children made their home at that school—and now Yuli was one of them.

Jaenelle walked into the study, gave him a look he couldn't interpret, then slumped in a chair in front of the desk.

"I have been given the honor of being the Official Liaison between the school and the Warlord Prince of Dhemlan," she said. "I was even given an official-looking piece of parchment, all signed and sealed, to acknowledge my new position."

"I see," Daemon said, working to keep his expression bland. "Didn't want to talk to me themselves?"

"Not in this decade. So. Do you want to see an extra report from the school? Do you require copies of the reports sent—and approved by the High Lord—from previous years?"

Daemon sat back, steepled his fingers, and rested the forefingers against his chin. "Is this a ripple caused by my note to the Province Queens?"

"Apparently. And even though they would prefer not to talk to you directly, the school's administrators seemed more puzzled than concerned by this sudden interest in the school."

A good sign that he wouldn't find anything wrong at the school when he paid them a surprise visit. And he would take the Official Liaison with him to avoid scaring the shit out of everyone.

"We discussed the necessity of Yuli receiving some individual tutoring, since I don't think he has much of the Dhemlan race in his bloodline and he'll mature faster than the other children," Jaenelle said. "It may be that he'll do better in a Territory like Scelt, but I'd prefer to keep him nearby for the time being."

"Was Yuli comfortable with staying at the school?" Daemon asked.

"A little frightened. But after he saw his room—and after Socks declared that it smelled like a good place—boy and puppy adjusted quickly enough. More quickly than the administrators, who are smart enough to realize what having a kindred puppy at the school will mean."

Daemon smiled. "That they'll now receive regular visits from adult kindred?"

"And that not all of those adults will be small or canine," Jaenelle said, returning the smile.

A small frown was added to his smile. "Socks? The puppy's name is Socks?"

Jaenelle rolled her eyes. "Yuli said the puppy looked like he was wearing white socks, so the puppy announced that that was his name—Socks."

"He's a Warlord, yes?"

"Yes, and that one will definitely wear a Jewel of sufficient rank when he goes through the Birthright Ceremony—and that means he'll most likely wear a dark Jewel at maturity."

The frown deepened. "Lord *Socks*? What was his name originally?"

A blush stained Jaenelle's cheeks. "I couldn't remember, and the puppy won't say. When I asked Ladvarian, he said, 'Socks is an easy name for humans to remember.'"

"The little prick," Daemon muttered.

She laughed.

Then she looked at him in a way that filled his stomach with butterflies. *Nervous* butterflies.

Everything has a price, old son. You made a promise. It's time to pay the debt. Time to pay off all the debts, actually.

"I have an appointment this evening," Daemon said. "I was waiting for you to return home before I left."

A subtle change in her eyes, in her psychic scent.

"An appointment," Witch said.

Not a question. Seventy-two hours had passed since he'd set his little game in motion. He had no doubt the first half of the debt had been paid in full. Now it was time to end it.

And Witch knew it.

"I've already informed Mrs. Beale that I won't be home for dinner." Informed Beale, actually. He'd hadn't wanted to be the one to tell Mrs. Beale—and her meat cleaver—just in case she'd already begun preparations for the evening meal. "After I return, I'm available for whatever help you want with your spooky house."

Her smile was female. Feline. More than a little bit terrifying.

"I'll look forward to it," she said.

Hell's fire, Mother Night, and may the Darkness be merciful.

After Jaenelle walked out of the study, he sat there for several minutes, giving himself time to grow some bone back into his legs and strap some steel to his spine.

He'd made a promise to his Queen. To his wife. And he would keep it.

But he had another promise to keep first.

⁂

Pressed into a corner, Jarvis Jenkell curled up a little tighter.

Her little surprises are now more in keeping with your intentions for this house. They all have teeth. That's what Sadi had said about Tersa's illusions. And he'd been right.

The beetles. The spiders. Even the skeleton mice.

The beetles were the worst. Swarming all over him whenever he tried to rest, swelling up, and then . . . Those *teeth*! Biting through his clothes. Biting through his skin. Chewing their way into him. Then gone, leaving no marks, no trace. But his flesh remembered the sensation, the pain. Just like the flesh remembered . . .

No scuff of shoe on wood. No sound at all. But he knew he was no longer alone. Knew what was going to happen. Again. Knew the pleasure would be as cold-blooded and merciless as the pain.

And no longer knew which was worse to endure.

The Sadist had arrived.

"Let this end," Jarvis whispered. "I'm begging you. Let this end."

The Sadist stared at him, a measuring regard.

"Yes," Daemon said softly. "The debt to the SaDiablo family has been paid in full." He took a step toward Jarvis. Took another. "Now it's time to pay the debt you owe the Warlord Prince of Dhemlan."

Witchfire took the house, and it burned fast and hard. Witchfire formed a carpet where grass had once grown, and burned fierce enough to partially melt the wrought-iron fence that surrounded the property.

Witchfire, fueled by a Black Jewel, burned through the spells and consumed the power that remained in the Blood who had been trapped in the house; it finished the kill and freed them to become a whisper in the Darkness.

With one exception.

The boy sneaked glances at the Warlord Prince who had rescued him from the house. The Prince had *said* he was the Eyrien Prince's brother, and the boy wasn't about to call him a liar—even if this Prince *didn't* have wings.

Besides, even though the man hadn't done anything to *him*, the boy was pretty sure *this* Prince was even scarier than the Eyrien Prince.

"Will I have to go to school?" the boy asked. "I'm dead, so I shouldn't have to go to school."

"That's something you'll have to discuss with the High Lord," the Prince said.

"Oh."

The man's eyes were glazed, and the boy had been taught to avoid Warlord Princes when their eyes were glazed because that's when they were the most dangerous. But since he'd ended up dead because the Jenkell man had tricked him into coming to the spooky house, he figured it was better to ask about things *now.*

"I like learning about some stuff," the boy offered.

A little warmth came into those cold eyes. "Then you should mention that." The Prince looked at the villagers who were running toward the fire. "Come on, puppy. It's time to leave."

He followed the Prince to the small Coach—and hoped the place he was going would be nicer than the spooky house.

Even if he did have to go to school.

Saetan felt the cold ripples in the abyss, rising up from the depth of the Black, and knew what was coming. *Who* was coming.

He set aside the stack of books he'd been cataloging and looked at Geoffrey. "Why don't you go into the other room and warm up some yarbarah for us?"

"Why would I need to go into the other room?" Following the direction of Saetan's gaze, Geoffrey looked at the door. Then he retreated to the small room that served as his office.

Saetan waited. Felt the storm coming closer.

When he'd heard what had happened in that Dhemlan village, he'd known why it was Lucivar who had come to the Keep to give him a report. And he'd known why—and when—Daemon would walk through that door.

The door opened. His beautiful, lethal son stood framed in the doorway.

Saetan stood very still as he studied those cold, glazed eyes.

"Did Lucivar tell you about the *cildru dyathe* boy?" Daemon asked.

"He told me."

"I brought him here."

"That's fine. I'll find a place for him."

He knew the brutality involved in a slow execution. There were times when the executioner also paid a price for the Blood's kind of justice.

"Is there anything else?" Saetan asked.

Their eyes met. Held.

"You were right," Daemon said too softly. "I'll never lose that edge."

Daemon walked away.

The library door closed with obscene gentleness.

Saetan felt the tremor run through him and allowed himself to indulge in a moment of queasiness—and sympathy. Daemon had killed before, and he had no doubt Daemon would kill again. But there was something different about a formal execution that was done because duty required it. That was done in a particular way because duty required it.

Extract the price. Make sure the blood debt was paid in full.

He didn't turn when Geoffrey walked back into the room and held out a glass of warmed yarbarah.

"You didn't ask him what he did," Geoffrey said.

Saetan took the glass of yarbarah and stared at the blood wine for a long moment before he looked at his friend.

"He's a mirror, Geoffrey. I didn't have to ask."

Daemon braced his hands on the shower wall and let the hot water flow over him.

He could no longer count how many of the Blood he had killed in his seventeen hundred years. Some had been a fast slash of temper; others had been exquisitely, hideously slow dances of agony.

He'd never felt dirty about making a kill. Until today.

Because it wasn't personal. The game he'd played with Jenkell? Yes, that was personal. He'd shaped the Sadist into a shadow and let him slip the leash. But the pain and terror he'd wrung from Jenkell during the execution . . . That hadn't been for himself. Hadn't even been for Rainier or Surreal. That had been done for those unknown people he had agreed to protect when he became the Warlord Prince of Dhemlan.

He hoped with all his heart that it would be decades before he had to do something like that again.

Since water would get his body clean but wouldn't cleanse his heart, he finished up and did his best to mentally prepare for the next part of the evening.

Jazen was waiting for him when he walked back into the Consort's bedroom.

"No costume?" Daemon asked, looking at the clothes laid out on the bed.

"The Lady felt your regular attire would best suit her plans for the evening."

Mother Night.

On the other hand, this was better than he'd expected.

"Consider yourself off duty for the rest of the evening," Daemon said.

"But—"

"Go. Or you'll be the next person who volunteers to help with the spooky house."

On behalf of his wife, he felt a little insulted at the speed in which Jazen left the room.

He dressed with care and even added some face paint to subtly enhance his eyes and make his lips more sensual. That wasn't for his participation in the spooky house; that was for the woman.

When he opened the connecting door and went into Jaenelle's bedroom, he was glad he'd made the extra effort. And he was glad there wasn't another male in this wing of the house because one look at her made him edgy and needy.

He chained lust, but it simmered in his blood. He chained need and let his senses feast on the woman before him.

The material looked like watercolors spilled over moonbeams that were then shaped into a gown. So vibrant and yet so delicate—he wasn't sure if it was real or an illusion. She wore a skin-colored sheath underneath the gown, but that, too, was so sheer he could see the shadows of her nipples through both layers of cloth.

He didn't dare look below her waist because that, he was sure, would bring him to his knees and break his self-control.

Her golden hair was long again and unrestrained, as it had been before she'd been injured last year. The hair was an illusion, and intriguing, but he was a trifle disappointed that it hid the spot on her neck that he found so enticing.

He crossed the room and stopped when he was close enough to touch her. But he didn't touch. Not yet.

"What do you want from me?" he asked, his voice having more of a seductive edge than usual. *Please want something from me.*

"I want you to help me keep a promise. Dance with me, Daemon."

He brushed his fingers over the sleeve of her gown—and still wasn't sure if he was touching something real. "That's all?"

She took the step that erased the distance left between them. Then she touched her lips to his in a kiss that was as warm as a dream and as soft as a wish.

"For the spooky house, yes, that's all." She wrapped her arms around his neck and added a little more heat to the kiss. "Afterward, we can have a late supper and a quiet evening alone to do whatever kind of dancing you want."

Heat flashed through his blood before he got himself under control again. "Promise?"

She smiled and linked her hand with his as she took a step back. "Promise."

TWENTY-EIGHT

Surreal had plenty to say to the man who walked into the sitting room.

"You have to talk to your brother."

"I talk to my brother all the time," Daemon said mildly. He crossed the room and stood next to the footstool in front of her chair.

"I mean it, Sadi. He's being unreasonable."

"*Lucivar* is being unreasonable? How can you tell?"

Smug, arrogant bastard. He was laughing at her.

"You don't know what it's like," she grumbled. "He comes here every day—*every single day*—and stares at me like I'm a roast and he's checking to see if I'm done." Which, she'd discovered, was *exactly* what Lucivar was doing. "He showed up earlier today and said that, after Winsol, I have to go to Ebon Rih and work with him to hone my fighting skills—especially defensive tactics."

Sadi looked politely interested, but it was hard to tell if his brain was really in the room.

"He *said* I can stay at The Tavern down in Riada, and he'll pay for room and board—as if I can't afford to pay for my own room—but if I get bitchy about this, he'll chuck me into a guest room at the eyrie and put shields around the room to make sure I stay there. *And* he'll chuck Daemonar in there with me. That's blackmail."

"No, darling," Daemon said. "Blackmail would be telling you that if you don't agree to Lucivar's terms, you will not only have to deal with him but with the rest of the males in the family who are unhappy because you got hurt. And that includes Chaosti."

Shit shit shit. Chaosti was the Warlord Prince of the Dea al Mon. Kin on her mother's side. Chaosti would be just as bad as Lucivar. Maybe worse.

Not worse. *No one* could be worse than Lucivar. Not individually. But if they ganged up on her . . .

"You're as useful as a bucket of piss," she growled.

Daemon just smiled. "Rainier is equally thrilled. He'll be joining you. You can whine together in the evenings."

She considered several extremely vile things to say to and about him, but he held out a white box tied with gold ribbon and she decided to wait and see if the bribe was worth holding her tongue.

"Chocolate fudge," Daemon said.

Hell's fire. She'd even be nice to Lucivar today for a box of fudge.

"If you don't want it . . ."

"You try to leave with that box, you'll be leaving without all of your skin."

Daemon grinned. "That's the witchling we all love. Now I know you're feeling better."

"Bastard."

He laughed and handed her the box. Then he handed her a familiar-sized envelope. "I'm delivering these in person."

Her hands trembled as she opened the envelope and read the invitation to the premier showing of Jaenelle and Marian's spooky house.

"You don't have to go," Daemon said gently. "We'll understand."

"I've seen worse, I've lived through worse, and I've done worse. I'd like to see what Jaenelle and Marian had intended. Maybe that will help erase the perversion of the other one."

She hadn't been sure she'd say anything, but as soon as she returned to Amdarh, she'd made it her business to find out everything she could about Jarvis Jenkell and the trap he had set for the SaDiablo family.

"I heard the house burned," she said, trying to sound casual—and hoping she was the only one who could hear the thunder of her heart beating. "Witchfire, wasn't it?"

He said nothing. Just looked at her with eyes that were suddenly a little glazed, a little sleepy.

"Was Jenkell still alive when the fire took the house?" she asked.

Still nothing. Then, "Why do you think I would know?"

"You'd know, Sadi. You would know."

He studied her for a long moment. Then he took that last step, bringing him right next to her chair. He leaned over. One hand cupped her face while his lips lightly brushed her cheek.

The Sadist whispered in her ear, "He was grateful when I let him die."

She shivered—and knew he felt the shiver.

Daemon stepped back. "I'll tell Jaenelle you'll be there for opening night. Rainier is planning to attend too."

He walked out of the room.

She set the box and invitation aside, then got up, wincing as her left side twinged in protest. Her main objection to this required training with Lucivar was that she didn't want her male relatives to know how weak she still was. Well, she had a few weeks before Winsol. If she could keep her relatives at bay until then, she'd be able to convince them that they had been fussing over nothing.

Although, come to think of it, they were probably getting daily reports from the Healer Sadi had hired to look in on her every day, and knew her condition better than she did. And Jaenelle would have understood every nuance of what the poison had done to her and how long it would take her to heal. While Daemon had been tucking her into the town house and giving Helton instructions about meals and visitors, Jaenelle had probably given the Healer explicit instructions of what to watch for to assure that the healing was progressing as it should.

So maybe it had been foolish stubbornness that had made her argue against having the finest Healer in Kaeleer keeping an eye on her, but Jaenelle was family. Right now Surreal would have felt smothered if she'd been fussed over too much by family. She considered it sufficient punishment that Helton was fussing over her. At least he was restrained by his position as the town house's butler and had to back off if she snarled at him.

Unfortunately, her *relatives* thought being snarled at meant her health was improving and that only encouraged them to be bigger pains in the ass.

They had her well and truly chained. Oh, they were giving her breathing room and the illusion of independence, but until she was fully healed, Lucivar and Daemon would continue circling, would continue to keep watch—and anything that was perceived as a threat would disappear before it got close enough for her to be aware of its presence.

So she would go to Ebon Rih, and she would find a way to

break the chains family had woven around her. She had a better chance of doing that with Lucivar, of getting him to agree to back off. If Daemon, on the other hand, felt a need to tighten those chains . . .

The look in his eyes. The sound of his voice when the tone was both seduction and threat.

Chilled to the bone, she stretched out on the sofa, put a warming spell on the blanket Helton had brought in earlier, and tucked it around her.

Was Jenkell still alive when the fire took the house?

Sadi hadn't answered her question.

Maybe that was for the best.

TWENTY-NINE

"Don't write in the dust, darling. That's rude."
" 'Hello, pree.' What does 'pree' mean?"
"It's 'prey.' 'Hello, prey.' " Pause. "Oh, dear."
"Mama, that's a mouse made of bones."
"Mouse? *Where?*"
"Bwaa ha ha!"

Surreal bit her lip as the ghost boy reached for the door he'd been told not to open. She wanted to scream at him, rage at him. But there was no one to scream at, nothing to rage at, so she turned and stared at sooty layers of cobwebs that were clotting one corner of the dining room ceiling.

She felt Rainier come up beside her, positioning himself so that he blocked even her peripheral view of what was happening.

"I know it's just entertainment," she said. "I know it isn't real, and I know Jaenelle and Marian created it before we walked into that trap, but . . ."

"I can't watch it either," Rainier said. He tipped his chin toward the cobwebs. "What do you think those are supposed to do?"

As if in answer, two spots began to glow and became eyes within a cobweb face shaped by a breath of air. Pieces of cobweb extended out, becoming an arm—and a hand with its fingers curled. The arm turned. The hand opened. And . . .

Surreal blinked.

"Bats?" Rainier asked. "Are those tiny bats?"

"Sparkly, Jewel-colored bats," she said. "Must be one of Tersa's spells."

By the time the last sparkly bat winked out and the cobwebs once again looked like sooty, clotted cobwebs, Surreal was ready to follow the rest of the guests who were leaving the dining room.

She found her balance as she wandered through the spooky house with Rainier at her side. Despite Jaenelle's skills as a Healer, he was still walking with a noticeable limp and needed the cane that had been a gift from Daemon.

He was lucky he was walking at all. Jaenelle had told her the Eyrien Warlord's war blade had cut halfway through the bone as well as severing the muscles in Rainier's leg. But he was healing, and she was glad he'd felt well enough to come with her to see *this* spooky house.

Jaenelle and Marian had created a house that was humor with a bite, scary with a wink. And some things were hauntingly lovely, like that voice in the upstairs hallway.

She saw the other illusions Tersa had added—and after watching eyes open up in the grapes, she was very glad she'd avoided those in the other spooky house.

In a way, this house poked fun at landens and Blood alike. And while some of it gave her a jolt—like that damn voice on the staircase—it really wasn't . . .

Sylvia rushed up to them, looking wild-eyed and horrified.

"They think we live like this?" she said. "Landens really think *we live like this?*"

All right. Maybe it *was* scary for some people. Just not for the expected reasons.

Rainier turned his back to deal with a sudden fit of coughing.

Sylvia turned in a circle, and in the course of that turn changed from wild-eyed woman to flame-eyed mother. "Where is Mikal? Hell's fire, if that boy has tried to make off with one of those giggling spiders, I will kill him flatter than dead."

Surreal watched the Queen of Halaway plow through a knot of stunned landens.

They don't know if she's part of the entertainment or a real mother, Rainier said.

Kill him flatter than dead? Surreal said. *What does that mean?*

No idea. But said in that tone of voice, it sure sounds impressive. And I think the landen mothers are committing that phrase to memory.

Surreal snorted.

They had seen most of the spooky house. Since they were family, they hadn't been required to follow a ghostly guide—and hadn't been herded back into a group by the shadow Scelties. It had been amusing to watch the other guests view the surprises, and she'd been entertained by watching rowdy landen boys come face-to-face with Lucivar. Even more amusing was watching the adolescent girls watch Daemon as he glided through the house. Unlike Lucivar, who had dealt with the boys by threatening to rip off all their poking little fingers and shove those fingers down their throats, Daemon had put a fading spell over a sight shield, so he simply faded away as he walked down a hallway, leaving all those girls wondering if he was real or illusion.

"So," Rainier said. "We've seen the woman in the cobwebs and the giggling spiders. We've heard the snarl in the cellar and—"

"The damn laughing staircase." She'd almost wet herself when she stepped on a stair and that voice rolled up from beneath her feet.

Rainier grinned but wisely said nothing. "And the eyes in the attic."

They had skipped the bathroom with the popping beetles. Thank the Darkness.

"That's the only room left to view."

They approached the door as a group of landens, led by their ghostly guide, also came to that part of the tour.

"This is the scariest room in the house," the ghost said.

The ghost stepped aside. The door opened without a creak or a squeak.

Surreal and Rainier entered the room and stood to one side. They would be able to stay and view the "surprise" in the room as many times as they wanted, so it seemed fair to let the "guests" have the better view.

Any ideas? Rainier asked.

She shook her head.

A beautifully decorated sitting room. Something she would expect in an aristo town house in Amdarh—or any of the sitting rooms at SaDiablo Hall.

Seconds passed. Nothing happened.

Then she heard the music. Faint at first, but growing stronger. And with the music, the dancers slowly formed out of mist until they became almost solid, almost real.

Jaenelle and Daemon, dancing. Just watching them, she could feel the heat of their love, could see their happiness at being together.

"Please tell me that gown is an illusion," Rainier whispered. "Jaenelle doesn't really own something like that, does she?"

"I'd heard she had to make the gown in the illusion more opaque," Surreal teased. "The real thing is even more sheer. But it's only to be worn for very private dinners."

"Thank the Darkness. If she wore that at a public gathering, Sadi would kill every male in the room just for looking at her."

The truth of that shivered through her bones.

She pursed her lips and looked around the room. What was . . . ?

"What's so scary about *this* room?" a boy asked.

The dancers stopped suddenly. Their bodies were still pressed together, but their heads turned toward the voice and they looked straight at the people in the room.

Mother Night, Surreal thought. She felt Rainier stiffen beside her. She felt the stillness ripple through the guests as each one recognized the danger. And she watched a feral quality add bite to Jaenelle's sapphire eyes while Daemon's gold eyes turned glazed and sleepy.

She'd known, had used that gauge for temper all her life. But because it was a constant part of her life, she'd never thought about it, had never seen it so clearly.

It's in the eyes. That's what changes the face from person to predator. That's the key to the truth about the Blood. The eyes say, "We aren't like you. We come from the same races. We laugh and love and grieve and cry. We have hopes and dreams and regrets and bitter disappointments. We feel the same things you feel. But we aren't like you. We are the guardians of the Realms. We are power. We are the Blood. Walk softly when you walk among us."

No one spoke. No one moved. No one even breathed until the dancers turned and simply disappeared as they walked away.

Then there was a collective sigh—and Surreal had no doubt that every landen in the room now had a gut-level understanding of the Blood.

The ghost had been right. It *was* the scariest room in the house.

She watched the landens file out, then heard nervous laughter as they walked out the front door.

"They set up refreshment tents," Rainier said. "Hot cider, ale, wine. A healthy dose of brandy to put some bone back in your legs."

"My legs are shaking," Surreal said. "I have lived in the same house as that man, and my legs are shaking."

"And that surprises you? Only a fool would play with that temper, and you're no fool. And while that temper is in everything that he is, it's not all that he is. Or any of us, for that matter. We saw a truth about us as well as him—and her."

"I know." She took a deep breath and blew it out in a gusty sigh. "Brandy. Then back to Amdarh for a late supper?"

"Agreed."

As they crossed the threshold, Surreal looked back.

Daemon leaned against the fireplace mantel, smiling at her with warm amusement. Then the door closed.

Surreal, Rainier said.

A small table had been positioned near the door, its top covered by a woven basket full of wood shavings. Sitting in the basket was a skeleton mouse waving bye-bye to the guests.

That explained the nervous laughter. Jaenelle, Marian, and Tersa had provided a last bit of whimsy to soften the frightening truth that danced in that beautiful sitting room.

Hell's fire, Surreal muttered.

Two boys were reaching for the skeleton mouse, and something about their expressions and the way they stood indicated an intention to damage the illusion in some way.

She took a step toward the boys, ready to smack some manners into their nasty little-boy heads.

Wait, Rainier said.

The two shadow Scelties suddenly appeared behind the boys and . . .

"Ow!" the boys cried. They hurried toward a knot of adults. "Those dogs bit us!"

A man—father?—looked at the shadows, who were now wagging their tails. "Don't be silly," he said. "Those are illusions. They can't bite you."

One of the boys turned toward the shadows, hauled back, and kicked with enough force it would have lifted a real dog off its feet. His foot went right through the shadow.

But Surreal saw a gleam in the dogs' eyes that made her knees go weak.

As the adults followed the ghostly guide up the stairs for the first part of the tour, the shadow Scelties moved in on the boys, nipping and herding until they had their quarry cornered. And there those boys would stay, missing the tour. Since the landen adults believed the illusions couldn't touch anyone, the Scelties were free to carry out their own brand of discipline.

Surreal and Rainier looked at the Scelties, then looked at each other and said in unison, "Now, *that's* scary."

Dear Readers,

This is a story about Surreal during the years when she lived in Terreille and made a good living as an assassin—before she moved to Kaeleer and acquired too many powerful male relatives. It was originally published in Treachery and Treason. *That anthology has been out of print for a few years, so I'm delighted the story was added as a bonus here.*

Anne Bishop

BY THE TIME THE WITCHBLOOD BLOOMS

It was a perfect place for my line of work. For both of my professions, actually, but I was there for only one of them.

The dining house catered to Blood aristos, so it exuded quality and comfort. The sunken main room had a rough-stoned fountain in the center that looked so natural you would swear they had built the room around it. Tables were scattered around the room with plenty of space between them—a sensible precaution, all things considered. The Blood's social structure is such a complicated dance, juggling caste, social rank, and Jewel rank, that an inadvertent nudge could turn into a violent confrontation in the space of a heartbeat. And spoil everyone's dinner if the end result was a little too messy.

Not that I would mind, unless something nasty landed on my plate. I enjoy carnage, especially when it's an aristo male being torn into little pieces. Unfortunately, I'm too much of a professional to indulge in things like that very often.

On either side of the sunken main room were large, comfortable booths discreetly shielded from the tables below by a wall of ferns and lightly spelled so that conversations remained private.

When I'd arrived that afternoon to look the place over, I'd chosen one of the booths for tonight's little game. The owner of the dining house graciously closed this section of the room so that I and my companion would have it all to ourselves. That wasn't difficult, since, even for the Blood, this was a late dinner, and the few people left in the main room were lingering over drinks by the time my companion arrived.

We settled into the booth, and the game began.

My companion was a Purple Dusk–Jeweled Warlord from an aristo family. That gave him some power. His serving one of the stronger Queens in this Territory gave him more. Enough so that he felt he could do anything to anyone as long as they didn't wear darker Jewels than his, didn't come from an aristo family, and didn't serve in a Queen's court.

Which was true. He *could* do anything to anyone and no one could touch him—unless, of course, they hired someone like me.

According to our most ancient legends, the Blood were given their power, their Craft, in order to be the caretakers of the Realms. The Jewels some of us wore not only acted as a reservoir for our power but also indicated how deep—and dark—that power was.

There are many words that could describe what the Blood have become. "Caretaker" isn't one of them.

Which is why, for me, business is so good.

My companion was a handsome enough man, if you found pigs erotic. Then again, whores don't choose clients based on how they look.

Neither do assassins.

"So, I was your first?" he said, dipping his fingers into the bowl of stained shrimp.

Idiot. I'm half-breed Hayllian, who are a *long*-lived race. My eyes have too much green in them to be pure Hayllian gold, but the light brown skin and black hair came from the son of a whoring bitch who had sired me.

I daintily cut one of my stuffed-mushroom appetizers. "Ah, no, sugar. Not *my* first." I laughed, soft and husky, and flashed him a look from beneath my lashes. "Your great-great-grandfather perhaps."

He grunted, ate another stained shrimp, and licked the sauce from his fingers in a way, I'm sure, he thought was erotically suggestive. "Might have been old Jozef. I'm a lot like him, you know."

I didn't doubt that for a moment.

He finished the last stained shrimp. The sweet-hot sauce produced beads of sweat on his forehead. Patting his face with his napkin, he shrugged and said, "They make it too mild here." His eyes wandered back down to my décolletage. "I like things really hot."

Ah, Warlord, I thought as I smiled at him, *soon enough you'll have all the fire you want.*

While we waited for the next course, I rested my elbows lightly on the table, tucked my chin in my laced fingers, and leaned forward to give him a better look at my breasts, which were barely covered by the silk of my dress. It was good he'd eaten all the stained shrimp. I would have hated for a serving boy to snitch the last one and suffer for it.

He patted his forehead with his napkin again. The look he gave me said the heat wasn't just from the stained shrimp.

"So now you're a tenant at a Red Moon house here?" He tried not to sound too eager, but his eyes wandered to my delicately pointed ears, the only physical evidence of my mother's mysterious race.

My ears make me unique, which means expensive, and I *do*

have a reputation for being the best of the best. When I choose to settle at a Red Moon house for a while, appointments are made weeks in advance, which is something no other whore can claim. Only half of what I do in bedrooms has anything to do with sex, but it's such *easy* bait.

"No, I'm not a tenant," I said. "This is a pleasure trip. I'm just passing through." Which I had told him when I invited him to dinner.

He still looked sulky and disappointed—because, of course, he hadn't believed it. His kind never do. Then a sly, calculating look came into his eyes. "But you won't be leaving until morning, will you, Sorrel?"

"Surreal," I said, correcting him. The bastard knew perfectly well what my name was. He was just trying to goad me into thinking I was too insignificant to remember so that I would be willing to prove I'm everything my reputation says I am.

That was fine with me. I was willing to let him play out his game, since it fit in with my own.

I smiled at the serving boy who brought the prime ribs. He placed my dish in front of me, the sharp blade of the knife carefully tucked beneath the meat. I glanced at the knife to confirm there was a small white enamel spot in the handle. My companion's knife had a small red spot.

Perfect.

Giving the boy a flicker of a warning smile, I picked up the knife and began to eat.

The Warlord grunted. "If the owner's going to have a dining house without rooms upstairs, the least he could do is have serving boys who aren't surly." He gave me a leering grin. "Or serving girls."

I gave him a saucy smile in return. "If you want to fill your belly, you come to a dining house. If you want to fill something else, you go to a Red Moon house. Besides, who wants to play with amateurs?"

A vicious light filled his pale eyes. "Playing with amateurs can be quite entertaining."

I just stared at him. He probably thought the vicious light in my own eyes was due to jealousy.

Fool.

I used Craft to chill the air around me, indicating my displeasure, and began to eat my dinner.

He chafed at the quiet censure, and his expression changed to thwarted-little-boy-turned-mean before he remembered that if a man wanted to be accommodated by a whore of my skill and reputation, part of the price was the illusion of courtesy.

Hiding his temper, he picked up his fork and wiggled it against the meat. "Meat's good. You can cut it with a fork."

I made a moue when meat juice splashed on the linen tablecloth. Finally realizing I wasn't impressed by his vigorous wrist action, he picked up the knife.

I flashed him a wanton smile of approval and settled down to eat.

His conversation was boring, being centered entirely on himself, but I didn't allow my attention to wander. Who knew what interesting tidbits he might let drop as he bragged about his connections?

I was admiring the bloodred, black-edged flower tucked into the fern pot opposite our booth when my companion noticed my gaze wasn't fastened on him.

"What's that?" he grunted, tearing a roll apart and dunking a piece into the butter bowl.

I looked away from the flower and shrugged. If he didn't know witchblood when he saw it, I wasn't about to tell him.

"Pretty," he said, probably thinking it would please me.

I almost laughed.

The meal, thank the Darkness, finally ended. After the brandy was served, he returned to his hoped-for agenda. "Listen," he said, leaning forward so he could stroke my wrist with his fingers, "since you say you don't have a room and this place is lacking in the finer points of service, I know a place—"

"Regrettably, Warlord, the hour is late, I'm expected elsewhere tomorrow, and my Coach leaves shortly."

His face immediately changed from leering soft to cruel hardened. Despite my youthful looks, I'm not a girl easily frightened into submission. I'm far more of a witch than he ever was a Warlord, and he was just a prick-ass who enjoyed hurting women, especially young women.

I dropped my right hand into my lap and used Craft to call in my favorite stiletto. It would have been a shame to gut him publicly, particularly after I'd gone to such trouble to do the thing so neatly, but he was going to be dead either way, and that was the point.

"What's this?" he growled. "*You* approached *me*. You think you can get me to spend good marks to fill your belly and then just—"

"As you say, *I* invited *you* for dinner." I leaned forward, looking at him with wide-eyed earnestness. "I wanted to meet you. You've a reputation among the ladies. In fact, one girl was left speechless after a night with you. Can you wonder why I'd want to meet you?"

"Since I changed my plans for this evening in order to come here, I expected something more than just dinner."

Of course he had. And he *was* going to get more than dinner. It just wasn't what he expected.

When he finally believed that I wasn't going to go anywhere with him, he started getting nasty, so I cut off his words. There were plenty of other things I wanted to cut off, but I restrained myself. "Since I invited you, it will be my privilege to pay for the meal in exchange for your company and conversation. Besides, I told you this was a pleasure trip, and I don't mix business with pleasure."

Making one more try to get what he had come for, he looked at my mouth and suggested that the booth was private enough for me to give him some small comfort. On any other night, those words alone would have earned him a knife in the gut, but tonight I simply declined. Mumbling something about my reputation having gone to my head to think I could waste a Warlord's time and not be accommodating, he left to find a Red Moon house with more compliant game.

When I was sure he'd gone, I slid out of the booth, plucked the flower from the pot, tucked it into my water glass, and settled back into the booth. While I waited, I called in a pen and the second of my little black books, and made careful notations about what I had done. Since the ingredients could be found almost anywhere in the Realm of Terreille, this would be another of my little recipes for death.

I vanished the book just as the owner of the dining house approached, a snifter of brandy in each hand. He set one in front of me before gingerly slipping into the booth.

It was always like this. Before, my clients are eager for the deed to be accomplished, and I'm treated with the deference due my skill. After . . . After, they begin to wonder if they might not one day be on the receiving end.

I stroked the witchblood petals and waited.

"It's done?" His voice shook a little.

"It's done." I continued to stroke the petals. "Legend says that the reason witchblood can't be destroyed once it's planted is that its roots grow so deep they're nourished in the Dark Realm."

"A plant from Hell?" He swallowed the brandy. "I want no ghosts or demons here."

Of course he wouldn't. "How is your daughter?"

"The same," he said, wiping his mouth with the back of his hand. "Always the same since that . . . since he . . ."

"How old is she?"

His mouth quivered with the effort to speak. "A child," he finally replied in a broken whisper. "A girl just beginning to be a woman."

Yes. I was twelve the first time I was thrown on my back, but the man was only strong enough to take my virginity. When he was done, I still had my Craft, still wore the Green Jewel that was my Birthright. I came away from that bloody bed still a witch, not just a Blood female. I've been paying men back in their own coin ever since.

The owner pushed a carefully folded napkin across the table. I lifted one edge, quickly counted the gold marks. As a whore, even with the fees I charge, it would take almost a month to earn this much. As a first-rate assassin, it was a pittance of my usual fee. But even I, at times, do charity work.

I vanished half the marks and pushed the napkin back across the table. The owner looked troubled—and a little frightened. I sipped my brandy. "Use the rest for the girl," I said with a gentleness harshened by my own memories. "A Black Widow is the only kind of witch who can heal what's left of your daughter's mind and possibly give her back some semblance of a life.

One with that much skill will expect to be paid well for her services."

"That has nothing to do with your fee," he protested.

I studied the witchblood. The plant will grow anywhere a witch's blood has been spilled in violence or where a witch violently killed has been buried. It's true that once it takes root over such a place, nothing can destroy it.

It's also true that if the petals are properly dried, it's a sweet-tasting, unforgiving poison that, like a flower opening to the sun, slowly lets its full force be known before blossoming into unrelenting pain. It is virulent and undetectable until it's far, far too late.

At this point, the Warlord would be feeling nothing more than a bit of a bellyache, and if, as I suspected, he was already entangled with a young whore, he wouldn't even notice.

The owner cleared his throat nervously. His son, who had insisted on being the serving boy tonight, placed two more snifters of brandy on the table, and then shifted from foot to foot. Glancing from his father to me, he said, "What should I do with the knife?"

"Cleanse it as I showed you," I said, "and then bury it deep."

The youth hurried away.

Actually there'd been nothing on the knife the Warlord had used but a glaze made from roots and herbs that would cause the mild bellyache. But they had wanted to see death being made, and since I wasn't about to tell them about the powdered witchblood I'd slipped into the bowl of stained shrimp, the mess I'd created in the kitchen that afternoon while I concocted the glaze had sufficiently impressed them. Besides, the Warlord will associate the bellyache with overindulgence and then forget it. By the time the witchblood blooms, no one will think of this place . . . or me.

I turned my attention back to the owner. "As for my fee, I'm keeping enough for expenses. I don't want the rest."

"But—"

"Hush," I said, smiling at him as I raised the brandy snifter in a small salute. "I was on a pleasure trip when you approached me, and"—I laughed, truly delighted—"as I told my arrogant dinner companion, I don't mix business with pleasure."